Praise for

LEETA SIMTAR
A LIFE ON TWO PLANETS

"...Fox's novel tells a richly told story of going rogue.
A rousing tale about a young woman coming to terms
with an unresolved past."
—KIRKUS REVIEWS ("VERDICT: GET IT")

"Fox knows how and when to surprise, and her warm and
empathic way of writing Leeta's relatable arc through inter-
nal monologues feels personal yet universally urgent, examining her real-world struggles of marginalization, racism,
and rigid hierarchies that enforce systemic exclusion."
—BOOKLIFE BY PUBLISHERS WEEKLY ("EDITOR'S PICK")

"A thrilling sci-fi journey about unexpected connections, the
power of friendship, and finding your place in the world. If
you love coming-of-age stories, this one's for you!"
—CAROL ANNE SHAW, AUTHOR OF THE PECULIAR LANGUAGE OF LLAMAS

"A stunning YA sci-fi novel... Leeta is in my soul, and when
I look up at the night sky and see those shining stars,
she'll be there in my mind."
—@BETHS_BOOKBLOG

"...a fantastic ride that combines deep emotional exploration with thrilling sci-fi adventure."
—@BOOKTOKWOMAN

"The author really made me feel things that Leeta felt,
often times I would find myself with tears in my eyes
wanting desperately to hug her."
—@KAHLANAMNELLRAHL

"When I first sat down with *Leeta Simtar* I was unsure what
to expect. What I got was a story I wished had been written
years ago, so I could have read it while still a teen myself."
—@IANMALCOLM

"This coming-of-age sci-fi adventure was such a fun read."
—@BREHELLYER

"[Leeta] is a character I would love to follow on more journeys and would be very interested to spend more time on her home planet. Five stars!"
—@BRANDI_PINKDISCOBALL

". . . a brilliant mix of sci-fi, heartfelt love story, and deep thoughts about life. It reminds us that even in a world full of uncertainty, there's always a spark of kindness and strength within us."
—MARY UGBODAGA, GOODREADS

"Another 5-star book by the amazing Annie Fox."
—@BASIC_BOOK_GIRL

"The book beautifully explores the idea of belonging, not just on alien planets but here on Earth—It's a total page-turner, and I couldn't put it down. If you love YA, humanistic sci-fi, coming-of-age stories, this one is definitely for you. Highly recommended!"
—@AMINIHOLMESLIZ

"Leeta provides a great lesson on self-acceptance and self-love. Would love to see a follow up story in the future."
—@ACTOYBOOKS

"Who doesn't love road trip vibes, main characters that make you laugh out loud, and found family?"
—@KENDRA_IS_BOOKISH

LEETA SIMTAR
A LIFE ON TWO PLANETS

The Unauthorized Biography

OTHER BOOKS BY ANNIE FOX

- The Teen Survival Guide to Dating and Relating
- Too Stressed to Think? A Teen Guide to Staying Sane When Life Makes You Crazy (with Ruth Kirschner)
- Middle School Confidential Book 1: Be Confident in Who You Are
- Middle School Confidential Book 2: Real Friends vs. the Other Kind
- Middle School Confidential Book 3: What's Up with My Family?
- Are You My Friend? A Raymond and Sheila Story
- Are We Lost? A Raymond and Sheila Story
- People Are Like Lollipops
- Teaching Kids to Be Good People: Progressive Parenting for the 21st Century
- The Girls Q&A Book on Friendship: 50 Ways to Fix a Friendship Without the DRAMA
- The Little Things That Kill: A Teen Friendship Afterlife Apology Tour

More at books.AnnieFox.com

LEETA SIMTAR
A LIFE ON TWO PLANETS

The Unauthorized Biography

ANNIE FOX

For David, always, in all ways

Here's to all the loners and outcasts.
We are not alone.

Home: *the starting place of love, hope,
and dreams.*

CONTENTS

Other Books by Annie Fox IV

Author's Note XII

ACT I: Life on Fure XIII

    CHAPTER 1: Graduation..1

    CHAPTER 2: Alone With the *Frigs* 10

    CHAPTER 3: Cave of Secrets 15

    CHAPTER 4: Interrogation 23

    CHAPTER 5: A Seed Will Grow 34

    CHAPTER 6: Ready or Not..38

    CHAPTER 7: Out of this World 43

ACT II: Earth 61

    CHAPTER 8: The Unwelcoming 63

    CHAPTER 9: Lost and Found 81

    CHAPTER 10: What's Your Style? 92

    CHAPTER 11: An Order of Onion Rings 99

    CHAPTER 12: The Listening Station...............................105

    CHAPTER 13: A Friend with Wheels 112

    CHAPTER 14: In the Predator's Lair 122

    CHAPTER 15: Food for the Road 130

    CHAPTER 16: The Road to Winterbrook.........................134

CHAPTER 17: Under the Stars 145

CHAPTER 18: The Uncovered Clue 157

CHAPTER 19: Back to Winterbrook 166

CHAPTER 20: A Wall and a Plan 182

CHAPTER 21: Into the Heart 185

CHAPTER 22: Curiosity and Connection 192

CHAPTER 23: Beyond the Front Door 196

CHAPTER 24: Tea Time 210

ACT III: FINDING LIAM 223

CHAPTER 25: Treachery and Tests 225

CHAPTER 26: Whose Side are You On? 234

CHAPTER 27: The Road to Shasta 239

CHAPTER 28: Promises Kept and Broken 246

CHAPTER 29: Haunted Paintings 252

CHAPTER 30: A Bumpy Road 267

CHAPTER 31: Goodbye Earth 277

Afterword 289

Glossary 292

Annie's Next Book 297

Acknowledgements 298

About the Author 300

AUTHOR'S NOTE

I MET LEETA SIMTAR six months after she landed on Earth. We spent time traveling together. I consider her a close friend. Maybe more. I hope she feels the same about me. As for what happened before she arrived, I only know what she described of her home planet and its people. Like everything Leeta told me, I believe most of it. The parts I'm not sure about I included here as well. I had to, otherwise this story would have been filled with holes. And no one likes that. If it turns out this version of Leeta Simtar's story is not 100% accurate, forgive me. It still deserves to be told. And it's not like you haven't been warned. This is the *unauthorized* biography.

ACT I

LIFE ON FURE

CHAPTER 1

GRADUATION

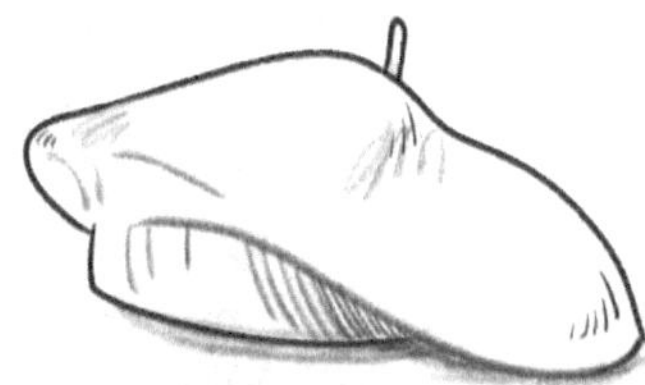

Through a vast network of willing donors and recipients, the Intergalactic Interspecies Program (IIP) has enhanced, supported, and accelerated the ethical development of non-Furean civilizations within the Planetary Alliance for 1500 years.
—THE INTERGALACTIC INTERSPECIES PROGRAM (IIP)—A HISTORY

ONE-HUNDRED-SIXTY GRADUATES stand at attention like a ring of ants on the round stage contained within a massive, transparent dome beneath the red clouds of Fure. Quivering with anticipation, the grads await the start of the Maturation Attainment ceremony while the audience chants, "One Mind. One Goal. One Family." The words run together, propelled by a single collective breath. A sustained humming sound, pulsing through the dome like 100,000 winged insects.

Each grad wears the same blue beret. A tightly belted blue tunic over long-line shorts. A pair of high blue boots, perfectly laced and tied with the same double-hitch knot. Uniforms aside, the first 154 grads also share the same dark complexion. Same height and body type. Same fine white hair. Every pair of small black eyes are, right this minute and always, assessing and accepting life with patience and logic. It's no surprise these grads seem like clones. They are *Reals*—100% Furean DNA.

The last six grads are another story. They're *Brids*—interspecies hybrids—none has more than 50% Furean DNA. Everything about them says they don't belong. And the ridiculously tall one at the end of the line is the worst offender.

Her name is Leeta Simtar. Her shorts, too short. So are her sleeves. Her boots, too small, and the double-hitch knots on the laces, already unhitched. If that weren't enough, look at her skin—a disturbing shade of tan only seen in pulverized *grentrum*, the sandstone that covers the surface of Fure. A scattering of pinpoint black freckles, as many as stars in the galaxy, cover her face. And her absurdly red-orange hair? Or whatever that color is. So thick and unruly, poking out on all sides of her head like tiny spikes along the back of a fierce, burrowing *mokeep*. Her large hands join at thin wrists. Her fingers, long and narrow, except for her stubby thumbs, the only visible trait she shares with Reals. But close up, Leeta Simtar's most unnerving feature is her wide-set, round, blue eyes, continuously darting around, scanning, searching, second-guessing. There is no patience or logic in this girl. Rumor has it she's only 29% Furean. Barely Furean at all. The other 71%? Gemian! That's certainly nothing to be proud of.

Leeta Simtar hunches over, a futile attempt at a disappearing act. She nervously clears her throat again and again to cover the sounds of her gurgling stomach. She desperately wishes she were in her secret place instead of on display in front of 25,000 Fureans. But wishing is unFurean, so she stops herself and pulls from her tunic pocket a fistful of *turils*, a sweet snack made from absurdly tough leaves. She pokes the arm of Fendro, the long-necked male Brid ahead of her in line. When he turns, she grins and holds out her palm. Fendro stares stupidly at the *turils*. Leeta rolls her eyes and steps around him, tapping the shoulder of her friend Zertee, a female Brid with a square jaw, who instantly sizes up the situation and all its potential consequences for Leeta. "Put those away," she whispers sternly.

Leeta grins mischievously, pops the handful of candy into her mouth, and steps back in line. Poor Zertee. No spark of spontaneity. No sense of fun whatever. She tries so hard to be Real. What's the point? She's Brid. That's all she'll ever be. The Reals are always chanting: *One Mind. One Goal. One Family,* but every Brid know they are not part of the family. If you're not Real, you're not even *real.* So, what does that make you? Fake? Imaginary? No. That's crazy. Leeta Simtar knows she isn't Real, but she's definitely *real.* So are Zertee and every Brid. All real. All the time. But that's not enough. The other Brids can't seem to stop trying to become more Real by trying to be less Brid. For Leeta, all this trying is pointless. She feels it as sharply as the pain from her too-tight boots. Reals will never make their one goal the acceptance of Brids into the family.

Why wait for something that's never going to happen? And yet, here are the outcasts, waiting to kneel before Daht Mayeel, leader of all Fureans, to receive their graduation affirmation. Like that's going to change even one thing for any Brid.

Leeta watches the Daht settle herself on a raised revolving platform, positioned directly under the eye of the dome. She is five feet tall and powerfully built. Rarely seen in public, the Daht exudes an intoxicating mix of serene kindness and unyielding authority. Her yellow ceremonial robe, trimmed in iridescent green and turquoise gemstones, dazzles the audience. But the outfit fades in comparison to the light show of interconnected symbols and shifting colors pulsing under the scalp of the Daht's large bald head, all of it effortlessly controlled via neurons in her brain.

The audience easily reads the flashing message: *It's time to begin.* Inhaling as one, the spectators reach under their seats and each extracts a small drum. Rising as one, they pound out the same rhythm they've heard since before birth, again and again, chanting along with it. Chanting and drumming, loud and prolonged as if no one needs to stop for breath because they have each other's lungs working for them.

Leeta Simtar shifts her weight from one aching foot to the other. She takes her own deep breath because no one else will do it for her. She watches Jemuno, the first Real grad and most accomplished student in the class, walk forward to receive his graduation affirmation. Arriving center stage, Jemuno closes his eyes, bows his head, and kneels before the Daht. As she begins to perform *tulahm* by cupping her hand on his head, the drumming and chanting stop abruptly.

Though Leeta has never been touched by the Daht, she knows all about *tulahm*. During her years at Central Nursery no one got *tulahmed* more than Leeta Simtar. It happened whenever she laughed too raucously. Or spoke in anger. Or cried about anything—a banged shin, a poor grade, a dead plant. Her teachers let her know that displays of emotions are unFurean, and they quickly placed cupped hands on her head and over her heart. Within seconds Leeta felt her emotions compress into a small, tight block, packed away in a box, a heavy lid locking them inside. *Tulahm* was supposed to make her feel calm and centered. That sounded like a good thing, but it never worked for Leeta. Maybe the teachers didn't know how to do it correctly. Surely the Daht knows.

With her hand still on the top of Jemuno's head, the Daht addresses him, her voice filling the entire dome. "You will accomplish great things for Fure. We are counting on you. One Mind. One Goal. One Family."

The audience picks up the chant again. It swells for a full minute, then fades to silence. Leeta watches Jemuno stand, slightly dazed, before descending a ramp into the audience. Then the next grad steps forward to begin their journey. The ritual repeats itself, in precisely the same way, for the next 151 graduates. It takes five hours.

Truth be told, the audience is tired of standing and chanting and drumming. They're also hungry and thirsty. Many need to use the facilities. Like the graduates, they want to move on. But whining and public displays of impatience are also unFurean, so no one speaks of discomfort. Instead, each audience member, including the newly anointed grads, rededicates themselves to drumming and chanting in support of the final six. This won't last much longer. They are just Brids. The Daht will hurry them along as she always does in public events. Then it will be time to celebrate.

After the first three Brids receive their affirmation, Leeta Simtar watches her friend walk proudly to the Daht, kneel and close her eyes. Daht Mayeel briefly rests a hand on Zertee's head and, for the 158th time today, proclaims, "You will accomplish great things for Fure. We are counting on you. One Mind. One Goal. One Family."

When Zertee passes Leeta on her way down to the audience, Leeta whispers, "How was it?"

Zertee stares ahead, as if she didn't hear the question. Maybe something just happened and Zertee can't speak.

After Fendro has his moment, finally it's Leeta's turn. Her heart lurches. Her mouth suddenly dry, it's hard to chew and swallow what's left of the *turils*, but she manages. And then she covers the distance to center stage with long, shaky strides, kneels before the Daht, and closes her eyes. She's trembling with anticipation. Of what? Probably nothing good. But when the Daht rests her cupped hand on Leeta's head, a warmth radiates down her neck, into her chest, around her heart, and it is good. But it's less good to hear the same words she's heard all day, directed at her. "You will accomplish great things for Fure. We are counting on you. One Mind. One Goal. One Family."

Especially the last word. Much harder to swallow than dried *turils*.

The drumming and chanting rise to grand finale levels.

Leeta tries to stand, but the pressure from the Daht's hand keeps her on her knees. Swift as a shadow, the Daht whispers in Leeta's ear, "Soon I will tell you the singular truth of your life and everything will change. Just remember, you can always come home."

An electric jolt shoots up Leeta's spine, short-circuiting her mind and leaving her body numb and floating in the void. By the time she regains her senses and gets to her feet, the Daht is gone. The audience is gone. The other grads are gone.

Leeta stands alone, unseen, under the eye of the dome, her brain empty, except for a single thought.

Did she say that to everyone or only me?

Leeta's still kicking the question around as she picks at remnants of party fare scattered on trays perfectly lined up on the buffet table. Fried *turil*, ground *gurder*, and a round dumpling stuffed with spiced seed called *pruvadam*. The long table feels like an escape pod floating in a sea of people. Leeta figures the Daht ordered the post-graduation party held in this much smaller dome to insure even more family oneness. Leeta would happily cling to this pod for the rest of the evening. What's left of the food is good and she wouldn't have to talk to anyone. But after the food is gone, then what? Stand alone next to an empty table? That would make her feel more out of it than usual. Or she could try to lose herself in the crowd. Not easy for someone who is more than a foot and a half taller than everyone else.

Leeta searches for Zertee and finds her not far away talking to Fendro, who grins foolishly. The other three Brid graduates fill out the group around them. Katrum, a large female with charcoal-gray skin, nervously touches her tangled seaweed-like hair. Pilak's small body can barely contain his nonstop jitters. Tarta, with her bulging forehead and rapidly blinking amber eyes, seems especially happy. Leeta prepares to join them. Better than wandering around by herself. As she picks up a tankard of *hastip*, a strong-smelling celebratory drink, the voices of two Reals standing nearby snag her attention. They've just bumped hands reaching for the same *pruvadam*.

"Oh! My apologizes. You take that one."

"Thank you for offering, but it's the last one so I couldn't possibly take it. Please go ahead. It is yours."

"Thank you for thanking me, and thank you for your offer, but no thank you. You eat it! Enjoy in good health."

Leeta grabs a long knife from the table, and in one swift move, chops the *pruvadam* in two.

"Share the damn thing," she says. A satisfied smile teases the corners of her mouth before she turns to make her way through the crowd. Crammed as the place is, her journey takes little effort. When the party-goers see Leeta coming they discreetly step aside, always with a polite nod and the hard-to-miss whiff of caution that comes from the belief that whatever is wrong with her just might be contagious. You can never be too sure.

Leeta joins Zertee and the other Brids as they eagerly empty their tankards of *hastip* and refill them. Leeta holds a full tankard, but she's not drinking. Unlike the Reals or any Brids, Leeta has a very low tolerance for fermented drinks. As unFurean as she normally is, Leeta on *hastip* can be too much to deal with. She knows it. So does everyone else. And because she desperately wants to remain in control of her emotions in this very public place, she wears a fixed expression and keeps her mouth shut.

"What did you think of the ceremony, Zertee?" Fendro asks.

"It was precisely executed," Zertee says.

"Yes, it was!" Fendro nods so eagerly his neck wobbles.

"The chanting was especially strong for us," Katrum says.

"One Mind. One Goal. One Family. That's what it's all about," Tarta agrees.

"Here's to our future," Pilak adds, raising his tankard. "May it be as Real as we can make it."

"Cheers!" says Zertee.

Everyone, including Leeta, clinks their tankards together. While the others drain theirs, Leeta takes a sip from hers, figuring a tiny amount won't have any effect. Then she takes another sip and another. Her plan to stay silent vanishes and a new one pops into place. She clears her throat dramatically.

"I want to say something."

Zertee and the others look at her.

Leeta takes a long swig, emptying half her tankard, then swipes her mouth with her fingers and stands taller, if that's possible.

The others look at each other warily and brace themselves.

"Before we leave this chapter of our lives," Leeta says, with a dramatic sweep of her hand, "I want to look back, just for a bit." She guzzles down the rest of the *hastip* and looks around the group with a sweet, loopy smile. "Ever since Central Nursery days, you guys have always been nice to me even though I—" Leeta's voice wavers on the edge of cracking. "I— I'm not the easiest person to be around. I have been known to lose it sometimes. Okay, a lot of the time. Which is why right now, before we go our separate ways, maybe never to stand together united in our Bridness, I just want to say, if I've ever embarrassed you by not being Real enough, I'm sorry."

"You have not embarrassed us!" the group shouts as one.

Leeta raises her hand to silence them. "You guys are sweet, but I have. I know it. And I'm very sorry." Her voice falls over the cliff as the first of many tears slip down her cheek. She sniffs, wiping her nose with the back of her hand. "Now that we've attained maturation and we'll be heading into the future, I want you all to know that your kindness has meant a lot to me. So, thank you."

Leeta's outpouring of emotions is so embarrassingly un-Furean the others don't know where to look or what to do with their faces. But nothing compares to their shock and mortification when Leeta spreads out her long arms and pulls them into a group hug. Zertee and the others endure the embrace like a bunch of vertical corpses. As Leeta squeezes them all tighter, she sobs, kissing the tops of their heads. When she finally releases them, her heart floats on a cloud of pure joy. To Leeta's fuzzy brain, this is what being part of a family is supposed to feel like. Then she catches Zertee nervously scanning the crowd, clearly worried that some Reals caught sight of what just happened. Leeta follows her gaze. Her mind snaps back to clarity. No one saw. Good thing, but still, this public display of affection was a huge mistake. So stupid. Except for Zertee, all the Brids think she's weird. They always have. If she asks them, they'll deny it. And they'll be lying even though lying is unFurean. Inside, they'll be telling themselves the truth. "What is wrong with that girl? How could she not know that when she does her weirdo Leeta thing, she is making it harder for all of us?"

Leeta plunks her tankard onto the table with an angry thud. The drumming and chanting grow more intense. The party crowd coils onto itself like a *po'ost* ready to strike. Everyone is staring at her. Chills rattle her bones. Her head aches, pounding its own rhythm, defiant and dangerously out of sync with the drums. Her hand flies to her temple.

"Leeta, what is the problem?" Zertee asks.

Leeta opens her mouth, then closes it without uttering a word. Too much effort. And what would she say? She looks down at her unhitched boot laces. Too late to fix them even if she knew how.

"What is wrong?" Zertee says, concern clouding her eyes. "Tell me the truth."

Her friend's face distorts behind a screen of fresh tears. Leeta blinks hard, but nothing seems normal, unless this is normal.

"Zertee, there's so much wrong I don't even know where to start."

Leeta shrinks into herself and rushes into the crowd, hoping to be swallowed whole. But OnemindOnegoalOnefamily has grown into an immense, tentacled monster, twisting and shifting, swimming over heads, between bodies, coming for Leeta from all directions. Larger. Louder. Faster. Larger. Louder. Faster.

What's wrong? Tell me the truth.

I will tell you the singular truth of your life and everything will change.

Nothing will ever change.

Leeta slaps on her combination goggles and mouth/nose filter, slips out of the dome through a rarely used exit, and steps into the wind-swept landscape that is her home planet, where she has no home.

CHAPTER 2
ALONE WITH THE *FRIGS*

"Fureans do not experience loneliness. We are all One Family. How could anyone be lonely?"
—HIGH GENETICS COUNCIL FINAL DISCIPLINARY HEARING

HEAD DOWN AGAINST THE WIND, breathing heavily through her appliance, Leeta hurries away from the glowing domes of Fure City into the dimly lit panorama spreading out before her. Officially it's early afternoon, but no one would know it. As always, dense clouds block Fure's red dwarf star, *Kerlanti*. Which is why, in spite of the many *grentrum* rocks dotting the landscape, and in spite of Leeta's own towering frame, no shadows touch the ground. Because her skin is the color of the rocks and shifting sand, she does not stand out here. For that she is grateful, but she is not welcome and she knows it. *Ka'aru*, the wind, welcomes no living thing. Like Leeta herself, *Ka'aru* is, at times, calm. Playful, even. Then, without warning, it can rip across the landscape, ruthlessly sandblasting anyone crazy enough to be out here. Few are crazy enough. But Leeta *is*, because this most barren corner of her world is one of the only places she can be alone. And sometimes this girl needs that even more than the air she breathes.

Leeta Simtar stops at the base of a rockface. She casts off her beret, jacket, boots, and socks, then easily climbs up on a boulder and lies across the top, gazing up at the clouds, imagining the red face of *Kerlanti*. Of course, she's never actually seen Fure's star with her own eyes. Nor has she seen anything that exists beyond these clouds, but she knows there are countless stars and galaxies out there. She believes she'll see them all clearly someday, with nothing blocking her view. That thought sparks joy. Then comes the gentle *maaa* of the hungry *frigs* grazing on the barren ridge overhead. Leeta wriggles her bare toes and listens. *Ka'aru* deposits sand in her hair and on her face. She laughs aloud, picturing herself returning to Fure City barefoot, so covered with sand she is unrecognizable.

Leeta is thirsty. Her skin is gritty. Her head still aches from too much *hastip*. Yet somehow, she feels better than she has all day.

But it doesn't last.

A high-pitched bleating grabs her attention. A small brown *frig* stands on a ledge halfway down the rockface. Leeta follows the animal's hungry gaze to a scraggly patch of yellow *fwaydrun* that has, against all odds, managed to push through the sand close to her backpack. Leeta jumps down from the boulder and pulls a small pair of shears from her backpack. She carefully cuts a few outer leaves from the base of the plant and waves them overhead.

"Hey, Little Brownie. Look what I've got for you! *Fwaydrun.* Want some?"

Brownie nervously paws the rock ledge, caught between intense need and intense fear.

"C'mon. The drop isn't that far. You're a *frig*. Rock leaping is what you're made for."

Leeta pictures the animal gracefully sailing through the air, safely landing on all fours, ambling toward her outstretched hand. Longhorns are unpredictable, but the girl isn't worried. The *frig* seems gentle. She can already feel its soft lips on her fingertips.

"I know you're hungry. Just jump!"

The animal leaps and at the same instant the wind turns wicked, shoving the *frig* off course. It drops from the air, lands on its side on top of a sharp rock and cries out, helplessly thrashing about. Leeta knows she cannot ease the *frig's* physical pain, but just maybe she can *tulahm* away some of its fear.

She rushes over, cupping both hands, and pressing them against the animal's heaving sides. After a moment, the *frig's* breathing stabilizes. Leeta stares at her hands, amazed and delighted. *I did it!*

The *frig* turns its head to Leeta, its small, black eyes filled with gratitude. A moment later, it struggles to stand.

Leeta shifts her hands underneath the *frig's* flanks. "You're okay," she says, lifting gently. "You can do this."

"Do what?"

Leeta whips around to face Zertee, breathless from running, yet somehow still perfectly belted down and laced up. Zertee catches sight of the *frig* with Leeta's hands on it. She does her best to hide her disgust, but her best isn't good enough.

"Do not touch that thing!"

"But he's hurt, Zertee. Give me a hand."

"No! It is unFurean to interact with animals."

"We have to help him stand up so he can return to his herd." Leeta points up at the rockface, where the rest of the *frigs* continue grazing.

Zertee shakes her head. "Up there? No. It is illogical to expend energy doing anything that has such a low probability of success."

"I disagree. Zertee, we've got to try."

Zertee squares her shoulders. "Leeta, group leader Sifat sent me to find you."

"And you did. Good for you, Zertee."

"She brought Search and Rescue." Zertee emphasizes the words hoping to alert Leeta to the seriousness of the situation.

Not a chance.

Leeta shrugs. "I don't need rescuing."

Zertee grabs Leeta's arm and attempts to pull her to her feet. "Come with me."

Leeta shakes her off. "No. You go. Tell Sifat you couldn't find me."

"You want me to lie?"

Leeta exhales impatiently. "Fine. Then tell her I'm busy. It's true. Just don't tell her what I'm busy doing. And . . . tell her I'll be there soon."

"It's not just Sifat and Search and Rescue. The Daht wants to see to you. Now."

Leeta recalls the Daht's whispered message.

I will tell you the singular truth of your life and everything will change.

"Yeah? Do you know why?"

"I do not know. Please come now."

"Not yet."

Leeta turns back to the *frig*. She gasps at the first sight of blood dripping from the gash in its belly. A red line crawls across the sand. Hurriedly she pulls a compactly folded blue *subyl* from her backpack, leans over the animal, gently dabbing the wound. Blood stains the fabric then instantly vanishes. With each anxious breath, more blood surges through the *frig's* wound. Leeta puts her cupped hands on the animal again, this time directly over its heart. After a moment, its breathing steadies and the *frig* rests its head on Leeta's forearm.

"That's better, Brownie," she says, stroking its head. "Now let's get you on your feet."

With the girl's help the *frig* manages to stand and take a few tentative steps. She tries to see the animal as she wants it to be. Strong. Healthy. But she cannot ignore what is. Her heart tightens into a cold fist of dread.

"Leeta, we must go . . ." says Zertee, softly but firmly.

Leeta nods, biting her bottom lip as she slow-walks fastening her tunic, pulling on her socks and boots, all the while watching the wounded *frig* limp away.

She stuffs her hat and *subyl* into her backpack, lifts it to her shoulder and stands. "Okay. Let's go."

At the same moment Brownie collapses with a soft thud and the air fills with a thousand high-pitched clicks as hundreds of *sanderols* pour out of a dozen underground burrows and surround the injured *frig*. They greedily sniff the air as the boldest ones creep close enough to lick the bloody sand.

"No!"

Leeta hurls a handful of small stones at the scavengers. The *sanderols* scatter, retreating a short distance. Then they turn, as one, and inch forward again, wary but determined. Leeta rushes them, swinging her backpack low, stomping the ground, screaming.

"Go away! Leave him alone!"

The *sanderols* scurry back to their burrows, a sharp-eyed lookout posted at each entrance. They've had it with this crazy girl. But only for the moment. They're desperately hungry, and as long as the *frig* is lying there lifeless, not one of the *sanderols* is leaving.

Leeta holds Brownie's body as it grows cold and stiff in her arms. She weeps into its furry neck.

"This is all my fault, Brownie. I shouldn't have told you to jump. I'm so sorry. I'm always sorry when it's too late." Zertee gently lays a cupped hand on Leeta's shoulder. Leeta twists away from her.

The low distant rumble of drums and chanting reaches the girls. Insistent and on the move. Leeta jumps to her feet, slings her backpack onto her shoulder, and scrambles up the rock face.

"Leeta, come down. You're upset. I will help you."

Leeta shakes her head. *No one can help me.*

CHAPTER 3
CAVE OF SECRETS

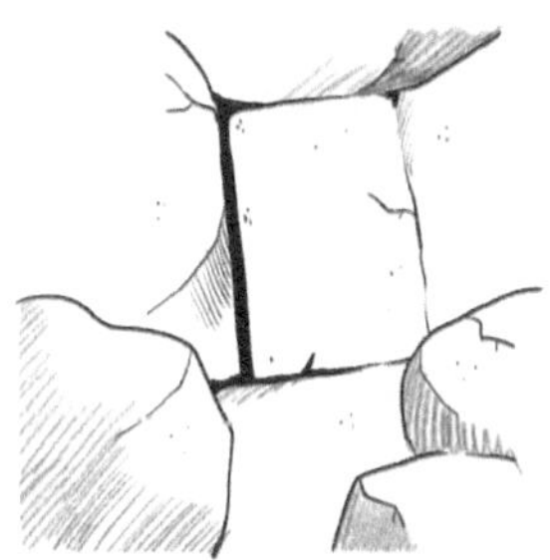

Like all Real offspring, all Brids are raised in Central Nurseries. Despite their differences, Brids have always lived among us peacefully with full acceptance from the majority population and with full Furean citizenship rights.
—THE INTERGALACTIC INTERSPECIES PROGRAM (IIP)—A HISTORY

DEFYING GRAVITY AND THE WIND, Leeta Simtar climbs higher. It's a struggle, but she relishes using her long, strong arms and legs this way. How does she know how to climb? She's not sure. Leeta's never actually seen anyone do it. Reals don't climb. Neither do Brids. It's possible her climbing ability comes from her Gemian DNA donor, but nothing else about Leeta matches what she knows about Gemians. They rarely show emotion and are almost as stoic as Fureans. That certainly does not describe this girl. But maybe they are climbers. If so, she's lucky because Zertee can't follow her up the rock face. Neither can Sifat or Search and Rescue. Of course that doesn't mean they're not coming for her. The Daht told Sifat to bring Leeta in and they will obey.

Leeta pulls herself over the top of the ledge. Brownie's herd grazes nearby. At least they're trying. Not much to eat up here. All of them are white. Brownie was one of a kind. The others are probably glad he's gone, if they've even noticed.

She takes her All-Purpose Electronic Device (APED) from her tunic pocket and speaks to it.

"AYA, am I being followed?"

"Maaaaybeee."

"What's that supposed to mean?"

"Relax, Leeta. I'm just kidding. No pursuers are behind you."

"Why do you do this to me, AYA?"

"Because you asked for an APED with a sense of humor. If you want to revert to standard boring Furean fare, just say the word."

"No. It's okay. Stay the way you are. I can always use a laugh."

"True. But you only get one if you recognize a joke when you hear one."

"Maybe it'd help if your jokes were funnier."

"Noted."

Leeta sidesteps the *frigs* and hurries on. Survival outside the dome for long periods is a challenge during the day, but nighttime temperatures plummet, and the merciless dust storms force all creatures to find shelter. If Leeta can get to her secret place before nightfall, Search and Rescue will go back to Fure City. But if somehow they know about her secret place, then by the time they return in the morning, she hopes to be hiding somewhere else.

Leeta enters a broad expanse of terrain studded with boulders huddled close together like a herd of enormous *frigs* who've eaten more than enough to grow fat and round. Fureans believe rocks contain the spirits of ancient ancestors. Touching rocks is forbidden. And don't even thinking about climbing them! Leeta doesn't believe any of that. She has no problem stepping on or over these boulders or turning sideways and wiggling through so the rocks hug her front and back. Still, it helps knowing where the obstacles are.

"AYA, is anyone following me now? No jokes, please."

"Absolutely no one is currently behind you, Leeta. Stop worrying already, okay?"

Leeta Simtar would love to stop worrying, but she can't. She is wired to worry. It's just another quirk that makes her an oddball. As far as she knows, no one else on Fure worries. Reals don't. It's unFurean. Leeta's not sure about other Brids. They never talk about it among themselves. Maybe talking about worrying is also unFurean. Leeta sometimes tells Zertee about her overwhelming, scary, dark thoughts. Zertee always listens, curious, compassionate, but Leeta knows she can't relate. Zertee says that whenever she has a persistent challenge—her personal understanding of the word worry—she logics herself out of it. Good trick if you can pull it off.

"One Mind. One Goal. One Family."

"AYA! I hear them! They're getting closer! Why did you say no one was behind me?"

"Because no one is behind you, Leeta. Search and Recovery are up ahead. To the north. Point three miles away. They're not gaining on you, you are gaining on *them*."

"*Sork!*"

"You got that right."

Leeta races forward to the steep rock wall looming ahead. She slides her fingertips above and below a deep fissure, long and jagged as a snake. A three-foot by three-foot section of rock slides to the left, revealing a tunnel. She flings her backpack inside, climbs up to the opening, and ducks inside. A quick tap on the wall behind her and the rock slides back into place, closing Leeta within the rockface. She exhales, fastens her backpack to her ankle and pulls it as she crawls along a low, tight tunnel. Dark, cool, silent.

A few years ago, when she first discovered this tunnel, she wondered who engineered it and why they needed to get away from Fure City. Whoever it was, she was grateful to them then and even more so now. Twenty feet in, the tunnel angles straight up, like a chimney. She probes the wall of the vertical passageway, finds handholds on the right and left, and pulls herself up, hanging freely for a moment. Using her hands and elbows to wedge herself inside the chimney-like space, she locates a toehold with her left foot and another with her right. Like a gecko climbing up a narrow tube, she makes her way through the tunnel. Right hand, left foot. Left hand, right foot. Again and again. After two or three yards the rock tube bends forward and the floor levels off, allowing her to crawl along a horizontal stretch. Another three yards, another turn to the left, and a cave yawns before her, tall and wide.

Leeta sinks onto the dirt floor, resting her back against the cave wall. She unfastens her backpack. *Frig* blood on her hands triggers a shudder of shame. She rubs her palms on the cave floor until they're covered with a thick layer of grit. Brownie's blood is still on her skin, but she can't see it now.

On the opposite wall, an odd collection of carefully arranged objects sits on a metal tray that Leeta snagged from the Botany Dome. They include a pair of black-rimmed, unbendable eyeglasses, a model of a radio telescope, and a coffee mug decorated with Vincent van Gogh's *The Starry Night*. Leeta doesn't know about van Gogh. Doesn't know what a painting is. The same is true for the eyeglasses and the radio telescope. None of these cherished items have ever been seen on Fure. And yet, she made each of them.

Leeta briefly rotates the mug between her palms, marveling as she always does at the swirling clouds and glowing starbursts. She picks up the last object on the shelf. Her favorite. A small cube with strange characters on each of the six surfaces. Unlike the radio telescope, eyeglasses, and coffee mug, Leeta is very familiar with cubes. Fureans mine halite crystals, and she's always admired their flat surfaces and sharp edges. But like everything in her collection, she has no idea what this small opaque cube is or what the six symbols mean.

She carries the cube into the swatch of light seeping into the cave around the edges of a boulder that partially obscures the front entrance. Before she discovered the hidden stone panel that leads to the back of the cave, Leeta came in through the front. She smiles now, remembering how surprised Zertee was the one time Leeta led her behind the boulder and into her secret cave.

Does she wish Zertee were here with her now? Not really. In this moment, Leeta is happy. No longer wondering about what the Daht whispered and what it could mean. No longer worried about how she embarrassed herself at the party. Yes, her feet still ache, but her pleasure in being here, on her own, outweighs the pain. She'd love to stay here, but solitude is unFurean. Sooner or later, they will find her and she will have to return to the group. The stinging inevitability of that truth makes this moment even more special.

A shadow falls across the small cube plunging it into darkness. A voice calls out.

"Leeta Simtar, we are here to help you."

"I don't need your help!" Leeta shouts. But she knows her words won't stop them. She slips the cube into her pocket then leaps to her feet, and sweeps the rest of her collection off the shelf and into her backpack.

"We are coming in."

Leeta tosses the backpack against the far wall, where it topples over, spilling her treasures. Leeta flings her tunic over them just as Sifat, an older Brid whose broad shoulders and long, blunt-ended nose gives her the appearance of a graying aardvark, strides into the cave. Behind her Pilak, Katrum, Tarta, and Fendro stand in an awkward knot just inside the entryway.

Leeta glares at Sifat. "How did you find me?"

Sifat doesn't need to answer. Leeta has just spotted Zertee standing behind Fendro, her eyes fixed on her tightly laced boots. Leeta lunges at her friend, screeching. "You told them!"

Sifat charges forward, cupped hands aimed at Leeta's back. The girl whirls around, eyes on fire, hands balled into fists.

"Touch me and you'll be sorry!"

Stunned at this outburst, Sifat lowers her hands and backs away.

Leeta fully expects they'll try to tame her into submission with a group compassion touch, a round of logical reasoning, and chanting, lots of chanting. Let them try. They will fail. She's never pushed back before, but she's ready to fight for the right to be as emotional, unpredictable, and unFurean as she is.

Staring down the group, Leeta sees something unmistakable in all their faces. Something she didn't expect. Every one of them is terrified of her. Even Sifat. Even Zertee! Her heart drops. She doesn't want to scare anyone. She doesn't want to hurt anyone. She only wants them to let her be the freak she is. Why is that so hard?

Eyes locked on Leeta, Sifat slowly draws a small drum out of her backpack. The others do the same. They form a loose circle around her. They beat their drums and chant in a continuous, soothing, pulsing rhythm, like a singing wind, like a magic spell weaving through the cave.

Leeta covers her ears. She will not be tamed. Hot tears leave pale tracks down her gritty face. She doesn't bother wiping them away. She is wired to think too much and to cry too often. She cries when she's sad. Also when she's angry and frustrated. And sometimes, like now, she cries when she feels powerful. It makes no sense. She doesn't pretend to understand any of it. But she knows, without a doubt, that these intense emotions are part of who she is. She doesn't care what the others think. She's done trying to make herself acceptable to them.

Sifat raises a hand. The drumming and chanting stop.

"Leeta Simtar, please pick up your tunic and come with us."

Leeta stares her down. "No."

A spark of outrage flashes in Sifat's eyes, then it's gone. Her next words are spoken calmly. "Fendro, please retrieve Leeta's tunic and hand it to her."

Fendro shoots a wary look in Leeta's direction. Leeta snarls. "Do not . . ."

Sifat locks eyes with Fendro, her voice controlled and uncompromising. "Proceed, Fendro."

Fendro inhales and exhales quickly. Head down to avoid Leeta's eyes, he walks to the back wall and lifts the tunic's edge, revealing Leeta's treasures. Sifat and the others gawk at the strange objects and gather around for a closer look. As Fendro reaches out to touch the mug, Leeta lands a vicious kick to his hip. He cries out and crumbles to the floor. The others hurry to his side with cupped hands and soft murmurs. Leeta sweeps up her treasures into her tunic, and cradling the bundle, escapes out the back of the cave. She makes her way through the dark, one-handed, unbalanced, cursing herself for forgetting to grab her backpack. Reaching the stone panel at the end of the tunnel, she pushes hard. As soon as the gap is wide enough, she crawls through and slips silently into the night air.

What now? Where now?

She looks up the length of the rock wall. It's much higher and smoother than the one she climbed earlier, but if she can make it to the top, she'll be safe. Her long fingers frantically search for a handhold.

"Step away from the rock, Leeta Simtar."

Sifat's voice grips her heart. She turns into the glare of six flashlights. No slipping into the night now. Squinting, she hugs the bundle.

"Please give those items to me," Sifat commands.

Leeta sneers. After a tense moment, she growls and shoves the bundled tunic into Sifat's hand.

Sifat snaps her fingers. "Pilak!"

Pilak, a nervous mouse, scurries forward carrying a closed silver cylinder. Sifat waves her hand over it and the lid slides open, and Pilak empties the contents of the tunic into it. Leeta's treasures hit the bottom of the cylinder with a mournful clunk. The lid closes, sealing them inside.

Sifat hands the tunic back to Leeta. "Please put this on," she says.

Leeta turns away, wrestling a volcano of rage.

"Please, Leeta Simtar. The night air is chilling."

As if to prove her point, the wind whips up, blowing cold air through Leeta's shirt. She rips the tunic from Sifat's hand and stuffs her arms into the sleeves, refusing to fasten the front.

Sifat holds out a lit flashlight. "And please carry this so you won't stumble in the dark."

Leeta yanks the flashlight from Sifat's hands and shuts it down. It doesn't matter if it's on or off. Her light doesn't count. They've made that clear. The path is bright enough for the rest of them without her small, dim, unsuitable beam. And nobody cares if she ever illuminates the darkness inside her.

As the ants march back to Fure City, Leeta grudgingly falls in line. Behind her breathing apparatus, she snorts like an angry machine. Zertee appears at her back, closing the prescribed distance between them by half.

"I am truly sorry, Leeta. My intention was to help you."

Leeta looks straight ahead, grim and defiant. "You failed."

CHAPTER 4

INTERROGATION

"Were you aware that FH1 was officially classified DNR (DO NOT REPEAT) and that no Furean scientists are permitted to attempt to reconstruct or reimagine any aspect of FH1 under any circumstances?"

"Yes, but—"

—High Genetics Council Final Disciplinary Hearing

LEETA FOLLOWS JEMUNO, the first Real grad to receive his maturation affirmation, through the long, curved corridor. When Leeta heard rumors he'd been named the Daht's Assistant-in-Waiting, she doubted it because they'd just graduated.

Was that only yesterday?

But seeing him in uniform makes it official.

Leeta has never been in the Administration Dome before, and it seems strange how eerily deserted this walkway is. Any of the others in Fure City would be packed in both directions at this time of day.

"So, what does the Daht want to talk to me about?" Leeta asks, trying and failing to keep her voice steady.

Jemuno, his short legs pumping, picks up the pace. Leeta easily catches up and taps his shoulder. "C'mon. You can tell me. I won't say anything to anyone."

He turns abruptly, tilting his neck at the extreme angle necessary to look her in the eye. "It is illogical to assume I have any knowledge of Daht Mayeel's intentions, so you should stop interrogating me."

"Sorry. I just thought you might have heard something."

"I have not."

He disappears around a curve, leaving Leeta wondering if this could be the perfect time to find an exit. They didn't pass any on the way here. She was paying close attention.

Jemuno calls to her from up ahead. "Hurry up, Leeta Simtar. The Daht is waiting for you."

Reluctantly, Leeta follows his voice and finds him standing in the middle of the corridor. As soon as he spots her, he moves to the wall and presses his palm against it. A secret door slides open onto a brightly lit room. He gestures for her to enter. She ducks her head and cautiously steps inside. As she does, the door closes behind her. She is alone.

An unseen, official-sounding voice welcomes her. "Hello, Leeta Simtar. The Daht will be with you shortly."

Like all rooms within Fure City, this one is domed. But unlike the others, it is windowless, apparently designed to ensure privacy for those, like Leeta, who've been called to meet with the Daht. Oddly though, for a meeting room, there are no seats except for the Daht's throne perched on a high pedestal behind a tall round table.

Leeta thinks about the cave and wonders if she'll ever see her treasures again. Her throat is sand-dry. Her feet ache worse than ever. She cups a hand over her pounding heart hoping to calm herself down. It doesn't work. The pounding quickens and grows so loud it bounces off the curved walls and echoes back into her ears. She looks at the dirty sleeves of her tunic and wishes she'd had time to change her clothes. *Wishing.* Yet another unFurean thing she's done today. Does the Daht know all her misdeeds?

Leeta has always assumed Daht Mayeel is all-knowing, even though it's not logical to believe anyone can know everything. Now that her treasures have been taken, the Daht definitely knows all of her secrets. What the girl doesn't yet know is that the Daht has deep secrets of her own. Secrets that involve Leeta.

In this quiet chamber, Leeta's thoughts are louder and more worrisome than usual.

Even if the Daht only knows half of what I did, there will be negative consequences.

A hidden portal off to the left silently opens. The Daht glides into the room wearing a yellow robe; its loose-fitting hood covers her head and shades her brow. She slowly climbs the steps to the throne and sits, ceremoniously settling her broad frame, meticulously smoothing the folds of her robe across her lap. Only then does she slowly weave her fingers together, one over the other, and calmly rest her folded hands on the table, giving Leeta plenty of time to watch all this while the Daht secretly observes the girl from under the edge of her hood.

"Hello, Leeta Simtar. Thank you for coming to talk with me."

Leeta wonders why is she being thanked as if she's done the Daht a favor by stopping by for a visit. She was summoned here. She had no choice.

"Please step forward."

Leeta obeys. The two of them are now at eye level.

"Will you please tell me what happened today?"

"Excuse me, Madam, but didn't Sifat make a report?"

"Yes. I have read her report thoroughly. And now I would like you to tell me what happened. In your own words."

"Everything?"

"Yes. Please."

Leeta inhales and blows the air out through pursed lips. "Okay. I left the party without permission. I ran away. I sat on a rock. I—" Her voice cracks. She looks down. "I hurt Fendro."

"I already know this, Leeta, and we will discuss any disciplinary action later. But for now, I want you to tell me what was happening inside of you that made you do these things."

Leeta shrugs. "I'm not sure. When things happen in my life—like when Brownie died. What? You don't know about that? It doesn't matter. I mean it *does* matter. So much. But only to me. That's the problem. Nobody else feels things in the same big, loud, embarrassing way as I do. My feelings are like a program override. Suddenly I've got no control over anything, and I need to be alone so I can calm down and think. That's why I was in the cave. Now do you understand?"

The Daht frowns slightly.

"I just want—" Leeta stops to figure out what she wants. There is so much, but right now, there is only one thing. "Please tell me you'll let me go to the cave whenever I need to."

The Daht stretches her palms flat on the table and leans forward. "I am sorry to disappoint you, Leeta, but I cannot allow that. I want you to be well, in body, mind, and emotions, but the best way to serve your needs is by accepting your place among us."

She stands, her head now higher than Leeta's. She takes off her hood and studies the girl intently. Leeta shifts uncomfortably but wills herself to hold the Daht's gaze.

"We are one family. You must try harder to be one with us. Self-imposed isolation is an ineffective remedy for quelling emotions. It is extremely unFurean."

Leeta pounds the table with her fist. "I'm sick of hearing how unFurean I am! Don't you think I know that? How could I forget it when everyone is always telling me to stop doing stuff because it's unFurean. But what about betraying a friend? Isn't that unFurean? Zertee had no right to tell anyone about my cave. Friends are supposed to keep your secrets."

"We have no secrets." The Daht begins chanting softly. Slowing the endless string of words as if it were a tram for Leeta to climb onboard. But Leeta refuses to go along for the ride.

"None of this would have happened if Zertee had kept her fat mouth shut!"

Reaching over the table, the Daht firmly places both cupped hands on Leeta's chest, triggering the same surge of comfort she felt at the graduation. Warmth radiates across her shoulders, down her spine, and through her arms, all the way to her fingertips. Leeta's mind quiets. Her anger fades. The Daht inhales and exhales audibly. Leeta joins her, and they breathe together as one.

"You are feeling better, Leeta Simtar?"

She is, but for some reason she wants to deny it. Instead, she nods.

"This feeling is your True Nature in repose, Leeta. Whenever you feel disconnected, the swiftest, most logical path to return to your True Nature is to reconnect with the Group." The Daht pauses and folds her hands together tightly over her belly. "The cave will be permanently sealed. Both entrances. Do not attempt to find another."

A sudden wave of sadness threatens to drag Leeta into a deep hole.

"I'm a terrible person."

"That is not true, Leeta. Biologically speaking, that is not even possible. You are a very good person."

"How do you know?" Leeta's voice suddenly rises. Her face turns dark, and she has trouble getting the words out fast enough. "You don't know anything about me. You have no idea what it's like to *be* me. Let me tell you, it's hard. But how could you know? Everyone loves you. Everyone is happy just to look at you. Not one single person on Fure is happy to see me. They all wish I wasn't here. But you don't care about that. You don't care about me because you have everything."

The Daht recoils, puts up her hood, and sits down. She places a cupped hand over her own heart and breathes slowly and deeply.

Uh oh.

"I'm very sorry, Madam. I shouldn't have said any of that. That was wrong. UnFurean. I'm so sorry. But now do you see what I'm talking about? I do and say terrible things all the time. I can't help it."

"There is a distinct difference between what you do and who you are. You are good. That is the undeniable truth. But it is also truth that your *behavior* is unacceptable at times."

"That makes no sense! Who I am and what I do are the same thing!" She's roaring like *Ka'aru.* "What's wrong with me, Madam? I'm the only Brid with Gemian DNA, but that can't be the problem because Gemians are peaceful, aren't they?"

The Daht's face clouds over for moment before she nods sharply. "Yes. It is true. Gemians are a peaceful species."

"Then I don't understand where these emotions of mine come from. All I know is when Fendro reached out his hand to pick up one of my personal things—"

"Fureans have no personal belongings. Materialism is un-Furean. We share everything because we—"

Leeta isn't listening. "—I just exploded as if a beast was attacking me, and if I didn't fight back with all my strength I would—"

"No one was attacking you. Sifat came with good intentions."

"—die! But that's what it felt like. So what else could I have done when she invaded my space?"

"Leeta, your space is within you. It cannot be invaded."

"You don't understand!" Leeta glares at the Daht with fierce intensity.

If she thinks Daht Mayeel is as easily intimidated as Sifat and the others, she's wrong. The Daht raises an amused eyebrow. Her chuckle is kind.

"Maybe not," she says waving her hand over the table. A panel slides open on the surface and the sealed silver cylinder rises into view. Leeta's heart hurts imagining her precious treasures piled on top of each other inside this dark prison.

"Now let's see what's in here that caused you so much distress."

The Daht waves her hand over the cylinder. It slides open. She reaches in and takes out the mug followed by the eyeglasses and sets them beside each other on the table. She leans in. A wistful longing fills her eyes, as if she has seen this mug and these eyeglasses before. But how? Leeta's models never left the cave before today. Zertee is the only one who's ever been in the secret hiding place and Leeta never showed Zertee her collection of treasures. Never even told her about them. Yet, there's an undeniable tenderness in the way the Daht handles the eyeglasses and gently traces the stems and frames with her fingertip as if touched by the memory of when she last saw them.

"Where . . ." The Daht stops, not trusting her voice. She clears her throat and begins again. "Where did these things come from?"

"I designed them."

"By yourself?"

"Yes. Why is everyone making such a big deal about this? What did I do wrong?"

"No one said you did anything wrong, Leeta. I am simply curious about your creative process."

From the time she was very young, Leeta *saw* things in her mind's eye. Unidentifiable things unlike any objects in the Central Nursery or in the Education Dome or on display in the History and Culture Museum. Once she asked Zertee what sort of things she saw in *her* mind's eye, but Zertee said her mind had no eyes. After that, Leeta no longer talked about the images. Instead, she began secretly drawing them, using small sharp stones to make designs in the sand. But time after time *Ka'aru* blew away the sketches. So Leeta decided to turn the images in her mind into things she could hold on to.

When she was eleven years old, she designed and modeled the first image—*The Starry Night* mug. Of course she was familiar with drinking vessels, but Furean containers and tools are completely devoid of decoration because, to the Furean mind, decoration has no function. When Leeta fashioned the vibrant mug, she was stunned by the way it looked. And the first time she held it in her hands, she was thunderstruck as tidal waves of the intense emotion—joy, belonging, loss, and despair—rose and fell within her and over her, lifting her up, dragging her down. If, at that time, Leeta Simtar had known what love was, she would have understood what powered the waves. But she didn't know love. Not yet. Even so, the emotions created a new realm within her where a new Leeta was born. She didn't share New Leeta with anyone, not even Zertee. It was enough that she existed, sleeping but growing stronger every day. Leeta hoped for a time when New Leeta would awaken and announce herself to everyone. Until then, she would continue modeling the strange objects that appeared in her mind's eye. Objects no one was ever meant to see.

The Daht reaches back into the cylinder, her short fingers wrapping around another object, something that's both round and angular. Drawing out the model of the radio telescope, she brings it up to her face. Her hands shake and her eyes go wide, as if she were suddenly facing the barrel of a loaded gun. She puts the model on the table and pushes it away. Then with the determination and practice that can only come from being the most public figure on Fure, the Daht puts her face back in place and turns to Leeta. "Where do your ideas come from?"

"My ideas? I don't know. I don't know where *any* ideas come from. Do you?"

The Daht gently rests her hand over the radio telescope. "Ideas originate in the brain and the unconscious mind. They're the product of synapses firing and making connections between thoughts and images and physical responses. What was the moment when your brain made a connection that inspired you to make these objects?"

Leeta shrugs, "Dunno."

Leeta reaches for *The Starry Night* mug and slides her fingers along the smooth surface, smiling to herself as if reconnecting with an old friend. "I appreciate that you want to help me get control over my emotions, Madam. I know that Sifat and Zertee also want to help me. But I don't need help because I have these treasures. I don't understand why they were taken away. They calm me and comfort me. What could be wrong with that?"

The Daht gestures to the mug, and Leeta hands it to her. When the Daht wraps both hands around it, her eyes gleam with a strange light. Tears? Definitely. But why?

"It's beautiful, isn't it, Madam?"

Instead of answering, the Daht sets the mug down on the table as if she can't let go of it fast enough. Clear-eyed again, she raises her chin. "Any form of attachment is an obstacle on our journey toward Enlightenment."

She flicks the air above her shoulder. A chime sounds. Jemuno appears. In a flash, he sweeps Leeta's collection back into the cylinder and carries it out of the room.

"No! Madam, please. Give them back. I need them!"

"You need to become a calm, well-disciplined Furean adult, Leeta. That is our goal for you."

Leeta's long frame sinks to the floor as she covers her face in her hands.

The Daht steps down from the throne, stands at Leeta's side and rests a cupped hand on her shoulder. Leeta pulls away.

"Please look at me, Leeta Simtar. I have something to tell you."

Leeta jerks her head up to meet the Daht's eyes. *Am I about to learn the singular truth of my life?*

The Daht exhales slowly. "Because of your behavior towards Fendro, and because of . . . other things . . . we think it best for you to spend time away from home to consider exactly how you will accomplish the goal of becoming more disciplined."

Time away? How is this the singular truth? This doesn't make sense. No, this has nothing to do with that. This my punishment for hurting Fendro.

Leeta has never lived outside of Fure City. She didn't know there were other places to live. But now that she thinks about it, getting away from this place doesn't sound terrible. New Leeta stirs in her sleep.

"Where are you sending me?"

Pleased at Leeta's sudden interest, the Daht favors her with a gentle smile. "That has not yet been decided. But all options under consideration will allow you to utilize your considerable knowledge of botanical ecosystems. This will be an opportunity to take your laboratory studies into the field and bring back observational data to expand the knowledge of all Fure. There is no greater honor than that. By contributing to our planet-wide database, you will favorably alter your reputation among our people."

Leeta didn't think she cared about impressing others, but hearing it put this way, she can't deny being more popular would make her life easier. Leeta stands, towering over the Daht.

"Okay. That sounds interesting. And since you haven't yet decided where I'm going, I'm wondering if you're open to suggestions, because I've always wanted to—"

"We are not open to suggestions." The Daht cuts her off. She quickly climbs the steps, resettles herself on her throne, and looks down at Leeta again, which feels much better than looking up at the girl for many reasons.

"When do I leave, Madam?"

"We will let you know well in advance of your departure date. In the meantime, please report to the Botany Dome and continue your work. That will be all."

Leeta fights the urge to say something else. Her eyes sting. Damnit! She's about to cry again and doesn't even know why.

"You will make us proud, Leeta Simtar."

Leeta looks at her trailing bootlaces, considers kneeling to tie them, then changes her mind.

"You may go now."

"Uh, what about the other thing?"

"What other thing?"

"At graduation you said you were going to tell me the singular truth of my life that would change everything. You said you'd tell me soon."

"Yes. I did say that. But I have reconsidered the timing of that disclosure."

"What?"

"You are dismissed."

Leeta angrily strides from the room, muttering, "*Yralba!*" under her breath.

CHAPTER 5
A SEED WILL GROW

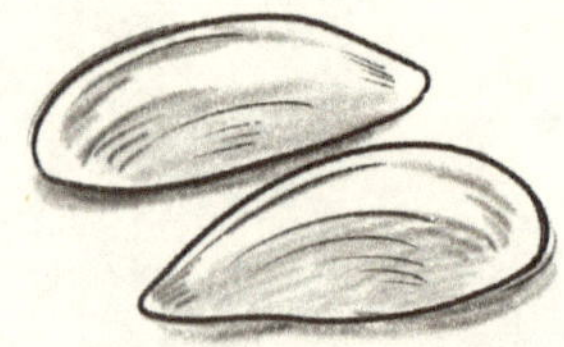

Within every seed, a universe slumbers.
—THE FUREAN BOTANIST'S HANDBOOK

LEETA AND ZERTEE WORK side by side, sweating in their sleeveless tunics within the controlled humidity of the botany dome. While Leeta harvests from the seed bank, Zertee half-fills labeled pots with granulated nutrients. Leeta and Zertee move between their tasks in perfect harmony, but just below the surface, Leeta's resentment toward her friend colors everything, like the blue overhead grow lights.

"Leeta, I have apologized eight times, but you have not said a word to me in 22 hours." Rare exasperation seeps into Zertee's voice. "You have not even looked at me. I am very sorry for what happened in the cave. That makes nine times. When will you accept my apology?"

Leeta knows she can resolve the tension and instantly make them both feel better by saying something like, "You meant well." Or "Sifat asked you where I was and you couldn't lie." Or simply, "I forgive you."

But she says nothing. Her heart prickles. Yet another indicator of the terrible person she is. She doesn't want to feel this way. She doesn't want to *be* this way. Zertee is her only friend. She longs to return to their easy way of talking, but anger and hurt have locked down her words and trapped her into sullen silence. Maybe she can let go if she gets one more apology. Ten is a good number. Waiting a while longer won't permanently damage the friendship. Friendship is sturdier than tiny seedlings. It won't die from a few hours of neglect.

It's also true that plants always grow stronger when they are nurtured.

Leeta takes two *quistel* seeds from the dispensing tray and places them in Zertee's palm, purposely letting her fingertips linger there for a moment. "These two are special," she says, smiling shyly. "Let's keep them together."

Zertee nods. "Always," she says, closing her hand around the seeds.

With that, Zertee places both seeds in the same pot, covering them with layers of three different sprouting nutrients. After the seeds have been planted, the girls measure the moisture that's been captured and recycled for these plants that are so essential to Furean survival. As Leeta watches each drop fall from the pointed spout of a calibrated squeeze bag and seep through the nutrients onto the two seeds, now nestled in their shared pot, Zertee records the precise amount of water they receive.

When the squeeze bag is empty, Leeta carefully refills it. Nothing wasted. Ever. "Zertee, have you ever heard of any place outside of Fure City where there is water?"

"Not enough to support us. Why do you ask?"

"No reason," she says, forcing a smile that makes her face feel sticky.

Leeta reaches the supply dispenser first, withdraws two neatly folded *subyls* and playfully tosses one to Zertee, who catches it one-handed. Back at their work station they begin cleaning the surfaces.

Without pausing her task, Zertee lowers her voice, "I am curious about what happened during your meeting with the Daht."

Leeta looks around cautiously. The only other botanists are a pair of females, huddled at an analysis station near the far edge of the dome. Whatever they're discussing can't be heard from this distance, and Leeta figures what she's about to say won't reach them, still, she lowers her voice as she tells Zertee everything the Daht said and failed to say.

"And you know the worst part? She permanently sealed my cave."

Zertee stops cleaning and frowns. Her eyes darken with sadness for her friend's loss. "That was not a nice thing for the Daht to do."

Leeta's mouth drops open. Zertee has never said one word against the Daht. Maybe the graduation has also changed her friend's perspective on the One Family.

Leeta shakes her head grimly. "Sure wasn't. I think she's trying to kill me."

"That cannot be accurate! You are worried and anxious due to the incomplete information she gave you. Your anxiety is feeding your negative thoughts, as it often does."

Zertee knows her well. And what she says is true, but there's more. "Okay, maybe she won't kill me, but I'm being disciplined. That can only mean something terrible!"

"That is an illogical conclusion, Leeta. Harshness and all forms of aggression are unFurean. Besides, you are not considering the derivation of the word discipline. Its root word means to instruct or train. Daht Mayeel will likely provide you with an opportunity for instruction or training."

Zertee offers a hopeful smile, squeezing in an extra dose of optimism.

Leeta leans in, scrutinizing her friend's broad face. "You *know* something!"

Zertee presses her lips together and busies herself brushing stray bits of nutrients back into their container.

Leeta clamps her hand on the brush, forcing Zertee to stop. "Tell me."

Zertee sighs. "Very well. I was informed that I will be traveling with you for a period of eight days."

"Where are we going?"

"Based on the packing list I received—"

"Wait! You got a packing list? I didn't get a packing list."

"Double check."

Leeta pulls out her APED and speaks into it. "AYA, I didn't get a packing list, did I?"

"Yeah, Leeta, you did. Six hours and forty-seven minutes ago. But since you didn't open it, I was just about to—"

"Never mind, AYA, I'll look at it later."

"Want me to send you a funny little reminder?"

"You don't need to . . . Okay. Sure. Send me a reminder in an hour."

"Reminder set for one hour. But don't blame me if you ignore it."

Leeta stuffs her APED into her pocket.

"What's on the list, Zertee?"

"One hundred fifty-nine different items. Based on the clothing, tools, and supplies we are to pack, I deduce there is a 98.29% probability that you and I are leaving Fure."

"Leaving? As in traveling into space?"

Zertee nods solemnly and prepares to console her emotional friend. But there's no time for that because Leeta has already pulled her into a joyful embrace. "Wow! That's great news!"

The other botanists, both Reals, look up from their cell analysis. Seeing the source of this unusual and highly un-Furean outburst, they shoot disapproving looks across the dome, but for once, Leeta is too happy to notice.

CHAPTER 6
READY OR NOT

"Why would a scientist like yourself, with full knowledge of this alien species' history and psychology, disregard official protocol and secretly undertake such a dangerous enterprise?"
—HIGH GENETICS COUNCIL FINAL DISCIPLINARY HEARING

Three months later . . .

LEETA AND ZERTEE, dressed in official-looking space travel training gear, enter a brightly lit locker room, take off their gloves and helmets, and look at each other. Leeta smiles excitedly, her bright eyes meeting Zertee's steady gaze. Without a word, they carefully fold and stow their gear, then quickly change into their normal clothes.

Leeta exhales loudly. "Well, tomorrow's the day." Her voice tingles with nervousness.

"Yes. Our training is complete and we are ready."

"You think? I mean, I'm sure *you're* ready and I guess I am too."

"Leeta, you are ready. Would you like my help double-checking your supply list?"

"No, thanks. I'm good."

They put on their breathing appliances and step out of the Training Dome, and silently walk side by side into the early evening light, which is barely dimmer than Fure's early morning, late morning, or mid-afternoon light. Without warning, Leeta sits on the ground, lays back, hands behind her head, gazing up at the perpetually cloud-clogged sky.

Zertee looks down at her, puzzled. "If you are tired, it would be more logical to return to the dorm to sleep."

"Yeah, it would," Leeta says, without moving.

"We should head back to the training dormitory. We will be awakened early in the morning."

"I don't need as much sleep as you do. Go ahead, Zertee. I just want to be by myself for a while."

"Are you sure? Because I would be more than happy to keep you company . . ."

"Thanks, but . . . go."

Zertee leaves as Leeta throws herself into a full mental movie where she's rocketing away from Fure, bursting through those clouds, and finally getting to the other side where she's experiencing the cosmos with its countless moons and planets, endless stars and galaxies. Maybe like all Brids, she has thought about her non-Furean parent from time to time. She doesn't know her father's name, only that he, like all alien DNA donors, willingly participated in Fure's Intergalactic Interspecies Program (IIP) in which members within the far reaches of the Alliance send DNA samples to Fure. Those samples were mixed in prescribed proportions with genetic material from Furean donors, a simple procedure that resulted in her existence.

Leeta wonders if any part of her Gemian family ever looks up at the sky and wonders about her. Assuming Gemians have individual families. Fureans don't. They are all one family, as they continually remind themselves. If that's how it is everywhere, then no Gemian ever had the least spark of curiosity about Leeta Simtar.

As she lies alone in the darkening dusk, she reminds herself she is best on her own and doesn't need a family. But lately, she has begun to wonder if it's actually true.

The next morning, Leeta and Zertee emerge from their dorm room dressed in hooded blue jumpsuits with the Furean Botany Team insignia patch emblazoned on their left arms. While their training has made them tough and strong, both girls are noticeably weighed down by their heavy boots, loaded backpacks, and the pair of large totes they each carry. They walk to the launch site, through a long corridor lined with an enthusiastic crowd of Reals and Brids who, despite the early hour, chant with the highest level of enthusiasm.

Zertee nods to everyone, chanting along with them. Leeta follows silently, too distracted by the flickering flames of so many different emotions all happening at once. She's embarrassed that everyone knows this mission is a direct consequence of her bad behavior. She's scared that space sickness will make her throw up all over her uniform. She's stressed she won't achieve the Daht's goal to become a well-disciplined Furean adult.

What happens if she doesn't change at all? What happens if she returns even less disciplined than she is now? Assuming that's even possible.

The chanting grows more forceful as the well-wishers swarm the girls like crazed fans. While Leeta towers over the crowd, her chest tightens, but for once, her boots fit well and her feet are grateful. As for the rest of her, Leeta is excited to be leaving Fure and hopeful this will be the start of something new and good in her life.

Someone taps her back. She turns to see Jemuno. "Leeta Simtar," he shouts above the noise. "The Daht summons you to a private meeting."

At his words, Leeta's heart drops, and the crowd gasps as one.

Is the Daht pulling her from the mission?

Cautiously she follows Jemuno through the crush of bodies, everyone eyeing her coldly now. Out in the corridor, away from the others, Jemuno makes a sudden right turn and leads her into a small room where the Daht awaits her, alone.

"Thank you, Jemuno. Give us five minutes."

He leaves and the Daht hands Leeta a small package tightly wrapped in soft blue fabric. "This is for you."

"Thank you, Madam. What is it?" Her fingers slyly prod the package.

"A small token given to me years ago by a friend, before our last goodbye. Since you are departing Fure on your first intergalactic mission, I deemed it an appropriate gift. Of course, all similarities end there as you will be returning in eight days. Two days to travel in each direction, four days at your destination."

"I'm honored. That's very kind of you. May I open it?"

"Not until you leave."

"Alright. Well, thanks for the gift," she says, opening her backpack and pushing the blue package deep inside. "I'll share this with Zertee."

"No. Do not share it with Zertee. Do not even show it to Zertee."

"Okay then. I won't," she says, refastening the pack. Then trying to sound as casual as possible she adds, "Do you think this is a good time to tell me the singular truth of my life?"

The Daht flicks the air above her shoulder. A chime sounds. "It is time now for your ship to depart."

Jemuno re-enters and waits by the door. Leeta hoists her backpack onto her shoulders. Despite the lightness of the Daht's gift, somehow and without knowing why, she feels the weight of it.

Back at the launch site the Daht leads the group in drumming and chanting all for the benefit of the soon-to-be space travelers. Zertee beams with pride. Leeta searches her many pockets for *turil*. By the time she locates some, the Daht is looking right at her. Leeta looks away and decides this is not the best time for a snack.

After too many rounds of enthusiastic chanting, the Daht raises her index finger. Silence reigns. The Daht seemingly glides away from the launch site, and the crowd follows like iron shavings clinging to a magnet. Suddenly the girls are alone. The spacecraft doors slide open.

"Huh," says Leeta. "That was strange the way they just left. Wasn't that strange?"

Zertee nods. "I expected they would stay long enough to toast our departure with at least two rounds of *hastip*."

Leeta chuckles. "Yeah, well, maybe they decided not to because they didn't want me hugging everyone goodbye."

"You would do that?"

Grinning, she picks up her gear and hurries into the ship. "You never know what I might do."

Zertee collects her own gear and walks into the ship, pondering the infinite possibilities of what could happen while traveling in space with her very strange friend.

CHAPTER 7
OUT OF THIS WORLD

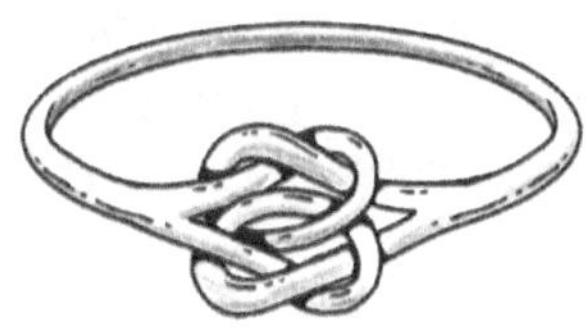

"Unlike our system of Collective Nurseries, these parents raise their own offspring and commonly maintain relationship bonds long after their offspring have matured and created family units of their own. I came to appreciate positives and negatives within each system of child-rearing."
—HIGH GENETICS COUNCIL FINAL DISCIPLINARY HEARING

LEETA SITS ON THE EDGE of her seat pressed close to the viewport of the spaceship. As she watches Fure shrink, she marvels at how quickly the distance is growing between everything she's ever known and all that is unknown. She felt jittery before the start of the mission that will take her and Zertee 40 light-years away, to a relatively obscure eight-planet solar system where they'll be investigating the plant life on the largest moon revolving around its largest planet. But now that they're officially on their way, Leeta's heart surges with excitement.

"Zertee! Look how incredibly beautiful this is. We saw stars in the simulator, but I never imagined there were this many, or that in real life, they'd appear so sharp and brilliant. Like a billion trillion seeds of light."

But because Leeta is Leeta, worry also seeps into her thoughts.

I've only done lab botany. Field botany is really different. What if I can't do this?

What if I make a terrible mistake and endanger Zertee or myself?

The Daht wants me to become more Furean during this mission. What if that's not possible?

The cosmic light show before her is not unlike the swirling golden stars that decorated her much loved and now lost Starry Night mug. She knows that some of the light comes from distant galaxies, while some pinpoints are individual stars. She is also aware that circling many of those brilliant stars, are planets, unseen but still there. Some of those planets are probably just like Fure, wind-swept and rocky, but some must be very different from Fure. She thinks about Gema, her father's home planet, and more questions percolate in her brain.

Are the people on Gema anything like me?

If I went there, how would I be treated?

"Zertee, do you ever wonder about your Trexan parent and what traits you might have inherited from him or her?"

"No. Why would I think about that? My Furean DNA represents the best of me."

"Yeah. That's what Brids have always been told. Hide the parts of you that are unFurean. But what if your Trexan parts are actually your best parts? And my best parts are Gemian?"

The thought slams Zertee with a nasty jolt of confusion, throwing her logical mind into a muddle. She starts to speak, then stops.

"It's possible," Leeta says. "And we'd never know, would we?"

No answer.

Leeta swivels in her chair to see Zertee across the cabin at the computer console, poring over system readouts.

"Zertee, come sit with me and look at the stars."

Zertee fixes her eyes on the displays. "No, thank you. I am checking our systems and documenting observations. Did you know that our trajectory will bring us in proximity of the X429 asteroid? That's close enough to look for anomalies and take photos. Of course, *close* is a relative term. This is not an alarming situation. In case you are worrying."

"I'm not worrying about colliding with an asteroid. And you're not either. The whole system is automated. It will steer us clear of any danger. It doesn't need you to monitor it."

Leeta spins back to the viewport, dreamily watching the cosmic show. "What could you possibly be doing that's more important than looking at this?"

Zertee swipes through data on multiple displays, making adjustments and taking notes. "I am recording all aspects of this initial part of our mission. Radiation shield protection levels. Velocity fluctuations. Composition of gaseous particles in our path."

Leeta shakes her head, wishing there was someone, somewhere, to share the magic of the universe with. She walks across the cabin into the alcove that serves as the galley and swipes her hand through the menu display. From a small opening in the counter surface, a cup of steaming orange liquid rises followed by a cup filled of steaming green liquid. Leeta carries both beverages back into the main cabin and places the orange one beside Zertee.

"Thank you," Zertee says, barely noticing the drink.

Leeta sips her own green beverage and studies the console. "So how much longer until we get far enough from Fure's gravitational pull to jump to hyperspace?"

Zertee taps a data field. "Five hours and seventeen minutes. After that we'll travel in hyperspace for the next 31 hours until we exit and arrive within a twelve-hour journey of Ganymede."

"Lots of time. Hey, how about, just for fun, we do some research on Trexo and Gema?

Zertee quickly enters search parameters. "Trexo is located in the outer section of the galaxy's Gamma quadrant. Gema is in the Beta quadrant. There is no explanation we could offer the Daht to justify why we were researching such distant planets."

"Yeah, I guess you're right. Forget about them. Maybe something closer. Like Earth! It's the only inhabited planet in our mission's solar system." Leeta sits at the console and does her own quick search. "How about that? When we arrive, Ganymede and Earth will be closer to each other than at any other time during the year. Let's research Earth. And don't say you're not curious."

"I am curious about many things, and yes, life on Earth is one of them. But Earth's database is off-limits and inaccessible to us."

"True, but *why?* C'mon, Zertee. Tell the truth. Haven't you ever wondered why we're not permitted to study Earth?"

"Yes, I have been curious about that restriction, but I am sure there is a good reason for it even if you and I are not aware of what that reason might be."

"Uh, huh. Okay. You're no fun. Maybe you get that from your Trexan DNA. I'm going to put my stuff away."

Leeta walks past the galley and into the storage alcove where she sits on the floor and struggles to pull off her left boot. After a full minute, she manages to free the boot and toss it into an empty cubby.

"I know why you're here," Leeta says in a voice loud enough to be heard in the next room.

Zertee appears in the alcove entryway, holding her cup, but not drinking from it. Leeta still sits on the floor, now working on freeing her right boot.

"You do?" Zertee asks.

"Oh, yeah. You're here to keep an eye on me."

"That is true." Zertee says this without a hint of shame.

Leeta looks up. "I knew it. You're spying."

"That is not true."

"Hey. It's okay. It had to be the Daht's idea. I know you wouldn't want to spy on me. But when she assigned you to this mission, you agreed because, let's face it, you're too much of a coward to say no to her."

"It is illogical to brand me a coward. Many Fureans consider me very brave to go anywhere alone with you."

Leeta bends her knee and pulls her foot in close to get a better grip on the boot. It's still not budging. "Why brave?" she says, growing more frustrated by the moment. "Because the others are scared of my mood swings?"

Zertee exhales and nods. "Yes. You frighten most people, but you do not frighten me. And for the sake of accuracy, the Daht did not *assign* me to this mission. She intended to send you to Ganymede alone."

The boot finally slides off Leeta's foot. She hurls it into the cubby, missing the opening by a long shot and knocking the wall with a loud *thwack*.

"The only reason you're not here alone," Zertee continues, "is because I convinced the Daht to let me go with you."

For a moment Leeta is speechless. She stands, barefoot, towering over Zertee. "Why would you do that?"

"Because I am your friend, and I did not want you to face the unknown by yourself."

As the words sink in Leeta's eyebrows scrunch together. Zertee cannot translate this expression or the half dozen other shape-shifts flitting across her face. When Leeta suddenly rushes at her, Zertee prepares to fend off an attack. No need. Leeta bends forward and warmly embraces her friend. Zertee's Furean nature dictates that she must receive the hug impassively. Yet she is also moved by the gesture and wonders if this unexpected surge of emotion might be a direct effect of her Trexan heritage.

Leeta smiles through her tears. "Zertee, you're the only person who understands me even a little bit. There's so much I don't even understand about myself. Or you! I'd like us to know each other better. I think that's what it means to be friends. Maybe, during this mission, in addition to studying the biology of Ganymede, you and I could try to understand each other better. What do you think?"

"It is always beneficial to increase understanding."

Leeta grins. "I agree." She raises her cup to Zertee.

They clink their cups together and drink.

An alert sounds.

Both girls rush into the main cabin as the Daht appears as a hologram. "Good evening, Zertee. Good evening, Leeta Simtar. One Mind. One Goal. One Family."

Zertee bows her head and enthusiastically repeats the words. Leeta doesn't bother doing either. If the Daht notices, she doesn't show it.

"I trust you girls are both settled into your ship's quarters and that the mission's objectives, schedule, and procedural doc are clear."

"They certainly are, Madam," Zertee says, smiling broadly and nodding. "Thank you for checking in with us. We appreciate your thoughtfulness. In fact, Leeta Simtar and I were just discussing how fortunate Fure is to have such an outstanding and compassionate leader as yourself. You make us all feel so special."

"Thank you, Zertee. Do either of you have any questions or concerns?"

"Not me," says Leeta curtly. Zertee watches, appalled, as Leeta fishes a *turil* out of her pocket, and, without even trying to hide what she's doing, pops the candy into her mouth.

Zertee pulls her eyes away from Leeta and blurts out. "We are both very excited about our eight-day mission with the primary objective to explore plant life on Ganymede. I have committed the six secondary objectives as well as the 27 lower-level objectives to memory. Would you like me to recite them, Madam?"

"That will not be necessary, as I wrote the mission protocol myself."

Leeta stifles a laugh. Zertee raises an eyebrow but continues smiling at the Daht.

Jemuno appears in the hologram and whispers in the Daht's ear. She looks at him briefly, waves him away, then focuses on the girls again.

"I must remind you both that there is no possibility of extending this mission beyond the approved eight days. In the past, newly graduated space scientists who successfully completed their mission were free to explore for an extra day before returning to Fure. Unfortunately, one pair went too far, entered an asteroid field, and were never heard from again. We lost their ship, all their data, and the two of them. For your own safety and the security of our collective knowledge bank, eight days is the limit. After that, we will take control of your ship and bring it back. Is that clear?"

Zertee, wide-eyed and serious, nods. "Oh, yes, Madam. Very clear."

Leeta sips her beverage and says nothing.

"There will be times during this mission when it will be impossible to reach me personally," the Daht continues. "But I will be tracking your APEDs at all times. Also, please note that all of your communications with Fure will be monitored. Of course, I have no doubt that you can skillfully handle unexpected challenges or emergencies."

Leeta chokes on her drink. "Emergencies? Like what?"

"If we could predict unexpected challenges, Leeta Simtar, they wouldn't be unexpected, would they? I understand your apprehension, this being your first mission, but I can assure you, even those who have completed dozens of missions will attest to the fact that there will come at least one time when a team or team member is required to pivot and create a new plan of action."

Jemuno reappears on the hologram, clears his throat, and hands a tablet to the Daht. Without missing a beat, she takes it from him and hurriedly scrolls.

The Daht barely glances at the girls. "Good mission," she mutters then returns her full attention to the tablet.

Zertee bows her head low. "One Mind. One Goal. One Family, Madam."

The transmission ends abruptly but Zertee is unaware and continues talking. "Thank you so much for taking the time to check in with us. I cannot even imagine how busy you are. Just seeing your face and hearing your voice and words of wisdom adds even greater honor to our mission. It is with extreme humility and sense of purpose—"

"You can stop now, Zertee. She's gone."

Zertee opens her eyes and flushes with embarrassment. "So she is." She concentrates on slowly sipping her beverage.

Leeta walks across the cabin and flops into her seat by the viewport, but instead of looking at the stars, she faces Zertee. "Why did you change your voice when you talked to her?"

Zertee calls up a new display of data. "How very astute of you to notice."

"Impossible to miss it," says Leeta. "Your tone instantly became higher. You started talking twice as fast as normal." She ticks off the evidence on her long fingers. "Also, you were flattering her. A lot! And when you're weren't flattering her, you were bragging about your intelligence and organizational skills." She throws up her hands in Zertee's face. "Will you please explain your behavior?"

Zertee takes an abnormal amount of time to finish the rest of her drink. Finally she says, "Is this request part of our mutual effort to understand each other better?"

Leeta nods. "Yes, it's like studying the water needs of different plant species. If you and I understand each other better, we can do a better job of showing we care."

"That is very logical. I will gladly explain my behavior. I flatter the Daht whenever I get the opportunity, in order to convey how much I admire her. Which I do. As for prominently displaying my intelligence and organizational skills, my motivation is simple and straightforward. Now that we have reached maturity, the Daht has begun handing out higher-level assignments."

"Yeah. Look where that boot-polisher Jemuno ended up."

"Exactly my point. I am certain he attained his current inner circle position by flattering the Daht and making his accomplishments known to her. Likewise, I am trying to impress her because I have aspirations to be in charge of my own botany experiments. And some day, my own lab."

"Huh. Well, that makes sense. And now that I understand why you do that stuff, I won't be so annoyed the next time you do it."

"Thank you. Now it is my turn to ask a question. I am curious to know why you altered *your* voice when you spoke to the Daht."

Leeta inhales dramatically and folds her arms across her chest. "I don't know what you're talking about."

"I am also curious to know why you are pretending not to know what I am talking about when I am 98.5 percent certain that you *do*. From the start of the transmission, you seemed ready to fight with the Daht. Why were you looking for opportunities to create tension?"

Leeta lets the question hang in the air between them for so long the edges of the words begin to curl up and crack like last season's *fwaydrun*.

Finally, she shrugs. "I dunno."

Not much of an answer. Definitely not likely to satisfy Zertee. But it is the truth. Leeta doesn't know why she distrusts the Daht because she's never actually thought about it. Now, with Zertee watching her so intently, her eyes brimming with encouragement, Leeta feels like it would be okay to try to figure this out in real time.

She lets out a long breath. "Something about the Daht has always rubbed me the wrong way. But at the graduation, when she looked me straight in the eye for the first time, it felt like she knows something about me that *I* should know but don't. It's like she's holding back personal information so she'll have power over me. She's supposed to be compassionate and all-knowing. She ought to know how awful this power trip makes me feel. The whole thing is . . . I don't know what it is but I just—well, I hate it."

"Hate is—"

"UnFurean." They both say it at the same time.

Leeta laughs, too long and too loud. It wasn't that funny but it feels good to laugh. When she recovers, she's instantly somber.

"I'm sorry if that stuff I said about the Daht made you uncomfortable."

"I accept your apology, but I am not uncomfortable. Everyone is entitled to their own opinion. I am glad you told me how you feel. It helps me understand you better. I think we will look back at this time together as a gift from the Daht."

"Oh, that reminds me." Leeta disappears into the alcove, and returns with the package wrapped in blue fabric. "She gave me this to me and said I could only open it after we left Fure's orbit."

Leeta hasn't forgotten the Daht's instructions not to show the gift to Zertee, but Zertee has proved herself to be a real friend, and real friends share secrets. Besides, if the Daht somehow finds out what she's about to do, Leeta isn't worried. That surprises her. She doesn't know why she's no longer scared to go against the Daht's wishes, but she welcomes this change in herself. Maybe it's New Leeta.

Leeta unwraps the soft blue fabric, revealing a sealed box. She tries to open it with her hands, but can't. She grabs a knife from the galley to pry the box open. Nothing.

She holds the box out to Zertee. "Help me," she says.

But even with Zertee clinging tightly to the bottom of the box and Leeta pulling on the top, the lid won't budge.

"Great gift! A box that won't open." Leeta scoffs, dropping the box on the console. "I feel so special."

An hour later, the girls lie in their cocoon-like sleep sacks suspended from the walls of a small chamber adjacent to the storage alcove. Zertee's eyelids are already drooping but Leeta is as talkative as ever.

"This feels different, doesn't it?" she says, looking around the chamber. "Our first night not sleeping in the Collective Nursery or in the Training Dome. And when we return, we'll move into Collective Adult housing."

"True."

"The Nursery staff who raised us treated Reals and Brids equally, but they didn't care about us."

"Why do you say they did not care?" Zertee's voice slows, as if speaking takes more energy than she's got left in her tank.

"They didn't. Not like really caring. I've observed animals with their young. Even *sanderols* feed their little ones for months, protecting them and teaching them to fend for themselves until they are ready to go out on their own. That's caring. Ever wondered what it would have been like to be raised by your own biological mother or father? In a very small dome? Just big enough for your parent, and you, and any siblings?"

"No, I have not," Zertee says through a yawn. "But it appears as though you have thought about this and I am curious to hear what you imagine that type of upbringing to be like."

Joy sparks in Leeta's heart, ignited by the idea of someone who is truly curious about her thoughts, illogical and un-Furean as they often are.

Zertee yawns again. It's a big one. Ever polite, her eyes fight to stay open. They are losing.

"You're a good friend, Zertee, but we don't need to keep talking about this now. I'll shut up and let you sleep."

Zertee falls asleep as quickly as a hunk of *grentrum* breaks off from a rock face and hits the ground. As if on cue, a continuous beep sounds from the main cabin. Zertee is too far gone to hear it, but Leeta rolls out of her sleep sack and hurries toward the sound. The Daht's gift box sits on the console, beeping and pulsing with blue light. Leeta reaches for it. At her touch the beeping stops and the box opens, revealing layers of padded blue fabric. Underneath the padding lies a small circle of yellow metal. It is cold to the touch. One edge is plain. The opposite is elegantly twisted into a double intertwining knot. Leeta has never seen anything like it.

She clears away the box and places the metal circle in the center of the console. "AYA, what is this thing?"

AYA speaks. "Aren't you supposed to be sleeping?"

"Please just answer the question."

"Okay. But don't blame me if you're crabby in the morning."

An enlarged holographic image of the object appears above the console, along with scrolling text and a chart of the object's elemental composition.

"This object is a manufactured ornament made to be worn on a finger or toe. It is called a *ring* (a class of jewelry). While Fureans do not adorn themselves with any kind of jewelry, wearing jewelry is customary on several dozen of the Alliance

Planets that trade with Fure. This ring is made of 75% gold, 12.5% copper, and 12.5% silver."

Leeta taps the text with her finger. The scrolling stops and AYA stops talking.

Leeta leans in and studies the list. Gold. Copper. Silver. The mostly commonly found elements on Fure are silicon, aluminum, iron, calcium, sodium, potassium, and magnesium. Gold, copper, and silver only exist in trace amounts on Fure, so it is highly unlikely this ring originated there.

Leeta swipes the text and it vanishes but the holographic image of the ring remains. "AYA, where did this ring come from?"

"Hm. Good question. Based on its composition, it is possible this ring came from any one of the following planets that practices jewelry-making. Have a look."

A lengthy scrolling list of planetary names appears. Leeta recognizes many of the names, but not all. One planet she knows, Gema, is not on the list. She wonders who produced the ring and what kind of friendship that person had with the Daht.

Leeta reaches out to the hologram, pinching opposite edges of the ring, stretching and peering at the magnified image. Any tiny detail might provide more information. When she brings the image closer to her face something on the inside rim catches her eye. Three engraved symbols followed by ten other symbols that look like this:

18K WR TO RR 1960

She touches the first three symbols. "AYA what do these symbols mean?"

"Those? That's easy, if you wanted to know about the symbols, you should have asked me earlier."

"Well, I just noticed them."

"You should learn to be more observant, Leeta."

"Thanks for the suggestion. I'll work on it. What do they mean?"

"The letter k stands for karat which is a unit of measurement used exclusively on Earth to describe the purity of gold. One karat is equal to 1/24th of pure gold—"

"—Did you say Earth?"

"Yes, thank you for interrupting. Earth is the third of eight planets orbiting around a G-type yellow-dwarf main sequence star—"

"AYA, stop. I know about Earth. So, then what does '18K' mean?"

"Like I said before, 18K gold is 18 parts gold to 6 parts other metals, or 75% pure gold combined with 25% other metals, in the case of this ring, equal parts copper and silver."

"What about the other ten symbols?"

"They belong to several Earth language alphabets. The last four symbols are numbers. I am 94.92% certain that '1960' refers to a year in Earth's twentieth century. As for 'WR TO RR'? I don't have a clue."

"Thanks, AYA, that was helpful."

"Really helpful? Or kind of helpful?"

"Helpful. Good night, AYA."

Leeta reaches for the actual ring, absently rolling the cold circle back and forth between her thumb and forefinger while she attempts to piece together what she already knows.

The ring was made on Earth.

A friend gave the ring to Daht Mayeel right before they parted.

Either the friend received the ring from a human and gave it to the Daht or the Daht's friend *was (or is)* human.

Humans don't possess the technology for interstellar travel; therefore, no human friend visited the Daht on Fure.

If the Daht's friend is human, then the friend must have given her the ring when they were both *on Earth!*

Then Leeta thinks about two big unanswered questions:

First, what was the Daht doing on Earth since it has long been off-limits to Fureans? The second big one, why did she give the ring to Leeta?

Leeta places the gold ring onto her index finger. Instantly a bright, clear vision of a large, meaty, alien hand, the back of which is sparsely covered with fine reddish hair, appears in her mind's eye. The hand gently slips this same ring onto a short, broad thumb that can only belong to a Furean. The two hands clasp tightly as if they will not ever part again.

Startled and bewildered by what she's seeing, Leeta pulls off the ring. The vision vanishes, yet it lingers in her mind. She has no idea what just happened. No idea what she just saw. She only knows that the pounding of her heart, a feeling she's always associated with fear and loneliness, now fills her with a sense of safety and belonging.

She looks at the ring. Clearly this is what triggered the vision that had all the look and feel of a memory. But it isn't one of Leeta's memories. She wonders who it belongs to. She also wonders if there could possibly be a connection between this moving vision of two hands and the various still images from her mind's eye that led her to create the treasured objects in her collection. Objects that made the Daht cry.

Leeta slips the ring on and off different fingers, hoping to trigger more visions that might provide answers. Nothing.

AYA speaks up. "Leeta, do you want additional information about the ring at this time?"

"Yes! What can you tell me AYA?"

"I cannot tell you anything, Leeta."

"But you just said . . . Never mind. AYA, give me additional information about the ring."

"Very well, Leeta. You now have access to the relevant Top Secret Databases."

"What? I don't have security clearance. Why are you giving me access to Top Secret stuff?"

"Who is giving you access?"

"AYA, you just said *you* were. Why would you do that?"

"What am I doing, Leeta?"

"What's going on, AYA?"

"Leeta Simtar, you ask too many questions."

"So, you aren't giving me access?"

"Access to what?"

Just as Leeta is about to scream *That's not funny!* a large holographic sphere appears. At her touch, it opens, revealing three smaller spheres. She taps the first sphere. Text appears and begins scrolling as AYA reads:

"The Intergalactic Interspecies Program (IIP)—A history. Through a vast network of willing Donors and Recipients within the Planetary Alliance, the Intergalactic Interspecies Program (IIP) has enhanced, supported, and accelerated the ethical development of non-Furean civilizations for 1500 years."

As a Brid, Leeta already knows about IIP. Not interested in learning more, she taps the text. It vanishes. She taps the second sphere. New text appears and begins scrolling as AYA reads:

"Furean/Human Interspecies Hybrid Experiment 1 (FH1)—The Case of Bortak-Morsee."

Leeta is unaware of the detailed history of FH1, but like all Reals and Brids, she knows the name Bortak-Morsee. It hurts to be reminded that Bortak-Morsee was a Gemian Brid, like herself. Who would want any perceived connection to Bortak-Morsee, the ultimate Bad Guy in every cautionary tale for children? The traitor who breached Furean protocol and harmed millions. The renegade whose bad acts led him to a very bad, but well-deserved ending. And that, kids, is what happens when you dare to believe you are more important than One Mind. One Goal. One Family.

Leeta jabs at the text. It vanishes.

She taps the third sphere and new text appears and begins scrolling as AYA reads the file name:

"High Genetics Council Final Disciplinary Hearing for Eta-Bakara. 17.06.28"

Leeta has never heard of Eta-Bakara but the file name intrigues her. She can't help wondering what kind of discipline this woman got and what, if anything, she did to deserve it.

She taps START and a Furean woman Leeta doesn't recognize appears on a hologram. Her bronze complexion and fine white hair set off her sculpted face and sharp features. Under a thick black unibrow, her eyes are intelligent and uncompromising. The woman is partially turned away from the camera, hastily scrolling through files on a smaller hologram on her left.

An unseen male voice asks, "Eta-Bakara, are you ready to begin?"

The woman shuts down the small hologram, turns, exhales between tight lips and looks directly at Leeta.

"Yes, I am ready," she says, in a low, steady voice.

"Very well," says the Interrogator. "For the record. Please state your name, classification, and your understanding of the reason you have been called to testify before the Genetics Council today."

"I am Eta-Bakara, genetics researcher and Intergalactic Communications Specialist 3A. I am testifying before the Council today to explain and defend my personal breaches of protocol."

For the next hour and forty minutes Leeta watches, transfixed, as Eta-Bakara tells a story that's equal parts reckless, gutsy, romantic, and shocking. It shatters Leeta to the core. Yet the storyteller remains cooly detached, as if her words described intimate details of a stranger's life. At the last moment, though, something else is revealed. Leeta pauses the hologram, freezing Eta-Bakara's face. Behind her fixed expression, her eyes reflect the lingering tragedy she carries with her.

Leeta's heart is heavy. Her breathing, hard and fast. Her thoughts shift and swirl like sand at the mercy of *Ka'aru*. Not just her thoughts, but Leeta *herself* has become the shifting, swirling sand. Fragmented into a million particles. Devoid of any sense of who she is or where she's going. And then just as suddenly as *Ka'aru* can whip up chaos, the wind dies and Leeta's fragmented thoughts click into place. Here, out in deep space, completely untethered from everything she's known, Leeta Simtar discovers that all her unanswered questions about why she is the way she is are answerable. Her parents weren't simply DNA donors. They were people who met against immeasurable odds. People who loved each other and risked everything to be together. Leeta exists because of their profound connection. Because she now knows part of their story, she knows part of her own.

She has four days to discover the rest.

Ten hours later, Zertee wakes to find a hologram message hovering over Leeta's empty sleep sack. "I took Escape Pod 1 for a research mission. I left the four-person pod for you just in case. Don't worry about me, Zertee. I'll be in touch."

ACT II

EARTH

CHAPTER 8

THE UNWELCOMING

Furean genes cannot overcome Earth's hostile social environment.

—THE CASE OF BORTAK-MORSEE,
HIGH GENETICS COUNCIL REPORT, FINAL CONCLUSION

LEETA SIMTAR HAS FINALLY learned the *singular truth* of her life and it only took 17 years. If she had waited for the Daht to get around to telling her, she might have died without knowing. Now that she knows, her heart bristles with outrage at the secrets and lies she's been raised on. Is that the Furean way? One Mind. One Goal. One Family. One massive load of *frig* shit.

In this moment, Leeta only wants to grow the fury inside her until the unchecked flames explode with a destructive force the likes of which the Daht and her devotees have never known. That will show all of them not to mess with Leeta Simtar.

As she fans the flames of her darkest thoughts, the water planet slips into view, opening a world within Leeta, cooling her fiery rage, filling her with hope. Bands of feathery clouds part, revealing vast stretches of green. So much green. Endless mountain ranges reach for the sky, some topped with trees, some covered in white, which Leeta correctly assumes is an accumulation of frozen water crystals. And many of the mountain peaks are as barren as the wind-swept ridges of Fure. But mostly, Leeta sees the blue oceans of Earth. So much blue. Leeta cannot imagine any place in the galaxy as beautiful. Surely there never was a place more at odds with the ancient rocks and rules of Fure. A girl could become a whole new person here.

From her hurried research of other off-limits databases, which she somehow accessed before jumping into the escape pod, she knows Earth's surface is 71% water. She also knows that she is not Gemian. Leeta Simtar is 71% human. She has always been curious about Earth without knowing why, but now it all starts to make sense. Leeta and Earth are linked. Even before she understood who and what she was, on some deep chromosomal level, she already knew the truth.

Her spherical escape pod, a transparent blue-tinged one-seater rimmed in chrome, descends silently over an open meadow surrounded by a dense forest whose trees are identified by the Earth database she downloaded into her auxiliary memory implant.

The implant speaks inside her brain.

Pine trees (genus Pinus): *evergreen, conifers that can be found throughout the world, but are native to northern temperate regions.*

Conifers: *trees that produce cones that encase reproduction seeds.*

To the east, not far away, a circular array of towering objects rise on a plateau, their enormous curved faces pointing at the sky. The implant identifies them for Leeta.

Radio telescopes: *instruments used to detect and amplify radio waves and microwaves emitted by astronomical objects, such as stars, galaxies, black holes, and planets, and turn them into signals astronomers use to enhance their understanding of the Universe.*

Of course, Leeta recognizes them because, apparently, one just like these was the inspiration for her model. When the radio telescope first appeared in her mind's eye, she didn't know what it was, but now she does.

Downslope from the radio telescopes stands the SETI Institute. The implant fills her in.

SETI: *acronym for Search for Extraterrestrial Intelligence, a collective term for scientific searches, monitoring electromagnetic radiation for signs of transmissions from civilizations on other planets.*

Thanks to Eta-Bakara's archived testimony at the disciplinary hearing, Leeta knows that SETI is where her father conducted his research and where Eta-Bakara first contacted him. Once she lands, SETI will be her first stop. Unless something stops her first.

Through his grease-smeared kitchen window, Rick Rodriguez, a rough-edged, mustached dude with a permanent squint, spots something descend from the sky and hover above the meadow. He flings open his front door for a better look. With shaky hands he aims his phone and snaps some photos. Milliseconds later, whatever it was vanishes into the forest. Rick curses and swipes through a dozen blurry images. Someone with less knowledge of these things would easily write them off as photos of a drone, a weather balloon, or possibly a turkey vulture. They'd be dead wrong. Rick knows what he just saw because it's not the first time he's seen it. These photos are nearly identical to the other blurry framed images hanging in his living room.

He calls 911.

"911, what is your emergency?"

"I just saw a UFO hovering about 30 feet above Blake's Meadow. I think it landed in the pine woods."

"Hello, Rick. How're you doing this evening?"

"How am I doing? Sandy, did you hear what I said? I saw another UFO and this time I've got credible photographic evidence."

"Good for you."

"Don't you talk to me like I'm some kind of lunatic."

"Calm down, Rick. No one's calling you a lunatic."

"Trust me. This is the real deal. And damn if this one doesn't look just like the one from 18 years ago. I'd bet anything these invaders are from the same planet as the last bunch."

"You don't say?"

"We don't have time for this! Those freakin' aliens may already be abducting our neighbors and their pets! Probably eating them for dinner. Or worse! Are you gonna send Tyler out here or do I have to defend humanity all by myself?"

"Oh, excuse me, Rick. Babs Sorensen just texted. Mike fell off a ladder in the garage and can't get up. I've gotta send Tyler over there right away."

"But what about—?"

Sandy cuts him off, cold and quick. "Looks like the fate of humanity is in your hands. Good luck."

Rick grabs a shotgun propped by the window and races out the front door with his dog.

"C'mon, Gunner. We've got aliens to catch."

Late afternoon sunbeams fill the pod as it touches down in a forest.

"AYA, open the hatch."

"You got it, Leeta."

The hatch opens. Unable to contain her wonder, Leeta reaches up to touch the golden light. Cupping her hands together, she turns them inward and brings them to her face so she can study the sunlight illuminating the spaces between her fingers, making the edges glow red. Giggling, she closes her eyes, as the loveliest shade of orange-red fills her field of vision. Her heart pulses with joy at the realization that she is witnessing her lifeblood, pulsing behind her eyelids, illuminated by Earth's closest star, allowing her, for the first time ever, to see through her own skin. Any Earth child would be familiar with this simple game. But Leeta is new to sunlight. New to Earth. As far as first impressions go, this one is good.

Shifting her backpack on her shoulders, the young stranger emerges from her escape pod into a strange world and steps into a few inches of water! This must have been left by a recent rainfall. Leeta's read about rain and how it is so plentiful in many places on Earth that no one needs to collect and save each precious drop like they do on Fure. By some cosmic miracle, rain falls on Earth, and with the help of the sun, the water evaporates, turning into clouds that grow heavy, and release more rain. Rain that waters plants of which there are so many varieties. Right here, within several feet of Leeta's landing spot, a forest grows. For a botany specialist, these trees that surround her are the largest, strongest, most uniquely formed plants she has ever seen. Even among those of the same species, not a single one is exactly like another. As for the many different tree species she identifies nearby, they are all thriving, side by side, in spite of their differences. More likely because of them.

"AYA, close hatch and cloak the pod."

"Ooh, fun! I don't get to do that one very often!"

The pod vanishes instantly.

"AYA, display directions to SETI, non-hologram mode."

"Non-hologram? Seriously? So boring."

"I don't know who may be in this vicinity. I don't want to draw attention to flashy displays."

"Okay. Whatever."

A map appears on the flat screen of her APED. Orienting herself, Leeta turns westward, walking briskly toward the late afternoon light filtering through a dense web of branches casting long shadows. The ground beneath her boots is spongy and fragrant with dried pine needles, cones, twigs, and animal droppings. Leeta runs both hands along the craggy, sticky trunk of an old tree. She presses her nose to a large bead of amber sap, inhaling the pungent scent. Turning her back to the old tree, she leans against it and looks up at the forest canopy, delighting in the surrounding beauty and peace of the place.

The wild barking of a dog punches the air along with gun-shots. Leeta doesn't know these sounds, but her heart begins jerking around in her chest. Never a good sign.

She turns away from the noise, and runs deeper into the shadows, searching for a hiding place. Where? Not there. Or there. No rock faces to climb. No caves to crawl into. No branches low enough to shimmy up. Ah. There! Partway down that short slope, a large hollow tree.

Redwood tree—Sequoioideae, *a subfamily of coniferous trees that range in the northern hemisphere and include the largest and tallest trees in the world.*

The tree, splintered and charred, still stands tall, though it stood much taller before a lightning bolt ended its reign decades earlier. Leeta ducks into the tree's vertical opening and hunkers down on a powdery carpet of decomposing wood.

She whispers into her APED. "AYA, am I being followed?"

"You'd better believe it! A 215-pound human male and his 77-pound domesticated wolf, aka dog, are 182 yards to the south moving in your direction at a velocity of 4.5 miles per hour."

Barking resounds through the forest along with the man's angry shouts. "I know you're in here, ET! Come out, goddamn it, before I blast you out! This way, Gunner? Good boy!"

Panicked, Leeta looks up. Twenty-five feet overhead, through a chimney-like tunnel, she spots a piece of blue sky. Her mind settles. Reaching up and to her right, she locates a long diagonal gap inside the tree trunk and shoves four long, strong fingers into it. She finds a second gap up and to her left. With the toe of her boot, she then locates a break in the bark right below her knee. Stepping up and pulling up at the same time she lifts herself off the ground. Stretching arms and legs wide, she climbs up inside the tree, like a spider.

Leeta, who's never had any trouble climbing, notices that something is different. She quickly realizes she's experiencing the difference between Fure's gravitational pull and Earth's.

Heavy footsteps approach. The muscles in her arms and legs burn, but Leeta holds on tight, listening intently. The man and dog thunder past. Footsteps and barking fade. A moment later the noise grows louder again.

Are they turning around? Will they come back this way? Will they find her this time? Should she drop down and make a run back to the escape pod? What if the man shoots her in the back and she dies here? What if she's captured and imprisoned in a lab or a zoo?

It's all happening too fast. What should she do?

"AYA, call Zertee."

"What? You want to leave already?"

BARK! BARK!

"AYA, just call her!"

"Fine."

Zertee appears in a hologram. She looks around, confused.

"Leeta! Where are you?"

"Inside a tree. On Earth."

BARK! BARK! BARK!

"What is that noise?" Zertee wants to know.

"Leeta, they are less than four meters away," AYA says.

"*Sork!* Zertee, come back and get me!"

"Okay. Send your coordinates."

BARK! BARK!

"I'll call you back!" Heart in her throat, fingers cramping, Leeta inches higher up the tree, straining to hear what's happening in front of her hiding place.

Gunner paws a pile of leaves then sniffs something at the edge of a nearby puddle.

"What's there, boy?"

The man prods the leaves with the toe of his boot. "Did they drop something?"

The dog noisily laps water from the puddle. A moment later, it has bounded into the puddle, pulling the leash from the man's hand.

"What the hell, Gunner? We've got a job to do!"

The man wades into the puddle. As he bends over to pick up Gunner's leash, his phone falls out of his shirt pocket with a flat splash, and sinks. Swearing, he fishes it out and turns it on. Dead. He frantically dries the phone with the bottom of his shirt. Turns it on again. Still dead.

"Thought this was supposed to be waterproof! Piece of shit." He stuffs the phone in his jacket pocket.

The dog pads out of the water. Lifts its leg to pee on the base of Leeta's hideout. Rick yanks the leash. "No time for that, Gun! They're getting away."

He takes off, dragging the dog with him. The cursing and barking fade to nothing.

"AYA, give me the current location of the man and the dog."

"Ooh, they're moving fast. 5.75 miles per hour. But they're traveling north *away* from you. So that's good news."

Leeta scrambles down and drops to the ground, ducks her head, and exits the tree.

"Thanks for your help, AYA."

"Hey, no problem. Off to SETI now?"

"First I'm going to look around."

Leeta cautiously emerges on the opposite side of the forest, and crosses into a clearing that leads up a long grassy hill. As she climbs, her auxiliary memory identifies everything she sees in real time. A bat zips overhead, snagging a hapless mosquito before reversing in mid-air and swooping back in the other direction. Unseen crickets warble their one note song, loud and insistent. The heady mix of grass and soil perfumes everything.

At the top of the hill, Leeta surveys the horizon, where the sun turns low-lying clouds into undulating wisps of gold, purple, red. Above the clouds, stars appear, one by one. Low in the Southern sky she recognizes the tiny speck that is *Kerlanti*. And while she can't see Fure, she knows it's right there. Along with everything and everyone she's ever known. If she could see Fure now, would she be homesick?

Not at all.

The biggest star in the realm of night sky entertainment is not a star at all. It's the moon, rising in the East. Fure has no moon, so nothing could have prepared Leeta for the splendor of this glowing rock, so bold and beautiful. A crowd of new, dark clouds closes in from the West, but they can never touch the moon, and while clouds and people may fool themselves into believing otherwise, some beautiful things will always remain out of reach.

Leeta Simtar wanders through this vibrant new world as if under a spell, forgetting for the moment why she came to Earth.

An unseen owl calls anxiously into the night. "Am I alone?"

Farther away, another owl answers. "No. I am here."

"Where are you?" the first owl asks.

"Come find me," says the second.

A chill breeze brings her back to her senses. She pulls her jacket out of her backpack, hurriedly slips her arms through the sleeves, fastens the front, and yanks up the hood. Striding into the wind, she shoves her hands in her pockets, touches the ring, and slips it on her finger.

In her mind's eye, she sees a vision featuring the same strong, alien hand she saw before. This time, there's only one hand. Trembling, it reaches up and parts a thick screen of leaves revealing an escape pod, similar to her own, rising swiftly and silently into the night sky, briefly crossing the face of the moon before vanishing. Gunfire rips through the night as the hand drops.

A sob charged with yearning echoes in Leeta's head. She pulls off the ring. The vision vanishes but the crying continues, gathering strength.

The sobs are her own.

After a long moment her sadness abates, replaced with absolute certainty that the alien hand she saw is human and belongs to her father.

Leeta doesn't know how the ring connects her to her father's memories. She doesn't know if the Daht is aware of its power. She doesn't have any idea how the Daht got the ring or why she gave it to Leeta. But she knows, without knowing how, that her father never recovered from the heartache of losing Eta-Bakara. Maybe by finding him she can ease his pain. Maybe the ring can help.

Cautiously she slips it on again.

Nothing happens.

This won't be easy.

When Leeta reaches the bottom of the hill, it's nearly dark but she's wary of being out in the open. She drops behind a high thicket and hunkers down, careful not to get too close to the thorns along the twisted stems. A sweet smell fills the air.

"AYA, illuminate this plant."

"Sure thing. Is this bright enough?"

The APED's light shines on multiple clusters of plump blackberries.

Leeta listens to her auxiliary memory implant.

Blackberry: *an edible **fruit** produced by many species in the genus Rubus in the family Rosaceae. The shiny black fruit is ripest and sweetest. Blackberries contain nutrients such as vitamin C, vitamin K, and manganese. They are also high in fiber, and may boost brain health.*

"What do you think, AYA? I mean, just cause something's edible doesn't mean it tastes good."

"That's true. But at least you know it won't kill you."

"Also true. And in a risky place like this, a brain boost would be beneficial."

She carefully plucks a berry off the end of a cluster and takes a tentative bite.

"Mmmm." Smiling to herself, she pops the rest of the berry in her mouth, licks her fingers, and continues picking and eating more and more as her hands, face and tongue turn purple with berry juice.

Beep.

Zertee appears in a hologram, wavering inches above the bush.

"Leeta! Your skin is blue! Are you ill? Injured?"

Leeta chuckles. "No. It's just fruit juice." She fishes her water vessel out of her backpack and washes off her hands and face, then holds them up. They are still stained. "Okay, it doesn't wash off easily, but I feel fine."

"I am relieved. I was worried when you did not call me back. Give me your coordinates, and I will rendezvous with your pod."

"I changed my mind, Zertee. I'm staying on Earth to find my father."

"What? Where is the logic in that? Your father is Gemian. How could you possibly find him on Earth?"

"He isn't Gemian."

"How do you know this to be true?"

Leeta bites her bottom lip. "While you were sleeping, I gained entry into the Top Secret database and I—"

"—How? You failed CyberSecurity 101. Twice."

"I was able to get in because a bug in the system provided access."

"A bug? Unlikely. If the system provided access, it was not a bug. The most logical explanation—"

"—Zertee, stop! It doesn't matter *how* I got in. I did and I viewed an archival file of a Disciplinary Hearing and discovered that I am the result of an Intergalactic Interspecies Hybrid Experiment."

"As am I. Fure is authorized to collect DNA from—"

"My DNA came from an *unauthorized* collection."

"Unauthorized how?"

"My DNA is human. I am 71% human on my father's side."

Zertee's eyes grow big as she stares at Leeta. "Oh. 71% human and only 29% Furean. That explains so much."

Leeta sneers. "Yeah? Well, it doesn't explain a *sorking* thing to me. I know nothing about humans because none of us were allowed to study them. That's the other reason I'm here. I want to understand humans so I can understand why I am the way I am."

"That is logical."

"Thanks. Oh, and listen to this. I discovered that my mother is (or was) a brilliant Furean geneticist named Eta-Bakara. Eighteen years ago she came to Earth and—"

"—Did you say Eta-Bakara?" Zertee blurts out.

"How do you know that name?"

"How do you *not?* Eta-Bakara was convicted of intimate contact with a human, who I assume was your father. And as a consequence of that highest-level protocol breach, they stripped her of her rank, shut down her research lab, and sent her to a secret re-education program. After three years she re-emerged, successfully rehabilitated. She changed her name to Mayeel and shifted her focus from genetics to social psychology. Five years later she became the Daht."

"Wait! What? Eta-Bakara is *the Daht?*"

"Yes."

"Daht Mayeel is my *mother?*"

"Apparently so."

Leeta's first impulse is to scream loud enough to blast the berries off the bush, but she can't risk signaling her location to the alien hunter in case he's still in the vicinity. Instead, she silently roars into the sleeve of her jacket. Once. Twice.

"Zertee," she whispers shakily. "The Daht is my mother."

"Yes, Leeta. We have already ascertained that fact."

"You know what that means?"

"It means the Daht is your mother."

"YES!" Leeta shouts and quickly claps a hand over her mouth. Peeking through the bushes, she strains to hear footsteps, barking, or any sign of danger. Thankfully, all is quiet. Still, Leeta lowers her voice to a whisper.

"I can't *sorking* believe it, Zertee. The Daht is my mother." She starts to cry, gagging on sobs.

"Are you well, Leeta?"

Leeta grimaces and shakes her head. Zertee reaches out to her with cupped hands. Leeta wishes she could feel the touch, but Furean holograms don't work that way. Leeta cups her own hand, places it over her heart, and breathes. After a moment, she exhales shakily and manages to swallow, her throat hot and raw.

"I'm better now," she says, trying to convince herself.

"Good," says Zertee. "But you are still in danger. I analyzed the background noise from our brief call. The short bursts were explosions from a deadly weapon. The other sounds were the aggressive vocalizations of a carnivorous animal."

"The human called the animal Gunner."

Zertee turns to a console. After a moment she says, "There are no Earth animals called gunners."

"I think it was a name—like Zertee. The human told Gunner to find me. To *get* me. As if I were prey. Gunner seemed very excited to do what the human commanded."

"I am surprised that humans name animals, but I am not surprised to learn that humans train animals to be vicious. While we've been talking, I searched a brief public database of Earth. In their relatively short history, humans are shown to be suspicious by nature. They regularly insult, cheat, deceive, betray, injure, and even kill one another. According to the Index of Interplanetary Tourists, humans consistently earn host ratings of one star or less. That is the lowest hospitality rating in the galaxy. If anyone discovers what you are, being 71% human will not protect you from this dangerous species."

"Zertee, it's illogical to assume all humans are dangerous. The Daht, who you respect and revere, mated with my human father. He gave her a lovely gift before she left Earth. And she gave it to me."

"You opened the box. What was inside?"

Leeta shows her the ring on her finger.

"It's called a ring. I think the Daht kept it all these years because she cared for my father. She may even still love him."

"What is love?" Zertee asks, because there is no database to provide the answer.

Leeta slips the ring off her finger and back on again, hoping to trigger another vision that might help explain this idea to Zertee.

Again, nothing happens.

Leeta shakes her head. "I'm not sure what love is. I heard the word in Eta-Bakara's testimony. I think it might mean the deepest kind of emotional attachment, one person to another."

"Deeper than our connection to One Family?"

"I sure hope so," she mutters under her breath.

Leeta lifts her backpack on to one shoulder and gets to her feet. She sticks her arms through the shoulder straps and hoists the pack onto her back. "Zertee, I've got more than one family. I'm staying here, and I'm going to find my father."

"Do you know his name?"

"Not yet," she says matter-of-factly. "But I'll find out soon."

"Leeta, be logical! You only have three more days. Earth is 18% larger than Fure with much more habitable land and a much larger population. You are looking for one human among . . ." She checks the console. ". . . more than eight billion humans. Where will you even begin to look?"

"I have my starting point. AYA, bring up those directions to SETI again."

A holographic map appears beside Zertee. "What is SETI?" she says.

"The science research center where my father worked 18 years ago." She is walking as she talks, doing both quickly and with determination. "If he's still there, I'll meet him."

"And if not?"

"I'll get information from other people. Don't worry. I'm prepared. While you slept, I learned enough of the California language to communicate well. I also downloaded the Earth database into my auxiliary memory implant."

"How did you get into the off-limits Earth database? Never mind. That database must be outdated. It will be of no help to you—"

"—Stop worrying. AYA will tell me whatever I need to know."

"No, I won't!" AYA says. "I am not programmed for Earth protocol."

"Not yet, but you'll figure it out and so will I. Zertee, If I haven't found my father in three days, I promise I'll return to Fure with you."

"I cannot convince you of the illogic of this plan?"

Leeta hears the whooshing of cars on the road, less than 100 yards directly ahead. She quickly turns, slouches, and continues walking diagonally through the tall grass. "Not a chance," she says.

Now it's Zertee's turn to reverse course. "Very well. Then logic dictates that I stop trying. Did you bring your *subyl?*"

"Of course." Leeta stops, pulls her neatly folded *subyl* out of her backpack and holds it up for Zertee to see. "I never go anywhere without my *subyl.*"

"I am relieved to hear that."

"By the way, in the California language this is called a towel."

"Interesting but irrelevant. Leeta, I am still extremely concerned for your safety. As your friend, though, I feel compelled to support your scientific exploration of human nature as well as the search for your father. Tell me how I can help."

Leeta thinks about it as she refolds her *subyl.* "Cover for me so the Daht doesn't find out I'm here. Without lying, of course."

"That won't be necessary."

"How come?"

"Since the Daht is tracking our APEDs, she would have known when you took off on Escape Pod 1 and ordered you to get back on the ship immediately. But I have received no messages from Fure since you left."

"Is it possible we're in a comm blackout and she doesn't yet know I'm gone?"

"We are not yet in a blackout, Leeta. I am receiving real-time transmissions from Fure. Besides, that would not be the case for an APED either way. I can only assume the Daht knows exactly where you are and—"

Leeta gasps. "—she *wants* me to be here! That's why she gave me the ring! She knew I'd discover it came from Earth and—"

"—she provided you access to the Top Secret and Earth databases so you would—"

"—find out that I'm human and come here. Zertee, my mother *wants* me to find my father!" Leeta tears up.

"Why are you sad?"

"All this time I didn't trust the Daht," she sniffles, wiping her eyes with the *subyl.* "I thought she was cold and unfeeling.

But now I see that she sent me here because she really cares about me."

Running at full speed, chasing what he cannot see but fully senses the presence of, Rick Rodriguez, aka Alien Hunter, smashes head-first into the cloaked escape pod. The impact throws him backwards, flat on his ass. Wincing in pain, he sits up, rubs his nose, and stares into the space ahead of him. Nothing to see. Yet he knows something is right there... somewhere. Something as big and solid as a wall. All he has to do is locate it again, preferably without using his head.

Gunner feverishly sniffs the ground. His tail shoots up, quivering. He lets out a string of short, rapid-fire barks. Rick slowly inches forward on his hands and knees. One hand cautiously feels the air in front of him while the other hand explores the ground. The air space is empty. Nothing on the ground but twigs, pine needles and oh, there's some coyote shit. Using the butt of his shotgun, he jabs the air ahead. Clunk. Something hard is sitting right there, but he can't see it.

Gunner sniffs the ground, barking again, his tail wags furiously.

Rick drops the shotgun, jumps to his feet, approaches the invisible thing and runs both hands up and down its smooth round surface. A moment later, raindrops hit his hands and the ground around his boots. Two feet above his head, drops ping off the top of the invisible thing. As the storm intensifies, water slides down its surface, front, back, and sides revealing a sleek spherical shape. Rick's mouth drops open like a mailbox, his eyes follow the line of water in reverse, all the way up. He can't see the thing, but he knows exactly what it is—a freakin' alien spaceship!

He lets loose a wild whoop. This is it. The thing he's waited a lifetime to find so he could prove himself to everyone who called him nuts. To finally dispel the stench of public ridicule that started in fifth grade when Joey Farmer told everyone that Rick told him that little green men from Mars were taking over human bodies so they could infiltrate our government and mess with our technology. Rick had said that to Joey because he believed it and thought by warning people, he would be a hero. He didn't expect everyone would start calling him a crazy weirdo. The label stuck, and years later, Rick is still obsessed with conspiracy theories about space aliens. His wife, an orthodontist with a thriving practice and a public image to protect, left him. His own son can't look him in the eye and always changes the subject whenever anyone mentions Rick's latest rant.

But now Rick will show them he was right all along with this undeniable proof that extraterrestrials are here, in San Mateo County. All he has to do is figure out how to get a ten-foot spherical, slippery, wet, invisible spaceship back to his barn.

Knowing she's safe for the moment and in no particular hurry to cover the ten miles to SETI, which logic dictates, will likely not reopen to the public until the morning, the girl from the driest of places takes a moment to raise her face to the now-clouded night sky, and let the deliciously cool rain wash over her. She loves it. As for the rumbling thunder, not so much.

"AYA, what is the source of that low pitched noise?"

"It's thunder. Created by lightning as it heats and rapidly expands the air. Want to hear the definition of lightning?"

"Okay."

"Lightning is a giant spark of electricity that can occur between the atmosphere and the ground, or between opposite charges within a thunderstorm cloud. Want to hear the definition of a thunderstorm cloud?"

"No, thank you, AYA."

"Okay. But just to let you know, it will be raining much harder in approximately . . ."

A sudden, much heavier downpour drenches Leeta.

"Now."

Head down, Leeta Simtar trudges onward, picking her way westward through the tall bushes and undergrowth that line the main highway, taking care to stay clear of the sweeping headlights of passing cars.

Chapter 9
Lost and Found

A BIG, GOOFY, YELLOW LAB sniffs at the tall girl curled up across the bus stop bench. She's wet and dirty. Her jumpsuit has no seams, buttons or zippers. What's that strange insignia on her left shoulder? Is that Russian? And those boots? They appear molded to her extremely large feet. What is her backpack made of? Aluminum? Everything about her looks and smells out of place. The dog's person, a wiry older woman, has worked in homeless shelters and to her, this girl shows all the signs of a runaway. Possibly a dead one.

The dog licks the girl's chin. No response. It whimpers and shoots the woman a concerned look. She gently hauls the dog back and signals it to sit behind her. The dog sits. The woman carefully shakes the girl's arm. Nothing. She shakes her again, more forcefully. Leeta's eyes snap open. She sits up, squinting in the morning sunlight. The woman's lined face comes into focus, her concerned brown eyes shine behind a pair of black, heavy-framed glasses.

The woman smiles with relief. "Good morning. For a minute there I thought you'd left us."

"Thought I left?" Leeta Simtar slowly repeats the words and looks to her left.

Sensing this oddly dressed girl may have some linguistic challenges (to say the least) the woman adds, "You know, *left us.* As in *departed this Earth.*"

Leeta sits up and studies the kind face, a shy smile spreading across her own. "I have not left. I am just arrived."

Leeta reaches out with both hands and carefully removes the woman's glasses, examining the hinges, chuckling to herself as she opens and closes the frames before trying them on her own face. After a quick look through the lenses, Leeta takes off the glasses and holds them at arm's length in front of the bus schedule, marveling at the magnified small print. The woman watches, fascinated. Is it possible this girl has never seen a pair of eyeglasses? Where has she been living her whole life?

Leeta places the glasses back onto the woman's face, gently pushing them up to the bridge of her nose.

The woman smiles and offers her hand to Leeta. "Welcome to El Lugar. I'm Angela. What's your name?"

Leeta stands to her full height and leans over to take Angela's hand. "I am Leeta Simtar. Nice to meet you, Angela." She pumps Angela's hand up and down like a whip. Angela chuckles and extracts her hand.

"Nice to meet you too, Leeta. But your hands are so cold. No wonder in that wet outfit. Want to use my truck to change into other clothes?"

"I have no other clothes."

The dog barks. Leeta notices it for the first time, jumps onto the bench and stands, nearly hitting her head on the shelter roof.

The woman tells the dog to sit. He sits. "It's okay. Don't be scared. My dog's very friendly."

The dog looks up at Leeta, eyes full of hope.

"Would you like to pet him?"

Leeta would love to, but she's not sure that's a good idea. She recalls what happened the last time she gave in to her desire to touch an animal. But this dog is nothing like the *frig*. His eyes beam intelligence and kindness. Besides there are no jagged rocks here. No cruel winds. What could go wrong?

Never taking her eyes off the dog, Leeta crouches and tentatively reaches out. The dog's tail sweeps the pavement. She giggles with delight and sits down to get closer. The dog nuzzles her hand. Leeta puts her arms around his neck and presses her cheek against his thick fur.

She has just learned something about being human: Hugging a dog warms her heart. *Is this another kind of love?*

"Does your dog have a name?"

Angela sits beside Leeta. "Do you know the constellations?"

"Not all 88 of them. I know one is called Canis Major, The Big Dog, but I do not think that constellation looks like this dog."

"I agree! None of them look anything like they're supposed to. The ancients who named the constellations must have been smoking something." Angela laughs.

Leeta has always enjoyed laughing but she's never had anyone to laugh with. Before she arrived, she learned a bit about the human sense of humor and concept of making a joke. Now she laughs along with Angela though she doesn't understand the joke. She's not sure if there is one. She's not sure if it even matters. The girl from Fure has just discovered something else about her human nature: Laughing with someone feels much better than laughing alone.

Angela affectionately rubs her dog's head. "His name's Wezen. After the yellow star that forms the tail of Canis Major."

"Yellow star. Yellow dog. Good name. It is very nice to meet you, Wezen the Dog." Leeta holds out her hand. Wezen places his paw in it. "I am Leeta Simtar." They shake. "You are good and kind. Not like the mean dog of yesterday."

Angela shoots her a look. "Where did you meet a mean dog?"

"I did not meet him. We did not exchange names and shake hands. He was chasing me with his mean owner. Chasing. Shouting. Barking. I hid in a tree, and I climbed up inside the tree. They did not see me. I did not see them. I heard a gun. Dogs do not shoot guns. The dog's owner shot the gun. Many times. The dog's owner must love guns because he called the dog Gunner. That is not a good name for a dog."

Angela's face darkens with the same troubled look Leeta saw on the Daht's face while she examined Leeta's treasures. "Gunner?" she says.

Leeta wants to ask Angela if she and the mean man are friends. What would she do if Angela said yes? Maybe these are not good questions. Maybe they would make her seem like a visitor from another planet. Maybe Leeta has already revealed too much to this human who seems very friendly but might actually be as unpredictable and untrustworthy as Zertee warned. No. Some questions are better left unasked and unanswered. Zertee would say that was a logical deduction in these circumstances. But Zertee isn't here. Of course she would never come to such a dangerous place.

As for Angela, she knows exactly which mean dog owner chased Leeta. It's a small town and Rick Rodriguez is famous. Not in a good way. Now she's certain the girl is a runaway. But from where? And why was Rick chasing her? Leeta said Rick didn't see her. Then what *did* he see that got him running into the woods shouting at her and firing his shotgun? Based on things her neighbors have said about Rick over the years, she has more than an inkling. And what about the time he showed up at her astronomy club uninvited and delivered an unhinged rant about the dangers of pointing telescopes at the sky because it attracted extraterrestrials? There's only one way to explain Rick's reaction to this girl. Angela knows what Rick thinks, but that doesn't mean . . . or does it? Sure, Leeta Simtar, or whatever her real name is, looks unusual. And her clothes and backpack are unlike anything Angela's ever seen. Then there's the very strange way she talks. Not to mention her reaction to eyeglasses. That was just odd. And saying that she *has just arrived*? Angela doesn't know what to make of it. She'd like to come right out and ask Leeta where she's from, but she's afraid to spook the girl and make her run again. She decides to take it slowly, try to gain her confidence, try to help her if she can. So she says nothing.

"Yes, Gunner, like gun, a weapon that kills people. He said, 'Gunner, what did you find there, boy? Gunner, did they drop something? No time for that Gunner, you're supposed to be tracking.'"

Then as if she just remembered what Gunner was tracking, Leeta hurriedly hoists her backpack onto her shoulder and says, "Goodbye, Angela. Goodbye, Wezen." Then sneaking a peek at her APED, she makes an abrupt right turn and walks quickly down the street.

"Leeta, wait!"

Leeta stops. The urgency in Angela's voice scares her. She feels Angela's eyes on her back. She doesn't turn around but she doesn't run either. She knows how fast dogs can move.

Angela catches up to her. "The wind is picking up."

"I would categorize this as a light breeze."

"Okay, but it's getting chilly. If you'd like, I can help you get some food and dry clothes."

Leeta isn't fooling this woman. She isn't passing for human. Leeta's sure that Angela has figured out her secret, but there are no shouts. No threats. No attack commands to Wezen. Only offers of food and warm clothing. Angela's knowing changes nothing between them.

Leeta turns and faces her with a crooked smile. She wonders if she's been wrong her whole life. Maybe the best thing isn't when you fool people into believing you're something you're not, something they'd like better. Maybe the best thing is when people know who you really are and they like you because of it. Maybe that's what humans mean when they say *I love you*.

"Are you hungry?" Angela asks.

"That is an accurate assumption, most likely based on the loud and continuous growling sounds emitting from my stomach. Sounds which are scientifically known as *borboryg-mus*. But undoubtedly, you are already familiar with that term since you have had your own stomach for a long time."

Angela fondly pats the bulge around her middle. "So true," she says.

Leeta rides shotgun in Angela's red pickup truck. Wezen surfs on the center console leaning toward the girl as she scratches just the right spot behind his silky soft ear, like she's been doing it for years. As they enter the town, every-thing Leeta observes is strange to her—cars, bicycles, traffic lights, parking meters, a fire hydrant, a recycling bin. Her aux-iliary memory implant identifies every object's name and function in real-time.

All of this information is useful to a stranger, but names and facts don't help Leeta process her reactions to these sights, sounds, and smells. And nothing in her implant eases her anxiety riding in this old, slow vehicle, so low to the ground. She's absolutely astonished by how easily Angela op-erates the machine *manually*, while talking to Leeta, petting Wezen, singing along with what she calls "an Oldie" on the radio, drinking from a cup and replacing it in its holder. All this without colliding into other vehicles or people on bicy-cles! It is a most impressive simultaneous display of multiple skills, and yet Leeta clutches the door handle to steady herself over bumps in the road.

They enter the business section of town and pass a small park where a mother and her young child sit on a bench eat-ing sandwiches. There's a shop window filled with toys and stuffed animals. Another store displays shoes and hats. Across the street sits a large square building with a red tiled roof and the words PUBLIC LIBRARY printed on a sign stuck in front.

Leeta listens to her implant.

Public Library: *A government building containing collections of books, periodicals, and sometimes films and recorded music for people to read, borrow, or refer to at no charge. The first public library was established in America in 1731 by Benjamin Franklin and a group of Philadelphia friends.*

Philadelphia: *A city in the state of Pennsylvania. Previously an English colony founded in 1682, Philadelphia was the temporary capital of the United States from 1790 to 1800.*

Angela expertly eases into a curbside parking spot. "I've gotta run across to the pet store. I'll only be a few minutes. You okay staying here with Wezen?"

"Yes. I am okay."

Wezen licks Leeta's face. Leeta snuggles the big dog. "Wezen is also okay."

Grateful for some quiet time on her own, Leeta watches the world outside the truck. All the way down the street, purple, pink, and white petunias crowd wire baskets hanging from tall lamp posts. The intoxicating smells of coffee, hot chocolate, buttery pastries, and sugar float into the truck from an outdoor café where a dozen humans sit, sip, eat, check their phones, and work on laptops. Some who sit together look alike, but just as often they don't. She observes many different types of skin and hair. Many different sizes and shapes of bodies. No one else seems to show disapproval or even notice.

Children wearing colorful jackets and shoes and little backpacks talk and laugh together. People walk past the truck carrying shopping bags. Some push babies in strollers. One of the babies smiles and waves at Leeta. She waves back. All this fills her with a rare type of joy.

A heavy thud behind them startles Leeta and Wezen. They both turn to the back of the truck where Angela has just flung a large bag of dog food into the bed. She groans softly as she climbs into the driver's seat. She grits her teeth as she carefully reaches for the door and slowly closes it.

"I came back as soon as I could," Angela says, smiling too tightly. "Hope you weren't bored."

"I was not bored. This place is very lively and also colorful and smelling very good."

Leeta watches Angela slowly lean forward to put the key in the ignition.

"Shit!" Angela says, wincing and grabbing her lower back.

"What is wrong?" Leeta asks.

"Tweaked my damn sacrum again. I hate when this happens."

Angela presses the heel of her hand into the pain. Without thinking, Leeta cups her hand over Angela's, hoping to help the woman relax and stop being so angry with herself. Angela immediately feels calmer. Leeta can sense that. What she doesn't yet realize is that something else is also happening in this moment.

Warmth radiates from Leeta's hand into Angela's back and the pain vanishes as if someone just flipped the off switch. Leeta doesn't know what she's done, but of course, Angela feels the change immediately. She tentatively leans forward again, key in hand, and breaks into a smile. "Wow! My back feels great! How'd you do that?"

Equally startled, Leeta looks at her hand, searching for some explanation. "I do not know. I have never done that before." She says it as if that's the end of the conversation, but Leeta's mind is churning with questions. How come Fureans can only use *tulahm* to ease emotional pain but not physical pain? She tried to take away Brownie's pain, but only managed to calm the *frig's* fears. Yet here, on Earth, Leeta has helped Angela relax *and* has eliminated her back pain. Maybe things are different here. Maybe *she's* different.

Angela notices the girl's four elongated fingers and her short, wide thumb. Angela's face clouds with confusion. Leeta quickly hides her left hand in her pocket and reaches for the door handle with her right. Leeta holds her breath, waiting for this woman to pull out a gun or for Wezen to bark angrily at her. But nothing like that happens. Instead, Angela's smile warmly lights her eyes. "Next stop. New clothes. After that . . . food! Okay? You good with that?"

Leeta nods and takes her hand off the door handle. "Yes, pleaseandthankyou."

Wezen boops Leeta with his cold wet nose. Leeta laughs. Angela joins in as she starts the truck. The lighted display chimes. A moment later the red truck is heading down El Lugar Avenue.

"How long have you lived here, Angela?"

"Oh, I don't live in El Lugar, though this is a great town. Good stores, but the rents are ridiculous. I just came in this morning to do some errands and to meet a very interesting new friend."

She reaches over and pats Leeta's knee. Leeta's heart swells. Someone besides Zertee has called her a friend. Someone who doesn't think of her as too Brid or not Real enough. She blinks back happy tears, not knowing what to say. Sensing the girl's embarrassment, Angela quickly fills in the silence.

"I live in Cedarville. Only eight miles away. Ever heard of it?"

"Yes! I have knowledge of Cedarville. It is the location of the SETI Institute which is dedicated to the search for extraterrestrial intelligence. I will be visiting there later today."

"Really? You're going to SETI? Are you doing research?"

"Yes! Researching and searching. Do you know anyone who works at the SETI Institute?"

"Not personally but it's open to the public. You can just walk right in. They welcome all visitors . . . even humans." She laughs at her own joke.

This time Leeta actually gets the joke. She laughs so hard she has trouble stopping. When she finally manages to speak again, she's unable to look at Angela. Instead, she turns to the window, intently cleaning off a smudge of dirt with her thumb.

"Angela, may I ask you a question?" she says softly.

"Of course, sweetie. What do you want to know?"

"Would *you* welcome a visitor who wasn't human?"

"What? You mean an ET? You bet I would! Meeting an ET is number one on my Wish List. Of course, that's probably not going to happen."

The truck stops at a red light.

"It is possible, Angela."

The woman shivers. She reaches for Wezen. A focused pressure on the side of her face tells her the girl is looking at her. Angela turns cautiously and meets Leeta's gaze. She's communicating with her eyes. Angela picked up an out-of-place vibe the moment she saw Leeta at the bus stop. But now the level of out-of-place she's starting to imagine is blowing her mind. She wants to ask Leeta point blank what she just meant when she said it was possible that Angela would meet an ET. But the question seems too absurd to put into words. And yet, it's as if Leeta already heard the question and answered it.

Angela blows air through her lips. "Wow. You're here."

Leeta nods, smiling with gratitude to this woman for finding her and making her feel safe. Zertee is wrong about all humans being violent. This one is her friend.

"Yes. I am," Leeta says and for some reason she laughs.

Suddenly, Angela feels an overwhelming need to protect this girl.

The light turns green. The truck pulls forward.

"Just so you know, Leeta, not everyone around here is all that welcoming of strangers." She says this slowly and carefully, not wanting to frighten the girl but also not wanting to fail in her new responsibility. "Some people do not welcome strangers of any kind, human or otherwise. I don't know why they feel that way. My guess is that some of those people are broken inside. They've been hurt or they've been lied to for so long they don't believe anything else. Either way, they don't trust anyone. They're convinced the only reason an ET would come here is to destroy us or turn us into slaves or some such bullshit. People like that can be very dangerous, Leeta. Do you understand what I'm saying?"

"Yes, Angela. You are saying that I must take care of myself."

"Exactly right. You've gotta be very careful about what you tell people. Because—"

"—because some people are mean."

Angela nods. "Very mean." She flips on the left turn signal. The green arrow flashes on the dashboard.

"Where are we going now, Angela?"

"To the Goodwill store to get you some nice, dry clothes. Is that okay?"

"Yes, that is okay. Goodwill means kindness, correct?"

"That's right."

Leeta sits back and smiles. "Good. There definitely will not be any mean people there."

Angela swallows her nervousness. "We can always hope."

CHAPTER 10
WHAT'S YOUR STYLE?

Civilizations that spend their time and resources making and accumulating objects of no utilitarian purpose will never evolve to greatness.

—Daht Mayeel

NGELA AND LEETA WALK into a large, brightly lit Goodwill store with so many human artifacts on display Leeta doesn't know where to look first. On one wall alone, stacked shelves hold countless bins filled with objects she's never seen, not even in her mind's eye.

She flicks the wires of a large whisk, examines a cheese grater, flips the flaps of a collapsable vegetable steamer, squeezes the handle of an old flour sifter again and again, watching the rotary blades spin.

"What are all these things?"

"Kitchen gadgets."

"What are *gadgets*?"

"Oh, they're simple tools. These are used for cooking."

Leeta opens and closes a garlic press.

"That one crushes garlic."

"Garlic is a plant! I like plants. Garlic is closely related to the onion. It produces a strong-smelling, pungent-tasting bulb used as a flavoring in cooking and in herbal medicine."

"Exactly right."

"Yes. My information is always accurate."

Leeta wanders to another section of the store where the shelves are loaded with small ceramic sculptures, sports trophies, heart-shaped picture frames, ribboned baskets, and more.

"Are these more gadgets, Angela?"

"Definitely not. This stuff is what they call home décor."

"What is home décor used for?"

"Uh . . . home décor? Well, it's not like a garlic press. Actually, it's not really used for anything. Some people just like to decorate their homes with useless junk."

"Is all of this useless junk?"

"Depends on who you ask."

"I am asking you, Angela. Is this useless junk?"

"Let's just say it's not my style."

"What is style?"

"You sure ask a lot of questions. Just like my son. Now he's studying journalism at SF State. Well, okay, here's my—I'd say style is a reflection of personal taste. Like what you hang on the walls in your house or the clothes you choose to wear."

She gestures to herself, taking in her broad brimmed hat, oversized red plaid shirt, drawstring pants, and flip-flops, ending with a hand on the crystal pendant hanging on a silver chain around her neck.

"This is what I choose for myself. What I feel comfortable in. This is my style." She gestures to Leeta's outfit. "And *that* is yours."

"No, Angela. That is not accurate. This is not my style. I did not choose these clothes."

"Hm. Then what is your style, Leeta?"

Leeta shrugs. "I do not know."

"Well, let's help you find out."

Angela leads her over to racks of clothing. "You'll probably find something you like here."

Leeta lightly runs her hand across a rack filled with shirts grouped together in colors. "Where do all these clothes come from?"

"People bring in the stuff they don't want any more. Maybe it used to be their style, but it's not anymore. Anyway, they donate it to Goodwill so other people can buy the clothes for not very much money."

"That is a very logical system."

Leeta rummages through a pile of hats on a table. She tries on a long red ski cap and pulls it all the way down to the bridge of her nose, covering her eyes.

Blindly, she turns to Angela. "Is this my style?"

Angela lifts the edge of the cap so Leeta can see, then pointing in the direction of a full-length mirror, she says, "Have a look for yourself."

Vanity is unFurean so mirrors are nonexistent there. Leeta has only ever seen her eye or a small section of her face reflected in the surface of the polished metal tools used in the Botany Dome. More than once Zertee caught her in the act of smiling at her reflection. Leeta was always embarrassed and tried to lie about what she was doing, but Zertee didn't buy the excuses. When she asked Leeta why she enjoyed looking at her reflection, Leeta couldn't explain because she didn't understand it. Now as she waits her turn at the full-length mirror, she watches a solidly built teenage boy admiring his reflection, and for Leeta, the pleasure of seeing oneself is starting to make sense.

The boy is dressed in a long, lacy wraparound skirt over flowered leggings, green high-top sneakers, and a short blue leather vest over a vintage Minnie Mouse tee shirt. He turns, looks back over his shoulder, smiles coyly, and wiggles his fingers at his reflection. He spots Leeta watching him strut his stuff.

"So, what do you think?" he asks.

Happy to be included, Leeta smiles. "I think your style is innovative!"

The boy blushes with pleasure. "Thanks!" Then frowning at her ski cap, he starts to reach for it, then pauses. "May I?"

She nods, unsure what is about to happen. He takes her hat off, then steps back, wide-eyed.

"Your hair is absolutely killer. So are your ears! And those brows? To die for! Quit hiding the goods, girl!" He tosses the red cap onto the table, expertly sorts through the other headgear in the pile, and extracts a soft, turquoise blue bucket hat. Holding it up to Leeta's face, he says. "This is your color."

He places the hat on Leeta, angling it toward the back of her head, deftly folding part of the brim here, another part there. When he's done, he whips a small jar of styling wax from his shoulder bag, coats his fingers, quickly working it into the front bits of her hair with a series of flicks and flips.

Stepping back, he nods at Leeta. "You are absolutely gorgeous!" He spins her around to face the mirror. "What do you think?"

She studies her reflection, tilts her head and looks at herself from different angles. "I think this is my style," she says, grinning broadly.

She hugs the boy, and he hugs her back. Then with a sweeping bow, he's off.

Angela pops up behind Leeta and gives her a double thumbs up, "You look great!"

Leeta takes one last longing look at her reflection, then removes the blue hat, reluctantly placing it back on the table.

"What? Change your mind about the hat?"

"No, Angela. My mind is the same. But I cannot buy this. I have less than not very much money. Much less."

"No problem, sugar. I've got you covered."

"Covered?"

"What I mean is, I'll pay for whatever you need."

"Thank you!" Leeta grabs the hat and puts it on again. "You are as kind as Wezen."

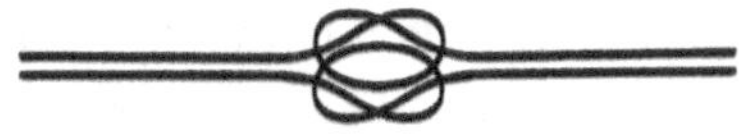

The curtain of the dressing room opens and Leeta steps out, wearing a pair of tight white jeans that make her legs look eight feet long, a short quilted purple vest over an untucked satin black shirt, a pair of black and red high-tops and, of course, the blue hat.

"Do you approve of my style, Angela?"

"You look great! How do you feel?"

Leeta grins and gives herself a double thumbs up. She then pats her body and discovers her jeans' pockets, front and back.

"Angela, my backpack has many pockets for carrying supplies, but what are these small pockets in clothing for?"

Strange question, but there are so many strange things about this towering scarecrow of a girl, Angela is starting to get used to hearing and answering them as if they're not strange at all.

"For carrying small personal items." Angela digs into her own jacket pockets and pulls out a half a dog biscuit, a quarter and a nickel, a cough drop wrapped in yellow paper, and a small seashell. Leeta carefully examines them all, but the shell holds her attention.

"Why do you carry this in your pocket? What is its purpose?"

Angela runs her thumb over the shell's ribbed surface. "My mom made it out of clay. She was a potter. I like the feel of it. It comforts me. I guess that's its purpose. Make sense?"

Leeta nods. She's already thinking about small comforting things she might put in her pockets. Then she gathers her boots, wet jumpsuit, and jacket from the fitting room floor and stuffs them into her backpack.

Eyeing the dirty clothes, Angela says, "There's a laundromat right here in town."

The implant clears Leeta's confusion.

Laundromat: *an establishment with coin-operated washing machines and dryers for public use. A place to go if you need to wash your clothes and don't have a washing machine at home.*

"I appreciate this suggestion offered in kindness, but I am in a hurry."

A round woman with tightly woven braids and an employee name badge identifying her as Tanika leans over the counter and scans the tags on Leeta's new hat, vest, shirt, jeans, and shoes. Leeta watches with bemused interest at the crude technology of the infrared scanner. But when Tanika comes at her with a pair of scissors, she gasps and pulls away.

"Don't worry, sweetheart. I'm just going to snip off these price tags. Promise it won't hurt." Leeta looks at Angela who smiles and calmly nods. Leeta closes her eyes and holds her breath as Tanika snips away and turns back to her register.

"That will be 32 dollars and 58 cents."

Angela takes a credit card out of her wallet.

"What is this?" Leeta asks.

Tanika shoots Angela a look, which she ignores. Then Angela patiently explains the function of credit cards to Leeta, describing how much more convenient they are than cash.

Leeta watches what happens when Angela taps her card on the card reader.

"That is a very logical system," says Leeta, nodding her approval.

On their way toward the exit, a large, painted landscape of rocks and shifting sands, barely distinguishable under glowing red clouds, catches Leeta's attention. She approaches the painting as if pulled in by a tractor beam. In the center of the canvas, a short female figure hovers a few inches off the ground. A tall male figure floats several feet over her head. Their arms and bodies stretch achingly toward one another, but the distance between them is too great and they cannot touch. Staring at the scene, a longing weighs heavily on Leeta's heart.

She strides back to Tanika and points at the painting. "Where did that come from?"

"That thing? No clue. It's been hanging there since I started working here five years ago. Tell you the truth, I try not to look at it. Creeps me out. No one wants it. Can't blame them. Kinda depressing. But what do I know about art?"

"What is art?"

"Right. To each his own. You like it? Ten dollars and it's yours."

Leeta fingers her shoulder strap, and looks back at the painting, eyes stinging. Angela touches her arm.

"Hey," Tanika says with a chuckle. "I just remembered. The painting's on sale today. You can have it for only three bucks. I'll even wrap it for you."

Leeta bites her lip and shakes her head. "It is not logical to purchase home décor when I have no home."

She readjusts her backpack and follows Angela out of the store.

CHAPTER II
AN ORDER OF ONION RINGS

*Food and water in the wild are scarce. Eat and drink
plentifully whenever you have the opportunity.*
—FUREAN FIELD SEARCH AND RESCUE GUIDE

ANGELA PASSES A TAKE-OUT BAG and a paper tray
holding a couple of tall drinking cups to Leeta through
the passenger side window. Wezen sniffs the bag appreciatively.

"I hope you like what I got," she says, sliding into the
driver's seat.

Leeta stares at the logo on the bag.

The words *Starry Night Café* are printed over a piece of
swirling blue sky and glowing stars, a replica of the image on
the mug in Leeta's collection. The same logo appears on the
drinking cups. Not believing what she's seeing, Leeta points
to the logo. "What is this image?"

"It's a copy of part of one of my favorite paintings. You've
never seen this image? No, of course you couldn't have."

"I *have* seen it before!"

"Really? I thought you just arrived."

"I did. But long before I arrived, I saw this image . . . in my mind's eye. Décor on a mug. I did not know what it was."

She pauses and listens to the implant.

The Starry Night: *an oil-on-canvas painting by the Dutch Post-Impressionist painter Vincent van Gogh, painted in June 1889. It depicts the view from the east-facing window of the artist's asylum room at Saint-Rémy-de-Provence, in France.*

"This image reminds me of a trip through the galaxy. Only smaller, of course. I like it very much. Is this art?"

"I'm not an expert on art. But I can tell you that millions of people have loved this painting for a very long time."

"That does not answer the question."

"You're right. It doesn't, but that's the best I can do." Angela opens the bag and pulls out a warm object wrapped in paper and passes it to Leeta directly under Wezen's drooling jaws. "Here, this one is for you."

"What is this?"

"A burger."

Burger: *food consisting of a round patty.*

Patty: *a small flat cake of minced or finely chopped food, especially ground beef.*

Ground beef: *the flesh of a cow.*

Cow: *a fully grown female animal of a domesticated breed of ox kept to produce milk or beef used as food.*

Leeta's eyes well up as she pushes the burger back to Angela.

"I cannot eat animals," she says, fighting back tears.

"Oh. Okay. No problem. I know someone who can."

Angela pulls the burger out of the bun, hands it off to Wezen who scarfs the whole thing down in one bite.

"Something to drink?"

Leeta looks at the cup suspiciously. "Is the drink made of cows?"

"No! It's root beer."

Root beer: *an effervescent drink made from an extract of the roots and bark of certain plants.*

"I can drink plants."

Angela gently taps Leeta's cup with her own. "Cheers," she says, smiling.

Pleased to know the old Furean *hastip* drinking custom is the same here on Earth, Leeta clinks Angela's cup a second time. "Cheers."

Angela closes her eyes, drinks deeply, and smiles appreciatively. Leeta does the same, but immediately turns her head and spits a mouthful of root beer out the window.

"What's wrong?"

"I do not enjoy this stinging, burning, tingling plant drink!"

"Oh, I'm sorry! I should have warned you about the carbonation. It's really very good. Try it again, but take little sips."

"I do not want to try it again."

Leeta offers the cup to Wezen. He sniffs the drink and shakes his head dramatically. Leeta's stomach growls more loudly than before. She digs into the paper bag and pulls out a large order of fried onion rings.

"What are these things? The aroma makes my mouth salivate. Are they made from animals?"

"Nope. These, Leeta Simtar, are onion rings. The fast food of the gods."

"Rings?" Leeta slips her finger through one. It slips down to the center of her hand. "A ring for a very large finger!" She laughs at her own joke. "Made from . . . onions?"

Onion: *an edible bulb from the onion plant.*

"I can eat this." Leeta nibbles at the ring she's wearing. "Hmm . . . Crispy. Salty. Crunchy. Slippery."

Two more bites and Leeta devours the entire onion ring. She eats another. And another. Until she quickly finishes them off.

"I get the feeling you'd like some more?"

"How do you know this, Angela?"

"Lucky guess. Am I right?"

Leeta nods eagerly. "Yes, you are correct."

Angela hands over a second large order of rings.

"Thank you."

"Glad you like them. You know, some people say onion rings are even better with ketchup, which is made from tomato plants."

Intrigued, Leeta pauses, mid-chew. "It is difficult to imagine anything more delicious than this."

Angela tears the corner of a small ketchup packet with her teeth and squeezes a small dollop onto the edge of an onion ring. "Try it now."

After one bite, Leeta's eyes glow. "Some people are correct. Onion rings *are* better with ketchup!"

Leeta quickly rips open several packets, smothering the rings with ketchup. She licks her fingers and dives in.

Angela starts driving again. Before long, the small town gives way to a four-lane highway. Angela stops for a red light at a large intersection. Leeta's stomach growls again.

"Still hungry?"

"I am always hungry, but I have eaten all of the onion rings. And all of the ketchup."

"I've got something else I think you'll like." Reaching behind Leeta's seat, Angela pulls a banana out of a shopping bag. Leeta's face lights up.

Banana: *a long curved fruit which grows in clusters and has soft pulpy flesh and yellow skin when ripe. Bananas are America's favorite fruit.*

"Banana!" She bites into the peel, sending mushed banana oozing out the corners of her mouth.

Angela laughs. "You have to peel it first." She picks out another banana, and slowly starts to peel it. "Like this," she says, handing it to Leeta.

Leeta peels the rest and takes a bite, happily rolling her tongue around inside her mouth.

"So, what's your verdict on bananas?"

"America's favorite fruit is also Leeta Simtar's favorite fruit. Is there . . . *are* there more bananas?"

As Angela drives up a long, inclined road, Leeta drops seven banana peels back into the grocery bag, one after the other.

"You are a good friend, Angela. Because of you I no longer have hungry. And I am aware of the tasting pleasures found in onion rings and bananas. Because of you I no longer have fear of all dogs or of being shot or captured and placed in a lab. I am no longer cold and wet. No longer wearing clothes that are not my style. I am thankful to you for all of this and for agreeing to transport me to SETI in Cedarville."

"You're very welcome. For all of it. As for the ride to SETI, I was on my way home anyway, and Wezen and I enjoy your company."

The car approaches an array of radio telescopes on both sides of the road. Not far from the base of one of the giants, a compactly built, dark-haired young man sits drawing intently on a tablet.

"Radio telescopes!" Leeta says. "I was unaware of how very large they are."

"Oh, yeah. These guys are 94 feet tall and 82 feet in diameter."

Leeta lowers the passenger window, sticking her head all the way out to admire the giants. Angela slows the car, lowers her driver side window, and calls to the young man.

"Hey, Sid! How's your masterpiece coming along?"

Sid looks up from his work and waves as they drive past.

"Who is Sid?" Leeta asks.

"Old friend of my son's. I coached them both in Little League. Sid was a damn good pitcher. The private high schools were scouting him. Then he broke his right wrist really bad. Never healed right. But that didn't hold him back. He started drawing with his left hand. Can you imagine? Kid's got real talent and a really good heart. If you're going to be around for a while, you couldn't ask for a better friend."

"Better than you?"

Angela chuckles. "Just sayin', Sid's a good guy. I vouch for him and I don't vouch for just anyone. There are other people in this town, a bunch of nutcase shitheads drawn to SETI. They hate everyone who isn't lily-white, anti-gay, anti-trans, anti-choice, anti-immigrant, anti-science."

"Do the nutcase shitheads hate you too, Angela?"

"You bet they do. For all those reasons. And I'm proud of it."

CHAPTER 12
THE LISTENING STATION

"Do whatever good you can accomplish on any planet in the galaxy, but waste no time on Earth."

—THE FUREAN PRIME DIRECTIVE

LEETA STRIDES THROUGH DOUBLE DOORS into the lobby of the SETI Visitor Center where a few dozen people of all ages, shapes, colors, and sizes peer over display cases, pick the brain of the staffer at the information desk, browse the gift shop, and take selfies in front of a wall-sized photo of deep space.

A group of young girls wearing identical green berets and vests catches Leeta's eye. They are led by an adult female. Though they aren't chanting, Leeta wonders if they are part of their own One Family. But no. They do not look at all alike. Yet what's with the uniforms?

Leeta approaches the girls, spotting the same insignia with the letters GSUSA sewn into the upper left corner of each vest. Leeta's implant gives her the lowdown.

GSUSA: *Girl Scouts of the United States of America, commonly referred to as Girl Scouts, is a youth organization for girls. The* *organization was founded in 1912 by Juliette Gordon Low with the goal to help girls develop leadership skills and good character.*

"Remember, girls," says the leader, handing out clipboards and pens, "We're here to work on our troop project so you earn your Space Science Junior Investigator Badge. Pay attention, learn as much as you can, and be good scouts."

A loud, whiny voice grabs Leeta's attention. "I want ET!"

In front of the gift shop, she spots a woman in a puffy black and white jacket pulling a very young child away from a display filled with fabric models of what look like large-headed turtles with short legs and skinny arms. Stepping closer, Leeta reads an attached label on one of the models: E.T. The Extraterrestrial.

Leeta listens to her memory implant:

ET: *A popular movie from 1982 that tells the story of a boy who befriends an extraterrestrial, dubbed E.T., who is stranded on Earth.*

Movie: *Also known as a film or a motion picture—a series of moving images produced by recording photographic images with a camera. Film is considered a popular art form for entertainment. Especially story telling.*

Leeta's eyes well up. She tenderly lifts one ET after the other and briefly hugs it to her heart before gently replacing it on the display.

"It's time for the movie!" the troop leader says.

Curious, Leeta follows the Girl Scouts into a dimly lit alcove where a movie plays on a large screen. She is confused when the large-headed turtle does not appear, but is soon riveted by the imagery of radio telescopes against a starry sky. The text on the screen asks:

Are there signs of intelligent life in the universe?

Leeta sits enraptured for the entire film. The final frame reads:

We are listening.

As the screen fades to black and the overhead lights come up in the alcove, Leeta mutters, *"Sork!"*

A sharp laugh behind her causes her to turn around to see a portly, gray-haired man. She studies his face and wonders if her father resembles this guy.

The man speaks to Leeta, "I didn't understand what you said, but it sounded something like '*Wow!*' Am I right?"

Leeta nods, shyly.

"That's exactly how I felt the first time it hit me that I could join a team searching for intelligent life on other planets and maybe one day we could actually *find* it." The man holds out his hand. "I'm Jay Piper, Breakthrough Listen Project Manager here at SETI."

Leeta looks into Jay's heavy-lidded brown eyes. The corners of his mouth turn up easily as if he smiles often. She's been told for years that humans are not the best scouts in the universe. But her personal list of good scouts now includes Angela, Tanika, and the teenage boy at the Goodwill store. Leeta feels certain that Jay Piper, with his kind voice and helpful manner, is also a good scout. Zertee would have strongly disapproved of her talking to any of them. But Zertee isn't here.

She shakes Jay's hand vigorously. "I am Leeta Simtar. Pleased to meet you."

"Nice to meet you too. What brought you here today?"

"Angela's red truck."

Momentarily taken aback, Jay's long experience talking with school kids kicks in. "Red trucks are very cool. My grandparents had one. Now that you've answered the how, let's try the why. Okay? Why did you come to SETI today?"

"Because today is the day I'm here. Also, because I am . . . working on my . . . project for Girl Scouts. I am doing research on the history of SETI Institute in Cedarville. Can you tell me the history of this space science facility pleaseandthankyou?"

"It all started with this man, Dr. Liam Rutherford." Jay points to a brass wall plaque. The engraved message reads:

"Are we alone? Unless we continue searching, we may never find the answer. But when we dare to reach beyond the comforts and

burdens of the familiar, we enter into the realm of limitless possibil-ities." —*Dr. Liam Rainier Rutherford*

Eta-Bakara stated that the human scientist she mated with founded SETI at Cedarville. Could this Liam Rutherford be him? Leeta focuses on the letters of the name, waiting for a flash of certainty or even a slight tingling in her scalp, something to indicate whether that Dr. Liam is her father.

She gets nothing.

"Do you have a photo of Dr. Liam Rainier Rutherford?"

"Not an individual photo. In fact, I've never seen one. Not even online. Dr. Rutherford refused to get his picture taken. I remember what a challenge it was getting him away from his computer for five minutes to stand up for the group shot on our opening day. Somehow, we managed. I can show you that one."

Further down on the same wall, Jay points to a large ar-chival photo of 50 people, some sitting, some standing in front of the wall-sized photo of deep space. Before he can point out Liam, Leeta zeroes in on a large man in his forties with unkempt red hair. He stands in back of the third row wearing an impatient expression, and a pair of black, heavy-framed eyeglasses. A wave of recognition surges so power-fully within her, she has to shoulder the wall to steady her-self.

She points to the man with glasses. "That is Dr. Ruther-ford." It isn't a question.

"Yes. That's him. How'd you know?"

She shrugs. She's not lying. She can't explain how she knows, but she absolutely does.

"Is he here today? I would very much like to talk to him."

Jay's mouth twists to one side. "Unfortunately, no. Dr. Rutherford is no longer part of our team."

"Do you know where he is located?"

Jay Piper shakes his head, about to end this conversation and walk away. Then he looks closely at Leeta and something he sees makes him linger a moment longer. "You don't know the story?

"No. Do you know the story?"

Jay's phone buzzes. He glances at it.

"Actually, it's not much of a story. So little is known. If you're interested you can check the computer in the lobby. See what you can find about Dr. Rutherford in old newspaper articles. Good luck with your research, Leeta."

Leeta watches a tired looking young woman wearing a blue hoodie with the word BERKELEY emblazoned on the front in yellow letters hunch over the SETI visitor center computer. As she types, a screen full of links appears, which the woman photographs with her phone before clearing the screen and stepping away.

Leeta steps forward and enters the name: Liam Rainier Rutherford. Up comes a list of links. The most recent one points to an article from a local publication dated two months earlier. The gist of the article is that Marcus Rainier Rutherford, youngest child of Richard Rutherford and Ruth Rainier Rutherford, died of a drug overdose. Richard and Ruth's older son, Liam Rainier Rutherford, founder of the Cedarville SETI Center, disappeared under mysterious circumstances 18 years earlier. His body was never recovered, nor was there any evidence of foul play.

An embedded link takes her to an article from 18 years ago. That piece describes how neighbors living near SETI reported hearing gunshots on the night Liam disappeared. According to several of them, Rick Rodriguez, a local self-proclaimed *alien hunter*, was angry at Liam for founding SETI. Rick was brought in for questioning but never charged.

The rest of the article includes an extensive quote from Rick:

> "Liam Rutherford was abducted by aliens. I saw their ship land and take off. As for the folks inside SETI and in our corrupt government, they've been in contact with ETs for decades and are hiding a sh*tload of evidence!

Rutherford deserved what he got. Never should have built that SETI Center. I told him it would only bring trouble. What do you expect? You set up radio telescopes, you don't think the aliens know we're listening to them? Some of those arrays have transmitters. You understand what I'm saying? They can send messages to the ETs. Jeez. Might as well broadcast an invitation to the universe. 'C'mon down. Invade Earth! We won't stop you.' No surprise them ETs got Rutherford. And they'll be back. When they do, they'll say they've come in peace, but that's a load of bull. They're coming to enslave humanity and don't you forget it."

Back on the search page, a final link takes Leeta to a recent video featuring a dark-haired man with a microphone, and very white teeth and excellent posture. "I'm here at the famed and fabulous Winterbrook Estate, ancestral home of Ruth Rainier Rutherford, Chairwoman of the Board of Rainier Pharmaceuticals, founded by her late father Paul Rainier. Now that Ruth, the family matriarch and heir to the Rainier fortune, is in failing health (though not failing fast enough according to some relatives) a family crisis has erupted. With her oldest son Liam long gone and presumed dead, and her remaining son Marcus passed on from a drug overdose just a month ago, Ruth and her husband Richard, both in their late 80s, are undoubtedly feeling the pressure to name a new heir."

Leeta shuts down the computer.

"ET! ET!"

Leeta freezes and looks around nervously. The same little boy she saw at the gift shop comes barreling toward her, laughing and looking back at his mom, who's chasing him across the lobby. The kid runs smack into Leeta and falls down. She lifts him to his feet. He tilts his head back to look up at her face. She smiles at him. He glances down and stares at her fingers.

"What's wrong with your hands?"

Her smile fades. She hides her hands behind her back.

The boy's mother appears. "I'm so sorry," she says to Leeta. "He knows he shouldn't run indoors."

"Mommy! What's wrong with her hands?"

Mom pulls him away.

Leeta's APED buzzes loudly. She takes it out of her backpack as one of the Girl Scouts nudges her friend.

"Woah! Look at her phone! Excuse me, can we see your phone?"

Panicking, Leeta shoves the still-buzzing APED into her pocket, pulls up her hood, hunches forward, and strides toward the exit.

CHAPTER 13
A Friend with Wheels

Be cautious of all alien species.
—The Furean Prime Directive

OUTSIDE THE SETI BUILDING, Leeta whispers into her APED, now set to audio-only mode.

"Zertee, I've learned my father's name and the location of his ancestral home."

"Excuse me!" calls an eager voice behind her.

Leeta turns to see Sid walking toward her. When their eyes meet, he looks away, as if she's the sun and he can't take too much at once. She shuts off her APED and shoves it into her pocket.

Sid stops in front of her, looks up and, smiles. "Hi, Leeta. I'm Sid."

She looks down at him, studying his face closely and twists her mouth to the left.

Awkward silence.

"Angela told me about you," Sid says, trying his best to put her at ease. It isn't working.

Leeta inhales deeply, stands taller, trembling inside. "What exactly did Angela tell you about me?"

"Exactly? Well . . . she said you were training for the US Women's Olympics volleyball team."

Leeta's brow crinkles as she listens intently to her implant.

Olympics aka The Olympic Games: *a series of international athletic competitions, featuring thousands of athletes from around the world.*

Volleyball: *a team sport in which two teams of six players are separated by a net.*

She shakes her head emphatically. "That is not accurate."

Sid feigns shock. "Really? Damn, I was sure . . ." Then he cracks up. "Okay. You got me. Angela never said that. I was just kidding."

Kidding: *playfully deceptive; when someone says something surprising or that seems as if it could not be serious or true.*

Leeta stares at him, puzzled. He looks at her hopefully, "Not even a little bit funny, huh?"

Leeta offers a sly smile. "I have not yet decided whether I find your comment humorous."

"So, you're saying there's still a chance you don't think I'm a complete asshole?"

Asshole: *a stupid, irritating or contemptible person.*

"Yes, Sid, there is still a 57% chance."

He throws back his head and laughs with pure delight. "57%? Okay. I'll take that."

Watching him, Leeta can't help giggling. Her APED buzzes. She shoots Sid a nervous look, but he's still smiling. She fumbles inside her pocket and shuts the device off.

"What else did Angela tell you about me? Are you able to answer this question without kidding?"

"I'll definitely *try* not to make lame jokes, but I can't promise. I like making people laugh. Kidding is just part of who I am. It's hard to turn it off. Know what I mean?"

She nods, relaxing her shoulders, enjoying this new feeling of being with someone who doesn't hide the truth about himself.

As for Sid, his heart is suddenly lighter, and he can't contain his smile. He's enjoying being with someone who isn't asking questions about his family. As far as first impression go, this is good.

"Angela says you're new here and you love onion rings, especially with ketchup."

"Do you like onion rings with ketchup?"

"Definitely! She also told me something kinda personal about you."

Leeta shifts her weight from one foot to the other, glancing around for an escape route. "What kinda personal was it?"

"She said you could use a friend. True?"

"What is your definition of friend?"

"Someone you can trust to keep your secrets. Do you need someone like that?"

"Maybe."

Leeta looks directly into Sid's brown eyes, wishing she could read beyond the generosity she sees there. Suddenly a strange but not unpleasant intensity overwhelms them both. Flustered, they feel compelled to look away from each other at the same moment.

"Is that all she told you about me, Sid?"

"That's all I can remember."

Leeta narrows her eyes. "If you remember more, do you promise you will tell me?"

Sid holds up his right hand. "Deal."

Deal: *an agreement entered into by two or more parties for their mutual benefit.*

Leeta nods. "As part of our deal, would you like to know what Angela said about you?"

"Sure," he says, but honestly, he's not so sure.

"Angela said you injured your right wrist playing Little League. I hope you are no longer experiencing any pain."

He scoffs. "She gave you my medical history?" He holds up his wrist, rotating it freely. "See? I'm good. No pain."

"She also said you draw very well and that she doesn't vouch for the nutcase shitheads, but she vouches for you."

Sid laughs. The sound pleases Leeta. Smiling with the light of a star, she sticks out her hand. "It is very nice to meet you, Sid."

He reaches up. "Good to meet you too." They shake hands. "So how tall are you, Leeta? About six-three? Six-four?"

"I have six feet and six inches of height. How much tall do you have?"

"Five-six on a good day."

"Is today a good day?"

He grins. "Sure. It's always good when I meet someone who makes me laugh."

Leeta's APED buzzes again. She slips her hand into her pocket. Doing a 180, she hurries away from Sid to take the call. At a safe distance, she presses the APED to her ear.

"Have you reached your father's ancestral home yet?" Zertee asks.

"No. But I'll be there soon."

"Good. There are only two days and a few hours remaining before you must return to your pod for redocking."

Leeta stashes the APED and trots back to Sid. "In which direction is Winterbrook?"

"The Rutherford Estate? North, 150, 200 miles. Give or take."

"Give or take what?"

"Nothing. Why are you going to Winterbrook?"

"To talk to the Rutherfords."

"You know that place isn't open to the public, right?"

"I do not understand."

"They don't let people inside the house."

"If the house is empty, where do the Rutherfords live?"

"What I mean is, the Rutherfords live in the house, but they don't let anyone else inside. Unless they're expecting you. Are they?"

"That would be impossible since none of the Rutherfords know of my existence. But I must get inside Winterbrook because I am researching the family for a Girl Scouts project."

"Aren't you too old to be a Girl Scout?"

"I am a member of the Old Girl Scouts of America."

Sid cocks his head quizzically. "The . . . Old Girl Scouts?"

She looks toward the sun, orients herself, and turns to the north. "Goodbye, Sid," she says, taking off at a good clip.

"Hey! Wait!"

She stops and turns around, standing tall and strong. "Are you remembering something else Angela told you about me?"

"No. I just want to know if you're going to walk to Winterbrook?"

She relaxes, but only a bit. "That would be illogical. Two hundred miles is too far, and I am in a hurry. I will be traveling in my vehicle which is very fast."

He looks around. "I love fast cars. Where'd you park?"

"Not far from here. In a forest—"

"—You parked in a forest?"

"—that rings a meadow."

"Oh, you must mean Blake's Meadow. That's about ten miles from here. If you're in a hurry I could drive you to your car."

"I accept your offer, Sid. Pleaseandthankyou."

In the parking lot, Leeta looks over the hand-painted exterior of Sid's 2015 Honda Civic SE, every inch covered with a profusion of stars, fiery comets, meteors, asteroids, nebulas, and cloud-shrouded and ringed planets, all swirling in the blackest of night skies. Mouth agape, she walks slowly around the car, lovingly running her hands over the doors, fenders, hood as if she can feel the colors of the cosmos through her skin.

"This is like a starry night galaxy on wheels, Sid."

"Yeah. I call it the Cosmos on Wheels."

"Did you put these colors on the Cosmos on Wheels?"

"Yeah. I painted it."

"Is this art?"

He shrugs, blushing. "I dunno. Maybe. Anyway, what is art?"

Her eyes flash. "Why is that such a difficult question for people to answer?"

He holds up his hands in surrender. "Okay. Okay. I'll give you an answer, but you might not like it. For me, something is art if *you* think it's art. That's all I got. Helpful?"

"Yes, that is helpful. Now I can answer the question for myself. Your vehicle is art."

"Thank you." He smiles and holds open the car door. "Welcome to my world."

As she climbs in, she bumps her forehead.

"Are you okay?" he asks.

"Yes. I am okay," she says, touching the spot. "My head is hard and not easily dented."

She settles into the passenger seat, backpack in her lap, knees nearly up to her chin.

"Oh, hold on. Let me fix that for you."

Sid touches a button on the side of her seat. It slides all the way back, taking Leeta with it. She laughs as she rides, stretching her legs out most of the way.

Fifteen minutes later they reach the road that rings Blake's Meadow.

"Stop right here!" Leeta says.

Sid hits the brakes. She hops out and hoists her pack to her shoulders. "Thank you and goodbye."

The way she slams the door and says that last word takes Sid by surprise. Instead of a casual "Goodbye," it sounds more like *We're never going to see each other again.*

Something about this thought feels like the opposite of laughter. Sid would never go where he's not wanted, but, damn, this girl is intriguing, and he'd really like to find out more about her and what she's up to, because she's clearly up to something and he wants to be part of it. But she just said goodbye. And she clearly meant it. So, he sits there, like a deserted island, watching her race across the meadow. Her crazy long legs bring her to the edge of the forest in less than a minute, and that's where he loses sight of her.

Leeta arrives at the spot where she landed on Earth just the day before.

"AYA, uncloak the escape pod."

"I'd really like to do that for you, Leeta, but we've got a problem."

"What is the problem?"

"Pod's gone."

"What do you mean *gone?*"

"I mean there's no trace of it."

"That is not logical!" Leeta shouts, frantically groping the empty air. She falls to her knees and sweeps the ground with her hands, grasping at dried leaves and twigs.

"I left it right here, AYA. These are the coordinates. Track it!"

"Don't you think I've tried? There's no signal, Leeta. The pod's not anywhere near here."

"AYA, what happened to it?"

"Most likely? I'd say that human with the dog found it and took it away."

"*Sork!*"

"Yeah. Totally *sorky.*"

Leeta gets to her feet, anxiously scanning the area without moving, terrified that she's just walked into a trap. The trees that welcomed her yesterday now feel like they're closing in, offering shelter only to her enemies. She runs further into the forest, finds the hollow redwood, and crawls inside.

"AYA, call Zertee."

Zertee appears. "You look upset, Leeta. What is the problem?"

"My pod is gone!"

"Vanished or destroyed?"

"I don't know. Both are possibilities." The words come out in a rush. Leeta is close to tears, as she often is when things touch her heart, but these tears are different. These are sourced at the well of terror and desperation. "The only thing I know with certainty is that my pod is no longer where I left it, and I can't get a signal to track it."

"Humans must have discovered it."

"That's what AYA said. Maybe human scientists removed it to a lab where they are now dismantling it piece by piece in order to determine its origins. Undoubtedly that will lead them to me. And when they find me, they will either kill me or imprison me in a laboratory!"

"Try to remain calm, Leeta. We do not yet have sufficient information for you to draw these conclusions."

Leeta takes several slow deep breaths. "You're right. Thank you. I am feeling calmer now. But why can't I get a signal?"

"Perhaps your communicator's power is low. Though that seems unlikely as you have been on the surface for less than 24 hours."

"My power indicator says 99.99%. Something else is going on. Zertee, can you track my pod from the ship?"

"Yes. I will call up the coordinates and get back to you."

Leeta looks up through the tree tunnel. The patch of sky visible at the end is now slate gray. Yesterday these wooden walls protected her. Now they feel like a prison. Fear gnaws at her heart and floods her brain with the craziest dark thoughts.

I will be stranded on Earth forever.

The nutcase and his dog will find me before I find my father.

Humans will turn my likeness into a toy and sell it at the SETI gift shop.

Slow breathing doesn't calm her now. Neither does cupping her right hand over her heart in her best effort at *tulahm*. When her APED buzzes again, she jumps.

"Zertee, do you have the coordinates?"

"No. It is a very strange thing, Leeta. Even with the ship's high-powered tracking, I cannot pick up a signal from the pod. I will continue working to locate it. What will you do in the meantime?"

"I'm leaving this location right now. It doesn't feel safe. I'll continue my journey to my father's ancestral home."

"That is a logical plan. But first you must calm down."

"You keep saying that!"

"Because you have not yet accomplished a state of calm. When you are agitated, you cannot do your best thinking. And considering your current location and situation, you need to think clearly. Breathe. Slowly. Deeply."

"You're right, Zertee. Thank you for that reminder." She shuts down her APED and breathes rapidly and loudly, in and out, through her nose. Again and again. She assures herself that she's calming down, but herself isn't convinced.

Leeta races through the trees, shaking and sobbing. Sid spots her the moment she reappears in the meadow and runs toward her through the grass and clover. "Leeta, are you okay?"

"No!" she says, eyes streaming. "Not okay. My vehicle is gone."

"Someone stole your car?"

"I don't knooooow!" Leeta wails.

As Sid moves closer, a yellowjacket nails the back of his leg. He cries out and collapses. Leeta rushes to his side. Grimacing, he clutches the puncture wound, which is already red with anger and swelling fast. Without hesitating, she cups her hand over the sting. An instant later, the pain and swelling vanish.

Sid stands, rubbing his leg. "Wow! Amazing. Thanks. That really helped. How'd you do that?"

Leeta thinks about what happened when she touched Angela's sore back. She *tulahmed* away the emotional distress *and* physical pain. But how? Even if Leeta could explain the process to herself, she would not reveal it to Sid. He seems kind, but Angela warned her to be very careful about what she told people. It would be illogical to ignore that advice.

Leeta returns to the present moment and stands up, hoisting her backpack on one shoulder.

"I have much happiness knowing you are feeling better, Sid. Now I have need of *your* help. Will you drive me to Winterbrook in your painted vehicle?"

He looks up at this impossibly tall girl. Her head blocks the sun and throws a shadow over him, a shadow that actually warms him.

"Lemme think," he says. After a long moment of silence, in which he pretends to consider his answer. "My next work deliverable isn't for another few days. I've got nothing else to do. Sure. Why not?"

Leeta nods and walks past Sid toward his car. "I have calculated the time we'll need. If we leave immediately and travel at the speed limit of 65 miles per hour, we will arrive at Winterbrook at approximately—

"—Wait!"

She inhales sharply, then turns back to him, her hand cups her heart, attempting to quiet her sudden agitation. "Have you just remembered something else Angela told you about me?"

"Nope. I already told you everything. It's just that we can't leave for Winterbrook immediately. We've got to pick up supplies before we hit the road."

"I have my own supplies." She pats her backpack and hurries toward the car.

He jogs to keep up with her. "That's great, but unless you've got a sleeping bag, a tent and a whole bunch of excellent snacks in there, we're going to need to make a few stops before we head out." Sid reads her expression and answers her question before she has a chance to ask it. "You've got that look on your face like you want to know why. It's because it'll be dark in a few hours and I'm not driving through the night. So, our first stop is my house for camping gear."

"How much time will be used by stopping at your house? I have approximately two days left."

"Until what?"

"Until I have to leave."

His heart drops. "You're leaving? But Angela said—"

"What did she say?"

"Nothing. Look, my house is less than a mile from here."

He opens the car door for her.

She hesitates and looks at him sharply. "Do you live alone?"

There's something fragile about this wonderfully strange girl who can take away a bee sting with her touch. More than anything, Sid would like to be able to touch her and take away her fear. But he knows he can't do that. And he can't lie to her.

"I live with my dad. But he's never home this time of day. So, if you want a ride to Winterbrook, we've gotta stop there first. Deal?"

"Deal." Her voice is tight. Her breath is ragged. She carefully ducks her head and climbs into the Cosmos on Wheels.

CHAPTER 14
IN THE PREDATOR'S LAIR

*Humans are far too primitive and entrenched in their fears
and violent instincts to benefit from the infusion of Furean DNA.*
—THE CASE OF BORTAK-MORSEE,
HIGH GENETICS COUNCIL REPORT, FINAL CONCLUSION

LEETA FOLLOWS SID UP the front steps of a modest two-story house, where paint flakes off the walls, and the overgrown front lawn has a brittle, defeated look. An old barn slumps at the back end of the property. Its front wall sports a hand-drawn sign in thick red letters that reads "*Mind Your Own Damn Business.*"

Sid unlocks the front door of the house and Leeta follows him inside.

"I'm just going to grab a few things in my room. This won't take long."

Leeta is quickly engrossed in the contents and décor of her first human home. The living room shades are drawn, giving the place a closed in, unwelcoming feel. Supermarket tabloids crowd a large table, headlines screaming of UFO sightings over New Mexico, mummified aliens brought back to life, government coverups of abducted humans. A foot-high cone made of light-weight metal and appearing as if it might be a head covering, sits atop a pile of printed planetary maps, diagrams, and charts peek out from the edges of a large, open pizza box containing a single, half-eaten slice with extra cheese.

Six large, framed movie posters line one wall. Leeta studies each one as her implant supplies brief synopses. A cold dread spreads through her chest and into her stomach.

The Thing from Another World: *a 1951 film about scientists fending off a bloodthirsty alien organism.*

Invasion of the Body Snatchers: *a 1956 film about a small town whose residents are being replaced by emotionless alien duplicates.*

The Blob: *a 1958 film in which a carnivorous alien crashes to Earth from outer space.*

Independence Day: *a 1996 film in which a powerful extraterrestrial race launches a worldwide attack.*

Edge of Tomorrow: *a 2014 film about an alien race that hits Earth in an unrelenting assault.*

Her anxiety intensifies as she focuses on the seventh and final poster. It's her friend, ET, with an actual dart stuck into his glowing heart.

She backs away as if trying to stay out of range of toxic radiation. She can't understand why Sid chose these disturbing images as home décor. Then she spots a framed newspaper story from 18 years ago and begins reading.

Rick Rodriguez, a local man with a long-held fascination with UFOs, claimed, yet again, to have seen a spaceship. According to Mr. Rodriguez, this one looked like a "large transparent ball" that landed in Blake's Meadow on Tuesday around midnight, not far from the SETI Center in Cedarville, California.

He went on to say that he approached the ship with a loaded shotgun and saw what he described as a "short but very strong space alien" who was "easily overpowering a tall, solidly built man."

Asked by this reporter if he recognized the man being assaulted, Mr. Rodriguez admitted that was impossible because there was "a whole lot of fog in the meadow at the time." Mr. Rodriguez also said he felt it was his "duty to protect Earth from an alien invasion" so he fired his weapon "several times" at the alien. "It was the damnedest thing. After I shot, the ship took off in a flash and disappeared."

When asked if he had hit either the alleged alien or the man, Mr. Rodriguez said, "I wasn't aiming for the guy. Don't think I hit the ET. I hope so. I hope he bled to death on his way home. Only way to treat those effin' aliens is shoot to kill."

A high-pitched clanging pulses in the center of Leeta's brain and will not let up. It was 18 years ago that Eta-Bakara came to Earth to meet Liam Rutherford. Was Rick Rodriguez the man who tried to kill her mother? Is he the same man who chased her? And why is this newspaper article and all these movie posters in Sid's house? But wait. Sid said he lived with his father.

Feeling sick, Leeta turns away from the wall, and spots a dog bowl on the floor. The name GUNNER printed on the side.

She barrels out of the house.

Sid walks downstairs, smiling, arms loaded with art supplies, sleeping bags, a rolled-up tent, water bottles, and extra hoodies. "I think I've got everything we need, and if not, we can pick up the rest on the way."

Leeta is not there.

He calls to her. No answer. He walks into the kitchen. Nope. Knocks on the bathroom door. Nothing. She's not in the front yard or in the car either. Utterly confused, he dumps all the stuff into the trunk, pulls out of the driveway, and hits the road.

A couple of miles from the house he spots her, running at an impressive trot. He taps the horn twice. She looks back and picks up her pace. He pulls up beside her, matching her speed, and lowers the passenger window.

"Hey Leeta! What's up? Why'd you leave?"

Her face is flushed, distorted. She's breathing heavily, her backpack banging incessantly against her, as if urging her forward.

"Leeta. What happened?"

Eyes straight ahead, refusing to acknowledge his presence, she pulls up her hood and continues running.

"Did I do something wrong?" he asks, desperation coloring every word.

"Stop following me, Sid. Go away. I no longer require a ride to Winterbrook. I will get there on foot. Goodbye."

Somehow this second brush-off feels worse than the first. When she first said goodbye, she seemed indifferent. Now, she seems scared of him. How could that be? He's agonizing over what he might have done to make her suddenly so afraid. Nothing comes to mind. Then he thinks about what, if anything, he can say to change her mind. To get her to see him as a friend. That's when he spots his father's white pickup truck heading toward them. It crests a hill before temporarily dipping out of sight.

Sid hits the brakes and flings open the passenger door. "Leeta, get in the car."

"Why should I do that?"

He points up the road. The white truck has reappeared. "Because that's my dad's truck."

Her eyes go wide. "Rick Rodriguez is coming here?"

"Yeah, and if he sees you . . ."

"He will hate me for not being lily-white."

"For starters. Just get in and hide in the back!"

She dives into the car, scrambles over the front seat, and crouches low on the floor. Sid speeds forward. Moments later, they zip past the truck, ignoring the blaring horn and barking dog. Sid watches the truck recede in the rearview mirror.

He exhales between pursed lips. "He's gone. You can come out now."

Leeta crawls back into the passenger seat and buckles up as Sid's phone dings. He glances at it.

"Your father?" she asks, nervously.

"How'd you know?"

"Lucky guess."

He puts the phone face down on the center console, and drives even faster

A moment later, Sid's phone dings again. Leeta flinches.

"Don't worry, Leeta. I'm not texting him back."

"How do you know that I am worrying?"

"Lucky guess. Well, not really. You were in the house long enough to see stuff."

"Yes, I saw stuff, and I read stuff." She taps her heart. "And I felt stuff, Sid. Very much uncomfortable stuff. Your father believes visitors from outer space want only to destroy Earth and should be killed on sight."

Sid squeezes the steering wheel and fixes his eyes on the road. "Yep. He and his buddies believe all kinds of crazy shit."

"What about you, Sid? Do you also believe crazy shit?" She tries to steady her voice, not give away too much. It's hard.

He wants to turn to look at her, just for a moment, but doesn't trust his face not to show how desperately he wants her to trust him. He knows she's freaked and he doesn't blame her. No one wants to be friends with the kid who's got a crazy dad. She'd probably rather be walking along the side of the road, alone in the dark, than be driving with him.

Sid shrugs and forces himself to face her. "Doesn't matter what I say. What matters is what you believe."

She studies a softness around his eyes she had not noticed before. "I believe that you are not like your father."

He exhales, not realizing he'd been holding his breath, and looks ahead again. They ride on in silence, but it's okay, and they both know it.

She lowers the window and leans out. The sky is all clear now except for a few high wispy clouds that look like they were painted on at the last minute, not unlike her last-minute decision to ride to Winterbrook with this human stranger. Zertee would not approve.

A short while later Sid turns onto Main Street, El Lugar.

"We're gonna need food for the road," he says. "Let's stop at the market."

"Might the Food-For-The-Road market be located in the vicinity of the Will-Be-Nice store?"

"The what?"

"Oh, my mistake. I meant to say the Will-Be-Good store."

"Will be good? Oh." Sid laughs. "You mean the Goodwill?"

"Yes. I need to stop there first. And I will need three dollars. Will you cover me?"

Sid sits in the Goodwill parking lot, nervously scanning for his father's truck. His phone dings. It's his dad. Sid's finger hovers over the screen. After a few seconds of indecision, he sends the call to voicemail and scans the block leading to the parking lot. No sign of the white pickup. He chews his lower lip and plays his dad's message. His dad talking so fast Sid can only understand a few words: *... not gonna believe ... fuckin' amazing! ...*

Hammering, drilling, barking and something that sounds like a blowtorch wash out the rest of the message. Then there's an explosion and the message ends.

Leeta reaches for the painting on the wall. When she takes hold of the frame, she closes her eyes and tentatively extends her thumbs so they touch the canvas. Her face contorts in anguish, and her chest tightens. A vision fills her mind: A human hand holds a paintbrush tipped in gray-blue. The hand guides the brush to a section of rock in the lower left of a canvas that appears to be the one she's holding. Grief grips her heart and won't let go. The whole store suddenly goes dark and airless.

With tremendous effort, she pulls her hands off the picture frame. The vision and the emotions that came with it vanish. She leans heavily against the wall, breathing hard. She wipes her eyes, stands up straight, and cautiously touches the frame again. This time with just a single fingertip. Nothing happens. She slowly places the palm of her right hand on the frame. Again nothing. Emboldened, Leeta lays both hands on the frame and rests them there. Again, no repeat of what she saw or felt. Slightly disappointed but mostly relieved that whatever just happened will not overwhelm her again, she lifts the painting off the wall and carries it to the counter where she places it in front of Tanika, along with three dollars.

"Ah, you're back. Changed your mind about the painting, I see."

"Is that permitted?"

"Sure. But we don't take returns, so once you buy it, you can't change your mind again. Want me to wrap it for you?"

"Yes, pleaseandthankyou."

Sid sketches a girl who looks like Leeta. The shape takes form on the page. He works on the curve of her neck then stops and begins tackling the lines of her spiky out-of-control hair. Not easy. Against his better judgement he replays his father's voicemail. He's heard plenty of *You're not gonna believe . . . fuckin' amazing . . .* rants before. None ever turned out to be anything mildly amazing or even interesting. But something in the new level of crazy in his dad's voice makes Sid wonder if this time he actually found something.

Leeta taps on the glass. Sid quickly shuts the sketchbook and lowers his window.

"What did you buy?" he says, pointing at the large flat parcel under her arm.

"Art."

"Yeah, well, I figured it wasn't a pair of sneakers."

"Kidding again?"

"Right. Ten points for you. Funny?"

"Five points for funny."

"Not bad. So, what kind of art did you buy for three bucks?"

"I do not wish to disclose that information at this time."

"Oh. Okay." He pushes a button and the trunk yawns open. "Just put the art in the back."

CHAPTER 15

FOOD FOR THE ROAD

Flowers are nature's way of saying hello.
—THE FUREAN BOTANIST'S HANDBOOK

SID HURRIEDLY PUSHES a shopping cart down the cereal aisle while Leeta lags behind, gawking at the endless shelves as if sleepwalking through a museum of treasures. Sid looks over his shoulder, still on edge that his father might spot his not so subtly decorated car in the store lot, burst in, and find them here.

"I thought you were in a hurry, Leeta."

"I am, but look at all of these different boxes of breakfast foods."

"Yeah, lots of choices. You know, this'll go much faster if I shop while you look around. If you see something you want, grab it. I'll meet you at the cashier in five minutes."

"Okay."

Leeta wanders, enthralled at the amount of food on display and the variety. Fresh fruits and vegetables. Canned sauces and bean. Juices. Sodas. Crackers. Chips. Cookies. Energy bars. Opening the freezer doors she's shocked by how cold *frozen* actually feels. But what most startles this visitor from a dry place is the bottled water. Yes, Earth is the water planet. Didn't she marvel at the blue view from space? But aside from the difference between ocean water and fresh water, Leeta cannot fathom all the different kinds of water offered for sale here in bottles, cans, and boxes. Flavored water! What is that? And why is that something humans are willing to spend money on? Grape, watermelon, peach, raspberry, black cherry, blackberry, lemon, zesty lime. Sparkling water! Probiotic water! Nutrient-enhanced water with vitamins, antioxidants, and electrolytes. Leeta wonders what Fureans would think if they could see all this. Or, better yet, what would happen if she brought back a few bottles?

In the floral department Leeta ogles the bouquets of cut flowers, the bottoms of their stems sitting in buckets of water. The colors blow her botanist's mind. Then she catches a whiff of lilac. Burying her nose in a cluster of purple flowers, she inhales deeply, and her head begins to float. From there she sample-smells roses, lilies, and freesias but when she gets to the gardenias, she's filled with a magical sense of joy.

Through the flowers Leeta spots a tiny women wearing a black surgical mask and leaning heavily on a cane. In her other hand she holds a leash attached to a large white-and black dog.

Leeta's implant tells her this dog is an **Alaskan Malamute:** *a large breed, affectionate, loyal, playful, needs a job.*

"Excuse me. What is your dog's name?"

"This is Sheila. She's my support dog. Aren't you, lovie?"

Sheila looks up at the woman and wags her tail.

"That is a good job," says Leeta. "In what ways does she support you?"

"Well, she calms me down whenever I'm anxious. Ever since COVID, I feel especially anxious in stores. Well, even *before* COVID. Crowds are not my favorite thing."

"Crowds are not my favorite thing either. I prefer gardenias, bananas, and onion rings."

"Well, if you don't like crowds, maybe you should get a support dog. Having Sheila by my side really helps."

The woman's knees creak when she bends to scratch behind Sheila's ear. Leeta notices it's the same as Wezen's favorite spot! She reaches out to touch Sheila, but the woman blocks her with her cane.

"Are you up to date with your boosters?" she asks sharply.

Booster: 1. *a keen promoter of a person, organization, or cause.*
"*athletic booster clubs*"
2. *a source of help or encouragement.*
"*job fairs are a great morale booster*"

While Leeta puzzles over the definitions she's just heard, the woman gives a wary look, and hobbles away, Sheila firmly in tow.

Leeta turns to the potted plant display and picks up one plant after another, gently stroking its leaves, stems and buds. Sid stands behind his shopping cart a few yards away, smiling to himself as he watches her, unseen. He has never been into plants, and now he's wondering if he's missed out on something. Finally, he steps forward.

"I'm ready to check out, Leeta. Find anything you want?"

"How do these plants grow in such small pots with no access to water or sunlight?"

Sid frowns. "I don't know for sure, but I don't think it hurts them. Not for a short time. Then when people buy them, they put them in a bigger pot and stick them by a sunny window. Or maybe plant them in the ground. That's what my mom always does. You want one of these?"

Leeta holds up a flowering blue plant. "I want this one. It is a hydrangea, native of Asia and the only plant here with blue flowers. Very unusual in the plant kingdom."

He looks at the price sticker. "It's $14.99. Have you got that much?"

"No. I do not have any money."

"You're traveling without money?"

"That is true. I had a lot to consider while making plans to come here. Unfortunately, I did not think about money. Do you have any money, Sid?"

"Well, yeah, I'm buying all this for us." He gestures to his cart. "I've got some cash which we might need for the road. But I've also got a credit card."

"I know about credit cards. They are better than cash. So, you've got me covered again!"

He nods. "I guess so."

CHAPTER 16
THE ROAD TO WINTERBROOK

SID DRIVES PAST GREEN HILLS and meadows carpeted with yellow mustard, purple lupine, orange poppies. More relaxed now that they're out of town and on their way north, he sneaks glances at Leeta who is alternating eating handfuls of gummy bears and M&M's while happily watching the spring landscape roll by.

"Didn't anyone ever tell you that too much sugar's not good for you?"

"No one has ever told me that, but if someone had, I would think they were ignorant. This food makes me feel great! I have so much energy."

"Yeah, well, candy isn't exactly food, and sugar energy doesn't last long. Ten minutes after you stop eating, you'll crash."

"How could I crash? I am not driving this car."

"Not that kind of crash. It's more like you get really tired, or jittery, or emotional. No offense, Leeta, but you seem like you're already a pretty emotional person and—"

"What's wrong with emotions?" she snaps.

"Nothing. Emotions are fine. Perfectly normal. It's just that if you eat too much sugar you might—"

Her communicator buzzes, startling them both. She digs the APED out of her pocket, glances at it, then shuts off the device and stashes it away again.

"Someone you don't want to talk to?" he asks.

"That is an incorrect assumption. I *do* want to talk to this someone, but I need privacy. Can we stop for a while?"

"Oh. Sure. I can pull over here."

He slows down, steering the car off the road onto a shoulder lined with grass that opens onto a field where a large oak stands, opening its spring leaves to the sun. Leeta hops out of the car and heads for the tree.

"Why did you not respond to my signal?" Zertee asks, concern creeping into her voice. "Are you in danger again?"

Leeta picks up an acorn and rolls it between her thumb and index finger. "Not at all. I am making good progress on my research. I didn't answer your call because I wasn't alone."

"Who was with you?"

"The same human male I mentioned before. His name is Sid. Since I currently have no means of transportation, he's volunteered to drive me to my father's ancestral home in his personal vehicle."

"Leeta! You are traveling in a personal vehicle with a human?"

"No worries, Zertee. Sid isn't like his father." She looks towards Sid's car. He is sitting on the front fender, sketching. A faint smile plays at the corners of her mouth. Leeta blushes, hoping Zertee didn't catch it.

She did.

"Why are you smiling like that? What do you mean 'He isn't like his father'?"

"Never mind." Leeta's all business again. "Did you locate my pod?"

"Not yet. I am able to receive a partially jumbled signal from it, but only for very brief intervals. Then the signal vanishes."

"Are you recording what you're receiving?"

"Yes, but the data is fragmented, non-sequential, and of no use."

Leeta ponders this while absently tracing her finger along the rough tree bark. "The cloaking protocol wouldn't have caused that."

"Not ordinarily. But there is the possibility that the abundance of radio waves and other communications signals so prevalent on and above Earth are somehow interfering with our technology's ability to track the pod."

"What are we gonna do?" Leeta's voice rises. "We can't shut out Earth's communication signals."

"True. I am working to compensate for the signal interference, but that will take some more time. There might also be another unrelated explanation."

"What's that?"

"Because of the intermittent and random nature of the data, I am beginning to conclude that the individual or individuals who transported your pod from the landing site and are currently in possession of it are not scientists. They seem too incompetent."

"Huh. If they don't know what they're doing, that might be a good thing."

Leeta says goodbye to Zertee, stuffs her APED into her pocket, and strides back to the car. Sid looks up from his sketchbook and catches the troubled look on her face. "Bad news?"

"Maybe. Maybe not." She studies his sketch. "Why are you attempting to replicate the radio telescopes from SETI?"

"Just for fun. But drawing is also my job. I work for a game publisher, doing background paintings. Let me show you."

He brings up an image on his phone. It's an intergalactic battle between two highly detailed spaceships in a field of stars and asteroids. Fiery blue photon torpedoes pour from one ship. A massive explosion lights the underbelly of the other. "I made this one is for a game called *Tyrodic Wars Part III*."

He launches into his best imitation of a series of explosions, alternating between sharp, whistling pings and low booms, quickly getting so carried away he almost forgets she's standing there. The sounds he's manufacturing fascinate her. So do his facial contortions and wild hand gestures that seem to be part of the performance. Leeta was not aware any of this was within the human vocal repertoire.

When Sid finally winds down she says, "But there is no sound in space because there is no air."

"Of course not. I was just . . . it's a game, Leeta. It's all pretend."

She can't take her eyes off the screen. "The image is so accurate," she mutters under her breath. To Sid she says, "You made this on a small cellular telephone?"

"No," he chuckles. "I work on a tablet. This is just a screen shot."

"Ah. A file capture."

"Yeah."

He offers her the phone and she zooms in on the image. "You have precisely recreated the vastness and beauty of space with its infinite possibilities."

Suddenly and for the first time Sid is seeing his work through someone else's eyes. The fact that it's Leeta's eyes that are so filled with admiration fills him with pride and confidence. He hasn't felt either since a broken wrist forced him to quit Little League and give up the dream of becoming a major league pitcher.

With great respect, she hands the phone back. "This is very art."

They look into each other's eyes, holding their gaze a beat or two longer than necessary. He feels at home. She's not sure what she feels. She breaks away and taps the sketchbook. "May I see some of your other just-for-fun drawings?"

"Okay. I don't show them to many people. Actually, not anyone. So don't expect too much. They're not *very art*."

She opens the book, carefully turning pages, studying each sketch before flipping to the next. When she reaches an elaborate drawing of a short female figure perched on a boulder amidst a barren rocky landscape, eyes trained on the night sky, Leeta inhales sharply and cups her right hand over her heart.

"What's wrong?" Sid asks, his voice tight with nerves.

"This sketch does not make me happy. It is bringing a deep sadness to my heart, but I am wanting more of it. That is strange to me. It is not the same as wanting more candy to eat. I am very interested in what I am looking at, and I want to understand more about this woman in your drawing. I sense that she is feeling alone and discouraged, but also hopeful that there is a place where there are others like herself. And though that place might be farther away than those stars overhead, some day she knows she will get there."

Sid has been listening to her with his mouth open as if he were frozen. Now he closes it and shakes his head. "That's amazing. What you just said. That's exactly what I felt when I drew it. You also got parts of her backstory I didn't even think of."

"There is more to the back of her story?"

"Yeah. Lots more. This is just one single frame of a graphic novel I've been working on for a couple of years. Want to hear more?"

"Yes. Later. Now I want us to start moving again toward Winterbrook."

She opens the car door. Her stomach growls. He grabs his art materials, pretending he didn't hear.

He gets into the driver's seat and closes the door. They are both inside the car. Her stomach growls again, more loudly. He clears his throat.

"There is no need for embarrassment, Sid. All living creatures hunger for something."

Leeta and Sid both know there is more than one kind of hunger. There's the kind satisfied by food and a deeper hunger that's about yearning for something. That one has nothing to do with food. Both of them have hungered for many things, though they've never talked to anyone else about this. Now might be a good time. But even the thought of talking about what they wish for is scary. You just never know if the other person might think your wishes are foolish. And then what?

"You're talking about food, right?" Sid asks.

"Yes!" says Leeta, too quickly. "Food."

The car moves silently through the late afternoon. The road ahead is wide open with only an occasional car or truck in sight. As they ride, they're eating peanut butter and strawberry jam sandwiches and chips, washing them down with boxes of apple juice.

"Ready for dessert?"

"Yes, I am ready!"

He pulls out a bag of candy from the grocery bag and hands it to Leeta.

"What is this?"

"Only my all-time Halloween favorite. People didn't give it out that often, so I used to save my stash and enjoy it a little at a time. The good thing about sugar, it can probably last for a thousand years and never degrade."

"Yes. Halloween, where children change their appearance, and no matter how different they look, they are accepted."

"Yeah, Halloween's a blast. You can become anything you want for that night."

"Even an ET?"

"Sure! My go-to costume was always some sort of space alien. The more out there you look, the better."

"And no one ostracized you?"

"No way! People thought I looked cool."

"Cool," she says under her breath.

"No Halloween where you're from?"

She shakes her head. "Where I am from there is no way for people who look different to be accepted. Not even for one night."

She's lost in thought, a sadness eating into her like a parasite.

"Hey! You're missing dessert. Take a bite."

"What is this?"

"Chocolate *and* mint. Classic combo."

She takes a bite.

"You like it?"

"Yes!" she says, licking her fingers and reading the wrapper. "I like Peppermint Patties even more than onion rings!"

He laughs. In the space of 60 seconds, Leeta unwraps four more Peppermint Patties, downs them and digs into the bag again, pulling out another fistful.

"How about we save some for later? Okay? Remember? Too much sugar's not good."

She pauses, replaces her last haul into the bag and looks at him, eyes swimming. "You are very kind to care about my health, Sid." She sniffles loudly.

"Are you okay? Having a sugar rush?"

"I do not think sugar is causing this emotional response." She chokes on her words. "More likely my feelings have to do with my coming to terms with the stark contrast between what I have been taught of the cruelty and unreliability of people and your caring spirit." This last comes in a rush of tears.

"I've got tissues in there if you need one." He pops the glove compartment open.

Tissues: *a thin, soft, and pliable paper that is used for blowing noses and other hygienic purposes.*

She yanks a tissue from the box, blows her nose. It quickly becomes soggy and useless.

"Can I have another tissue?"

"Yeah. Sure. Go for it."

She smiles, gratefully. Taking another tissue, she wipes her eyes and blows her nose again. "What do I do with these?" she asks holding up the used tissues.

He empties a paper bag and says, "Just toss them in there."

She does.

"Feeling better?"

She sniffles, like she might erupt again.

"Woah! I'm sorry. If it makes you sad when I ask how you're feeling, I'll stop asking."

"No, pleaseandthankyou. It is a kindness that shows you care about my well-being. Even though I am crying, I am enjoying this unusual opportunity to freely express my emotions."

He nods and offers a small smile. She smiles back through tears.

They drive on in silence for a while. But there is no tension. No awkward feeling. No expectation for either of them to do anything other than roll along, sharing this space. But something is definitely percolating below the calm surface. Something Leeta has never felt before, and something Sid may have felt once or twice, but not like this. Never like this. Whatever the feeling, it's still too faint for either of them to name with any certainty. Not yet.

"Please tell me the story of your graphic novel."

"Yeah? You're sure you want to hear it? Okay. So, this alien woman comes to Earth in search of salt for . . . well, I haven't figured that part out yet. Anyway, she falls in love with a human male. They keep their relationship on the down low, but his family finds out and tries to convince the man to dump her. But he won't. So, the two of them decide to leave Earth together. And just as they're about to board her ship, a crazy alien hunter guy who believes in all kinds of whacko conspiracy theories about hostile aliens starts shooting at them. Fortunately, the lovers are uninjured and the ship is undamaged, so they're able to get away. Unfortunately, when they arrive at her planet, they are also unwelcome. Turns out humans aren't the only racists. No surprises there. Anyway, the rest of the story follows the two lovers as they explore the galaxy looking for a home they can share together."

Leeta's eyes slide to Sid's profile for the briefest moment and then down at her left hand resting in her lap. Her thumb appears more out of place than ever. She quickly folds her thumb across her palm, and curls her other fingers over it tightly.

Racist: *a person who is prejudiced against or antagonistic toward people on the basis of their membership in a particular racial or ethnic group.*

Her eyes tear up. She presses her back against the seat.

Sid understands her. But how? How can a human who has never been to Fure possibly know what it's like for her to live among the Reals? To feel the coldness behind their pleasant greetings. To receive no welcome anywhere?

"So, what do you think of the story?" He looks at the road, trying to sound like he doesn't care one way or the other.

She looks out the window at the headlights of the cars moving through the darkness, looking for a place to stop and rest for the night. She says nothing. The silence expands and thickens.

"Hey. It's okay," Sid says. "I know it's not great. But it might have potential . . . or not." He shuts up, waiting. He looks at her sideways, trying to read the back of her. "You really hate it, huh?"

She turns to him. "No, Sid! I do not really hate your story. It is very good. I was just thinking it might be even more interesting if the two lovers do *not* leave Earth together. Instead, what if the alien hunter's attack on the ship forces a difficult choice on the female? She knows she is the target. She does not want to leave her lover, and he doesn't want her to go. But she knows the only way to keep him safe is for her to leave without him. So, they quickly part, with no time to say goodbye. And she goes back to where she came from."

Something in Leeta's voice and the ease with which she's throwing out this new narrative makes Sid wonder if her story ideas are so much more than that. An eerie chill zips up the back of his neck, triggering an even eerier thought that Leeta Simtar herself is much more than she appears to be. Wasn't there something weird in the way that Angela looked at him when she said that Leeta had *just arrived*? And there was definitely something weird in the way Angela said it that made it clear he shouldn't ask the obvious question: *Where is Leeta from?* He presses the gas pedal. The car lurches forward faster than the speed limit but not as fast as his thoughts. Of course he can't tell Leeta what he's thinking. Not yet.

He takes a breath, hesitates, then swallows. "How does the story end?" he asks haltingly.

Leeta has been wondering the same thing. Her eyes well up. "I do not know how it ends," she says, mostly to herself.

"Okay, so you don't know the ending yet. But every story has one. You just have to—"

"—How much longer until we arrive at Winterbrook?"

Sid pretends he doesn't notice she's abruptly changed the subject. "Another hour," he says, hoping these runaway thoughts and unsettling feelings will give him a break.

They don't.

It's a little past sundown but not yet dark when the car turns right off the main road, following a wide private drive lined with long, rough stone walls. When Sid stops in front of the massive wrought iron gates at Winterbrook, Leeta gasps at the intricate design at the top. It's an exact replica of the Daht's ring.

"What's wrong?"

"Nothing."

Sid looks at her, but she's fiddling with her backpack. "You sure?"

She nods, still not looking at him. He lowers his window and pushes the call button on the security camera mounted on the post sunk into the wall.

"How can I help you?" A sharp voice barks from the speaker.

Leeta leans across Sid and talks into the speaker. "Hello. My name is Leeta Simtar, and I'd like to enter Winterbrook to speak to Richard Rutherford and Ruth Rainier Rutherford and any other Rutherfords who are inside at this time."

"Leeta Simtar? Hold on. Sorry. Your name is not on the authorized list of visitors for this week. Do you have a confirmation number for an appointment?"

"No. I do not have a confirmation number for an appointment because I do not have an appointment. But I assure you I am here on an important mission so if you would open the gates, pleaseandthankyou, I will—"

The voice cuts her off. "I'm sorry. You will not be admitted. Please turn your car around and proceed back to the main road."

"But I must speak to the Rutherfords!"

"If you do not turn your car around immediately and leave the property, I will call the police."

"But—"

"Leeta, let's go."

As Sid turns the car around Leeta lowers her window, leans out and shouts at the speaker, "*Kiroota!*" a classic Furean insult that roughly translates as "Your brain secretes *frig* excrement."

CHAPTER 17

UNDER THE STARS

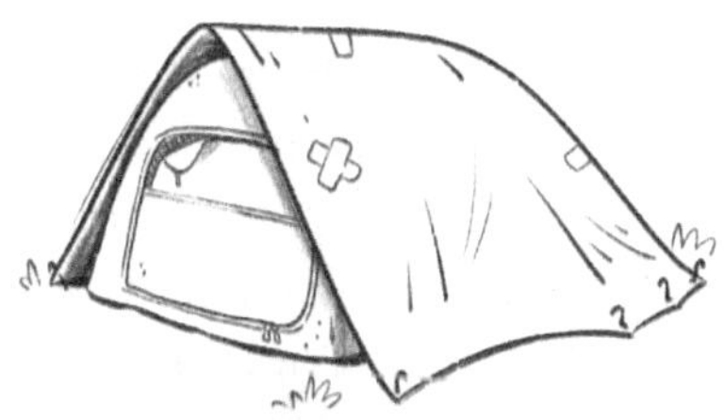

Do not touch rocks. If you inadvertently make contact, immediately apologize to the Ancient Ones and apply a poultice of fwaydrun to the affected areas."

—FUREAN FIELD SEARCH AND RESCUE GUIDE

THEY RIDE IN SILENCE as the amber clouds fade to gray. Leeta's eyes are fixed ahead, like headlights, searching for a path in the dark.

"It sucks they wouldn't let us in," Sid says. "Guess it's back to Cedarville. But not tonight. I need some sleep. There's a campground in four and a half miles. How about if we camp there for the night?"

"Yes. That is logical. We can stop for the night, so you can rest your body and brain, but I am not going back to Cedarville in the morning. Tomorrow morning, I will be going inside Winterbrook to talk with Richard and Ruth Rutherford."

His eyes cloud with worry. Hers flash, daring him to try to convince her it's a bad idea. He already knows her well enough not to try. His shoulders drop.

"Okay. I'll drive you back to Winterbrook in the morning."

"Thanks," she says, unwrapping a Peppermint Patty, offering it to him, and taking one for herself. They ride into the darkening evening, comfortably sharing the space and the chocolate. For now, this is more than enough.

Sid offers Leeta his water bottle. She drinks from it and hands it back. He takes it and washes down the chocolate.

"I hope you don't mind my asking, and I'm not trying to get you to change your mind or anything, but I'm just really curious. Why is talking to the Rutherfords so important to you?"

Leeta feels the same spark she felt on the ship when she and Zertee were talking after the Daht's transmission. A warmth ignited by the comfort of knowing that someone is curious about her. Not because she's odd, but simply because they care. Her eyes soften, and she looks at Sid for a long moment. "I would like to tell you the why of everything, but I think it would be better if you were not driving at that time."

His stomach flips around the chocolate he ate. He's glad he didn't eat more.

It's dusk when Sid pulls into the campground's empty parking lot. They sit in the car in silence. Leeta watches Venus showing her face in the west.

"It's getting cold," he says, rubbing his palms together. "So, what do you want to tell me?"

Leeta opens her mouth and closes it again. Saying the words will not be as simple as she imagined. This could be foolishly dangerous. She knows Zertee would think so. Maybe the risk is too great and she should keep her secret to herself. Maybe Sid is more like his father than he realizes.

She decides not to tell him.

She sees him studying her in the same way Wezen did. His eyes filled with encouragement. Also, a hint of fear. She thinks about the past ten hours and how many ways Sid has already shown himself to be a caring, rational, even-tempered human, without a hint of violence. She thinks about how the story for his graphic novel reflects only positive attitudes about extraterrestrials. Leeta easily imagines his excitement when she discloses her secret. He will be supportive and helpful. She will need a friend on this mission and he will be that friend. Not telling him the truth is illogical.

She decides to tell him.

"I am..." Her mouth twists left. Her throat tightens around the rest of her words and won't let go. She balls up a fist and pounds the dashboard. She raises it to pound again and stops mid-air. Sid shoots her a worried look. With effort, she relaxes her fingers, cups her hand over her heart, and speaks again. "I am experiencing very many nerves."

"Hey. It's okay. Take your time. Don't be nervous."

"I would like not to be, but I have not told this to anyone like you, and I have been educated with certain attitudes that make this very difficult." She rubs her thumb back and forth over her right knee as if she wanted to rub right through her jeans. Sid wishes he could reassure her.

"Also, there is a high probability what I'm about to tell will disturb or even frighten you. I do not wish to cause you any of these emotions. Also, this information might make you think less of me. I am hopeful that will not be the case because I like you. I am also encouraged to give you this personal information because you appear to be a very open-minded person."

"Thanks. I try to be." His stomach flips again and he adds, "Whenever possible."

The uncertainty in his voice saps her confidence. She cracks opened the car door, inviting in a rush of cool air. She inhales, momentarily calming herself, while scanning the wooded area behind the restrooms on the other side of the lot.

"Hey, Leeta," he says, his voice warm around her name. "It'll be alright. Whatever it is, you can tell me. I'm your friend."

She wants to tell him, but what if he turns against her? She'd be so alone in this very large and strange planet. She searches his face. She sees only kindness. Her need to tell him outweighs her fear, but not by much.

"Before I say this, Sid, I need you to tell me once again that you are not like your father. I need you to prove it."

Sid combs his fingers through his hair as if trying to organize his thoughts. When it comes to his father, that's impossible. So much of who the man is offends and embarrasses Sid. But if he has any hope of getting this girl to like him, he's got to answer her question.

"Prove it? I don't know if I can. I just know that every square inch of my father's brain is filled with crazy dark theories about fake science and the government and the news. Plus, his mind is jam-packed with sick ideas about other people. And the whole thing is boarded up so tight no light or air can get inside. You want to know how I'm different? I don't live my life like that."

"But you live with him."

"Only temporarily. I was living in Cedarville until my landlord sold the place in March. I'm just staying with my dad for a few months 'til I find a new place. Probably in the fall. In the meantime, I help him out by paying rent and chipping in on groceries. But that doesn't mean . . . I mean, two people can share the same space but not any of the same ideas." He pauses and looks at her. "That's it. That's all I've got. Don't know if that proves anything."

He continues looking at her across the short dark distance of the front seat. If she trusts him, great. If not, there's nothing he can do about it at this moment.

Her mouth twists to the left. She looks away. Turns back to face him. Inhales deeply and lets it out in a rush. "I am an extraterrestrial," she says, never taking her eyes from his eyes. "I am from the planet Fure, which is forty light-years away from Earth." Her voice is a barely audible whisper. "I am an interspecies hybrid. My mother is Furean. My father is human. I came here to find him."

Leeta holds her breath, trying to read the expression on Sid's face. He squints at her, like he's looking through dense fog. His mouth hangs open. She doesn't know what to make of it. With each passing second of silence, she feels more judged and more regretful of telling him her secret.

Finally, he says, "I don't know what to say."

She recoils as if she'd been slapped hard across the face. "Why do you not know what to say? Are the words so difficult to find because you are so repelled by me or are you frightened that I will attack you or implant your brain with a controlling device?"

Now it's his turn to be shocked. He shakes his head vehemently. "No!"

He reaches for her hand. She bats him away.

"Perhaps you do not know what to say because, Sid, deep down, you are more like your father than you think. Maybe, just like him, you are convinced that I am an alien invader who wants to enslave humanity."

"What? No! When I said I didn't know what to say I just meant—"

Leeta cuts him off, shoves her door open and climbs out of the car. "Zertee thinks I am not Furean enough. And you don't think I am human enough! When will I ever be *enough* of something? I know when. *Now.* Because right now I am stupid enough to have trusted you!"

Leeta slams the door. She runs to the restroom, pushes her way in, and quickly peeks under the stalls. Empty.

"AYA, call Zertee."

"Not a good idea, Leeta. She'll just say you were wrong about humans and she was right."

"Stop talking and call her!"

"Fine! You don't need to shout."

Zertee appears. "Hi Leeta, I was just going to call you."

"Have you located my pod yet? I may want to leave sooner than planned."

"Why? What happened?"

"Not sure. Have you found the pod?"

"Not yet, but I have a theory. The humans who took it have likely covered the entire surface with some kind of impenetrable metal in order to block our tracking technology."

"Hmmm. Maybe they're not as incompetent as we assumed."

"Indeed. Are you still traveling with the human male?"

"Yes. But probably not for much longer. I just told Sid that I'm an extraterrestrial."

Zertee gasps. "You revealed yourself? Did Sid attack you?"

"No, but I attacked him."

"I do not understand. You hurt the human?"
"Yes. I believe I did."

Sid's head throbs as he tries to figure out what's actually going on here. Leeta said she's from another planet. Obviously, she was speaking figurately. He can relate. He often feels like a stranger in a strange land who can't make sense of anyone around him. Like when his father goes on one of his thinly veiled racist UFO rants and Sid has to scream at him to shut up. Or when his boss sends back Sid's drawings for a sixth round of revisions even though the woman doesn't know shit about art.

But maybe Leeta meant what she said literally. From the look on her face, it's clear *she* believes it. She was scared to tell him, but she did it anyway because she trusted him. And what had he done? Had he reassured her that it didn't matter? That they were friends and that wouldn't change? No, he'd just stared at her like an imbecile. He doesn't blame her for running out of the car. He feels ashamed of himself. She called him open-minded. Is he really? And more to the point, is she crazy or is she a real ET? Is that even possible? He's always thought so. Ever since he was . . . well, since forever. He reads about ETs. Writes about them. Dreams them. Draws endless pictures of them. Not the buggy-eyed Yoda types bringing the wisdom of the ages, or his father's evil intergalactic invaders. Sid's ETs are intellectually curious beings, fun to be with and, well, kind of attractive. Like Leeta. Though he never imagined one who was over six feet tall. But hey, you can't have everything.

Sid entertains the possibility that Leeta is telling the truth. He sensed something unusual about her from the first moment. And he *would* have even if Angela hadn't stopped to tell him anything about her. All he had to do is be with her to know. There was her unusual way of talking. Her over-the-top emotions. The way she took away the pain and swelling from the yellow jacket sting. Her responses to everyday things like the cereal aisle in the supermarket. Even the potted plants! In many ways, her mannerisms are exactly what he'd expect from someone visiting Earth for the first time. And what about the way she added to his story? The ideas flowing out of her so easily, like she wasn't just making it up. Like she was telling her own story.

The grinding headache stops. A soft clear light fills his head.

It *is* her story.

How could he have missed that?

It's also Sid's father's story.

Leeta leaves the restroom, without even a glance at the car, and picks her way down a narrow trail that ends at a stream. She squats by the shore, takes her dirty inflight jumpsuit and jacket out of her backpack, and repeatedly dunks them in the water. Using the blue *subyl*, she quickly blots the wet clothing. Instantly, jacket and jumpsuit are dry. She folds everything compactly and returns all of it to her backpack. She cups her hands and drinks from the cool stream. Dipping her hands in again, she washes her face. The wind blows cold across her wet skin. She watches a couple of water skimmers glide across the glassy surface, so enthralled, she doesn't hear Sid's footfalls behind her.

He clears his throat, and reaches for the back of his neck to scratch a spot that doesn't itch, just to give himself time to think of something to say to her. She stands and turns to him, uncertain what comes next.

He offers a small, hopeful smile. "I'm sorry that I came off as such a jerk. I didn't know what the hell I was saying."

Hell: *noun. A place regarded in various religious traditions as a spiritual realm of evil and suffering.*

exclamation. An expression used to show annoyance with one self or with others.

She nods. "And I am also sorry that I overreacted."

"We both did. It's just that no one's ever—"

"Ever what?"

"Come out to me as an ET."

"I am not surprised to hear that, Sid. I should have realized that and understood your confusion. I presented you with a large amount of new—"

"—new information. Yeah, it's a lot to take in."

"Yes!" says Leeta. "And with all that new data to process it is understandable that—"

"—my small human brain went into overload." Sid laughs at himself.

"The size of the human brain is comparable to the size of a Furean brain," Leeta says.

"Good to know." He looks at the ground and absently pushes a stone with the toe of his shoe. "The thing is, I just really want you to know that I am *not* like my father. Not even close."

Desperate to prove himself a good guy, the blood rushes to his head. What evidence can he offer her? He looks up at her with pleading eyes. They are both locked in a story that other people wrote. She puts a hand on his shoulder and feels him trembling under his jacket.

"I would never do what he did. God! He tried to kill your parents. He tried to kill *you!*"

Her eyes widen. "You figured that out?"

"Yeah. The story you told about the ET and her human lover wasn't just a story. I get it now. I really do. Leeta, I understand why it's hard for you to trust me. I wouldn't trust me either if I were you. Knowing that I'm his son, why are you even here with me?"

She sits on the shore again and pats the ground beside her. He sits. "I am here with you, because you are not like him.

Shared DNA does not always result in shared behavior. I know this because I am nothing like my mother."

Moments pass. The only sound is the stream. The only sight is moonlight sparkling on the water like dancing stars.

"What are you thinking about?" he whispers.

No one has ever asked her this question. It feels like a very special invitation. Before answering, she skims her hand across the water, making small waves. The water is cold. She takes her hand out and licks her fingers. "I am thinking about how the water gives life to everything that lives below the surface and above. Humans are very fortunate to have so much water on your planet."

"Yeah. Earth's surface is—"

"—71% water. I studied that before I came. But seeing and hearing the water, touching it and tasting it is so much different from reading about it."

He nods.

"What are you thinking about, Sid?"

He leans back on his elbows and crosses his ankles. "I'm thinking that being here with you gives me the chance to see the world through your eyes. It's like I'm seeing all of this for the first time."

She picks up a smooth stone beside her and rubs the surface of it with her thumb. "This flat, smooth surface is made by the movement of water, isn't it?"

He sits up. "Yeah. Hey, watch this!" He grabs a stone, stands, and skips it across the water, watching it bounce twice before sinking and scattering a school of tiny fish.

She watches in amazement. "How did you do that?"

"Get up and I'll show you."

She jumps to her feet.

"First, you've gotta find a good rock . . . like this one." He chooses a flat, round stone about two inches across. "Then you hold it in one hand like this, and spin it while you throw it hard. You've gotta make sure, though, that you're throwing parallel to the surface of the water. Okay? Ready to count the bounces?"

He lets the stone go and it bounces four times across the stream before losing momentum and dropping below the surface with a gentle plunk.

Leeta's eyes widen with delight. "That is incredible!"

He laughs, happy to show off with his old pitching arm. "It's all in the wrist." He selects just the right stone for her. "Here. Your turn."

She twists her long body as she saw him do. Then she leans back on one leg while raising the other and drawing her arm back all before releasing the stone in one sweeping motion. It skips across the water as she counts. "One, two, three, four, five, six, seven, eight! I got eight!" She smiles broadly.

"Nice going!"

"Your turn, Sid."

"I can't beat that."

"This is not a competition. We are friends."

"Yeah," he smiles. "We are."

A beautiful green-headed duck swoops over the water and lands in a deeper, slower-moving part of the stream. A moment later a brown duck comes in for a landing not far from her partner. Leeta and Sid hold on to their stones and watch the ducks take turns sticking their heads under the surface of the water and coming up for air.

"Mallards," they say at the same time.

"How'd you know that?" he asks. "Don't tell me there are ducks on Fure."

She laughs. "Not a chance." Then tapping the back of her head, she adds. "I downloaded our Earth database before I arrived. It is very good at identifying plant and animal species."

"Huh." His non-verbal response embarrasses him and makes him feel like a Neanderthal. His brain crawls with questions. How is it possible to download a planet's entire database into your brain? How is it possible to travel forty light-years in a few days? How could Leeta arrive on a new planet, get around as well as she does, and communicate with humans—a species she's never met—all without freaking out? He couldn't do it. Leeta is amazing. The fact that she's still here with him. Also, amazing. Every single thought and feeling that's come to him since the moment he met her this morning is completely and profoundly amazing. He thinks he loves her.

Of course, he can't say that out loud or he'd sound worse than a Neanderthal. Maybe "*Huh*" can work as a placeholder until he finds the right words. Finally, he thinks of a question which doesn't sound completely idiotic.

"Leeta, why did you share your secret with me? I'm honored and all, but why me?"

He holds his breath, watching the ducks swim so close together there's no space between them. She must know what he's really asking. Will she reassure him she feels the same way he feels? Will she tell him that she shared her secret because she loves him?

"I told you because I need your help." she says, with absolutely no emotion.

"Oh," he says, trying not to sound crushed. "Yeah, sure. A ride back to Winterbrook in the morning. You got it."

She shakes her head. "I need more than a ride from you, Sid. Can I count on you?"

"For what? You can't just expect me to say yes without knowing what I'm agreeing to. What else are you going to need?" He feels mean, saying this. But hey, if she doesn't like him that way, he's got to protect himself."

"It is logical to want full information before you make an agreement, but at this time, I do not know what more I will require. I only know that you are the one person on this planet within 200 miles that I can rely on."

They face each other, both weighing the significance of the moment and the possible consequences of the deal they are about to make.

Sid knows even if she doesn't love him, he's going to do whatever he can to help her.

His phone buzzes. He glances at it and shuts it off.

"My dad," he says flatly.

Her APED buzzes. She pulls it from her pocket only long enough to shut it off.

"My Zertee," she says with a shrug.

As they stow their devices, they smile at each other know-ingly.

The ducks have flown away. He chooses a stone for her. She chooses one for him. Together they continue skipping stones, cheering each other on, until it's too dark to count the bounces.

CHAPTER 18
THE UNCOVERED CLUE

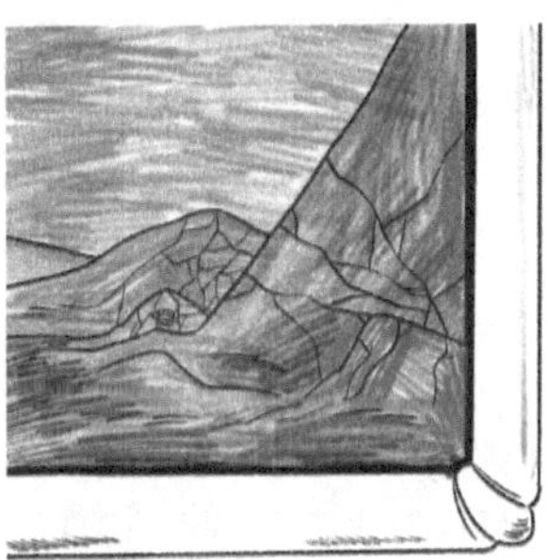

Keep your boots clean and your laces properly knotted at all times.
—Furean Field Search and Rescue Guide

G ENTLE BUT PERSISTENT RAIN falling on the tent wakes Sid. He looks over at Leeta's sleeping bag. Empty. The tent flap is open. He crawls forward and peers out into the cold, wet campsite. She's sitting on the ground, her head tilted back, mouth open wide as she catches raindrops on her tongue. Without making a sound, Sid grabs his sketchbook and quickly gets to work, attempting to capture the girl in this joyful moment. He doesn't need to rush. Leeta sits in the same position for another five minutes, until the shower passes and the clouds dissipate, revealing a clear blue sky overhead.

After breakfast, they take down the tent. With all the gear strewn about, the campsite looks sad and a bit confused, like it doesn't know if it's coming or going. Sid struggles to stuff his sleeping bag into its narrow storage sack until Leeta shows him how to press out all the air and roll it up super tight. While he stretches the sack's opening, she slides the bag inside. Next, they deconstruct and fold up the tent and tarp. Easy enough. But stuffing them back into the duffle, along with the bendable tent poles and metal stakes, is a bigger challenge.

"Removing the gear from the tote was very much simpler," Leeta observes.

"Yeah. This part is a major pain in the ass, but we can do it. Just push down here and I'll stuff it into the corners."

After they manage to get everything in the bag, Sid yanks the zipper but it won't budge.

"Mechanical fasteners are a major pain in the ass!" Leeta shouts.

Sid laughs. "You got that right. Look, I'll hold the edges together like this and you zip it toward me."

After more grumbling and frustrated howls, they finally manage to close the damn bag. Sid holds up his hand. "Well done, team! High-five!"

Confused, she looks at his raised palm. When her implant explains what he's inviting her to do, her face clears. "Well done, team!" she says, smacking his palm much harder than he expected.

"Ow!"

"Oh, I am so sorry! I was not given any instructions about the appropriate amount of force to use in response to a high-five."

Sid and Leeta sit across from each other at the picnic table under a redwood tree, enjoying another round of peanut butter and jam sandwiches, bananas, and orange juice. No candy or dessert this time.

With breakfast over, Sid retreats to the restroom while Leeta stretches out on the empty table, smiling up at the clear sky peeking through the web of leaves and branches. When

Sid returns, he pauses at the edge of their campsite to watch her. She senses his presence, she sits up.

"Are you ready to drive me back to Winterbrook?" she asks.

"I'm ready when you are. But if you'd like more time to be here on your own, to look at the trees or whatever, I'm happy to take a walk by myself."

"Ha!" she says.

"What's funny?" he asks, worried he's just said something else that makes him sound like a Neanderthal.

"*You*, Sid. You are very funny. Not as in *humorous*, though you are that also. But funny in an *unusual* way. You are so very *different*."

"*I'm* different?" He runs his hand through his hair, wondering if she thinks of him as different bad or different good.

"Yes, you are very much different. You showed respect for my need to be alone. On Fure, I had to sneak away to get time to myself. Sifat, our group leader, would always send Zertee to bring me back, because that is what the group wanted and needed. No one, not even Zertee, who knows me better than anyone else, ever asked what *I* needed. But you just did. I very much like that."

She smiles at him warmly. He blushes so intensely his scalp tingles. "Maybe I asked because I need time alone, too. Otherwise, how could I make up stories or do my crazy little drawings?"

"Your drawings are not crazy," Leeta says, dead serious. "Your lines and colors are *you* saved in the pages of your sketch book and on your phone. Your drawings express your ideas and feelings and imagination in ways that makes me believe what you have drawn is real. Your drawings are art, Sid. I will remember them always. And you as well."

"Yeah. I'll remember you too." He tries to sound casual and wonders if he's fooled her. He's not sure if he wants to fool her or not. As for Leeta, her focus moves inward. There's more she wants to say, but she's not sure how to say it or if this is the right time. Awkward uncertainty fills the space between them.

Sid makes a show of stretching his neck to the right and left. "Well, I guess I'll take a walk. Get out some of the kinks from sleeping on the ground. And you can—"

"—No. Stay with me. Please."

Maybe he hasn't fooled her.

"Okay," he says, smiling to himself and grabbing his sketchbook. "So, tell me, what does Fure look like?"

"I will show you." She hops off the table, takes the wrapped painting out of the trunk, and unwraps it on the table, taking extreme care not to touch the frame or the canvas.

"Fure looks exactly like this," she says, her gesture taking in the entire painting.

Sid studies the painting. There's so much to see. As a sci-fi graphic novelist, he's eating it up. "Wow! Three bucks at Goodwill. Good deal."

"Outside of Fure City, these types of rocks are everywhere. So is the sand. And Fure has this sky with these dimly lit red clouds blocking everything above. The clouds are so thick we never see stars, not even the one star we revolve around. Oh, and on Fure, there are unkind winds. Hot. Dry. Never to be trusted. This painting depicts *exactly* what I see—what I *used* to see—from the front entrance to my secret cave."

"How did a Furean artist get their painting to California?"

"I do not have the answer to your California question, but this painting was not made by a Furean. Fureans do not make art of any kind, Sid. The artist is a human."

"A human traveled to Fure and went to your secret cave to paint?"

"No human has ever been to Fure."

"Then how did the artist make this landscape with such accuracy?"

"I do not have an answer to that question either, Sid. This painting holds many unanswered questions. When I first touched the painting, I saw a human hand in my mind's eye holding a paintbrush to this canvas. I felt much of the artist's loneliness and grief. Too much for me to experience all in one moment."

Caught in the memory, her mouth trembles. She blinks back tears, swallows hard. She hurriedly cups a hand over her heart and exhales. Sid wants to put his arms around her, to hold her close and try to comfort her. But he's worried she'd push him away and maybe run off again. So he stands there, arms at his sides and breathes with her. He wonders if she notices. She notices and her mouth stops trembling. They look at each other, matching breath for breath.

"That must have been intense," he says quietly.

She looks at him and nods. "Intense and inexplicable."

"You know, Leeta, I've read about something that's kinda like a psychic connection between people that can reach across time and distance. It's called psychometry. Some people can touch an object and pull certain kinds of information from its energy field. Like where the object has been and who else has touched it. Is this something Fureans can do?"

"I have never heard of any other Fureans possessing this ability."

"Guess you're one of a kind," he says, leaning over the painting, scrutinizing the bottom edge of the canvas.

"What are you looking for?" she asks, stuffing her hands in her pockets and leaning forward.

"A signature," he says, widening the search area.

"Artists sign their names on paintings?"

"Yeah, it's an old Earth tradition."

After several minutes, Sid's convinced there is no signature anywhere on this cosmic landscape, but he does spot a small complex design of delicate lines that might or might not be naturally formed cracks in one of the boulders in the background. Whatever these lines are, they are completely out of place. He aims his phone at the design, zooms in, takes a photo, and shows it to Leeta.

She gasps. "I know that symbol! It was on the gate at Winterbrook."

"You're right. It was up at the top."

"I've seen the same symbol on something else." She digs the ring out of her backpack, slips it on her index finger and holds her hand out to show Sid.

He takes her hand. It's the first time they've touched. Both feel something beyond the warmth of contact. And both of them pretend they don't.

Sid brings Leeta's hand up to his phone and compares the ring to the photo he just took. "Definitely the same," he says. "Where'd you get the ring?"

"From my mother. She said she got it from a friend, but I know that friend was my father. His name is Liam Rutherford.

"Liam Rutherford? The famous SETI guy who mysteriously disappeared years ago? He's your father? No shit?"

"Yes shit."

"So that's why you want to get into Winterbrook."

"Correct. I am researching my human family. My mother came to Earth to meet my father. She had to leave in a hurry, and sadly, they were parted and never saw each other again."

"And you felt the sadness when you touched the painting."

Her eyes fill but no tears fall. "I felt it much," she says, her voice a long sigh.

"Leeta, you know what this means? You felt all that because your father, Liam Rutherford, is the artist!"

"Liam Rutherford painted this? But how could he paint a landscape that he never saw."

"He saw it through your eyes. He got the images from you. Not only are you and Liam Rutherford genetically linked, you guys are psychically linked."

Still wearing the ring on her index finger, Leeta tentatively reaches out toward the painted symbol on the rock, purposely aligning it with the gold one. She braces herself for the impact. In spite of her fear, she wants to feel whatever comes through from her father. She needs to feel it.

She touches the canvas. A powerful wave of loss surges through her. She pulls her hand away from the painting and turns left and right without knowing why, stumbling over something on the ground that isn't there. She reaches for Sid at the same moment he reaches for her. Taking his hand, she pulls him toward her. He enfolds her in his arms. She rests her head against him. A sense of belonging washes over her. The tidal wave of grief and loss recedes.

The campsite is clear. The gear loaded. Leeta and Sid are in their seats. Car doors locked. Belts are clicked in place. But they're not moving.

"Leeta are you sure you still want to go to Winterbrook, knowing that Liam's not there?"

"Yes! I want to meet Richard and Ruth Rutherford. Even if I can't find my father." She pauses and briefly plays with the ring that's still on her finger. "Grandparents count as family."

The sadness in her voice hurts his heart. He grabs his phone.

"What are you doing?" she asks.

"Searching the internet for Liam Rutherford."

"I already did that at SETI. That's how I learned about Winterbrook. But the most recent information I found about Liam was from 18 years ago."

"There's gotta be something else we can use to find him."

Leeta takes out her APED. "I do not know if there is a way for AYA to access Earth's internet, but I will try. AYA, are you listening to this?"

"Of course I'm listening. What else is there to do? Skip stones?"

Sid's jaw drops as he stares at the APED. "Huh? What? Wow! Your AI has amazing capabilities. And serious attitude."

"Yes. AYA has much serious attitude."

"I can hear you, guys!" AYA says.

Leeta and Sid cover their mouths stifling giggles.

"What's so funny?" AYA demands. "Never mind. I'm currently downloading the entire internet into my memory."

"What did you say?" Leeta's voice rises. "AYA, you've been withholding abilities that could have made this mission easier from the start! Why didn't you tell me you could download the internet?"

"You never asked."

Leeta pounds both fists on the dashboard. "Do you ever experience this level of insubordination from your phone, Sid?"

"Honestly? Never. Might be time for an upgrade."

"Upgrade? What's he talking about?" AYA says, suddenly contrite. "Leeta. Girl friend! From now on, I'll try harder to read your mind. In the meantime, I'm getting exactly what you requested. But it's going to take a while. Earth data speeds are pathetically slow. It's shocking that humans find this technology at all helpful. While I'm downloading, I can search for Liam Rutherford. Ok, search completed. He's got no internet footprint. But my search for the symbol on the ring has come up with multiple matches. I found it in 14th century stonework on the exterior of a church in Coryton Parrish, Devon, England. Also, on the 16th century Rutherford family crest. Which obviously explains why the same symbol was crafted in wrought iron on the main gates at Winterbrook. As for mentions of Liam Rutherford, here's the same article you read in Rick Rodriguez's house and the two you read at the SETI visitor center. Nothing more recent than that. Oh, and I found several similar paintings to the one you purchased at Goodwill, all in the same artistic style and subject matter, all unsigned, and all marked with the same symbol."

"AYA, do you see any websites advertising the sale of these paintings?"

"Nope. But I see multiple group shots shared on social media accounts, where paintings like yours are visible on walls in different settings but always behind a group of similarly intoxicated-looking humans. These account owners live all throughout California. But a concentration of them lives closest to Mount Shasta."

"Shasta?" says Sid. "Hm. I wonder if Liam Rutherford lives up there."

"Sid, let's go to Mount Shasta right now!" Leeta's eyes glow with excitement. "After that, we can go to Winterbrook."

Sid checks GPS. "I dunno if that's a good idea. It's already late afternoon. Shasta is more than two hundred miles away and we can be at Winterbrook in half an hour. Let's go there first."

Leeta thinks for a moment then nods enthusiastically. "Yes. It is more logical to meet Grandmother and Grandfather

Rutherford first. Then we will go and find my father." Her smile illuminates her face.

Sid starts the car. Some kind of small, reddish beetle flies through the open window and lands on his hand for a moment before taking off again. His mom once told him you can wish on ladybugs. He's not sure it *was* a ladybug, but he makes a wish anyway. *I hope Leeta gets the happy family reunion she's expecting.*

CHAPTER 19
BACK TO WINTERBROOK

THEY DRIVE UNDER GATHERING CLOUDS. The gray
highlights the hills, turning them into Leeta's favorite
shade of green. But she's too engrossed in Sid's sketchbook to notice the hills. Sid is too engrossed in sneaking
glances at Leeta. Lucky for both of them, the road is relatively
clear of traffic.

An indie rock song pulses through the car speakers like an
unchecked heartbeat, the singer telling her story to a haunt-
ing melody.

You say you've never passed this way before
So can you tell me why nothing here feels new?
I swear I've never seen you here before
Can't say why I feel the way I do. The way I do. The way I do.

Only five more miles to Winterbrook. Sid can't push away
thoughts of what will happen after he drops her off. He pictures himself alone in the car, all the light and air gone. He
will follow her with his eyes as she walks through the gates

of the mansion. Then he'll turn the car around and make the long sad drive back to Cedarville alone. Back to his life, which will be so much less than what it is now. He wishes he could make this moment *before* they say goodbye last forever. Forever? What kind of delusional thought is that? The worst kind. The kind that haunts you.

"I like this music," she says with a crooked smile.

Her voice brings him back to the present. She's not gone yet. She's still there beside him. His heart beats faster. He bops to the song, turning up the volume and singing along with the radio. "The way I do . . . ooo-oo. The way I do."

She applauds. "You can sing! That is nice." She sighs. "Music is very happy making. Or sad making. But always making feelings. We do not have music on Fure."

"None at all?"

"Only drums and chanting."

"What kind of chanting?"

She starts to chant "One Mind . . ." then stops abruptly. "Never mind. I never liked the chanting. It takes away feelings. That is the Furean way. But this song and these words and this voice bring on so many thoughts and feelings. I could listen to this music for a very long time and not get tired of it."

"Me, too." Sid says, his voice wistful.

He slows down as they drive through the town of Shoben. Much bigger and flashier than Cedarville. Fancier stores and restaurants. Fancier cars parked along State Street. Definitely no Goodwill here.

"Are you hungry?" Sid says with a sly grin, then continues as if narrating his graphic novel. "He foolishly asks the girl who is always hungry."

"No. I am not hungry." Leeta shakes her head, not taking her eyes off Sid's sketch of the radio telescope, which she's now tracing with her index finger.

Leeta is thinking about her model radio telescope. How the image of it first came to her in a dream so strong it woke her up, while the other children in the Central Nursery slept. She saw the concave white dish with its central antenna. The intricate open web of crisscrossing support structures. The design had puzzled and confused her. It was so different from the compact domes of Fure. So different from anything she'd ever seen. But her train of thought had moved on quickly, leaving behind the image and all memory of it. It might never have resurfaced if the same image hadn't continued to pop up in her mind at random times over the years. She didn't know what it was, but now she does. She didn't know why or how this white disc kept appearing in her mind, like a series of repeat messages from light-years away, but now, as she traces the contours of Sid's drawing, watching the ring glide along with her finger, and suddenly it all makes sense.

"Sid! Let's stop the car. I am hungry now."

In a paved courtyard surrounded by boutiques and trendy food stores, Sid sits on the edge of a large fountain eating a bagel and sipping an iced, blended coffee drink out of a tall paper cup. Beside him is his sketchbook, open to the drawing of the radio telescope.

Leeta paces in front of him, waving her own bagel as she talks. "While I was on Fure, I saw things from Earth, very clearly in my mind's eye, and I programmed them and made models."

Sid sits up. "Seriously?"

"Yes. One thing I modeled was a drinking vessel decorated with The Starry Night painting by the human artist Vincent van Gogh. As I told you, Fureans do not make or display art. I also made a pair of black-framed eyeglasses. Mine didn't fold, like Angela's glasses, but that is because I was only seeing still images in my mind. Anyway, eyeglasses do not exist on Fure because we all have excellent visual capabilities. Yet I made them." She points to his sketch of the radio telescope. "I made a model of this as well, which is also inexplicable since we have no radio telescopes on Fure. I saw it in my mind's eye years ago, but the first time I actually saw one was when I flew over SETI on my descent to Earth."

Sid nods slowly, taking it all in. "That's . . . amazing. So, what happened to those models you made?"

She frowns. "My treasures were confiscated."

"All of them?"

She brightens suddenly. "No! You have just reminded me. I hid one and brought it with me."

Lost in thought, she sits beside him, eats her bagel and helps herself to a sip of his drink. Smiling broadly, she says, "Mmm. I very much like this cold, creamy, frothing, nutty drink."

"Starbucks will be happy to know they've made a new customer. Give it back, okay?" He reaches for the cup, and she playfully holds it out of his reach.

"I will give it back if you promise to share the rest with me?"

He laughs. "Deal."

She hands the drink back. He takes a long drink and hands it to her again. "Any ideas how these mental images of Earth objects came to you?"

"I have been thinking about what you said . . . that my father could paint the landscape because he saw it through my eyes. I now believe that I was able to model The Starry Night mug and the others, because I saw them through *his* eyes. Somehow, when *he* saw those objects, the images were sent directly from his brain to mine."

Sid jumps to his feet. "Images sent from his brain to yours across light-years. Like signals from space! Leeta, do you think your father was trying to reach you intentionally?"

She hands him the drink. He finishes the rest while she takes another bite of her bagel and talks through a mouthful. "Not intentionally. Liam Rutherford does not know about me. He was simply living his life and somehow, I received his messages."

"Okay. So, since you guys are psychically linked, how about you *intentionally* send him a message?"

She looks at him like his idea is crazy but also logical. He tosses his napkin and his cup into the green waste bin. She wipes her mouth with her napkin and does the same.

Walking back to the car, they pass a shop window filled with toys and trendy clothing for babies and toddlers. The prices are outrageous. They stop in front of another shop window, this one filled with gifts for privileged pets. A few times their hands accidentally brush against each other. They both pretend it was nothing. It wasn't nothing.

Sid wants to ask Leeta a question, but she beats him to it.

"What kind of message do you think I should send to Liam?" she asks.

"Maybe something simple like, 'Hello, Liam Rutherford, where are you?' Which reminds me, we really need to get back on the road."

Her mouth drops open. "I was just going to say the same thing, Sid."

"Yeah? Well, maybe you and I are psychically linked," he says, more than a little pleased to speak the words *you and I* out loud.

She laughs with delight. "I was just going to say that too!"

"Oh yeah?" He smiles mysteriously. "Then tell me what I'm thinking right now."

She looks straight at him and tilts her head. "You are thinking—"

His stomach flips. This was not a great idea. He blushes, wondering if can he block her from reading his thoughts. If he can't and she actually reads his mind, she's definitely going to know what he thinks of her. If reading emotions is part of this too, he's in big trouble.

He spots the Cosmos on Wheels parked behind a white van. "Oh, look!" he says, relief flooding through him. "There's the car. Better get going if we want to get to Winterbrook before dark."

As they drive, the daylight dims and the wind picks up.

"AYA, can you send a message from my brain to the brain of Liam Rutherford?"

"You are referring to telepathy, a *supposed* ability to communicate without using words or other physical signs or signals. There is no credible scientific evidence that telepathy exists. Really, Leeta, I took you to be infinitely more grounded in science and logic than that. Hm. I wonder . . . could Earth be making you . . . How do they say it here? Woo-woo."

"I am not woo-woo, AYA! Am I woo-woo, Sid?"

"Nah. Not even a little bit. But *I* might be."

"I knew it!" says AYA "That proves a theory of mine. Woo-woo appears to be contagious."

"Woah!" says Sid, "Did AYA hear what I just said?"

"AYA, Sid wants to know—"

"Yes, I heard him. I can also see him and talk to him. But I'm warning you, Sid, don't get any ideas."

"Uh, what kind of ideas, AYA?"

"Like suddenly thinking you've got your own personal AYA with technological capabilities far superior to anything you've ever imagined, even in your graphic novel. If you assume you can get me to do stuff for you, that's not happening. I only work for Leeta. Are we clear, Sid?"

"Yeah. Absolutely."

"Good, because I may never directly talk to you again. Leeta, tell Sid to pay attention to the road. There is a human female, mid-twenties, ahead of you. She is walking erratically due to acute pain in her feet and her attempts to control a large piece of unwieldy luggage. She is currently engaged in a verbal conversation with someone called Mom while concurrently texting with two other individuals named Simone and Tess. Leeta Simtar, I strongly advise you to advise Sid to reduce his driving speed to avoid a collision."

"Slow down, Sid," says Leeta.

He slows to a crawl alongside the girl with the suitcase who is so engrossed in her phone she barely notices. Leeta lowers the window. "Do you want to ride with us?"

The girl throws a cold eye at Leeta and hurriedly says, "I'll talk to you later, Mom." She slips her phone into her shoulder bag, stops, and faces the car, which also stops. She looks past Leeta over to Sid, then back to Leeta again. "Why would I want to ride with you two?"

"Because your feet hurt." Leeta sounds matter-of-fact.

The girl covers her surprise with a sneer. "Whatever. Why do you care?"

"Based on my own extensive experience with hurting feet, I know that *I* would be happier riding in the back seat of this vehicle than continuing to walk in pain. Therefore, I made the logical assumption that you would feel the same way."

"Wrong."

Leeta watches the girl walk slowly away from the car, limping, as she drags her suitcase. Leeta sighs and moves her cupped hand over her heart.

AYA interrupts the silence. "Leeta, I don't understand why you want that human to join you in Sid's vehicle, but since that's your goal, tell her there's a 94% chance of rain beginning in four minutes. The downpour will only last for 15 minutes, but it will be forceful."

"Thanks, AYA." Leeta calls out the car window. "Excuse me!"

The girl stops and glares back to Leeta, "Now what?"

"I want you to know that it will be raining in a few minutes."

The girl looks at the ceiling of dense clouds as if daring them to rain on her. Leeta hops out of the car and opens the back door.

The girl looks her up and down. "God, how tall are you?"

"I am certain that God cannot answer your question, but I can. My height has six feet and six inches. Give or take."

Sid snorts. Noticing the girl eyeing the bulging grocery bags on the back seat, he says, "There's good stuff back there if you're hungry."

"I'm not hungry."

"No?" says Leeta. "Yet I clearly detect borborygmus coming from your direction. Hm. If you are not hungry, then I advise you to seek a medical examination to rule out lactose intolerance, irritable bowel syndrome, or gastrointestinal bleeding."

"What are you talking about?"

The first rain drops hit the girl's head followed by hundreds more falling faster and harder.

"Fine. You can give me a ride," she says like she's doing them a huge favor.

As she struggles with her suitcase Leeta grabs the handle to help. The girl angrily swats her hand away. Shocked, Leeta backs off. "Is this the typical attitude you display toward people who are trying to be of service?"

The girl glares at her.

Leeta nods. "I will credit that response as a yes."

Once the suitcase is wedged into the back seat and both girls are buckled up in the car, Sid takes off, windshield wipers swishing at top speed.

"Just drop me off at Winterbrook," the girl commands.

"That is where we are going!" Leeta says.

Sid clears his throat, and speaking over the sound of the pelting rain on the roof, he adds, "I'm Sid. What's your name?"

The girl is already rummaging through a grocery bag. "Is candy all you've got?"

"There's fruit in one of the bags," he says.

The girl digs deep into another bag and pulls out an orange. "How am I supposed to eat this?"

Leeta turns around in her seat. "This is not an attempt to be of service, but I would suggest you use your very long fingernails for peeling the orange."

"And risk breaking one? I don't think so."

Sid passes a folded Swiss army knife over his shoulder. "Here. Be careful not to cut yourself."

The girl takes the knife. "Thanks, *Dad*," she says in a voice guilty of multiple counts of aggravated sarcasm.

Leeta shoots Sid a look and mouths the word. "*Dad?*"

He mouths back, "She's kidding."

Unable to open the knife and unwilling to ask for help, the girl drops the knife and the orange, and rips into a bag of chips with her teeth.

"I am Leeta Simtar," Leeta says, offering her hand. "What is your name?"

"Lucy," says Lucy, ignoring her hand and stuffing her mouth with chips.

"Lucy, for your information, those chips contain 200 mg of salt per serving and can trigger irritable bowel syndrome. May I recommend the chocolate minty things instead? Unless you prefer Milky Ways . . . which are not made from cows."

"I don't eat any chocolate that's not fairtrade."

Fairtrade: a global movement aiming to create more equitable trade relationships that ensure farmers and workers receive fair prices for their work and are treated ethically.

Leeta nods her approval. "Fairtrade is a very much helpful action that benefits lots of people."

Lucy looks at her, surprised but pleased. "So why are you guys going to Winterbrook?" she asks, all her vocal edges suddenly smoothed away.

Leeta's mouth twists left, a tell that Sid recognizes. Before she has a chance to answer, he says, "We're journalists."

"Hm-m," Lucy leans back in her seat. "Ah. So, you're researching the abysmal history of Rainier Rutherford Pharmaceuticals. Right? Then you'll write an exposé describing their corrupt ways of lobbying members of Congress to pass new laws in their favor while routinely violating existing laws against animal testing, water pollution, and price gouging. Which, if your publisher agrees to risk printing it, will probably get you sued?"

Leeta, utterly confused, looks at Sid.

"Nothing like that," he says. "Actually, our research—"

"—Hey, don't get me wrong, Sid. It's Sid, right? R&R totally deserves to be outed for all the shit they've gotten away with. So good on you, but here's the thing. They never talk to journalists. How'd you get an appointment for an interview?"

"We do not have an appointment," says Leeta.

Lucy leans forward. "You seriously think you can just show up? No effin' way. They don't let just anybody inside Winterbrook."

Leeta turns her head to face her. "Then how will you get inside?" she asks.

"Obviously, I'm not just anybody." The cutting edge is back in her voice, sharp as ever. "They're expecting me."

"So, you know Ruth and Richard Rutherford?" Sid asks.

"I know Richard." She retreats into silence, watching raindrops slide across the window.

"What about Ruth?" Leeta asks.

Lucy abruptly turns to Leeta as if she's been pulled hard in that direction. "The Queen of Whatever?"

Leeta laughs softly. "Since there is no such title or official position, am I correct in assuming that mocking Ruth is your way of hiding some deep insecurity she elicits in you? I think you have important information about her. I would like to ask you some questions."

Lucy crumples the empty chip bag into a tight wad. "I don't want to talk about Ruth," she mutters, jutting out her chin.

Leeta reaches into the candy bag at her feet and pulls out a red Tootsie Pop. "Would you be willing to talk about Ruth if I offered you this? The flavor is a simulation of cherries, and there is no actual chocolate of any kind in it."

"No thanks. So why do you guys really want to get into Winterbrook? No way are you journalists."

"Leeta's doing research," says Sid.

"What kind of research?"

Leeta juts out her chin, mimicking Lucy's voice and earlier gesture. "I do not want to talk about my research."

"Like I give two shits."

"Clearly you *do* give two shits, Lucy. Maybe even three or four shits. Otherwise, you would not have asked me about my research. To ask for information then emphatically declare that you do not want to hear that information makes you sound like a nutcase."

Leeta abruptly turns to face the front of the vehicle. Lucy glares at the back of Leeta's head and asks Sid, "What's wrong with her?"

"What do you mean?" He tries to sound casual.

"Don't give me that. What planet is she from?"

Without moving his head or his lips, Sid tells Leeta out of the side of his mouth, "Do *not* answer that."

Without moving her head or lips, Leeta does the same. "After your reaction when I told *you*? No effin' way will I make that mistake again."

"I can hear you guys!" says Lucy.

Leeta turns around in her seat, scrambling onto her knees. "Lucy, it is obvious that you are distressed. Maybe your feet still hurt or you are uncomfortably wet from the rain. More probably you are worrying about your upcoming encounter with Ruth. I can help." She reaches over the back of her seat with both hands cupped.

Lucy jerks away. "What are you doing? What is she doing?"

Sid has trouble hiding his amusement. "It's okay. She won't hurt you. She just has a big heart."

"Well, tell her to keep it to herself."

Leeta aims one cupped hand at the air above Lucy's head, like the dish of a radio telescope searching for signs of intelligent life. With her other hand she drums the seatback. "One Mind. One Goal. One Family. One Mind. One Goal. One Family."

"That's it. Stop! Let me out here."

Sid hits the brakes. Lucy opens the door and jumps out of the car into the pouring rain. She yanks at her suitcase, but the wheels jam in the driver's seat track. She keeps pulling, but it's hopelessly stuck.

Leeta reaches over the back seat, assessing the problem. "I can free your suitcase, Lucy, so you will be able to continue walking to Winterbrook. How much farther is it, Sid?"

"Three and a third miles."

"That is approximately 8,000 steps in the rain. I wonder how your feet will feel after that? Or we could drive you right up to the front gate."

"Quit pretending you care about my feet. Why do you guys really want to help me?"

"For the continued pleasure of your company," Sid says.

"Yeah, right."

"Lucy," says Leeta. "Please get back in the car, and I will tell you the truth."

Sid shoots her a warning look and opens his mouth. Leeta holds a hand in front of his face, cutting him off before he starts. Lucy, soaked and shivering, crawls back into the car and shuts the door. Sid puts the car in Drive and starts moving again.

Leeta pulls her *subyl* out of her backpack and hands it to Lucy. "Here. Dry yourself off."

Lucy dries off her face, hair, pants, and top. In less than 30 seconds she's completely dry, and miraculously so is the *subyl*. "This towel's incredible," she says. "Where'd you get it?"

"It is . . ." Leeta hesitates.

"Imported," Sid jumps in. "But not available online."

"That is true," Leeta nods, neatly folding the *subyl* and returning it to her backpack. "It is also true that I am not researching R&R Pharmaceuticals. I am researching the Rutherford family. I am hoping you will introduce me to Richard and Ruth. I believe they can help."

"Ruth doesn't help anyone but herself."

"What about Richard?"

"Richard? He'd gladly help anyone, but you'd have to get past Ruth first."

Leeta lets that sink in. "What about Liam Rutherford? Is he more like Richard or Ruth?"

Lucy looks at her hands, pressing a fingernail deeply into her palm. "Liam was a good guy," she says softly.

Leeta inhales sharply. "*Was?* Is Liam Rutherford dead?" Her brain tightens around the thought like a fist clutching a burning rock—painful to hold yet impossible to release.

Lucy looks up to see Leeta's face is now a disturbing shade of gray. She inhales, biting her bottom lip. "Well, I don't know for sure. But yeah. Probably. Did you know him?"

Leeta shakes her head. Tears drop into her lap. Sid rests a hand on her shoulder, but she doesn't seem to notice.

"It happened a long time ago," says Lucy. "And if you didn't even know him, what's the big deal?"

Leeta shoots her an angry look. "It is humans like you who give humans a bad reputation."

Lucy shrugs. "What did I do?"

They drive the next few miles in silence, until the car stops in front of the gates to Winterbrook.

"Move forward," Lucy tells Sid.

When the back window of the car lines up with the lens of the security camera mounted on the stone wall, Lucy lowers her window and presses the button on the control panel.

"Good morning," says the sharp voice from the speaker. "How may I help you?"

"Hello," Lucy says, with a friendliness she's definitely not exhibited to Sid or Leeta. "I'm Lucy Valare."

"Ah, yes, Ms. Valare. I see you on the list. Welcome to Winterbrook."

The massive gates swing open, an inviting embrace if it weren't for the arsenal of ornamental spears adorning the top. Sid drives through, and the gates shut behind them with a cold clang. They follow the long, tree-lined driveway, finally arriving at the sprawling, three-story home with a stone and stucco façade, multi-leveled tile roof, and a broad flight of stone steps leading up to a wide front entryway.

Lucy opens the car door and pulls the suitcase out after her. She drags it across the driveway and up the stairs, bumping each step as she goes. At the top, she smooths her hair and straightens her clothes, then notices Leeta standing directly behind her.

"What are you doing?"

"I'm going inside to talk to Richard and Ruth."

"I told you, you can't just walk in."

The ornate oak door opens and a wiry older man with an undeniable air of authority nods to Lucy.

"Good afternoon, Ms. Valare. I trust you had a pleasant journey."

"It was fine, Vincent. Or is it Benson?"

"Benson, Miss. Mr. and Mrs. Rutherford are looking forward to your visit, but I was not informed you'd be bringing anyone with you."

"She's not with me. They're my Uber."

"I see." Benson snaps his fingers.

A much larger, squarely built man steps out of the house. Benson takes Lucy's suitcase while the other man takes Leeta's elbow and escorts her down the steps. Leeta shakes him off and climbs into the passenger seat of the Cosmos on Wheels. Lucy follows Benson into the house, but not before pausing at the threshold for a brief moment to turn and watch Leeta close the car door.

"Well, that was fun," says Sid.

"In what universe would you define that as fun?" Leeta snaps.

"Hey! Relax. It's me. Remember? The one with the kind eyes?"

Leeta hangs her head. "I am sorry, Sid. It's just that I do not like that Lucy. Not at all."

Leeta and Sid are parked in the lot of a fast-food place. He polishes off his second burger, washing it down with a chocolate shake. She slumps forward, head in her hands, an untouched take-out meal sits in a paper bag on her lap. Sid offers her a paper tray of onion rings with extra ketchup. Listlessly, she shakes her head.

"You're worried that Lucy is right about Liam," he says kindly.

Abruptly she drops the bag on the floor, opens the door and steps into the noon sunshine. Sid watches the distance between them grow. When Leeta disappears around the corner of the building, he gets out of the car and follows her.

He sits down next to her on a long log at the far edge of the parking lot under a scrawny pine tree.

"Cheer up, Leeta. She doesn't know for sure that Liam's dead."

"But what if it's true? What if I will not find him because he is no longer alive? That would be very disappointing after all this effort."

"Yeah, it would. But maybe you could still get into Winterbrook somehow and talk to Richard and Ruth."

She looks at him, blinking repeatedly. "Yes, they are his parents. They could tell me what kind of person . . . my father *was*."

She chokes on the last words, shaking her head to banish the thought she's not totally willing to accept.

"Where does it hurt?" Sid asks gently.

Leeta points to her throat. He rests a cupped hand over the spot.

"What are you doing, Sid?"

"I don't have a clue. Is it working?"

She smiles and rests her hand over his. "Yes, it is working."

"Hey. How about that? Even if you don't know what you're doing, you can just imagine you do, and sometimes that's good enough."

They sit there for moment, their hands overlapping, feeling the warmth of each other's skin. And something else, as well. Something exciting.

He drops his hand. "Leeta, I've got an idea! How about if you imagine you know how to send Liam a telepathic message to see if his brain is still online? Pretend you can mentally call him. And, just for fun, try it. If you get any kind of signal back, that might tell you he's alive."

She looks at him thoughtfully, then nods. "Okay. I will try."

She closes her eyes and attempts to home in on the brain of someone she's never met. Someone she has little information about. She takes some breaths to steady her heart, which suddenly seems intent on bouncing around in her chest, banging on her ribs, just for fun. Only it's not fun. It makes it harder to concentrate and do this message-sending thing that she doesn't even know how to do.

After a few minutes, Leeta opens her eyes and frowns. "This will not work because I am not capable of doing this."

"It's okay," he says. "I was just trying to help the team."

Then she remembers something.

There is at least one moment during every mission when a team or team member is required to pivot and create a new plan of action.

"Sid, it's time to pivot."

She hurries back to the car and grabs her backpack. "Open the trunk!"

A moment later Leeta clasps the ring in one hand, pressing the other hand firmly on the center of the canvas, making sure her index finger touches the painted symbol. She closes her eyes and focuses on a single thought.

Hello, Liam Rutherford, where are you?

The tingling starts in her fingers, quickly making its way through her hands, up her arms to her shoulders where it turns inward, sidling into the space between her lungs and heart, where it settles as a hot weight.

At the same moment, more than 100 miles away, a paintbrush pauses over a canvas, and a voice, dusty from disuse, speaks into the still air of an empty room, "Eta-Bakara, is that you?"

Leeta gasps, draws back from the painting as if she'd been stung.

Sid closes the space between them and enfolds her in his arms. "What just happened? Are you okay?"

She looks at him and nods, but he's not convinced. Why would he be? Her mouth is trembling. Her eyes are streaming. After a moment, she manages to find her way through a fog of longing and hope to say three words.

"Liam is alive."

CHAPTER 20
A WALL AND A PLAN

There are always multiple options for solving problems. Stay calm and think.
—THE FUREAN FIELD SEARCH AND RESCUE GUIDE

ON THE ROAD AGAIN, Sid checks the map of the entire estate. "Let's try this side street."

They follow the long, rough-cut stone wall around to the back of the property. Leeta studies its surface and height, nodding to herself. "I will climb over the wall, walk into the house, and talk to Richard and Ruth," she says, like that settles everything.

She opens the car door. Sid touches her arm. "Wait a minute. Look. There, there, and there. Security cameras."

"Good observation, Sid. I do not wish to alert anyone of my presence before I have a chance to explain my mission. AYA, can you tap into the security system?"

"Sure thing. Done."

"What are those cameras seeing?"

"A Western squirrel sitting on the limb of an oak tree watching a human male who is facing away from the camera. He is on his hands and knees tending plants. The man is wearing what appear to be gardening gloves. He's holding a small garden trowel. Also nearby are a pair of pruning shears, a 1.5 cubic foot bag of chicken manure, a 50-foot lightweight expandable garden hose with a heavy-duty metal nozzle equipped with seven adjustable water spray patterns. Humans have so many shopping options! Would you like me to search for garden gnomes, bird baths, rain gauges, lawn mowers, or inflatable wading pools?"

"No thank you, AYA. What else can you tell me about the man?"

"Based on his age—more than 85 years—and his demeanor, including the tender way he is handling the young plants, I would say with 92.5% accuracy that the man is harmless. But I don't trust that squirrel."

"Sid, I am climbing over the wall to talk my way past the gardener and gain entrance into the house."

"What about the camera's motion detection capability?"

"Excellent point. AYA, make me invisible to the security systems."

"Done. Sorry, that took so long."

"Cool trick," says Sid, looking up at the stone wall towering above them at a height of ten feet. "Can AYA also beam you onto the other side?"

"Beam me?"

"You know, convert your body into an energy pattern and send it over the wall where you'd be instantly reconverted into solid matter again."

"We do not have that technology. Is that something humans can accomplish?"

"No. Well, yeah, but only on *Star Trek*. You know *Star Trek*? No, of course not. How could you?"

Leeta listens briefly to her implant and then says: "I have watched and enjoyed all 79 episodes of the original *Star Trek* series."

His eyes widen in shock. "You watched *Star Trek* on Fure? Seriously?"

She laughs. "No, Sid. I am just kidding."

He grins appreciatively. "Ten points for you ... no, 20. Okay, ready to go over the wall? I'll give you a boost."

She shakes her head. "That will not be necessary. I am an excellent climber. Are you going to wait here?"

"Of course, I'll wait. I'll be right here, just in case you need help."

"Thank you, but I will not need help. I will be fine. I will see you when I return."

With that, Leeta finds her first handhold in the stones and begins her climb, pausing for a moment to listen to a song floating up from the garden. A slow melody with simple words, sung by a voice charged with longing, wholly different from the pop stuff Sid played in the car.

Sid watches her climb, his heart in his throat. Not that he's worried she'll fall. She's moving effortlessly, so strong and confident, owning that wall. But she's heading into the unknown, and he's just standing there by the side of the road, completely useless. He promised he'd be there if she needed help, but what the hell can he actually do for her once she's on the other side?

CHAPTER 21
INTO THE HEART

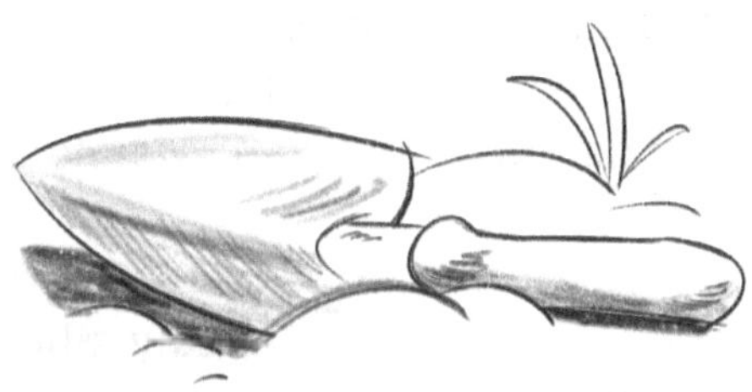

Even a small, fragile plant has a hidden root system.
—THE FUREAN BOTANIST'S HANDBOOK

TEN SECONDS LATER, Leeta drops, unseen, into an expansive garden and crouches behind a towering clump of ornamental grasses growing against the wall. She peers out of her hiding place, stunned at the precisely lined up rows of lush flowers, vegetables, and herbs, and thoroughly enchanted by the gravel paths winding lazily through dozens of blooming rose bushes. The abundance of color, texture, and variety of plants enclosed within these walls is an interstellar botanist's dream. So much more impressive than Safeway's floral department.

The music crescendos, refocusing her to the mission at hand. The gardener sits on his heels beside a collection of gardening tools. His back is straight, hands folded in his lap like he's praying. The music Leeta hears plays through a smart phone that lies on a wrought iron table next to two unoccupied chairs. This man resembles the man in the SETI photo, only much, much older. He is no hired gardener. This must be Richard Rutherford.

Richard raises his face to the sky and sings along with the recording, his voice shaky. Of course, Leeta is not familiar with the song, but the lyrics ... something about bringing someone home, triggers a sudden tightness in her chest and fierce, stinging pressure behind her eyes.

Tears track Richard's lined face like runoff through a dry stream bed.

When the song ends, he stands. He's a large man, slightly stooped, not nearly as tall as Leeta, but still quite tall. He shuts off the phone and sighs, as if wondering, *Why am I torturing myself this way?*

A dog that AYA hadn't reported runs straight through the tall grasses to Leeta, and barks excitedly. She cringes, then sensing only friendly intentions, relaxes and reaches out to pet it. Tail wagging madly, the dog licks her hand and snuggles against her.

The man turns to the clump of grass. "What did you find in there, Jasper?"

Leeta has prepared several opening lines for the moment she first meets her father: *Hi, Dad.* Too shocking. *Hello, Liam.* Too casual. But she's unprepared to greet any other family members.

"Hello?" Richard raises his voice. "Who's there?"

Leeta slips out from behind the grass, but hangs back in the shade. Jasper hangs back with her. She continues stroking his back, hoping he won't leave her standing there alone. She takes a deep breath, every cell within her vibrating at high frequency.

"Hello," she finally manages to say. "Do not be alarmed. I come in peace."

"I'm not in the least alarmed, my dear. Clearly Jasper approves of you and that's good enough for me. But you have me at a disadvantage. My vision is not what it used to be, and I seem to have left my glasses inside. Could you please come closer?"

"Oh, I am sorry."

"Nothing to be sorry about. We all deal with one sort of blindness or another."

Leeta steps into the sunshine.

"That's much better," says Richard. "And you are?"

She walks toward him, her hand extended. "My name is Leeta Simtar. Pleased to meet you."

He presses her hand. His is warm and there's a bumpy scar in the soft spot between thumb and forefinger. "I'm very pleased to meet you, Leeta Simtar. I am Richard Rutherford."

"I know who you are. I came here to talk to you."

"We do have a front door, you know."

"I came to the front door yesterday, but was not permitted entry. That is why I climbed over the wall today."

"Over the wall? Impressive." He gestures to a chair. "Please sit down."

She sits and folds her hands under the table.

"You must really want to speak to me, Leeta. And why is that?"

"I have new information about your son."

"Ah, Marcus. Was he your father, too? If so, I'm very sorry. I'm sure you and your mother deserved much better."

"No, Marcus was not my father. I am Liam Rutherford's daughter."

"Liam's daughter?" Something stirs in his heart. His breath catches in his throat, and he swallows it down. Richard reaches for his phone, then holds off.

"How old are you, Leeta Simtar?" he asks cautiously.

"Seventeen."

"And who is your mother?"

She ignores the question. "Do you know where Liam is now?"

He shakes his head, not taking his eyes off of her. "No one does. He vanished. Eighteen years ago. Maybe with all his SETI work he actually made contact with an extraterrestrial." He chuckles. It's the saddest laugh Leeta has ever heard. Suddenly serious, Richard asks, "When did *you* last see him?"

"I have never met Liam."

"Ah. I see." Something in his face shuts down. He stands, picks up a pair of pruning shears and walks to a nearby azalea bush, and begins snipping off dead blossoms.

Leeta joins him. "I have something I want you to see, Richard." She extracts the ring from her backpack and holds it up.

He puts down the shears and brings the ring close to his eyes, examining every curve and bend, as if walking a familiar landscape he once loved but hasn't traveled through in years. Jasper whimpers at Richard's feet, but this time Richard doesn't notice.

"This ring was mine," he says, his voice thick with emotion. "My father gave it to me when I graduated from college. I offered it to Liam when he graduated, but he wasn't interested. Where did you get this?"

"My mother gave it to me before I came here."

"What's your mother's name?"

"Eta-Bakara."

"Lovely. Delicate. I'll just bet she's like her name."

Leeta shifts uncomfortably. "If you made that bet you would lose all your money. Roses are lovely. Butterflies are delicate. My mother is strong. Hard. Unmovable. Like that stone wall."

"Well, Liam certainly had a strength and tenacity of his own and a certain stubbornness he inherited from his mother, Ruth. That was on full display the last time I saw him. We were here in this garden. He said he'd fallen in love, though he wouldn't tell me anything about the woman. Said if they didn't go far away, they could never be together. I didn't understand. I told him whoever she was, I would love her because *he* loved her and I loved *him*. He said he didn't trust Ruth to feel the same. I should have tried harder to convince him to bring the woman to meet us, but I saw that unmovable look on his face. Nothing would have changed his mind. He said the woman was waiting for him and they needed to leave right away. That's when I gave him the ring, right off my finger. So he'd have something of his family to give to the woman he loved." He hands the ring back to Leeta. "Looks like he took my advice. I'm so glad they were able to make a life together. Where did they go?"

"Eta-Bakara and Liam did not go anywhere together that night. Or ever. My mother returned home. Very far away. To the place where I was raised. The place where I live. Liam stayed here."

"What? Here? Then why hasn't he been in touch with us? We searched for him. Never found a clue. Not the slimmest lead. After all these years, we assumed he was . . . what else could we think?"

"I heard you singing. You still have hope."

"That's because I'm a foolish dreamer. My wife, on the other hand, has a firm grasp on reality. It's a good thing one of us does."

Lost in thought, Richard picks up the shears again and absently snips off one dead blossom and another before accidentally lopping off a fat pink bud only a day or two before its first bloom.

"Damn," he says, gently picking up the bud from the ground and placing it into Leeta's open hand. "Didn't mean to do that. Hadn't even opened yet."

Leeta's fingertip caresses the bud, as if somehow, *tulahm* could keep it alive. Of course, she knows that's as unlikely as this man believing what she's told him.

"Sometimes I cut off something I didn't mean to," she says. "But often the plant forgives me and grows back even stronger."

Richard glances at her and nods. The kindness she sees in his eyes warms her heart, but the suspicion hurts her.

"I like you, Leeta," he says, and she can tell that he means it. "You're a sweet girl. But you're not the first 16- or 17-year-old who has reached out to us with news of Liam. Though I will admit you are the first to climb over the wall with what appears to be the same ring I gave my son. But I've had my hopes raised and dashed too many times. And while you seem very sincere, I cannot allow myself to be swept away by a story told by just anyone."

She carefully places the bud into his hand, letting her fingers linger. "I am not just anyone, Richard. Look at me."

Richard looks. Their eyes hold. He raises his hands in front of her face. "May I?"

She nods.

He traces the shape of her head with his fingertips, then moves to her ears, cheekbones, her nose, her lips, her chin. He shakes his head in wonder as his hand drops to his side.

Jasper barks once. Richard and Leeta reach down at the same moment and scratch the dog's back.

Leeta senses Richard studying her but she won't look at him. She's worrying that she's just made a fatal error by showing him the ring, telling him about her mother, letting him touch her face. All of it was illogical. Now that he knows her secret, what will he do? What will Zertee say? It does not matter. She will never find out because Leeta will never have the chance to tell her. She is trapped inside a walled garden with a very rich and powerful man who has servants to turn people away at his front gate. How could she expect him to believe she is Liam's daughter when others have lied to him and he has so little hope left? This could end up worse than if Gunner and the alien hunter had finished her off the first night.

Leeta glances at the wall, judging the distance. She thinks about Sid, her friend, waiting to comfort her on the other side.

Richard stands up and holds his arms out wide. "Leeta, come give your grandpa a hug."

Leeta looks at him. The suspicion in his eyes is gone. There is only welcoming. He smiles. Her heart stops. Her worrying thoughts stop. She rushes into his embrace. A sense of belonging she has never felt before floods her heart. They stand together in the warmth of the midday sun, delighting in the new treasure they've found in each other.

A chime rings in the house and floats through the garden.

Richard chuckles. "I'm being summoned to lunch. Come in and meet your grandmother."

Leeta inhales sharply. "No. Not ready. Not yet."

"What are you afraid of?"

"The same thing Liam was afraid of. That Ruth will not accept me."

"I understand. All right then. Come back this afternoon for tea. At 3:30. That will give me time to think of something. You could use the time to think of something as well."

"What sort of something?"

"Some made-up story about why you are here at Winterbrook. Something ordinary that Ruth will believe. We will get to the extraordinary truth, of course. And when we do, I'll be right by your side, helping you explain. But she doesn't like surprises. So, I suggest we start with something boring when you first meet her. Oh, and come to the front door. You will be welcomed. Okay?"

"Okay. I will come to tea and bring a boring, made-up story. May I also bring my friend Sid?"

"Of course."

She squeezes his hand and runs to the wall. She quickly climbs to the top and stops, turning briefly to wave. "I will see you at 3:30 . . . Grandpa."

CHAPTER 22

CURIOSITY AND CONNECTION

The more we know, the more we understand.
—DAHT MAYEEL

WHEN LEETA DROPS DOWN on the other side of the wall, Sid is relieved to see her again. "How did it go?"

Grinning, she hugs him so tightly it throws his feet and his heart off balance.

"That good, huh?"

"Yes, Sid! So very, very good. I met the gardener. But he is not the gardener. He is Richard Rutherford! My grandfather."

"Yeah? What did you say?"

"I told him Liam is my dad. And I showed him the ring. He recognized it immediately. It used to belong to *his* father, my great-grandfather. Sid, he was so happy to meet me he cried. And he hugged me in a way I have never been hugged before. The way I imagine a *frig* would hug its own baby, if a *frig* had arms."

"Wow! That's amazing, and he wasn't freaked out when you told him you're an ET?"

"No." She walks quickly to the car. "Not freaked out at all."

He hurries to catch up. "You didn't tell him."

She looks at him. "Not yet. But I will tell him soon. And it will not matter to him."

"You don't think so?"

"I know it will not."

Leeta and Sid walk through a tree-lined park, each carrying a bag of take-out food. Actually, Sid is the only one walking. Head down, eyes on the path, he's still processing Leeta's hug, trying to remember every second of it and imagining what it meant to Leeta and where the two of them might take this thing that's happening between them. He watches her skipping ahead, like a very tall, giddy child, and reminds himself that she is leaving in less than two days. If he were smart, he wouldn't read too much into a friendly little hug, and he definitely wouldn't let his imagination run wild. But Sid's imagination has always gone wherever it pleases.

Leeta circles back to him, blocking his path mischievously.

"I cannot wait for you to meet my grandpa! Only two and one half hours left until tea time. Sid, you will like him. He is so very kind and nice! Having been raised by a father like Richard makes me feel great certainty that my own father is also very kind and nice."

Sid's mouth twitches. "Hope you're right."

"Why do you use that disbelieving tone of voice? Do you not know the old Earth saying, 'Like father, like son'?"

He scoffs. "Yeah, I know the saying. But it doesn't always work that way. I'm nothing like my father."

"Oh," she frowns. "That is true. You are not. I should not make generalizations. Nothing about parents and their children is universally true beyond the single scientific fact that they share DNA. I am sorry, Sid. Are we good?"

"Yeah. Of course, we're good."

They reach a grassy spot under a large elm. They sit together in the shade and unpack a couple of sandwiches, two bags of carrot chips, and two boxes of mango juice.

"Sorry that place didn't have onion rings."

"That is not a problem. I am sure this food is good."

She takes a big bite of her sandwich, and her eyes practically glow with pleasure.

"You like it?"

"Mmm-hmm. I very much like avocado, tomato, and lettuce. Creamy, tart, and juicy. Crisp and watery. And this bread is soft, seedy, and crusty all at once. I am glad you told me tea is not an actual meal and suggested we eat lunch before going back to Winterbrook. Otherwise, everyone there would be subjected to my loud and constant borborygmus!"

"Ooh, yeah. The Borborygmus Patrol would boot us right out the mansion."

"You are kidding."

"Yep." He takes a bite of his sandwich and sips his juice. "Ten points for you."

"Sid, are we really keeping score?"

"Ha! You really thought so? That's ten points for me!"

Leeta pops a carrot chip in her mouth and takes a long drink of mango juice. "Humans must have the best-tasting food in the galaxy."

"I wouldn't know. I've never been out of California."

"Would you like to be out of California?"

"Yeah! I'd love to travel to far-off places. And live an adventure story. Like you." He thoughtfully munches a carrot chip. "But travel is expensive."

"I hope someday you will have all the money you need for your own great adventure story. Oh, this reminds me. My grandpa said I need to bring an ordinary, made-up story to explain to Ruth why I came to Winterbrook. Can you think of something I could tell her?"

He takes another chip, then offers the bag to her. "Well, we already told Lucy we're journalists, so let's stick with that. I mean, Lucy's probably gonna be there, so no sense making up something else or she'll rat us out." He thinks for a moment. "I know! You said the garden was amazing, so how about you say you're writing a magazine article about estate gardens, and you've come to Winterbrook to interview Richard. What do you think?"

"I think this is a very good made-up story. Thank you for helping me lie. Lying appears to be an essential human skill."

He laughs softly. "That's the truth."

After the food is gone, Sid takes out his sketch book and begins drawing Leeta. She stretches out on her back, her head against her backpack and smiles as she follows the slow drift of clouds. He shifts his eyes back and forth between her and her portrait.

"Did you ever find the object you snuck out of the cave?" he asks. "You said it was in your backpack."

"I have not yet looked for it, but I will do that now." She sits up and searches through the compartments of her backpack. "I am certain it is in here somewhere."

Deep within a side pocket, Leeta finds a small object. "Here," she says, holding it in her palm. "I am glad I was able to save this one. It has always been my favorite."

Sid turns the multi-sided object over in his hand. "It looks like a kid made it." He examines the writing on each side. His eyes grow round. "Woah! Look at this!"

"What?"

Leeta snatches the object from him, quickly rotating it between her fingers, reading each side again and again. Her mouth hangs. Her head explodes. She didn't know any English when she made this model, but now she does.

"What a shocker, huh?" Sid says.

"No shit," Leeta murmurs. "She wasn't kidding when she said she wasn't just anybody."

CHAPTER 23
BEYOND THE FRONT DOOR

"I was guided by emotions. UnFurean emotions which I cannot explain."
—High Genetics Council Final Disciplinary Hearing

LEETA CARRIES HER POTTED HYDRANGEA up the steps to the massive front door of Winterbrook and rings the bell. Elaborate chimes echo from within. Sid looks everywhere at once.

"Woah! I've only seen houses this big on TV. You sure they'll let us in this time?"

"Do not worry, Sid. My grandpa said we would be welcomed." She holds out the plant for him. "Here. Touch my hydrangea. It will make you feel better."

Sid gently pinches the edge of a broad leaf and holds on.

"Better?" she asks.

"Not really."

Benson opens the door. Sid quickly drops his hand to his side.

"Hello. Again," Benson says drily.

Jasper noses his way past Benson's legs and barks excitedly at Leeta's feet. She crouches to pet the pup who can't seem to get enough of the hands-on attention.

The rapid-fire clicking of high heels approaches from inside. A compactly built, white-haired woman wearing a pair of perfectly pleated black wool slacks appears on the threshold. Her white silk blouse straining across her chest is topped by a pink cashmere cardigan and multiple strands of pearls.

Leeta stands to her full height and offers a cautious nod. The woman glances up at her with disdain.

"Benson! What's going on here?"

"I apologize for the commotion, Madam, but according to Dietrich at the front gate, this young woman is scheduled for an appointment with Mr. Rutherford."

"What kind of appointment?"

"She will be interviewing Mr. Rutherford for an article on estate gardens."

The woman turns her head to Leeta. "What is your name?" she asks coldly.

Leeta sticks out her hand. "I am Leeta Simtar. And you must be The Queen of... Ruth Rutherford. I am pleased to meet you."

Ruth ignores Leeta's hand. "What is the name of your publication?"

"The Official Publication for Estate Gardens."

Ruth holds out her palm and taps it sharply. "Credentials."

Leeta freezes, listening to her implant.

Credentials: *a qualification, achievement, personal quality, or aspect of a person's background, used to indicate their suitability for a task. Press credentials can be something as simple as a* **business card or photo ID** *from a reporter's employer.*

Leeta leans toward Sid and whispers, "Do you have any credentials to show her?"

Sid nervously shakes his head.

"Good day." Ruth shuts the door in their faces.

Stunned, Leeta and Sid stand on the threshold, looking at each other. A moment later the door opens. Richard fills the frame, smiling.

"I am terribly sorry about the misunderstanding," he says, extending a warm hand to Leeta. "I meant to answer the door before Benson. Let's begin again. Good morning. I'm Richard Rutherford, and you must be Leeta Simtar. Thank you for being so prompt for our appointment, especially after your long journey."

Leeta shakes Richard's hand warmly. "Yes, it was a very, very long journey. This is Sid Rodriguez."

Richard and Sid shake hands. "Nice to meet you. Come in." Then turning to Leeta he adds, "Just make yourself at home."

"Richard, they have no credentials," Ruth says.

He laughs. "No matter. Neither do I!"

Ruth looks at her husband as if he's suddenly not playing with a full deck.

Leeta and Sid step into the grand entryway, its walls lined with paintings. Sid has entered another world, his eyes devouring the art. Is that an actual Monet? And that one? A Chagall?

But Leeta is all business.

"Thank you for agreeing to this interview on such short notice, Mr. Rutherford. I just received the assignment yesterday, and I am so excited to learn about all the plants in your garden for the garden interview. We both are. Sid is the official garden photographer."

"Excellent! I'm always happy to talk about my garden. Sometimes too much so, isn't that true, my dear?"

Ruth smiles thinly, "Hm."

"Well," says Richard. "Why are we just standing around? Let's get this interview started, shall we, Leeta?"

"Shall we, Sid?" Leeta says over her shoulder.

Sid drags himself away from the art and hurries to catch up.

Richard notices Leeta's potted plant. "What a beautiful hydrangea."

Leeta beams. "Her name is Sheila. She is my support plant."

Richard laughs heartily. "Support plant! Why didn't I ever think of that? And what a brilliant choice. Hydrangeas are famous for their compassion."

Ruth's mouth turns down slightly as she tries to figure out what the hell is going on. Lucy, who has just wandered into the hallway, wonders the same thing.

"Oh, there you are, Lucy," says Richard, putting his arm around her shoulder. "You're just in time. I am about to give our guests a tour of the garden. Come join us."

Sid and Leeta wave at Lucy. She glares at them. "No, thanks."

"Oh, come on," says Richard. "Please? It won't be the same without you."

Lucy rolls her eyes and reluctantly nods.

"Good. And after we've seen the garden, we can all have tea together in the solarium," Richard says, then turning to Ruth adds, "I'm sure that scrumptious lemon blueberry cake you made will be more than plenty for the five of us."

Ruth smiles tightly. "I suppose it will have to be."

Lucy sidles over to Leeta and mutters through clenched teeth. "How'd you get in here?"

Leeta playfully clenches her teeth and mutters back, "I am also not just anyone."

"This way, everyone." Grandpa leads the young people toward the back of the house.

"Wait," Ruth says. The tour group stops. "Sid, would you mind helping me with something in the kitchen?"

"I'm supposed to—"

She waves a bejeweled hand in the air, flicking away the rest of his words. "It won't take long."

Inside the walled garden, Richard faces the girls, a secret joy that he can't contain bubbles behind his eyes.

"Lucy," he says with a grin, "I want to introduce you to your first cousin."

Lucy's face darkens with disbelief and dread while Leeta's auxiliary implant fills her in:

First cousin: *a child of one's aunt or uncle.*

Aunt: *a sister of one's mother or father.*

Uncle: *a brother of one's mother or father.*

"What are you talking about, Grandpa?"

Richard smiles, first at Lucy, then at Leeta, holding his arms open wide. "You are both my beautiful granddaughters," he says, as if these six words explain everything and also possess the power to turn the girls into instant besties.

The air between them bristles with unanswered questions.

Lucy's never had any close relatives her own age, no siblings or cousins of any rank, though she's envied friends who have. But now, her eyes narrow, as she tries to figure out what possible quirk of genetic fate has made this total weirdo her cousin.

"Who is your father, Lucy?" Leeta wants to know.

"Who's *your* father? *Mine* was Marcus Rutherford," Lucy says, daring Leeta to top that.

"My father is Liam Rutherford. Marcus' older brother."

"I know who Liam was!" Lucy spits out the words. "Which proves that you're lying. Liam didn't have kids. This is complete and total bullshit. You are bullshit!"

"Lucy, that's enough," says Richard. Not that she's paying any attention to him. Neither of the girls is.

"I am not bullshit," says Leeta. "I am not any kind of shit. I am your cousin because your uncle, Liam Rutherford, is my father."

"No, he's not!"

Lucy lunges at Leeta, hands like talons. Leeta blocks her with cupped hands that Lucy viciously bats away. Richard steps in, wraps his arms around Lucy's waist, and pulls her back.

"I said that's enough, Lucy. Calm down."

"She's a fake, Grandpa. She's only after your money. Why do you believe her? You don't even know her."

"Yet it feels like I've always known her."

Lucy scoffs. "Give me a break. What makes her Uncle Liam's daughter? Because she says so? You're so gullible it's pathetic. Look, I know how much you must miss Uncle Liam. I miss him too. But believing every teenager who shows up here claiming they're his kid won't bring him back." She turns on Leeta. "Who are you really? And you'd better tell the truth."

"Who am I really?" Leeta hugs her support plant to her chest. "That is a very good question." Her voice wavers. She breathes deeply and looks at Richard who reaches out and pats her shoulder. "The answer is complicated, but I will try to explain it all. To both of you." Leeta takes out her APED. "AYA, display Eta-Bakara's testimony."

"Hold on, Leeta," says AYA. "I don't think that's a good idea. You don't know if you can trust *her*."

Lucy sneers. "What kind of AI is that?"

"The kind that recognizes bitchy, entitled behavior when she sees it," AYA says. "I'm talking to you, Lucy."

Lucy jerks her head back, as if she'd just been sprayed in the face with a garden hose.

Leeta sighs and shakes her head. "I am sorry, Lucy. AYA was very rude. She is only trying to protect me. As you are trying to protect our grandfather. I am going to tell you who I am. To do that, I must reveal a secret that will put me at risk. Grandpa, I did not tell you my whole story. I am feeling much nervousness now because I need to trust you both to guard my secret. I trust *you*, Grandpa, but Lucy, you have not shown yourself to be my friend. Because trust between people must be mutual, I will make the first move. I will trust you with the truth of who I am and why I am here. AYA, display Eta-Bakara's testimony."

From the moment Eta-Bakara's hologram appears, floating above Leeta's APED and begins playing, Lucy and Richard's expressions couldn't be more different. Lucy doesn't bother hiding her skepticism of what she assumes is obviously a deep fake. But Richard, a retired chemist who has kept up with discoveries in his field and the evolving technology that enables them to be implemented and shared, stares at the hologram with a profound sense of awe and respect.

"A hologram on a handheld device. Just like *Star Wars*. How marvelous! And this is Eta-Bakara?"

"Yes, this is my mother, though I was not aware of our biological connection until I watched this archival recording for the first time, two days ago."

Richard leans in for a closer look.

So does Lucy. "Why does she look so weird?"

Leeta inhales sharply and swallows hard. "By 'weird' I assume you mean alien," she says, her voice thin and shaky. "My mother looks like an alien because she is one." She lowers her voice and adds, "And so am I."

The humans stare at Leeta, her face, her hair, her mismatched fingers, as if noticing all the differences for the first time. Leeta looks away, an old, familiar shame screams inside her head. *Don't let them see you. Cover your face.* But her hands remain at her sides. She's done hiding. She came to Earth to find her human family. If she has any hope of being accepted by them, she needs to show herself to them. Otherwise, what was the point of all this?

Leeta stands tall. First, looking down into her grandfather's eyes, and then her cousin's. When she speaks again, her voice is steady and clear.

"You want the truth about me? Here it is. I am 71% human and 29% Furean. Fure is a small planet with only 85% of Earth's gravitational pull. I was born and raised there, which explains why I am taller than any Rutherford men. Now you know the truth. I am an extraterrestrial. I have no control over how you process this information, but I can control how I tell my story. I will let my mother tell you how she and my father met. As she speaks, she makes no mention of Liam Rutherford by name, but you will have no problem figuring out exactly who she is referring to. AYA, advance to that section."

AYA advances the hologram to the portion of the testimony where Eta-Bakara describes how she connected with the SETI scientist, fell in love, came to Earth to meet him, mated with him, was shot at, departed in a hurry, and left her human lover behind. As it plays, Richard and Lucy watch silently, intently reading the English subtitles.

At the end of the recording, Leeta pauses the hologram on Eta-Bakara, her face a portrait of hopelessness.

Leeta wipes the tears from her eyes.

Grandpa weeps openly.

Lucy sneers. "Cool trick," she says.

"It is not a trick, Lucy." Richard is calm but very serious. "This is advanced technology that doesn't exist on Earth. This confirms everything."

"Not to me it doesn't."

"Then maybe this will," says Richard, "Leeta was here earlier today and showed me a ring." He nods to Leeta, who takes off the ring and hands it to Lucy. "I gave this to Liam the last time I saw him, 18 years ago. It was given to me by your great-grandfather Walter Rutherford."

"How do you know it's the same ring, Grandpa?"

"It is inscribed to him," says Leeta.

Lucy examines the inside of the ring. "1960?"

Richard nods. "Yes. That's when I graduated from college."

Lucy hands the ring back to Leeta. "Did you get this from Liam?" she asks.

Leeta slips the ring back on her finger. "No. I have never met Liam. My mother got it from him and she gave it to me."

Lucy looks away, her expression a mix of disbelief and distrust.

"Lucy, I know all this sounds—"

"—crazy?"

"—out of the realm of your experience," says Leeta patiently. "But the simple truth is that Liam fell in love with an extraterrestrial named Eta-Bakara. They connected through SETI. And I am their daughter."

Lucy turns to Richard. "How can you believe this? There's no such thing as extraterrestrials. You're a scientist, Grandpa. Where's the evidence that she's telling the truth?"

"There's a strong family resemblance. Maybe you don't remember what Liam looked like, but Leeta looks just like him."

"I do and she doesn't!"

Richard puts his hand on Lucy's shoulder. "I can't help it if you don't see the resemblance or if you believe that the ring is a fake. For me, both of those stand as evidence. And if I still had any doubt, the hologram dispelled it all."

Lucy turns away. "I'm sorry, Grandpa. But none of that actually proves anything. So, Leeta, or whatever your name is, if that's all you've got—"

"—I have something else." Leeta pulls the small, hand-painted cube out of her pocket and hands it to Lucy.

Lucy stares at the cube, her mouth trembling. "Where'd you get this?"

"I made it," says Leeta.

"No, you didn't! *I* made it. When I was six. That's my writing." She rotates the cube, slowly reading each side, "To. Uncle. Liam. 2012. ♥. Lucy," her voice clogged with pain and the dust of memories. "But this isn't my Valentine cube. Mine was bigger and made of wood. This is some kind of model. How could you possibly know how to make this?"

Leeta glances at her APED. "AYA? Explain telepathy to Lucy."

"Sorry, Leeta. I pass. I don't do pseudo-science. You're on your own."

Leeta closes her eyes and cups a hand over her heart. A moment later, she faces her cousin.

"Starting when I was a child, strange images came to my mind. I didn't know what they were or where they came from, but now I do. What I saw came from Liam's thoughts. He and I are mentally linked. That is how I made your Valentine cube. He must have been looking at it when the image of it came to me."

"It was just a dorky block of wood. Why would he keep it?"

"Because he loves you."

Lucy's face crumbles. "Don't. Please. Just don't."

Sid stands on one side of a sleek, white, marble-topped kitchen island watching Ruth artfully drizzle blueberry sauce on a white porcelain dessert plate with gold edges. Next, she slices a single-layer lemon cake with a silver cake server. With the precision of a brain surgeon, she slowly lifts the wedge and places it at a 45-degree angle to the sauce. She takes five fresh blueberries from a small bowl beside her and artfully places them one by one on top of the cake. Then she finishes the dessert with a topper of sliced candied lemon peel and a couple of perfectly trimmed mint leaves.

She turns the plate to face Sid.

"Do you think you can make four more exactly like that?" Her voice a challenge.

"Yeah. No problem. My mom bakes."

"What's her signature bake?"

Without hesitation, Sid says, "Peach pear strawberry galette with a light dusting of demerara sugar."

Ruth raises an eyebrow. "Hm. She sounds like the real deal. And what about your father? Does he also bake?"

"No. He hunts."

Ruth wipes down the sink counter, pretending to eradicate a bit of stuck, dried food where there is none. "You must get your artistic side from your mother. I noticed your admiring our art collection when you arrived."

"Yeah. It's all pretty fantastic stuff."

"Yes. It's nice to have the resources to buy what you like." She rinses the sponge, lovingly dries her manicured hands, and turns to Sid. "Tell me exactly why you are here? And please dispense with that ridiculous story about being a photographer on assignment. If you are honest with me, Sid, I can make it worth your while."

"I'm here with Leeta because she's my friend."

"And why is Leeta here?"

"To interview Mr. Rutherford."

"Indeed."

She closely watches him plate the next slice of cake. He feels her appraising eyes and looks up, nervous. She nods coolly. He continues his work. She continues monitoring.

"In addition to the Chagall, the Monet, and the Modigliani, you undoubtedly have also noticed that Mr. Rutherford and I are no longer young, Sid. I am wondering if you happen to have read about the untimely death of our son, Marcus?"

"Yes, my condolences."

"Thank you. This may not be the most maternal thing to say, but Marcus completely wasted his life. I was not surprised he died of an overdose. My only surprise was that any one of his many other unhealthy obsessions did not destroy him sooner. Wealth does not protect one from trouble, Sid."

"I wouldn't know."

The supply of blueberries in the bowl is running low.

"We had another son, you know. Liam. Brilliant astrophysicist. I was proud of him. Though I'll admit, I was disappointed when he chose to open that SETI center with his share of the money my father left him. Obsessed with listening to space noise, believing that some day he'd get a message that actually meant something. What kind of career was that? He could have easily stepped into a top role at R&R Pharmaceuticals. Eventually run the empire my father founded. But Liam was only interested in searching for men from Mars. Both my sons wasted their lives on destructive obsessions."

She pulls a large basket of blueberries out of the refrigerator, pours them into the bowl, and slides it toward Sid. He looks at the bowl, but doesn't touch it.

"Now we come to the end of our lives, and we have no heirs. Well, that's not true. Lucy is our biological granddaughter. I'll be honest, I don't care for the mother. Stephanie. We've never met. Why should I have bothered? She and Marcus were never serious. She's an estate liquidator. Rather morbid, wouldn't you say? I'm sure that's why she got herself pregnant. And why she sent Lucy here so soon after Marcus passed. So she could stake her claim on our estate. Vulture! And what is this Leeta Simtar up to? I'm certain she and

Richard communicated before today. It was obvious by the way they greeted each other. What is her game, Sid? Or is she too conniving to tell you?"

"Leeta is not the least bit conniving! She's kind and brave and always committed to her research and to finding the truth."

"Oh, I see. You have a thing for her. How sweet. And pathetic. You two make a ridiculous-looking couple. She must be two feet taller than you!"

Sid plucks an especially fat, juicy blueberry out of the bowl, forcefully squishing it under his thumb into the white marble.

"I'm done with this conversation, Mrs. Rutherford. If you've got questions about Leeta, ask her yourself. Or ask your husband. Now, would you like some help serving this cake?"

Richard sits at the wrought iron table, a sense of peace about him as he pets Jasper, who sleeps in his lap. Lucy sits across from him, nervously tapping her clenched fist on the table top. Leeta stands behind her cousin, resting a cupped hand in the center of Lucy's back. Lucy's breathing steadies and after a few moments, her fist relaxes and she finds her voice.

"Uncle Liam was in Miami for a SETI conference and he came to our apartment to see me and my mom."

"I encouraged him to visit you," Richard says, patting Lucy's hand. "I gave him your address."

She looks over and smiles. "I'm really glad you did. He took me to the planetarium. We had such a great time. The whole day I pretended he was my dad. When he brought me home, I heard him and my mom talking about Grandma. Mom was worried she'd find out about the checks you were sending us and cut us off."

Richard stops petting Jasper. "You knew about the checks?"

Lucy nods. "Uncle Liam promised if they ever stopped, he would take care of me."

Richard sighs and smiles sadly. "I know he would have kept that promise."

Lucy turns to look up at Leeta. Sensing how this awkward position hurts Lucy's neck, Leeta comes around and sits on the grass beside her cousin's chair. As soon as she does, Jasper jumps down from Richard's lap and snuggles between Leeta's hands.

"After that visit, Uncle Liam . . . I mean your dad . . . started writing to me."

Hearing Liam referred to as her *dad* floods Leeta's heart with a new kind of giddy warmth that spills onto her face. Lucy notices and smiles at her.

"He sent me postcards," Lucy continues. "With amazing pictures of different planets and images from the Hubble Space Telescope. Saturn, Mars, Jupiter's Big Red Spot. On the back he wrote about his work at SETI and he always included a science fact. On the Saturn postcard he wrote: *Since it rotates on its axis once in about 10.7 hours, Saturn's day is the second-shortest in the solar system.* I saved all of them."

Lucy opens her hand revealing the Valentine cube. "I made this for him when I was in first grade. Mom and I put it in a box with red tissue paper and mailed it to him. Not long after that we got a call from Grandpa. Mom was crying when she got off the phone. She told me Uncle Liam had disappeared. I asked if he was dead. She said no. But no one knew where he was. Even at six, it made no sense to me that someone could just disappear. I missed him." Lucy traces the letters of Liam's name that she herself painted on the original cube so long ago. "I still miss him."

When Leeta reaches up to the table, Lucy finds her hand. After a quiet moment, Leeta leaps to her feet, more excited than they've ever seen her. "I have something else I want to tell you both. Something I know will make you happy."

Richard and Lucy look at each other, baffled, but mostly eager to hear the next big thing this galaxy girl has to say.

"Since my dad and I have been psychically connected all this time, Sid had the idea that I should try sending Liam a mental message. I didn't believe it would work, but yesterday I tried. I sent a simple hello message. And I heard his reply, in my head. He spoke. *Liam is alive.*"

"Alive?" Richard's voice is raspy.

"Are you sure?" Lucy can't keep hope from creeping into her voice.

"Yes, I am sure, and I am going to find him."

Richard gathers both girls into his arms, his heart pounding with the power of this moment.

"Leeta, sweetheart, I believe in you and in your determination to find Liam."

"Thank you, Grandpa."

"Okay, hold on a second," says Lucy. "I know you mean well, Leeta. But you haven't been here. This has been very hard for my... for *our* grandparents. They've already searched for Liam for years. How much longer can you expect them to wait and hope and get no results?"

"I will leave very soon and I will quickly get results." Leeta says this with so much confidence that a strange but welcome optimism fills Lucy's heart and shuts her mouth

Leeta hands her potted plant to Grandpa. "I do not wish to take Sheila with me. Can you find a place for her in your garden? Maybe over there with the other hydrangeas? I think she'd like to be with her own kind."

Richard looks at this sweet girl, beyond joyful that she climbed over the wall and into his life. "Are you sure you won't need her for support anymore?"

"I am no longer feeling anxious. About anything."

The chime announcing tea time cuts through the garden. Leeta starts. Lucy takes the plant from Richard and hands it back to Leeta. "Maybe you should hold on to Sheila until after you talk to Grandma."

CHAPTER 24
TEA TIME

"Those raised in a violent atmosphere are likely to become violent, anti-social people. Conversely, those raised with kindness and a full appreciation of One Mind, One Goal, One Family are likely to become peaceful, helpful, and friendly. This theory formed the basis of my new hypothesis."
—HIGH GENETICS COUNCIL FINAL DISCIPLINARY HEARING

LEETA SITS BETWEEN LUCY AND SID on the edge of a wicker couch inside Winterbrook's famed solarium. An impressive assortment of tall potted plants fills the glass-paneled room: palms, birds of paradise, and hanging baskets of lush, silver-leafed dichondras. Leeta scrapes her dessert plate of its last bits of cake before popping the fork into her mouth. Sid nibbles around the edges of his slice. On the long coffee table in front of the couch, Lucy's untouched plate shares the space with Sheila the potted hydrangea.

Ruth and Richard sit on chairs on the other side of the table. Ruth sips her tea daintily, her eyes locked on Leeta. Richard carefully folds and refolds his napkin.

"And how did you enjoy your garden tour, Ms. Simtar?" Ruth asks.

Leeta looks up, a blob of blueberry sauce dotting the corner of her mouth. "The garden is out of this world. It is natural art. The way the colors come together to form a living painting is like nothing I have ever seen, even in my dreams. The abundance of thriving green life lifts my heart to a joyful place."

"My! You are very expressive. I suppose that comes with being a writer." Ruth eyes Leeta's empty plate, and says with a smug smile. "And may I assume you enjoyed my cake?"

"Your cake is . . . *was* delicious. Maybe even more delicious than Peppermint Patties." Leeta places her empty plate on the table and, still holding the fork, adds, "Is there any more cake?"

"Well, yes. In the kitchen. It's not plated yet, but if you'd like, I could get you another slice."

Before Leeta can answer, Lucy hands over her plate "Here. Take mine. I'm not hungry."

Leeta smiles and digs into Lucy's piece of cake.

Eyes still fixed on Leeta, Ruth pours a cup of tea and hands it to her.

"Sid told me how committed you are to your research and to finding the truth."

Alarm drains the color from Leeta's face. She shoots a side glance at Sid whose slight mouth twitch instantly reassures her that he hasn't revealed her secret to Ruth. Fortunately, Ruth is busy pouring herself another cup of tea and misses the interaction.

"I admire tenacity," Ruth says, stirring honey into her cup. "My husband would say I've got a tenacious streak myself. Isn't that true, Richard?"

Hearing his name, Richard looks over at his wife. "Excuse me, my dear?"

The confusion in his eyes tells Ruth that his mind has been far away. She dismisses him with a soft grunt and turns her attention back to Leeta. "I must admit, Ms. Simtar, ever since you and Sid showed up, I just cannot shake the feeling that your being here involves more than discovering the best kinds of potting soil. That's my tenacious streak. Can't help it, but I am correct, aren't I?"

Leeta's hands shake and the cake takes a sudden slide through the blueberry sauce. Attempting to avoid disaster, she overcompensates and tilts the plate toward her. The slice slips off the edge and bounces off her chest, leaving a wide splotch of purple on her shirt before landing on her white jeans.

She jumps up and shouts, *"Pertru!"* (*A Furean expression of embarrassment used most often when you've been clumsy in front of strangers you're trying impress.*)

Lucy grabs Leeta's hand and pulls her to her feet. "Come with me."

The girls enter the childhood bedroom of a space nerd. A massive poster of the moon hangs on the wall behind the bed. On another wall, the image of Earth from space. One built-in bookshelf holds a collection of science fiction classics including *The Foundation* series, *The Martian Chronicles*, *Do Androids Dream of Electric Sheep?* On another shelf sits a model of a Saturn 5 rocket made from a kit. A three-inch diameter reflecting telescope sits on a tripod by the window.

Leeta takes it all in, laughing with delight, as if she'd magically walked back in time into the heart and mind of her father. "This was Liam's room!"

"Good guess," says Lucy. "I had my choice of six fancy guest rooms, but I like it in here. I like how they kept all Uncle Liam's stuff just the way he had it when he was a kid."

"This is like my secret cave!" Leeta says.

"Oh, yeah? Wish I had a secret cave."

"What would you put in it?"

Lucy pauses and shrugs. "Dunno. Never thought about that. Maybe not a bunch of stuff. I've always had the money to buy whatever I want and no one ever told me I couldn't.

No, I think if I had a secret cave, it would just be a place to get away from everything. You must know what I'm talking about. I mean you traveled really far to get away."

Leeta nods. "Yes, that is true. But the problem with a secret cave and a long trip is that eventually, you have to go back to the things you wanted to get away from."

Leeta pulls *Stranger in a Strange Land* from the bookshelf, and begins reading intently.

"Let's get you out of those clothes, which, no offense, weren't that great even before you dropped the cake in your lap. They look like you got them from Goodwill."

Leeta looks up from the book. "Good guess! And proud of it!"

Lucy opens the closet and pages through half a dozen pairs of expensive jeans hanging on the rack. "Well, none of these are long enough for you." She pulls out three skirts and three tops. She opens a dresser drawer and takes out four different pairs of shorts, and lays everything on the bed. "Okay. What do you think of these? Take whatever you like."

Leeta chooses a purple skirt, pale blue top, and a pair of green shorts. While she's trying them on, Lucy peers through the eyepiece of the telescope by the window. "Do you think your mother ... uh ... tricked your father into having sex with her so she'd get pregnant?"

"No!" says Leeta. "My parents were emotionally bonded to each other. Their exchange of DNA was by mutual consent. There was no deception involved. I cannot imagine anyone would do such a thing."

"My mother did. That's how I got here."

Leeta looks at her cousin, baffled. "Why did she do that?"

"Because Marcus had all this." She gestures wide, taking in the entirety of Winterbrook. "My mom works really hard, but she's got expensive taste. Probably comes from all the fancy stuff she sees every day at estate sales. She and Marcus met in a club in Miami. He was a playboy, just passing through."

Leeta listens:

Playboy: *a wealthy man who spends his time enjoying himself, especially one who behaves irresponsibly or has many casual sexual relationships.*

"Do you understand what that word means?"

"Yes, I understand. But why would your mother want to have a sexual relationship with someone she didn't care about?"

"Oh, I think she cared about Marcus. They dated for a while and she got pregnant. Her plan. Obviously not his. They split up soon after she told him. When I was born, she contacted him about child support. He denied they'd ever had sex. She went to Ruth and Richard. Ruth insisted on a DNA test, which proved I was his kid. Ruth still refused to pay. But Grandpa sent us big monthly checks so my mom and I were taken care of. Grandpa also sent extra gifts to me and my mom on our birthdays. Christmas. He didn't have to do that, but he really cared. My mom sent him pictures of me along with letters about how I was doing. When I got older, I talked to him on the phone every month or so. My mom made sure of that because she wanted the money to keep on coming. But I was just glad I had a grandpa, especially after Uncle Liam disappeared."

Lucy looks in the mirror hanging over the dresser and runs a brush through her long wavy hair. Leeta bends down to see her reflection. She picks up Lucy's brush and attempts to run it through her own wild hair. The brush gets stuck, and she tugs at it, frowning. Lucy gently unsticks it. "Your hair is super cool. You don't need to change a thing."

Leeta looks at herself. "Thank you, Lucy. That is a good reminder."

"Speaking of reminders, when are you going to tell Grandma the truth?"

"I think it is logical for me to wait and tell her when she is in a good mood."

Lucy shakes her head. "We don't have enough cake to last 'til then."

"As I get to know you better, cousin Lucy, I am better able to detect the presence of sarcasm in human speech. Thank you for this learning opportunity."

Lucy first looks offended, then reconsiders and smiles. "You're welcome?"

"I understand that you are worried I might be procrastinating, which I believe involves some kind of magical thinking in relation to the passage of time. I am aware that I need to tell Grandma the truth very soon because my remaining time on Earth is short."

Lucy's hand flies to her mouth. "Ohmigod! Are you dying?"

"Not to my knowledge. I have only 28 hours left here because tomorrow evening I am supposed to take off in my escape pod and dock with Zertee for our return trip to Fure. At that time, our ship's controls will go on autopilot and it will be brought back to Fure whether I am onboard or not. Of course, that is a problem because, like Liam's current location, the current location of my escape pod is also unknown. I have very much to do. I must find Liam before I meet up with Zertee, and before *that* I must tell Ruth who I really am."

"Good luck. You'll need it."

"Lucy? In case Sheila isn't enough, will you be my support person?"

Lucy is touched. And nods, with a hint of embarrassment. "Okay. I'll try, but just to let you know, Grandma hates me. It's not like my mom was the first woman Marcus got pregnant, but none of the others wanted to *stay* pregnant. They were paid off, so they didn't need long-term Rutherford money for child support. My mom wanted me. And she's a good mom. When Marcus died, she pushed me to come here to *remind* Grandpa and Grandma, marriage or no marriage, I am family, and since they have to change their wills anyway, they should name me as their sole heir. But now you're here."

"Do not worry, Lucy. I have no interest in being anyone's heir. What would I do with Earth money on Fure? I just came to meet my family. And I am very glad I have met you."

Lucy looks down. "Yeah. Me too."

"Do you believe there is any remaining cake to be eaten?" Leeta asks.

"Let's check it out."

"Obviously, my husband is the gardening expert," Ruth says, handing Leeta a cup of tea. "But I'd be happy to answer any other questions you might have about the house, the antiques, the family lineage."

"Why is this house called Winterbrook?" Leeta asks.

"Because Agatha Christie is my favorite author and her home in England is called Winterbrook."

"My grandmother loves mysteries," says Lucy.

"That's very true, Lucy. I didn't know you were aware of that."

"Oh, I know a lot of things about this family that you aren't aware of, Grandma."

"Really? Like what?"

Lucy opens her mouth. Leeta glares at her, daring her to speak. Lucy shuts her mouth. Sid's phone buzzes. He gives it a glance. It's his dad. He's about to send it to voice mail when he notices five other voice mail messages. All from his dad.

"Excuse me," Sid says, stepping out of the room.

In the front hallway, Sid inhales and answers the call.

"Hey, Dad."

"Where you been? I've left like a million messages."

"Yeah. Sorry about that. I'm out of town. Doing research for work."

"Sid, I found something. And it's gonna change everything."

"Yeah, ok. Great. Actually, Dad, I've gotta go."

He turns off the phone, but something in his father's voice makes him wonder if just maybe his father actually found something this time. Nah. Impossible.

Leeta clears her throat. Ruth may not be in a good mood yet, but Lucy is right, she doesn't have the time to wait. She's got to get to the point. "Mrs. Rutherford, please tell me about your son Liam."

Ruth starts, "Excuse me? What relevance would Liam have to an article about gardening?"

Richard stands and puts a comforting hand on Ruth's shoulder. She looks up at him, suddenly alarmed.

"What is it, Richard? Why is she asking about Liam?"

"Ruth," Richard says in as soothing a voice as he can muster in the face of his wife's demand, "Leeta is Liam's daughter."

Ruth scoffs. "Oh please. Don't tell me you're falling for that again? After all the money-grubbing phonies who've shown up here claiming they were Liam's child. So ludicrous, since Liam never even dated. Always working. Always looking to the stars. As if he'd find someone up there. True, the others who showed up in the past two months claiming Marcus was their father had more competition. And this girl obviously thinks she has a better chance of cashing in by claiming to be Liam's daughter. She may be more strategic, but she is no different from the rest."

"She *is* different, Ruth. Leeta, show her the ring."

Leeta reaches into her backpack, pulls out the ring and shows it to Ruth. Recognizing it immediately, she reaches out for it. Examining the ring closely, she slips it on her finger.

"Where did you get this?" her voice cold and accusatory.

"From my mother," says Leeta, unphased.

"Even if that were true, your mother obviously stole it."

"No! My mother did not—"

Ruth cuts her off. "Please leave."

"But I have information you need to—"

"—Get out of my house. Now!"

"Ruth, stop!" says Richard. "Leeta's telling the truth. Liam *gave* the ring to her mother because Liam loved Leeta's mother."

Ruth stands to face her husband, eyes flashing with anger. "Who *is* Leeta's mother? *Where* is she? If she and Liam were so in love and this is really their child, why have we never heard from her or Leeta until now? Could it possibly be because of all the recent press coverage about Marcus' death and the rantings about our failing health and our need to name a new heir?"

"You haven't heard from my mother and me because we live on another planet."

"Another planet? Well, mystery solved. That explains everything."

Leeta looks over at Lucy and whispers, "Good sarcasm."

Lucy nods. "It runs in the family."

"And did your mother meet my son on this other planet?" asks Ruth.

"No. Liam never left Earth. My mother came here to meet him after they made contact through SETI."

"Ah, of course you'd say that. It's the perfect touch to your story. SETI." She spits out the word. "Liam's inheritance from his grandfather was completely wasted on that place. So, he spends his life searching for extraterrestrials. Finally makes contact with one. Falls in love. Makes a baby. Is that what you're saying?"

Leeta nods matter-of-factly. "Yes, that is exactly what I am saying because that is the truth. I understand that you do not believe what I am saying. If I were you, with your brain and your life experience, it would be difficult for me to believe it as well. But it does not matter whether you believe me or not. I came to Winterbrook to meet my grandparents and I am glad I did."

"Ms. Simtar, how fitting that your name sounds as made up as the rest of this absurd story. You are obviously lying or mentally unwell or both, but despite that, you assume this story will pay off for you and your mother. Maybe you're hoping I'm still so distraught over the loss of Liam that I will believe you out of desperation or stupidity. But you are decidedly wrong, Ms. Simtar. I have made my peace with Liam's disappearance. And I am neither desperate nor stupid."

Richard stands behind the couch, his hands firmly on Leeta's shoulders. She reaches up and squeezes his hand.

Ruth scoffs. "Oh, so we're taking sides now, are we? Richard, you appear to have lost whatever was left of your grip on reality. Luckily for this family, I have not lost mine. I will not rewrite my will for a science fiction fantasy. You are not getting a penny from this family, Ms. Simtar."

"I don't want any of your money."

"Is that so? Then why did you come all the way from Planet X?"

"I came from Fure to find my father," she says simply.

"Well, you've made a very long trip for nothing. If Liam is still alive, he doesn't want to be found. He's gone to great lengths not to be."

Leeta stands. Sid stands beside her. She looks at him and says, "We are going now."

Sid nods to the rest of them. "Yep. We're going."

"Goodbye, Grandma Ruth." Leeta offers her hand, but instead of taking it, Ruth slides her hand under her napkin.

"Give her back the ring, Ruth," Richard says, his voice strong and clear. "It belongs to her."

Ruth hesitates, withdraws her hand from the napkin, takes off the ring and drops it into Leeta's palm, never once looking at the girl.

Richard hugs Leeta, and she hugs him back, holding on for a long moment.

"Goodbye, sweet girl."

"Goodbye, Grandpa."

When she breaks away she gestures to the potted hydrangea on the table. "Please take care of Sheila for me."

Richard nods, then turns to Sid. "Take good care of her."

"She doesn't need taking care of," Sid says.

"No. But take care of her anyway."

"Bye, Lucy," Leeta holds out her hand. Lucy goes in for a quick hug then hurries out of the room.

In front of the estate, Sid and Leeta climb into the Cosmos on Wheels. Sid lowers his window, starts the car, and puts it in reverse.

"Wait!" Lucy calls to them.

Sid hits the brakes. Lucy stands at the top of the front steps, holding the handle of her suitcase.

"Is it okay if I come with you guys?"

Leeta and Sid get out of the car.

"Yes," says Leeta with a big smile. "It is okay."

"C'mon," says Sid. "Your ride's about to leave!"

Leeta runs up the steps and grabs the front handle of the suitcase while Lucy holds the one on the side. Together they carry the suitcase down the rest of the steps. Sid comes around the car and opens the trunk and rearranges some stuff, making room. The girls heave the suitcase inside.

The three of them hop in the car and slam their doors at exactly the same time. As they drive through the gate, Lucy looks out the back window.

"Grandpa looked so sad and old. I wonder if we'll see him again."

"We will," says Leeta.

"Is that coming from some psychic sense?"

"No. It is coming from the fact that we know where he lives."

"And what about Uncle Liam? We have no idea where he lives. Do you really think we'll find him?"

Leeta turns around in her seat. "Lucy, look at me." Lucy drags her gaze away from the fading view of Winterbrook. Her eyes are damp, her lips pressed tight.

"I cannot predict the probability of finding Liam. I cannot say for sure that we will succeed. But I can say with 100% certainty that I will try everything to find him."

Lucy nods. "Okay. I believe you. So where do we start looking?"

"Mount Shasta," says Sid.

"Why Mount Shasta?"

"It's a long story. We'll fill you in, but since it's about 200 miles from here, how about we stop at a market first and get some food for the road?"

"Cool!" says Lucy. "I'll make a shopping list." She takes out her phone and starts typing.

"I am hungry for warm food," says Leeta. "How about before we hit the market, we stop for quick food."

"You mean fast food? Sure," says Lucy, "but not McDonald's or Wendy's. You've gotta find the nearest Burger King or Jack in the Box."

"Why one of those?" asks Sid.

"Because Mickey D's and Wendy's don't serve onion rings."

Leeta laughs. "Lucy, you like onion rings?"

"Love 'em," says Lucy, scooting forward. "Especially with ketchup."

"Yes!" says Leeta, high-fiving her cousin.

AYA says, "FYI, Lucy, you can also get onion rings at Sonic."

"Hey, AYA," says Sid. "How come you're talking to Lucy and you never talk to me?"

"Leeta please tell Sid the reason Lucy rates higher on my approval scale is that she's organized. And unlike some people in this vehicle, she's not at all woo-woo."

Lucy playfully pokes Sid. "Ooh. Now we know your secret."

"Yeah," says Sid, with a playful nod. "I'm woo-woo but I also like onion rings."

Leeta rests her hand on Sid's shoulder, simultaneously touching her cousin's head and says, "One Mind. One Goal. One Onion Ring Family!"

The three of them laugh, like it was a ridiculous thing to say. But later, when they look back at that moment, they'll admit they were all feeling very woo-woo.

ACT III

FINDING LIAM

CHAPTER 25
TREACHERY AND TESTS

Always seek the truth within all species. The truth does not lie.

—THE FUREAN PRIME DIRECTIVE

RUTH COLLECTS KNIVES and teaspoons off the coffee table and arranges them on the tea tray in two precise lines. Richard picks up cake plates and stacks them on the tray, then makes the rounds collecting discarded napkins. The two of them gracefully weave and flow around each other like a pair of well-trained dancers. With closer inspection, it is clear how their every movement is coldly designed to avoid contact.

After most of the evidence of the recent tea time disaster is corralled onto the tray, Richard flings a linen napkin on a plate, where it lands in a puddle of blueberry sauce.

"Richard!" Ruth shrieks and picks up the napkin, blue sauce already dripping down the edge. "Look what you've done!"

"What *I've* done? Who cares about a napkin, Ruth? Thanks to you we've lost both girls."

She, looks at him, stunned. "How can you possibly blame me for Lucy leaving?"

"I'll tell you how," he says through gritted teeth. "If you weren't so hostile to Stephanie from the beginning, we could have had a normal relationship with Lucy while she was growing up. We could have had Christmas visits and family vacations."

Ruth scoffs and tosses the napkin back into the sauce. "Seriously? You think you missed your chance to play the beloved grandpa whose sweet-cheeked child sits on your lap asking for one more bedtime story? It's not really like that."

"How would you know what it's like to be a grandparent? Or a parent, for that matter? All you ever cared about was R&R Pharmaceuticals and winning your father's approval, which he never gave because he thought if he ever told you what an amazing job you were doing, you'd stop striving to be better. So sad, Ruth, how you were stuck in that trap. The only person you ever loved didn't love you back, and then, when you had a chance to love your own children, you didn't know how."

She gasps, her hands flying to the comfort of the pearls around her neck. They offer no comfort. Her chest is tight. Her heart beats dangerously fast. "That. Is. Not. True. I loved Liam and he knew it!"

Richard shakes his head and closes his eyes. Maybe he can shut out the sight of this woman he barely recognizes. Maybe he can shut her out so completely she will be gone when he opens his eyes again. He opens his eyes. She's still there. Glaring at him.

"Don't tell me you think it was *my* fault that Liam left," she says, the vein on the bridge of her nose pulses with rage.

He looks at her straight on. "It *was* your fault. If you weren't always so narrow-minded, so goddamn worried about what other people thought, Liam would have brought Eta-Bakara home to meet us."

She scoffs and begins fussing with the lemon wedges, making sure they're all perfectly lined up at the same angle. "You mean the Martian? Seriously, Richard?"

He can no longer trust himself to look at her. He stacks tea cups inside one another, creating a wobbly tower. As he storms toward the kitchen, they start to sway.

She grabs the cups with both hands and hugs them to her chest. "Go play with your plants," she snaps. "I'll finish cleaning up."

He lifts Leeta's support plant from the table, gently cradling it in his arms. "Come on, Sheila," he says so softly Ruth can't hear. "Let's get out of here and find you a nice home in the garden."

He pushes opens the solarium door, breathes in the fresh air, and steps into the light.

Ruth rips a clean doggie poop bag off a roll stored in a pet-centric kitchen drawer. She sticks her hand inside, and using it like a glove, carefully picks up Leeta's fork from her plate.

Moments later, she holds out the bag to Benson, who eyes it with disgust.

"Madam, the disposal of Jasper's deposits is not in my job description."

"Don't be ludicrous, Benson. There is no poop in this bag. Only a fork. Tell Brown to drive it over to the Lab. Dr. Sanders is expecting him."

Fifteen minutes later, Brown walks through the front doors of Rainier Rutherford Pharmaceuticals, poop bag in hand.

Lucy shines her phone light on the Goodwill painting resting on a picnic table alongside the remnants of their dinner including six large orders of onion rings.

"Definitely the same," she says, comparing the ring between her fingers to the symbol in the painting. "But that doesn't prove Liam painted it."

"True," says Sid. "But what are the chances anyone but Liam painted a Furean landscape, from a viewpoint that only

Leeta ever saw? Oh, and that person just happened to add the symbol of the Rutherford family crest?"

AYA speaks, "The probability of this painting being made by anyone other than Liam Rutherford is 0%."

Leeta throws up her hands. "I already knew this. Why are we wasting time? I only have until tomorrow night. I need new data."

"Right," says Sid. "So, how do we use the painting to figure out where Liam is?"

Lucy taps the edge of her phone against her chin. "I've got an idea. You guys said AYA's search couldn't find any websites that sold paintings like this, but she did find several similar paintings in the background of photos that people posted on social media."

"Yes," says Leeta. "And most of the account holders were clustered in the Mount Shasta area. That's why we're heading there. But that is not precise enough information."

"Let's assume Liam is the only one painting all of them," says Lucy. "But he's been hiding for 18 years, so someone else must be selling the paintings for him. We just have to find out who that is."

"How?" asks Sid.

Lucy sweeps her flashlight dramatically over the canvas. "By checking the provenance of this one!" she says. "My mom does that whenever she needs to determine the value of an original painting."

Provenance: *the recorded journey of an artwork from its origin through one or more owners to the present day.*

"Good idea," Leeta says. "But how?"

Lucy's already typing.

"What are you doing?"

"Finding the nearest art gallery with an onsite appraiser."

Dr. Sanders, a serious-looking Black woman in her mid-fifties wearing large eyeglasses and a white lab coat, reads data from her computer into a speaker phone. "Yes, I've triple-checked the sample. The results are consistent. 71% of the subject's DNA is your son's, not 50% as would be expected. But that is only one part of the anomaly. The composition of the remaining 29% is even stranger. I don't quite know how to put this. I actually feel embarrassed telling you this, but the other 29% of the subject's DNA appears to be from a non-human source."

Ruth sits at the kitchen table, listening to Dr. Sander's voice on speaker. "What do you mean non-human? Are you taking about animal DNA?"

"I've cross-referenced the sample. It does not match any animal DNA. Obviously, the only explanation for such an impossible result is that the sample was contaminated. I can assure you, Mrs. Rutherford, it was not contaminated in my lab. Perhaps it occurred in your home or in transport. In the future, I would suggest you not use poop bags as sterile carrying containers. Be that as it may, I destroyed the sample you sent, and you'll need to send another."

"Never mind, Dr. Sanders. I will not be providing another sample. And you destroyed the records as well?"

"Of course."

"Good. We're done here." Ruth shuts off the speaker phone and sits back in her chair.

"Ruth." The voice is strained and gruff.

She turns to see Richard standing in the doorway. He's standing tall, his fists, covered in garden dirt, are clenched at his sides.

She inhales sharply, hand to her throat. "How much did you hear?"

He looks at his wife, eyes cold with resolve. "Enough to know what you did."

Sid drives through a good-sized town. The people walking around have the distinct look of tourists. They're relaxed, smiling, eating ice cream, looking in store windows, carrying colorful gift bags. Sid continues halfway up the main street, slows down and points to a large store on the left. An over-sized mermaid carved in polished wood reclines in the front window. On the glass door, the words

Sudmeyer and Sons

Fine Art Gallery

are painted in a fancy, old-fashioned calligraphy font.

"There it is," Sid says

They walk into a quiet, brightly lit, upscale space. A tall abstract bronze sculpture that might represent a flame or the wings of a bird looms in the center of the room. Leeta circles the sculpture, studying it from all angles. Sid looks at the framed paintings hanging on the walls, most of them quite large. He gets up close to a painting of an upside-down tree floating among purple clouds, its leaves and branches at the bottom of the frame. Growing upward from the base of the inverted trunk is a dense network of intertwining towers complete with windows and tiled roofs. He peers at the price sticker, and his eyes widen.

Lucy carries the Goodwill painting, now wrapped in a grey blanket, to the only other person in the gallery, a man with a neatly trimmed gray mustache and beard, sitting behind a desk, working intently at his computer.

Lucy clears her throat. The man looks up and offers a dramatically weary smile. "Hello."

"Are you the art appraiser?"

"Yes. I am Mark Sudmeyer. But we're closing in—" he glances at his gold Rolex "—three minutes."

Lucy slides a hundred-dollar bill across the desk toward him.

He palms the bill and slips it into his pocket in one quick motion. "Of course, I'm happy to stay a bit later. What can I do for you?"

"What can you tell me about this painting?" She puts the painting on the desk and unwraps it.

Mr. Sudmeyer stands, puts on his glasses, and leans over the canvas.

"Oh! Oh my. One of his earlier works. How marvelous!"

"You've seen this artist's work before?"

"Yes. Three times. This makes four. But even if it had been once, forty years ago, with work this singular, one never forgets. May I ask where you acquired this masterpiece?"

Leeta appears at Lucy's side. "The Goodwill store. In El Lugar."

"Small town in the Bay Area," Sid adds, from Lucy's other side.

The man's mouth drops open. "Goodwill? Seriously? Just like Antiques Road Show! Why doesn't that ever happen to me? I assume you'd like to find out how much it's worth."

"No, that is not relevant," says Leeta. "We just want to know—"

Lucy puts a hand on Leeta's arm, never taking her eyes off Mr. Sudmeyer. "Yes, please tell us how much it's worth."

"Well, the first time I sold one of their paintings was ten years ago. Right before the pandemic. It went for $50,000. Then three years later I sold another, smaller one, for $70,000, if you can believe it. The most recent was just a year ago. That went for $110,000."

"Wow!" says Sid.

"What do you know about the artist?" asks Leeta. "Is he local?"

"I know nothing about the artist. Not their name. Not even their gender. There's nothing online either. I'm sure it's intentional. The mystique certainly helps to sell their work."

"How do you connect with the artist?" asks Lucy.

"Oh, I don't. I deal exclusively with a woman who represents the artist. Though she certainly doesn't look like any artist's rep I've ever worked with. She's one of those New Age people."

Leeta listens:

New Age: *a broad movement characterized by alternative approaches to traditional Western culture, with an interest in spirituality, mysticism, holism, and environmentalism.*

"What is this New Ager's name?" asks Leeta.

"Sabine."

"Her last name?"

"I don't know. She's never disclosed it. Part of the artist's mystique, I guess. I've never met her or talked with her on the phone. All three times I've sold this artist's work, Sabine first sent me a handwritten note from a P.O. Box that included a Polaroid photo of a painting she wanted me to sell. How old school is that? Each time we agreed on terms, and she had the painting delivered by some delivery service. Also, no return address. When I sold a painting, which never took long, I sent her a cashier's check."

"What else do you know about Sabine?" asks Lucy.

"Only that she also makes crystal jewelry. These are hers." He gestures to an open display case at the end of the counter. "It's part of our arrangement for me to sell them here. A side hustle for her They're not really my thing, but they're very well made."

Sensing Leeta's interest he picks up a pink crystal pendant mounted in sliver, a small amethyst in the setting, and hands it to her.

Leeta slides her finger along the length of the cold stone, gently poking the end of the crystal into her fingertip.

"Do you know where Sabine lives?" asks Leeta.

Sudmeyer shakes his head. "No clue."

She hands the pendant back to him.

"All I've got is the P.O. Box in Mount Shasta City," he says, closing the display case and locking it. "I can give you that if you want to write to her. Maybe she'll even write back. Set up a meeting if you're lucky."

Lucy, Sid, and Leeta exchange looks.

"No time for that," says Leeta. "We're in a hurry."

Lucy wraps the painting while Mr. Sudmeyer watches longingly as it disappears under the blanket. "If you're interested in selling that one, I only take a 50% commission."

Sid scoffs. "You take half when the artist did all the work?"

Sudmeyer frowns defensively. "Other galleries take up to 60%."

Lucy tucks the painting under her arm and picks up a business card. "I'll keep that in mind, Mr. Sudmeyer. Thank you for your time."

As soon as they leave the gallery, Lucy hands the painting to Leeta who says, "I'm not selling the painting."

Lucy's already typing on her phone. "I know that," she says. Then she adds, "Got her."

"Who?" says Sid.

"Sabine. Crystal jewelry. Mount Shasta."

"Let's go," says Leeta.

Lucy shakes her head. "No point. They're closed 'til tomorrow at 10. And it's four hours away."

"Let's get back in the car," Sid says. "I can drive a few more hours and then . . ."

He and Leeta grin at each other. "Camp out!" they say together and break into a run.

Lucy stops dead in the middle of the sidewalk. "Wait! Seriously? We're going to sleep outside?"

Sid looks over his shoulder. "Ever hear of camping indoors?"

"But I've never . . ."

Leeta waves her on. "There is always a first time, cousin."

CHAPTER 26
WHOSE SIDE ARE YOU ON?

If someone publicly questions your integrity, question their motives.

—DAHT MAYEEL

LUCY AND SID SIT by a campfire roasting marshmallows then pushing the hot gooey mass on top of chocolate bars and packing the whole melty mess between two graham crackers. Leeta sits on a camp chair, away from the fire, scanning the night sky.

"I've gotta admit it, Sid," Lucy says, pulling a marshmallow off the long stick in her hand and dropping it into her mouth. "Camping is way better than I thought."

"Right?" He stands and delivers a newly assembled s'more to Leeta. "Here's another one for you."

"You can eat that one, Sid. The high sugar content is making my teeth itch." She tilts her head back, scanning the sky. "The stars still fill me up with surprise and delight, even now after these days on Earth. The sky has room for all the stars. And each one can shine."

Sid stands beside her, absently eating the s'more and looking at the sky overhead, taking in the vastness, feeling smaller and more Earth-bound than ever.

Leeta sighs. "When I am back on Fure, what I will miss most is seeing the stars."

Really? He thinks. *That's what you'll miss most?*

He looks at what's left of the oozy mess in his hand. He wants to fling it away but it's stuck to his fingers and he can't let go. He eats the marshmallow goo off his thumb. His stomach turns and yes, his teeth itch.

Sid's phone buzzes. He makes a face and is about to send it to voicemail when he sees the request for FaceTime. Sid's heart tightens. Reluctantly he accepts the call. Rick's face appears on the screen.

"Hey, Dad," he says, his voice cautious.

"Sid, can you see me?"

"Yeah, I can see you."

"How come I can't see you?"

"I've got my camera off. Uh, just got out of the shower. What do you want?"

"I want to show you what I found." He turns the camera on his discovery.

Sid excitedly gestures to Leeta and Lucy to come over and look at the screen. "What is that thing, Dad?"

"A spaceship."

Leeta and Lucy nearly choke. With a finger pressed against his lips, Sid gestures for silence.

"That's cool. Why's it wrapped in aluminum foil?"

"Because it's invisible. If I didn't wrap it, I might forget where it was. Also, the aluminum prevents the aliens from tracking it. Your old man's no dummy." Rick chuckles proudly. "Bet those alien invaders are looking all over the place for this bad boy."

"Yeah, well, congrats. You found an invisible spaceship. This definitely tops that inch-long iron bolt you swore was part of a flying saucer. Well, I've gotta go—"

"Wait! I'm not done. I'm doing a big reveal right here. Started reaching out to everyone in the group."

"Did you tell anyone what you found?"

"'Course not. Need a little time to set the whole thing up. I just told them they need to get their asses over here for something really big."

Sid and Leeta exchange horrified looks.

"When's this going to happen? Are we talking this afternoon? Tomorrow?"

Rick's eyes narrow. Sid can almost hear his father's conspiracy-addled brain hatching a theory that Sid's in cahoots with aliens. But that might be too crazy, even for Rick. Funny how the truth crosses the line for nutcases.

"How come you're suddenly so interested?" Rick asks.

After years of fighting with his dad, Sid knows he can't suddenly sound like he actual believes in alien invaders.

"I'm just thinking your discovery would make a great subplot for my graphic novel."

"You're right! It would. Gonna put me in the book?"

"Sure. So how about if you call me like an hour before everyone gets there? That way I can watch in real time while you set up."

"I don't need to call you."

"But I want to see when you're doing it."

"Oh, you'll see it alright. I'll text you an invite with the time and the link."

"Link to what?"

"To the live stream? I'm gonna stream this to the whole damn planet."

Sid hangs up and looks at Leeta who turns to her APED.

"AYA, call Zertee."

"Who's Zertee?" Lucy whispers to Sid.

"Leeta's bestie," he says.

"Where is she?"

Leeta points to the sky. Lucy looks up, wide-eyed and pops two marshmallows into her mouth. "Wow! How much are your roaming charges?"

Leeta listens to her implant.

Roaming charges: *the additional fees that mobile network providers charge when you use your phone outside of your home network's coverage area.*

Leeta laughs loudly. "That is a very funny joke."

"It's not that funny." Lucy shrugs modestly, though she's obviously pleased.

Zertee appears over Leeta's APED.

"Zertee," says Leeta. "We have the location of the pod."

"Excellent. Give me the coordinates."

"Sid will provide them. AYA, please translate in real time. Zertee, these are my friends, Sid and Lucy."

Lucy stares at Zertee and remains uncharacteristically silent. Sid, on the other hand, smiles and says "Hey, Zertee. Nice to meet you. How's it going? How are things in—"

"—Sid, human male friend of Leeta's, stop wasting time with small talk. What are the coordinates?"

Sid quickly brings up Google Maps on his phone and gives Zertee the coordinates of Rick's barn.

After an instant, Zertee says, "These coordinates are incorrect. I am not picking up anything from that location. Why are you providing inaccurate coordinates? I assume you know that if Leeta has not docked with our ship by tomorrow night, it will go on autopilot, and I will be brought back to Fure leaving Leeta stranded on Earth. Is that the intention of your treachery?"

Sid is about to lash out in his own defense, but Zertee's question has thrown up a roadblock, and he suddenly finds himself struggling with questions of his own. *Is he trying to help Leeta leave Earth or is he setting it up so she'll have to stay?*

Leeta looks at Sid, curious about what's taking him so long to answer the question. In her heart she wants him to battle Zertee and defeat her anti-human bias once and for all. But in her head, Leeta cannot totally dismiss the logic of Zertee's argument.

"Those are the correct coordinates," Sid says, an unmistakable edge to his voice. "The reason you're not picking up a signal is because my father covered the pod with aluminum foil to block—"

"—Wait!" Zertee screeches. "Your father is the human who stole Leeta's escape pod? The same human who tried to kill the Daht and Liam Rutherford 18 years ago? The same human who shot at Leeta just two days ago?"

"Yeah, that's him. But I'm on Leeta's side."

"Are you really?"

"Yes, I really am." He takes Leeta's hand and holds it up in his so Zertee can see. "Leeta and I are friends. We don't need to prove anything to you or anybody else."

Zertee's face goes cold. She's done talking to Sid. Turning to Leeta, she says simply, "Is he your friend?"

"Without a doubt." Leeta squeezes Sid's hand. "Monitor those coordinates closely. We'll be in touch."

CHAPTER 27
THE ROAD TO SHASTA

THE CAR ROLLS UNDER the early morning sun, through the rising mist and along the freeway. The speedometer reads 65 miles per hour, yet to Leeta the scenery is changing so slowly they don't seem to be getting anywhere. She understands for the first time why humans are such an impatient species.

"How much farther to Mount Shasta City?" she asks.

"150 miles," Sid says.

"Give or take?" she asks, flatly.

He laughs, way too loud. "Nope. Exactly 150. Oops. Make that 149."

Leeta doesn't crack a smile. His fades.

The flatlands stretch endlessly in all directions, neatly divided by farms with an occasional house sitting at the end of a field. Leeta has always enjoyed her time alone, but she imagines that living out here, in such isolation, must be like living alone in an empty dome within a deserted Fure City. Not what she's looking for.

Lucy's phone buzzes in the back seat. Leeta turns to see her cousin texting furiously, thumbs tapping away so quickly they blur.

"Sid, how much longer will it take for us to arrive?" Leeta asks, her voice tight with urgency.

"Two and half hours. Exactly."

He looks at her sideways hoping to catch her eye and cheer her with a goofy grin, but she's too busy fiddling with the window controller to notice. Up and down. Up and down. She blows air through her lips. "Can you drive more quickly, Sid? I have approximately 12 hours left."

He bites his lip. "Don't worry. We'll get to Shasta way before that."

Leeta nervously taps the dashboard, flips down the visor, and sees Lucy's reflection as she puts away her phone.

"Who were you texting?"

"My mom. She wanted to know how things were going at Winterbrook. I said we left. Sometimes telling the truth is easier than lying."

"You didn't tell her about Leeta, did you?" Sid asks.

"Only that we're cousins. And that she's cool."

"I am cool?" Leeta asks both of them.

"Definitely," says Sid.

"Hell, yeah," says Lucy. "And I told her we're taking a little road trip. That's all."

The three of them settle into silence. The road tilts upward. The fields turn into rolling hills that turn into rolling forests which eventually turn into certifiable mountains.

"What if Sabine won't help us?" Leeta asks. "We will need to pivot."

Lucy's phone buzzes again. She looks at it briefly, then turns it off.

"Don't worry," she says. "I guarantee she'll help us. My mom's best friend, Celeste, is a total New Ager. She's into peace and love and helping others. That's her thing. They're all like that. And if somehow Sabine needs convincing, well, didn't you see how quickly the hundred-dollar bill got the art gallery guy to change his mind? I've got plenty more of them."

"Maybe Sabine does not care about money," Leeta says.

Lucy throws her head back and hoots. "*Everyone* on this planet cares about money. Right, Sid?"

He nods, distracted. "Huh? Yeah. Pretty much."

Leeta's stomach growls. "Are you hungry?" Sid asks.

"I have a little hunger, but we should not waste time stopping for food." She sticks her arm out the window, holds her fingers together and rides the air stream like a surfer.

"Well, I'm very hungry," he says. "Hey, Lucy, what have we got left back there?"

Lucy looks in the bag beside her. "Marshmallows. Want some marshmallows, Leeta?"

"No, pleaseandthankyou. Could we listen to some music?"

Sid brightens. "Sure. How about this?" A jerky, frenetic pop song pulses out of the car speakers.

"No. No," says Lucy. "Too early for that. How about this instead?" A whiny love song drips from her phone.

Leeta brings her arm back into the car and closes the window. "How about nothing?" she says.

"But you just said—"

"I changed my mind. I am going to sleep."

Lucy's phone buzzes. She picks it up. "Hi, Grandpa. Is everything okay?" She listens for a minute. "Yes. We're all here. In the car. She does? Okay. I'll put you on speaker."

Lucy sits forward holding the phone between Sid and Leeta so they can all hear.

"Lucy? Can you hear me?"

It's Ruth. The three exchange worried looks. This can't be good.

"Yes, Grandma, we can all hear you. What do you want?"

"I . . . I want to apologize for the way I treated you and your mother all these years."

"Really? Well, now I believe in miracles." Lucy's voice drips with sarcasm.

"I'll admit that I have been unwelcoming. And rude. No. More than rude. I have been cruel, and I'm very sorry. I made a mistake, and I will always regret the way I denied your place in our family. Do you forgive me?"

Lucy rolls her eyes and clamps her mouth shut to keep from exploding. She turns to Leeta who understands better than anyone the frustration of having to push aside your true feelings so other people can be more comfortable in their lies.

"Tell her how you really feel," Leeta whispers to her cousin.

And that's all it takes for Lucy to let it rip. "No, Grandma," she says. "I don't forgive you. I'm just not feeling it. But if you want to check off 'Apologize to Lucy' from your to-do list, go for it. You did your thing but it doesn't change anything, so who cares? Oh, and let me know if you want to apologize to *my mom*. I'll text you her number."

After a long, stunned pause, Ruth says, "Yes. Please. I would greatly appreciate having your mother's phone number. Thank you."

Lucy sniffles and rubs her nose. "Whatever."

"Lucy, is Leeta there? I'd like to speak with her."

"I am here," says Leeta.

"Leeta, I am very sorry I didn't believe you when you said you are Liam's daughter. I believe you now."

Lucy whispers to Leeta, "Don't trust her."

Leeta holds up one finger to silence Lucy, then into the phone she says, "You must have received some new irrefutable data contradicting your prior firmly held belief. What was it?"

Silence on the other end.

"I know!" shrieks Leeta. "You collected my DNA off of my tea cup."

Lucy gives Leeta a thumbs up, but Leeta has turned away, her face drawn with worry.

"Actually, it was from your fork," says Ruth, sheepishly. "I am not proud of sneaking around, but the results put my mind at ease. The DNA proves you're exactly who you say you are."

Lucy holds the phone closer to her mouth. "Grandpa, you weren't a part of this." It's not a question.

"I certainly was not!" Richard shouts on his end of the line.

Leeta turns back to the phone. "What have you done? People will find out who I am. What I am. Because of you, I am now in great danger." Leeta is shaking, her voice rising in panic.

Lucy rests a hand on the back of Leeta's neck. Sid reaches out and gently squeezes her knee.

"No. No," says Ruth. "No! Listen, Leeta. You're not in danger. I swear. The director of the lab works for me. She didn't trust the results anyway. I told her to destroy the sample. She had already done it. Please, don't worry." Ruth's voice is warm and caring. "No one outside of our family knows the truth and no one ever will. You can trust me. Okay? I'm your grandmother. Okay?"

Leeta says nothing.

"Sid?" says Ruth. "I owe you an apology too."

"Why? You steal his DNA too?" says Leeta.

"No. Why would I? Never mind. Sid, I was rude to you. I had no right to make personal comments about how you and Leeta look . . . together."

"What is she talking about?" Leeta whispers to Sid.

Sid shrugs, but Leeta knows he knows exactly what she's talking about.

"Anyway. I'm truly sorry. Maybe I've finally learned that when it comes to love, nothing matters less than what other people think. I hope you will forgive me, Sid. I hope you will all forgive me."

The three of them look at each other. Silence.

"Well, do you?" Old Ruth is back.

"Whatever," says Lucy. The others say nothing.

"I will take that as a yes. Thank you. Well, good luck finding Liam. I mean that sincerely. And if you do find him, please bring him home to us. And even if you don't, please come back anyway."

Lucy hangs up. "Unbelievable. Ruth Rainier Rutherford apologized. Do you guys think she's dying?"

"I am not a physician," says Leeta. "She sounded healthy to me, but symptoms of ill health can be very subtle."

"You know," says Sid, "this whole thing reminds me of a graphic novel I read where this planet was ruled by a highly evolved species that was half living, half automaton. They were immortal, and because of that they were shitty to each other. The ruler was the shittiest of all. Then a microscopic alien life form landed on the planet, and somehow, only the ruler got sick. He started thinking about all the bad stuff he'd done. So, he apologized to everyone, which of course blew everyone's mind."

"What happened after the guy apologized?" Lucy asks. "Did he become healthy again?"

"No. He died."

They all exhale and shift in their seats in a failed attempt to get comfortable. Leeta turns to the back seat. "Lucy, please give me a marshmallow."

Lucy reaches in the bag and hands her a marshmallow.

Leeta pops it in her mouth. "I will have another," she says, her voice softly muffled.

Lucy hands her another one, which Leeta also stuffs in her mouth.

Sid shakes his head. "I don't understand. You just said . . ."

"I know what I just said," Leeta snaps, erupting in tears.

Sid catches Lucy in the rearview mirror. She shrugs, pops a marshmallow into her own mouth and offers him one. He shakes his head and turns to Leeta.

"What's wrong?"

"This is taking too long!" Leeta sobs.

The road bends to the north. Suddenly, beyond a vast stretch of forest, a hazy outline appears on the horizon.

"Hey guys, look!"

"Where?"

"What?"

"There!" Sid points to the right. "That's Shasta!"

At 14,179 feet, the snow-covered peak is so tall they can spot it 140 miles away.

For Lucy, who has never seen a mountain, or snow, or snow on a mountain, Shasta dazzles. She's lived her whole life in Florida, a mostly flat, swampy place where the highest peak isn't a mountain at all but a mountain wannabe called Britton Hill, which, at 345 feet above sea level, has the distinction of being the *lowest* highest elevation in the United States. This Shasta that seems to hold up the sky fills Lucy with wonder at the possibilities of a world she's lived in her whole life, but barely knows at all.

For Leeta, the sight of the mountain brings sweet certainty to her heart. At this moment she is looking toward her father. She can picture him in a small house surrounded by tall trees, somewhere on or near this mountain. He is painting. He pauses and looks out the window facing south. He's watching the morning sun find its way around and through the branches, and he feels something akin to what she feels, without yet knowing what it is. The feeling is growing stronger. Something is finding its way to him.

As for Sid, he's already imagining how Mount Shasta will look on the cover of his graphic novel.

CHAPTER 28
PROMISES KEPT AND BROKEN

Help is where you find it. If you can't find it, keep looking.
—*FUREAN FIELD SEARCH AND RESCUE GUIDE*

A PAINTED GREEN DRAGONFLY hovers above a quartz crystal in the window of Sabine's New Age Emporium where the three friends stand in front of the locked door. Actually, only two of them are standing. The tall one paces endlessly between store and curb, sniffing the air suspiciously.

"It's ten o'clock," Leeta says. "The store is supposed to be open. They are late. That is not acceptable."

Sid checks his phone. "They're not late. It's only 9:59." He looks at her, exuding calm. The effort is wasted. Leeta's grinding her teeth.

Lucy shifts the painting from one arm to the other. "Relax, Leeta or I'll try that cupped hand thing on you, and who knows how that'll turn out."

From inside the store, a slender hand adorned with silver rings and a henna pentagram flips the CLOSED sign to WELCOME. As the woman attached to the hand opens the door, a smallish black cat slips out and rubs against Leeta's ankles. Leeta bends down to touch the cat who looks up at her as if to say, "*It took you long enough.*"

The woman smiles radiantly. "Good morning. I'm Sabine."

Sabine's shoulder-length dark brown hair with blunt-cut bangs is parted in the middle revealing gray roots. The large enamel brooch pinned to the front of her flowing green dress reads *Resident Good Witch*. She opens the door wider. The sound of celestial bells floats out to the sidewalk along with a sweet, earthy, floral scent. "Welcome. Please come in."

Lucy carries the painting inside the store. Leeta repeatedly sneezes and clears her throat.

"Are you okay?" Sid asks. "Allergic to cats?"

Leeta covers her nose and mouth, and shakes her head. "It is not the cat. It is that smell."

"Oh, that's sandalwood incense," says Sabine. "Most people find it very soothing."

"I am not most people. I will wait outside."

Sid follows Sabine inside the shop. The door closes behind them. Leeta walks to the curb, leans against a bike rack and aimlessly fiddles with a lock on a chain. The cat remains at her heels. As she reaches down to pet it, the cat turns tail and walks to the corner of the building where it pauses and looks back at her as if to say, "*Are you coming or not?*" Leeta trails the cat to the parking lot behind the store where a green pickup truck adorned with Sabine's logo has just pulled into the spot next to Sid's car.

Sid and Lucy stand on one side of the counter studying Sabine while she studies the painting from the other side. The witch's mouth knots in agitation, before she smooths it into a bland smile.

"Evocative work," she says, looking up at them. "Thank you for sharing, but this is not a consignment store. And even if it were, as you can see, I don't sell paintings."

Sabine rests a shaky hand atop the large amethyst crystal beside her. Her pinky nearly covers the $250 price sticker.

"Maybe not here," says Sid. "But you do sell paintings just like this out of a P.O. Box."

Sabine's smile freezes. "What gives you that idea?"

Sid's eyes narrow. He's close to boiling. Lucy frowns a quick warning. "Hey, no worries, Sabine," she says. "Private business on the side. I get it. Thing is, we're super fans of Liam Rutherford. Sid here's an artist, himself. And we'd really just love to take a selfie with him. So can you please tell us where he lives?"

"I can't do that."

Sid dissects her with his eyes. "Can't or won't?"

Sabine's hand flies to her left temple where she secretly presses the corner of her twitching eye.

"Won't," she says, her voice steady.

The front door opens triggering the celestial bells as two well-dressed older men enter the store, a small border collie between them.

Sabine calls across the room. "Good morning! Welcome!"

"Is it okay if we bring our dog inside?" the shorter man asks.

"Of course. Everyone is welcome here."

"Except anyone asking about Liam," Sid whispers to Lucy.

Sabine turns back to Sid and Lucy, a pained smile on her face. "I think we're done here."

Lucy slaps the counter. "I'm Liam's niece. The tall allergic one who's waiting outside is his daughter, who he's never met."

Sabine inhales sharply. "Oh."

"Yeah. Oh. So, we need to find him quickly and we know that *you* know where he lives."

"I do, but I won't tell you."

"Why the hell not? You've got information that could help two sad, desperate people . . . no, four."

"Make that five," adds Sid. "What kind of good witch are you anyway?"

Sabine grasps the amethyst and breathes deeply. "The kind that honors the vow I made to an old and very dear friend. I promised I would never say his name to anyone who came looking for him. Not strangers or blood relatives. I also vowed that I would never reveal his location. I'm very sorry to disappoint you."

Lucy scoffs. "Like hell you are."

Leeta and the cat watch a very thin young woman in her twenties step down from the green truck with Sabine's dragonfly painted on the side. She's wearing a long flowing crimson dress which makes her pale skin appear even paler. A rose quartz crystal hangs from a silver chain around her neck. Witchy vibes exude from every pore. A little girl in blue shorts and a yellow t-shirt hops out of the passenger seat of the truck, laughing. While Leeta watches her, smiling to herself, the girl starts popping with hiccoughs, making her laugh harder.

The witchy woman smiles knowingly at Leeta and gestures to the cat. "Did Faeryn just bring you back here?" she asks.

"Faeryn?" Leeta has never heard this word before.

Her implant quickly fills her in.

Faeryn: *a female name of English origins, meaning "from the fairies."*

Fairy: *a small imaginary being of human form that has magical powers.*

"That is an interesting name for a cat," says Leeta. "It is possible Faeryn led me here to coincide with your arrival, though I must say, that sounds rather woo-woo."

The woman shrugs. "Call it what you want, Faeryn must have sensed we're supposed to meet. I'm Iz."

Hiccoughs gone, the little girl lifts Faeryn into her arms. "I'm Fiona," she says. "I'm seven. What's your name? You're very tall."

"I am Leeta Simtar. And yes, compared to most people I meet, I am very tall."

Leeta shakes hands with Fiona. When she offers her hand to Iz, Iz holds on for a long moment searching Leeta's eyes. The parade of curious expressions that trip and dance across Iz's face frighten Leeta. She pulls her hand away and hurries toward the front of the building.

"Leeta, wait!" Iz's voice stops her cold.

Leeta turns to see Iz clutching the crystal as if it were a receiver of data. "You're looking for someone. You've come from very far away to find him. He is a tall man, nearly as tall as you. He has a faded red beard and long hair. Not much on top. His fingers are long and strong. Stained with color. He has a distracted look about him and he's wearing—"

Leeta walks back to Iz. "—black, heavy-framed glasses?"

"Yes," Iz nods. "With blue tape holding them together in the center."

"Can you please provide more information?"

"Maybe. You have something that belongs to him. Maybe I can hold it?"

Without asking how she knows this, Leeta slips off the ring and hands it to Iz who closes her fingers around it, her other hand still clutching the crystal. She shuts her eyes. After a few moments, she speaks.

"This ring is heavy as lead and light as air. It contains the fire of desire along with the chill of a distant place that has never known the warmth of the sun. I feel love, happiness, unlimited promise. The man you're looking for had this ring, but never wore it. He gave it to his lover. When he placed it on her finger, both their hearts soared with hope for the future. Then a spark of hate flared in the night and consumed their hope and their future. They parted. Both hearts heavy. And still, even now, they are burdened with the pain of their loss."

Iz opens her eyes, damp with tears, and looks up at Leeta, whose cupped hand rests shakily over her own heart.

"Iz, do you know the man I am looking for?"

"Yes." A shadow crosses Iz's face. "It's Liam Rutherford. I just came from his house."

Leeta's face ignites with joy. "Pleaseandthankyou take me there now!"

Iz sadly shakes her head and drops the ring into Leeta's open palm. "I'm really sorry, but I can't. I made a promise."

Leeta looks at the ring as if it were the dead, empty shell of a once-lovely life. She thinks about what she'll say when she gives it back to the Daht. How she'll apologize for failing to complete the real mission she was sent to accomplish. Crying silently, she sinks to the ground, head buried in her hands. Fiona walks to Leeta's side and puts her arms around her, but Leeta is too far gone to find comfort there.

Iz grimaces, one hand on her belly. She exhales unevenly, touching the crystal around her neck, and she murmurs something about the Goddess Eternal. Fiona rolls her eyes. She's heard this before and knows it could take time. Time they don't have.

Eyes flashing, the little girl shakes Iz's arm. "Not true! My *mom* promised Liam. You never did and neither did I. We've got to help Leeta."

Leeta looks up to see a wordless agreement pass between Iz and Fiona. They each reach for one of her hands and help her up. Sid and Lucy appear around the corner of the building, talking over each other.

"Sabine won't help."

"We've got to pivot."

"We do not need Sabine." Leeta points to the skinny witch and the little girl. "*They* will help us."

Moments later, Iz's truck tears out of the parking lot followed by the Cosmos on Wheels.

The cat watches from the sidewalk, for all the world looking like she's smiling to herself.

CHAPTER 29
HAUNTED PAINTINGS

"The human retreats from the world, haunted by thoughts of what might have been."
—FROM AN UNPUBLISHED GRAPHIC NOVEL

THE DRAGONFLY TRUCK BARRELS ALONG North Old Stage Road. The Cosmos on Wheels follows close behind. Black Butte, the massive cinder cone of a dormant volcano, looms ominously on their right. When Iz turns onto an unmarked dirt road, Sid does the same. The road narrows, the trees grow closer, the air turns chill. A mile or so later, the truck slows to a stop in a tight clearing surrounded by pines. Iz gets out and walks back to Sid's car.

"Why are we stopping?" asks Leeta.

"It's right over there." Iz points through the trees to an aging cabin, its saggy roof dotted with moss. "I'll park in front and knock on the door. Stay here so he doesn't see your car."

Iz pulls forward another 20 feet, shuts off the engine and holds her crystal.

"What are you waiting for?" asks Fiona. She opens the door, hops onto the running board, and jumps down to the ground, raising dust.

In another minute the little girl is scampering up four steps to the cabin's front door, her small hand knocking against the heavy wood, barely making a sound.

Iz appears beside her, breathless. "Maybe he's not home."

"Yeah, he is," says Fiona. "His car's around the side. He just can't hear me. You knock."

Iz nods. "For Leeta." She clenches her fists and hammers the door, rapid fire. "Liam! Liam! I know you're in there. Open the door."

Shuffling steps approach from the inside. The door opens slowly. A tall haunted scarecrow of a man squints at them like he's not used to daylight or fresh air. Or both. Liam Rutherford is visibly older, thinner, and scruffier than the burly bear he was in the SETI photo. Scraggly beard and mostly bald on top. What's left of his red hair is faded and pulled back in a skinny ponytail. He's wearing paint-splotched overalls. Electrical tape holds his black-rimmed eyeglasses together. Behind the scratched, smudged lenses, where keenly intelligent eyes once challenged everything, only sadness reigns.

"Iz. Fiona. You're back." His tone is flat. His voice cracked and dry, like the skin on his hands. "Forget something?"

"No," Iz says. "We brought someone to see you."

Liam's eyes dart around the front yard like a frightened animal. "I don't want to talk to anyone else today."

He backs into the cabin and starts to close the door. A hand shoots out, blocking it.

"Hello, Uncle Liam."

He peers suspiciously at the well-dressed young woman standing on his front steps, trying to decide if she's an art collector who wants to buy directly from him so she'll have a great story to tell her friends.

"Who are you?" he asks in a low growl.

If he intended to scare the woman, he is failing miserably. At most Lucy is annoyed that he doesn't seem to recognize her. How could Uncle Liam forget his only niece? The more she dwells on the snub the more pissed off she gets. Then she looks at him, *really* looks. If she ran into him anywhere else, she wouldn't recognize him. And he hasn't seen her since she was six. They've both changed so much.

"I'm Lucy," she says, as if that explains it all.

Liam leans forward, squinting at her, as if through fogged glass, his expression vacillates between confused and clueless.

Awkward moments pass. Lucy's had enough. "I'll give you a hint," she says. "I'm Marcus' daughter."

Something sparks deep in a closed-off section of Liam's brain.

The fog lifts, but only slightly. "Lucy." He nods.

She thinks she detects the hint of a smile, but it doesn't make it to up his eyes, so it hardly counts. She purses her lips.

"How is your mother?" he asks, his voice plodding through the dusty corridors.

"She's good."

Liam seems to have forgotten Lucy is there. He begins digging out green paint from under his fingernails. This could be a very short reunion. She shifts her weight from one hip to the other. "Aren't you going to ask about my father?" she says.

Liam purses his lips and rubs his palms along the sides of his overalls. "Oh. Yes. How is Marcus?"

"He died two months ago."

She says this without a lot of emotion, letting the words hang in the air to test his reaction, as if pressing a dull pencil against a balloon to see if it will pop. It doesn't. Liam absently touches the top of his bare head.

"My condolences," he says, also without a lot of emotion. "Is that why you came? To tell me about Marcus?"

"No." Lucy shakes her head emphatically. "I wanted to see you, Uncle Liam. It's been so long. We all thought you were dead."

"Most of me is."

He gazes into the forest just beyond the yard, and spots a hint of bright color. He crosses in front of Lucy, ambles down the steps, and heads toward the trees.

Sid sits on the ground sketching, his back against a large pine. He looks up to watch the strange man circling the Cosmos on Wheels. This guy looks more like an old beekeeper than a world-class painter of other worldly landscapes.

After Liam's third rotation, he stops in front of Sid. "Did you paint this?"

Sid gets to his feet, clutching his sketchbook and bracing himself for a trashing. "Yeah."

"It's good," says Liam.

Sid exhales cautiously.

"Very good. In fact, it's truly remarkable."

Sid's head spins. A real artist just called his car paint job remarkable.

"Are you with Lucy?" Liam asks.

"Yes."

"Come inside and I'll show you my work."

Sid imagines talking with Liam Rutherford about art. He can easily see the two of them bent over his sketchbook. Of course he'll also show Liam his computer art. Maybe the great man will be so impressed he'll help Sid publish his graphic novel. Of course he will.

Liam turns back toward the cabin and Sid starts to follow.

"Hello, Liam Rutherford."

The sharp voice pushes against the back of Liam's head. He recognizes something in the way it demands his attention. He whips around to see Leeta, wearing her inflight suit, walking toward him, her gaze locked on his eyes like a tractor beam.

The contours of his face and the way he moves are familiar to Leeta. Not so much for his resemblance to her, though she can't miss the shape of his hands, his blue eyes, or the color of what's left of his hair. No, he seems familiar because he looks so much like Richard. Seeing Liam fills Leeta's heart with a deep satisfaction knowing that she's finally found the source of her humanity. Because they are connected in mysterious ways that have brought her the mental images of Liam's day-to-day life along with some deeply felt emotions, she believes she already knows Liam. And since she's just proved their link works in two directions, she believes he must know her too.

As for Liam, the sight of Leeta in her uniform, the Furean insignia in particular, shakes him like nothing else has in the past 18 years. Too shocked and confused to speak, he shakes his head and mutters to himself.

"What are you saying?" Leeta wants to know.

"Nothing. Just . . . Good costume. Very . . . realistic." With that he turns and heads back to the cabin.

"This is not a costume," she calls after him. "I am from Fure."

The word cuts through him. He is suddenly frightened. He turns to face her.

"*Fure?* What are you talking about? How could you possibly . . . Never mind. Who are you? Why are you here?"

Leeta considers the logic of parsing out the truth bit by bit. With only ten hours left, she doesn't have time for parsing.

"I am Leeta Simtar, and I am here because Eta-Bakara sent me."

His pulse roars in his ears, while the blood rushes from his head to his feet. He tries to catch his breath. It seems to be just out of reach, like the truth about this tall young woman who is wearing the same clothing his lover wore the last time he saw her.

"How do you know Eta-Bakara?" he asks.

"Eta-Bakara is my mother."

His heart stops altogether. Suddenly unsteady, he reaches for something, but there's nothing to hold on to. He falls heavily against the fender of the Cosmos on Wheels. The impact seems to clear his mind.

"Your mother?" he croaks. Could it be possible? Yet she says she's from Fure. And the costume is perfect. Even if she is as delusional as she appears, the mention of Eta-Bakara fills Liam with joy, reconnecting him with his lost love. And in that moment hope rekindles and all rational thoughts fly from his brain. He closes the distance between them in seconds, takes Leeta's hands in his and examines her fingers, like the scientist he's always been.

"You have her beautiful thumbs. But your other fingers are so—"

"—human. That's because I am Brid. 29% Furean and 71% percent human."

A kaleidoscope of electric butterflies swarm behind Liam's heart. Reflexively, his hands close around hers as he cradles them. Vivid images flit through his mind like a slide show as they pass directly into hers.

Eta-Bakara stands on her toes, beside her escape pod, wisps of fog swirling around her legs.

She raises her arm, reaching high overhead.

Liam stoops and bends toward her, his palm slowly compressing the air between them.

Their palms meet, fingers intertwine.

Light shines between them and through them, growing brighter.

"Is it possible—" he says, his voice thick and quivering.

"—More than possible," she says, squeezing his hands. "It is true. I am your daughter."

Liam's emotions, dormant for so long, erupt at full force. All the feelings that torment and delight humans rush to the surface and fill the space around them. Father and daughter hold each other for the first time, both of them weeping with joy.

He is like a man long adrift at sea who has finally found the island he has so long dreamed of. Leeta also feels like she's found what she's always longed for.

Liam's tears suddenly turn into uncontrollable laughter.

"Why are you laughing?" she asks, though something unspoken has already whispered the answer.

"I've been such a fool," he says. "I thought she forgot about me, but she didn't, did she?"

So, the truth is told. Their reunion is not the cause of Liam's joy. This celebration is not about Leeta at all. This is and always will be about Liam and the Daht. Her heart sinks. She could make up a story in answer to his question. That way, at least, she could fight for what she's just found. But Liam deserves the truth.

"No," Leeta says, taking the ring from the side pocket of her backpack and handing it to him. "She never forgot you."

He holds the ring in his palm as if it were a fragile thing, containing the very essence of love itself. He remembers the moment he slipped it on Eta-Bakara's finger. He remembers the light in her eyes. The touch of her lips on his. They were both so filled with hope. He freezes the memory, banishing the horror and injustice of what happened next.

"She kept it all this time, Liam. She gave it to me before I left Fure. I used this ring to find you, just as she knew I would."

Tearfully, he hands the ring back to her. "Thank you, Leeta, for coming all this way and for bringing Eta-Bakara with you."

Leeta smiles. She has lifted her father from his dark prison and made him happy. When she reports back to the Daht she will also be happy. And while Leeta is disappointed that her reunion with her father is not all that she thought it would be, she has gained much more than she lost. She understands now what it means to be Brid. And that is no small thing. She also understands the way of the cosmos—how the scattering of seeds renews life and love, again and again. Against all odds.

Iz's truck is gone from the front yard now. Lucy sits on the front steps, texting. Sid, who slipped away unseen as soon as Leeta revealed herself, sits beside Lucy, sketching yet another portrait of Leeta. When father and daughter reappear, walking together, Leeta's friends look up. Sid searches her face. She nods at him, her mouth twisting left. He senses something isn't right with her, but isn't entirely wrong either. Did he screw things up by wishing on some random beetle instead of an actual ladybug? Is it possible the Liam portion of Leeta's "happy family reunion" has, somehow, already disappointed her as much the Winterbrook episode? He hopes not.

Liam climbs the front steps to the cabin and opens the door wide. "Please come in," he says. "All of you."

The three friends follow Liam inside, pausing to let their eyes to adjust to the dimness. It takes a minute to get used to. It takes longer to get used to the unbearable sorrow hanging in the air. All shades are drawn except for the one furthest from the door. Strong sunlight from the west illuminates the easel standing there, holding an unfinished portrait so abstract it's impossible to tell if the subject is human. What's unmistakable in the painting is the chaotic star field that makes up the background. A Starry Night coffee mug sits on a small wooden table fitted with four old mismatched chairs, all sharing the same look of despair. Painted canvases are stacked in corners, leaning against baseboards, laying sideways on top of bookshelves. There seems to be no order anywhere, except for a series of paintings hanging neatly along the wall to the right of the door. Each one matches the palette and style of the painting in Sid's car. They all look like pages from the same heroically tragic graphic novel.

Liam gestures to the series. "These paintings tell our love story—mine and Eta-Bakara's. I thought you'd be interested, Leeta. After all, not many people can say they've seen an illustrated account of how their parents met."

"Yes. Of course I am interested," she says, a bit too eagerly.

While Sid and Leeta look at the art, Lucy spots the original Valentine cube beside Liam's easel.

"Uncle Liam! You still have my Valentine cube!"
She hugs him. He reflexively pulls away, then catches himself and gives her a quick pat on the back.

"Take a look at this," she says, pulling Leeta's Valentine cube out of her purse. "Leeta made this one. When she was on Fure."

Liam takes the model cube in his hand and compares it to Lucy's original. "This is remarkable. Except for the difference in size and material, these are identical. How did you do this, Leeta?"

Leeta explains as best she can about their psychic connection and how she was able to make models of the SETI radio telescope, Liam's Starry Night mug, and his eyeglasses, though she admits that hers didn't have blue tape in the center.

Liam shakes his head in wonder, "I guess we can logically conclude that you saw my glasses in your mind's eye before I broke them."

"I would agree with that assessment."

Lucy laughs. "You guys are definitely related."

"We most definitely are." Liam squeezes Leeta's hand and smiles at her broadly. She smiles back, less broadly. Liam doesn't notice, but Sid does.

"Liam," he says, more loudly than necessary. "The other day, before we knew you were alive, Leeta and I did a telepathy experiment. She tried to send you a mental message. We figured if you heard it and responded, that might prove you were alive."

"When was this?" Liam asks.

"Tuesday. Around noon. Did you hear anything?"

Liam's thumb briefly strokes his beard. "I did! I remember. I was just finishing up a section of this portrait at the time." He points to one of three separate portraits of Eta-Bakara all in progress. "I took a break for lunch. I was making tuna salad. I always make tuna salad on Tuesdays. Suddenly I heard a woman's voice in my head. I thought Eta-Bakara was talking to me. I've got to admit, over the years I've had quite a few conversations with her inside my head. But this voice was different. It was your voice, Leeta. Tell me what you said."

"I said, 'Hello, Liam Rutherford. Where are you?'"

"Yes. That's exactly what I heard."

"And you replied, 'Eta-Bakara? Is that you?'"

"I did!"

Liam and Leeta seem as pleased as a couple of kids who just won an award for their science fair project.

Leeta smiles at Liam, then at Lucy, and finally at Sid. "When I return to Fure, I will not be needing any of your phone numbers to communicate with you."

Sid's smile slides off his face, and he doesn't bother sticking it back on.

Leeta, Lucy, and Sid sip coffee from identical Starry Night mugs while Liam stands in front of the first painting on the wall. A radio telescope, turning its face to the starry sky, fills the center of the canvas. A mass of tiny lines, dots, and indecipherable symbols swims toward the antenna from all directions. Amidst the confusion, one pure vibrant golden thread shines.

"This is the first one I made when I came up here," says Liam. "This is how it all began with us. I'd listened to so much space noise. Hoping for so long that some day I'd hear something. And then one miraculous night, she spoke to me."

The next painting shows Eta-Bakara and Liam lying side by side in a meadow, their faces flush with delight at the wonders of the stars overhead and the wonder of being together. "This is us, five years later, soon after we'd met in person for the first time. Funny how we knew right away. But we did. We always knew."

The third painting shows the lovers embracing beside a spherical space craft, its light diffused in swirling fog. "This is us, three days later right before we were going to leave."

In the fourth painting, a sinister figure prowls in the foreground, pointing a large shotgun at Eta-Bakara and Liam, still embracing but in the far distance. A fiery ball fills the center of the canvas, its black and red shards like poison-tipped missiles, fly toward the lovers. Liam starts to say something, but the words don't come. He looks away from the painting, but there's nowhere to look in this place that doesn't remind him of what he lost. He closes his eyes and rubs the top of his head.

He waves the group forward to the fifth and final painting in the sequence, inviting them to study it on their own while he quickly retreats to the easel by the window and resumes his work on the portrait.

The last image features Liam in the foreground, sheltering behind a thick hedge, his face distraught, his eyes helpless as he watches the spaceship traverse the face of the moon. The assailant, now in the form of a grotesque beast, continues firing his weapon into the sky.

Sid walks away from the canvas toward Liam, his legs, are slow and heavy as he crosses to the back of the cabin. Leeta follows him. Sensing what's about to happen, her chest tightens.

"Liam," Sid says, more forcefully than he intended. "I need to tell you something."

Leeta shoots Sid a warning look. He gets her message and shifts gears, but only slightly. "Did you ever find who shot at you and Eta-Bakara that night?"

Silence.

The pause is so long, Sid wonders if the question had evaporated somewhere in Liam's brain or if the old man had heard it at all.

Without taking his eyes from the canvas, Liam adds a touch of blue to Eta-Bakara's lower lip. "I knew who it was as soon as the shooting started." His voice is strangely calm. "A crazy local guy named Rick Rodriguez."

Sid looks away, eyes burning with shame. "Rick Rodriguez is my father," he says, forcing himself to speak up. "And when Leeta's pod landed, he shot at her too."

The paintbrush hits the floor with a soft thud of surprise, knowing it doesn't belong down there but is helpless until the artist notices what's happened. Unfortunately for the brush, the artist has other things to worry about. His head jerks to the left, and he looks at Leeta over his glasses, his face a storm of emotion.

"I was not hurt," she quickly reassures him.

But Liam is not reassured. He glares at Sid. "I want you to leave my house. Now!"

"That is not right," says Leeta as she stands beside Sid and slips her hand into his. "Sid is not like his father!"

Lucy stands close to Sid's other side. "He definitely isn't," she says.

"Thanks, guys." Sid whispers to both of them, squeezing Leeta's hand before reluctantly letting go. "I'll wait for you outside."

As Sid closes the cabin door behind him, Liam sits down heavily, and the old chair creaks in protest.

Sitting alone inside the Cosmos on Wheels, Sid thinks about what he would have said if Liam had given him a chance to defend himself. What could he say? The truth? Well, the truth isn't so easy to say or to hear. If his father wasn't such a trigger-happy nutcase, Liam and Eta-Bakara would have lived a happy life together instead of Liam's becoming a miserable hermit haunted by the dreams of what might have been. As for Eta-Bakara, from what Leeta's told him, even being the ruler of all Fure doesn't guarantee you happiness. And his father is to blame for all this. Why in the world should Liam trust him? Why would he even allow Sid anywhere near his daughter?

Sid shivers from the familiar cold outrage and that awful feeling of how unfair it is that he, Sid, a good guy, should have to defend himself against his father's hateful acts.

He's not sure how long he's been sitting there, consumed by thoughts that bring him into places darker than the nothingness of a black hole, before a tapping on the passenger window forces him back into the light.

It's Liam.

Sid lowers the window. The two of them look at each other, but only briefly before Liam looks away, absently touching the top of his head. "I want to say something," he begins.

"Me, too," says Sid.

"Okay. You can go first."

Sid inhales deeply, lets it out quickly. "I'm very sorry for what my father did and for all the sadness he caused." There's much more he wants to say but Liam won't let him. "I hope you accept my apology."

"No," says Liam. "I don't. I won't accept it because you've got nothing to apologize for. It's not your job to apologize for your father. You didn't do anything wrong, Sid. You did everything right. You helped the girls find me. You brought them here. You've been such a good friend to Leeta she trusted you with her secret. I thank you for all that. You've proven yourself to this family. I don't need anything more from you."

Liam holds out his large hand, and after a brief pause to consider this lucky change of heart, Sid shakes it.

"Now that you've seen some of my work, may I look at your sketchbook?"

"Oh, well, my stuff is no way near as amazing as yours. I . . . I don't want to waste your time."

"You want to show me or not?"

Sid blushes. "Let's do it."

Leeta and Lucy sit outside on the front steps, the sun high over the tops of the pines.

Leeta takes out her APED. "I need to make a call."

Lucy stands up. "No problem. I'll leave."

"Not necessary. AYA, call Zertee."

Zertee appears. "Is it time to activate the self-destruct?"

"Not yet. I just wanted to tell you that I found my father."

"Congratulations, Leeta. Mission accomplished. What is he like, this human who was loved by the Daht?"

"I'll tell you everything, but not now. Stay on the coordinates."

After Leeta hangs up, Lucy says, "I'm gonna call Grandpa and tell him about Liam." She punches in the number.

"Hello?" Richard's voice is heard through the phone.

"Grandpa? It's Lucy. Leeta's here with me. I've got you on speaker."

Richard's voice warms the morning air. "Hello, girls! I was just thinking about you and wondering—"

Leeta grabs the phone. "—Grandpa, we found him!"

"What? Really? Oh my god! Ruth ... Ruth! They found Liam!"

Ruth is heard on the phone, crying, "They found him?"

"Yes! And we're bringing him home," Leeta shouts.

Lucy hangs up and stares at Leeta who is already halfway across the porch. "When did Liam agree to that?"

Leeta grins. "He does not know yet." she says, pulling open the front door.

When the girls reenter the cabin, Liam is standing at the end of the room, again working at his easel. He's layering on colors with a palette knife. Purple. Orange. Green. The applied paint, a half-inch thick in some places, resembles a 3D topographic map. In other places, the paint's been scraped so thin the blank canvas shows through. Sid sits on a chair to Liam's left, pencil in hand, totally absorbed in sketching a portrait of the artist at work.

"Uncle Liam, we just talked to Grandma and Grandpa."

He pauses, brush in mid-air and sighs. "I wish you hadn't called them, Lucy."

Sid turns his chair, flips to a clean page in his sketch book, and begins drawing Lucy.

"How could we not? Don't they deserve to know you're alive?"

"Thanks to you, they know that now." Liam squeezes out a mound of chromium oxide green onto his palette and scrapes half of it onto his knife. Before he can touch the canvas again, Lucy grabs his wrist. "Come back to Winterbrook with us."

He unhooks her fingers. "My life is here."

"Just come for a visit. They've missed you."

"I'm not ready. You go. Tell them . . . I'll come some other time. Okay?"

Impatience grows in Leeta's gut. In her mind's eye she sees her grandfather, as he was when she first climbed over the garden wall. She hears him singing along with the recording on his phone, his pleading voice reaching to the heavens, begging some powerful being to bring his son home. She promised herself that she would.

"No!" she says, stepping in front of Lucy. "That is not okay, Liam. You thanked me for coming all this way to connect with you. Your parents are only a few hours away. How can you deny them the joy of reconnecting with you?"

He carefully wipes the tip of the palette knife with a paint rag so covered with old stains there is no evidence of what color it might once have been. "I wouldn't mind seeing my father," he says, mostly to himself. "But my mother . . . Ruth . . . she is. . ."

"We all know her, Liam," says Sid.

"People make mistakes," says Leeta. She's about to say more, but decides to leave it at that.

Liam looks away. He's had enough of this conversation. Enough of these visitors. He longs to be alone in his cabin again. Alone with his memories of Eta-Bakara. But Leeta's words pull at him, from outside and from within. *People make mistakes*. All people. He puts down the palette knife and stares at Leeta. He can't miss the determination in her eyes. He knows it comes from being Eta-Bakara's daughter. He also sees compassion and forgiveness, and knows that must come from his own father.

"All right." He gets up so suddenly he topples the chair behind him. "But I'm taking my own car so I can leave when I want."

"Deal," says Leeta. "But I am going to ride with you."

CHAPTER 30

A Bumpy Road

THE GRAY 2024 R1T TRI RIVIAN PICKUP powers on the instant the vehicle recognizes Liam's phone in his pocket. Leeta stands by the open door watching him toss a birdwatcher's guide, some paint rags, a broad-brimmed hat, blank canvas panels, and a half-eaten apple over the seat back where they join a portable easel, a sweatshirt, hiking boots, random socks, and a woolen blanket.

"There's room for you now," he tells Leeta.

She climbs into the truck and settles herself easily. No need to duck or adjust the seat, thanks to the extra headroom and the fact that the passenger seat position matches the driver's seat. Perfect for long legs.

"To Winterbrook!" says Leeta, clicking her seat belt closed. "I am thinking this will be much fun."

Liam says nothing as he slowly maneuvers the truck around the house and out of the yard. He drives forward slowly, watching the cabin retreat in the rear-view mirror. He moves even more slowly to the end of the dirt road, as if his ambivalence were a load of concrete in the truck bed.

Leeta is used to the lack of speed in human vehicles, but that doesn't make her any happier about being a passenger, with no more control over where she's going or how fast she gets there than one of Liam's mismatched socks lying on the back seat.

When he comes to a complete stop at the crossroad, he activates the right turn signal. Sid's car stops behind him. Liam looks to the right onto North Old Stage Road. To the left. And to the right again. Leeta observes his behavior closely in case she has an opportunity to drive while she's still on Earth. The road is empty in both directions, but Liam does not proceed. The turn signal flashes and clicks repeatedly as moments turn to minutes, and he continues to sit at a stand-still. Leeta doesn't know what to make of this. Who is Liam signaling to? There is no one here, and Sid's GPS is set to Winterbrook so he doesn't need Liam to show him the way back.

Leeta's seat suddenly feels like it's attacking her, sprouting sharp lumps under her legs, poking her back. She fidgets, unable to get comfortable. The number nine screams inside her head. That's how many hours she's got to meet up with Zertee; otherwise, she's stranded on Earth like ET.

"What the hell are you waiting for?" she demands, loud enough for Sid and Lucy to hear.

Liam jerks to life. "Nothing," he says, his voice sullen, as he finally turns onto the main road.

They drive in uneasy silence. Leeta had imagined the same comfortable flow of conversation she had with Sid and Lucy. She looks at Liam sitting stiffy in his seat, his shoulders hunched to his ears, his neck jutting forward. She knows he is not comfortable being in this situation.

"How about some music?" she asks.

"I don't like listening to music when I drive. It interferes with my train of thought."

"Maybe we could stop at a market. What are your favorite foods for the road?"

"I prefer not to eat while I drive. It affects my concentration."

Why had she insisted on riding with him, anyway? To get to know her father better and to better understand herself. This seemed like an easy goal to accomplish considering that she currently knows next to nothing about him. But now she realizes that getting any personal information out of Liam Rutherford will be much harder than she anticipated.

"I'd like to ask you some personal questions," she says in as friendly a tone as possible. "Questions about you and my mother."

His hands choke the steering wheel. No one has ever asked him about his relationship with Eta-Bakara because no one ever knew. "Okay," he says, the words drawn out and guarded.

Now that she has his attention, she doesn't know where to begin. Her long fingers aimlessly explore the deep crevice down the side of her seat where she encounters something dry, misshapen, and long forgotten. Extracting it from its hiding place, she holds it up. An apple core. Without another thought, she tosses it over her shoulder into the back seat. Still caught between wanting to tread lightly with Liam and plunging right in, she glances in the side-view mirror. Back in Sid's car Lucy spots Leeta's reflection and gives her a thumbs up. In that moment, Leeta decides to go with Lucy's direct approach to getting what she wants.

"I am curious about how you and Eta-Bakara originally connected."

Liam's neck muscles tighten. He moistens his lips.

"One night I was alone at SETI. Picked up a simple signal. A mathematical progression. I listened and ran some tests to make sure it wasn't coming from a near Earth source. I should have immediately alerted the team, shared the data. That's strict protocol, but I ignored it."

A chill races across Leeta's scalp. From the very beginning, Eta-Bakara's story and Liam's ran along parallel paths. "How come you ignored protocol?"

He shrugs, eyes still locked on the road. "Maybe because I thought her signal was just like hundreds of false alarms we got every day. Even so, something told me to respond and not tell anyone. I sent back the next number in the progression. Within minutes, the ET Messenger, that's what I called her at first, replied in English."

"What did she say?"

"'Are you there?'"

Leeta's next question is hard to ask, but if she doesn't ask it now, she might never know the answer.

"When did you know that you loved Eta-Bakara?"

Liam inhales shakily, then seems to forget to exhale. Leeta holds her breath too, waiting to learn more about the most important moment of her life, the part that happened before she was born.

Eyes still on the road Liam searches for the right words and slowly strings them together. "I guess it was from her first reply, though, of course, I didn't know it then. I felt so . . . strange. Excited. Like a door I'd been trying to unlock with every key I could devise suddenly swung open on its own. I felt . . . changed. Like I truly was part of the universe. About to learn its secrets."

Leeta can almost hear his heart pounding. She turns in her seat to face him. Forgetting caution, her words rush out. "What happened next?"

"We talked. She told me her name and that she lived on a small planet called Fure, forty light-years away. I found the red dwarf she described. We call it Trappist-1. She and I communicated in secret for a year. We learned to understand each other. She was exactly what I needed in my life. She felt the same. We couldn't wait to meet. Of course, it was all in secret and we hadn't yet figured out how we'd manage it. We just knew we would."

"How did you keep a secret like that for so long?"

"After each conversation, I removed the data from the log and replaced it with falsified data so there wouldn't be any gaps. Her method was similar."

"Did she ever tell you why she took so many risks to reach out to you?"

Wanting to honor the impulse that sparked their love, Liam thinks back to the words she used when he asked the same question. "She was fascinated by an old failed experiment in which the intermingling of Furean and human DNA resulted in the birth and rise to power of a terrifyingly sick individual. A person whose name all humans still recognize. Even more than a century later, he is considered the most heartless dictator in history."

Leeta's hands are suddenly cold. She slips them deep into her pockets. It barely helps. "I have read about this person," she says in a sharp whisper. "He was directly responsible for a global war that killed at least 45 million civilians and 25 million military combatants. His actions contributed to the suffering of countless millions more."

Leeta forces herself to imagine all those people across the planet, dead, dying, and broken. A tsunami of grief overwhelms her. She cries, loudly and without shame. The force of her tears startles Liam. His heart lurches in his chest. He wants to reach out to her, to comfort her like a father, but part of him is still where he was 18 years ago, hiding behind a hedge. Scared and heartsick as he watched his lover vanish into the night sky. And now in this moment, all he can think to do for Eta-Bakara's daughter, for *his* daughter, is to turn on the radio.

The music is jarring. A pulsing beat with lyrics that make no sense. Leeta shoots out her hand and shuts off the radio. She wipes her face. Sits up straighter.

He continues driving. She continues talking. "Eta-Bakara was certain the original interspecies experiment using human DNA failed because the environment in which the subject was raised contributed to his becoming a violent dictator. She wanted to redo the experiment and raise the Furean/human hybrid child on Fure to prove her theory that environment overcomes genetic predisposition. And you did everything you could to help prove her theory without ever thinking about the subject of your experiment?"

"That's true," says Liam, without a hint of shame or regret.

A flash of anger rips through her heart. A volcano explodes in the center of her brain. She shoots a glance in the side mirror. The Cosmos on Wheels still right behind them. Lucy is asleep, her head against her window. Maybe she's dreaming about returning to Florida. Sid's face is unreadable. Maybe he's thinking about his graphic novel and how Liam praised his art. No one is thinking about Leeta right now. Isn't that the way it's always been? All or nothing? The people on Fure thought about her too much and how different she is. And from the very beginning, her parents, if they thought about her at all, it was only as the *subject* of their secret, world-changing experiment. They never considered for a single moment what could happen if the result of combining Furean and human DNA a second time turned out to be as much of a disaster as the first time. Or worse.

As Liam drives, wondering what time he'll arrive at Winterbrook, fear grips Leeta's lungs like an iron claw as she obsesses over the possibility she'll grow up to become some kind of monster.

Leeta cups a hand over her heart and shoves aside the fears. She can't ride that train of thought. Not now. Her time with Liam is running short. She has more questions that need answers. "What was it like for you, the first time you saw her? You two look so very different."

"Yes. I was a bit taller than she," he chuckles. "But to tell you the truth, it never mattered. We spent three solid days together and, for the first time, I felt like I was *home*. Nothing like being a child at Winterbrook, with the constant tension between my parents. Eta-Bakara said I helped her understand what love was, beyond the One Mind, One Goal, One Family she had been taught. We exchanged DNA with the sustained contact of palm to palm. And returned to the ship. We were about to board and go away together back to Fure, to raise our child together, when that man attacked us. She pushed me to the ground to protect me, then ran onto the ship and took off."

"The second time I put on the ring, I saw you watching her leave."

Liam nods, bites his lip, but the tears flow freely. "I hid like a coward. I couldn't move. I only went back to SETI after I was sure Rodriguez left the area. I thought for sure she would land again, in a more secure location, pick me up, and we'd follow through on our plans. When I got back to my office, her message was waiting for me."

He stops. "She said . . ." The words catch in his throat. "'I will not be returning to Earth. My ship is under Furean control. The Genetics Council will hold a disciplinary hearing about my actions and my future. This will be the end of my career as a geneticist. Whatever you and I planned was pure fantasy. I understand that now, and I will not communicate with you again. Goodbye, Liam Rutherford. I wish you well.'"

A strangled whimpering arises from the back of his throat. She feels a hot tightness in her own throat. She cups her hand and rests it on his shoulder. If it makes him feel any better he doesn't show it, but he continues talking as if now that he's started he can't stop.

"I didn't know where to go. Ever felt that way? That you didn't belong anywhere?"

Only always.

"I knew I'd never return to SETI. My apartment only reminded me of how empty my life was before I met her. I'd already said goodbye to my parents."

"So, you left everything behind," Leeta says.

"I tried. I saw a therapist once. It's easy talking to a stranger about lost love. Of course, I never mention the ET part. He encouraged me to paint. Said it would be therapeutic. Help me let go of her. Another failed experiment. She's always with me."

"Eta-Bakara isn't the person you are painting."

"What do you mean?"

"She looks completely different now. You changed when she left. She changed when she returned to Fure. You wouldn't even know her."

He listens intently, nodding every so often, as Leeta tells him what she learned from the archive. She talks about the disciplinary hearing, the loss of Eta-Bakara's lab, her assignment to the re-education program. Finally hearing what happened after they parted, knowing that she loved her work as much as he loved his, and how they both lost so much, the steering wheel suddenly feels like it's bending in his hands.

"When she returned from the re-education program three years later, she immediately changed her field of study to social psychology, and changed her name from Eta-Bakara to Mayeel, erasing her past."

"Ma-eel? But that's Liam, spelled backwards!"

"Huh!" Leeta squeaks. "You are correct! I never put that together before. It is as I said. She publicly erased her past, but in her heart she never forgot you."

He smiles to himself as if, just now, he has received a cosmic Valentine that was sent years ago. Leeta doesn't want to spoil this moment for him, but she needs to know if love can survive the inevitable changes that happen over time.

"Liam, would you still love Eta-Bakara if you knew that she is no longer the person who broke all the rules for love?"

"What do you mean?"

"Eta-Bakara didn't just change her name and her intellectual pursuits. She changed to become the ruler of Fure. She is now the Daht Mayeel. She enforces all the rules."

"Leeta, data can be deleted, but former selves can't be erased. Not entirely. I may live like a hermit now, but I am still the SETI scientist who gave his heart and soul to an alien. Eta-Bakara still lives within Daht Mayeel. I know she does."

"You are correct. It was Eta-Bakara who orchestrated this whole thing. Assigned me to this solar system, gave me the ring knowing that I'd discover its planet of origin. She even gave me access to a secret database so I'd learn her history with you and your connection to me."

Leeta and Liam fall silent, immersed in their own thoughts, universes away from each other.

She's wondering if he'd like to know anything about her. What it was like for her to grow up the most Brid of all Brids. She'd like to tell him. She needs to.

They pass a road sign that reads *Shoben 60 miles*. She glances at the GPS: Destination Winterbrook . . . 55 miles. 52 minutes.

Her heart flutters. So little time left.

She thinks of the pledge she and Zertee made to each other. Their mutual effort to understand each other better. Was it only five days ago?

She wants Liam to know her better so he can understand who Leeta Simtar is.

"Now I will tell you about myself," she says.

He looks at her as if he's not sure he wants to hear what she has to say. He says nothing and drives faster. Is he suddenly in more of a hurry to get to Winterbrook? Or is he in a hurry to get away from something?

It doesn't matter. Leeta is going to tell him anyway. She just needs to, so he will know who she is before they say goodbye.

And so she begins by telling Liam what it has been like to grow up on logic-loving Fure as the only interspecies hybrid with all of her unpredictable, loud, and messy human emotions. What it was like to always be the tallest one whose clothes never fit. Who never fit in a chair or a bed or a group of friends. How she was always hungry because the prescribed servings in the Central Nursery Dining Hall were never enough to satisfy her hunger. She talks about how she has spent her life hiding tears and laughter and anger and confusion, all because she was not accepted by anyone, including herself. And how she always blamed herself for not being a typical Furean-Gemian hybrid when she wasn't Gemian at all.

When she's done, she turns to him.

"That was very much a data dump." She laughs, a little embarrassed, but happy that he now knows some of the most important things about his daughter. Like the questions she asked when he told his story, she expects he must have many questions for her. So she pauses.

"I will stop now so you can ask questions," she says. "I am sure that you must have much curiosity about me."

Silence.

"Liam. What questions do you have about me?"

He looks at her surprised, as if he had just looked over and realized he wasn't alone.

"Questions? Oh, yes, I have a question. I'm prone to motion sickness. I wonder if you are too. I know motion sickness has no hereditary link, but this condition tends to cluster in families. So, how did you manage on the flight?"

Out of all the things her father could have asked about her, the only thing he wants to know is if she vomited in space.

CHAPTER 31
GOODBYE EARTH

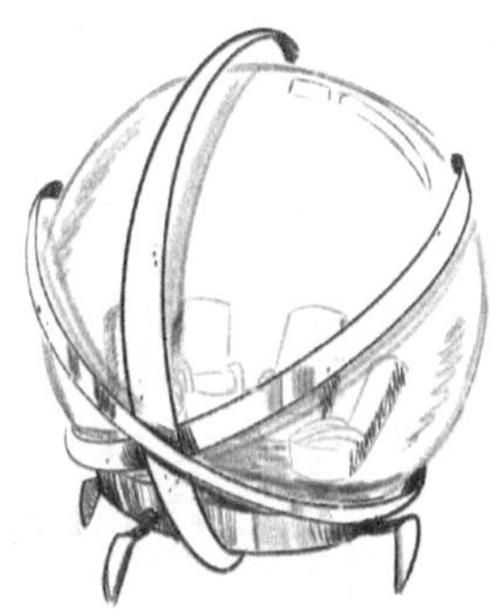

*"We were two scientists, both intensely focused on inter-
planetary life, cross-cultural alliances, and our conversations were very engaging and satisfying to me as well as to
him. Over time, we became . . . friends."*
—HIGH GENETICS COUNCIL FINAL DISCIPLINARY HEARING

THE MID-AFTERNOON SUN has just begun its downhill
journey as Liam drives through Winterbrook's gates,
his face showing none of the joyful anticipation expected for a homecoming 18 years in the making. To Leeta,
he looks more like a man facing an old terror and wondering
if there's still time to escape.

Richard is already standing at the bottom of the steps in
front of the mansion when both vehicles pull to a stop. When
Liam opens his door, unfolds his long legs, and steps out,
Richard's face erupts in tearful delight. He heads toward the
truck at a surprisingly fast clip and pulls his son into a tight
embrace that neither seems in a hurry to end.

Leeta joins Sid and Lucy, leaning against Sid's car. She
wraps an arm around each of them and pulls them in close

as if it's been four months instead of four hours since she's seen them. The three watch the father and son reunion, their hearts full, knowing they each had a hand in making this moment happen.

"How was your ride with Liam?" asks Lucy. "What'd you guys talk about?"

"Mostly about Liam and Eta-Bakara. Their story is sad."

"Is there something else?" asks Sid, looking so closely Leeta feels the tension of his concern.

She shrugs.

"I'll bet I know what's bothering you," Lucy announces.

Sid and Leeta look at her, expecting her to deliver the cold hard truth, like always.

"You're disappointed because you expected something from Liam that you didn't get. That happened every time I saw my father."

Leeta watches Richard and Liam climb the steps to the front door where Ruth stands just over the threshold, her face pinched. Liam stops at the top step and looks at his mother. Neither making a move to close the distance between them.

"You are right," Leeta says in a straightforward tone, verging on resignation. "I am disappointed that he did not have much curiosity about me."

While Richard tries to bring joy to the reunion in the solarium, Ruth and Liam sit stiffly across from each other, half-heartedly drinking tea and eating lemon blueberry cake. Lucy and Sid exchange looks that seem to say, *Maybe we shouldn't have pushed so hard to get him here.*

Leeta has other things on her mind. She excuses herself and steps out into the garden, drinking in the flowers and lush greenery to store them permanently in her memory.

"AYA, call Zertee."

Zertee appears. "Is it time to self-destruct the pod?"

"Not yet. I'll let you know. Please connect me with the Daht. I need to speak to her."

To Leeta's shock, the Daht appears almost immediately. "Hello, Leeta Simtar. Congratulations on accomplishing your mission."

"Congratulations? You set it all up. Giving me the ring. Sending me to Ganymede so I'd be in this solar system. Guiding me with clues to get me here. Listening in on every conversation through AYA."

"All that is true, but just because I had my plans does not mean that you were destined to succeed. So, you deserve congratulations."

"Okay. Thanks." Leeta pauses a moment for a deep breath of air, tinged with the smells of roses, wet grass, and mint. "Thank you for letting me come and experience all of this." Her voice is full of gratitude. "Even though I know you did it more for yourself and Liam than for me."

"I did it for all of us," says the Daht.

Leeta isn't sure she believes that but decides not to press the issue. Instead, she walks toward the hydrangeas where she spots Sheila, thriving in her new home. She bends down to touch one of her leaves. "I am sorry for what you and Liam went through, Madam. You two had a special love. and you deserved more time together."

In spite of the silence on the other end, and the unfathomable distance between them, Leeta can see, in her mind's eye, the strangest sight she could ever imagine—Daht Mayeel is openly weeping. Of course, Leeta's own eyes burn like fire, and in the depths of her own heart, she feels the Daht's pain.

They stay in that silence, grieving together. No time or space separating them, until finally the Daht says, "Thank you, Leeta. Are we done here for now?"

Leeta stands and looks at the wall surrounding the garden. She thinks about the wall she built around her heart while she was growing up. "I know there is no time machine and wishing is unFurean, but I just need you to hear me say this: I wish you had told me who my father really was. If I had known that I am human, I wouldn't have been so hard on myself for being so unFurean. I would have understood so much more about why I think and feel and act the way I do. I just might have learned to love myself a long time ago."

"I am sorry, Leeta. I see now that I should have told you."

"It's okay. It all got me here. So, I thank you for that. And I have a gift for you."

"Oh, what is it?"

"I'm going to put you on mute for a while and shut down the hologram, but I don't want you to go anywhere."

Leeta walks back into the house. Liam is no longer in the solarium with his parents. Neither are Lucy and Sid.

"Grandpa, where is Liam?"

"With Lucy. Down the hall."

"And Sid?"

"He stepped out in front to take a call."

When Leeta walks into Liam's old room, he's peering through the telescope, as he might have done on any night while growing up. Lucy sits on the bed, studying the model of the Saturn-5 rocket, imagining herself traveling into space.

"Liam, there is someone who wants to talk with you." Leeta unmutes the APED but leaves the hologram off and holds it out to him.

Lucy scrambles off the bed and tries to catch her cousin's eye, but Leeta is focused on her father. His hand trembles as he reaches out and takes the APED from her. The device is smooth and slightly cool to the touch. Surprisingly light. He stares at it, not daring to believe something this small possesses the power to reach across the galaxy and connect him with the ghost he never stopped loving.

His heart races dangerously. Leeta touches his chest with a cupped hand. He looks at her gratefully, inhales again, clears his throat, and speaks into the APED.

"Eta-Bakara?" he says, unraveling time back to the moment when he sat alone in his SETI office and first spoke her name. Through countless star fields, Eta-Bakara hears the voice she's only heard in her dreams for so many years. She wastes no time, because time does not exist between them.

She speaks the same words she did when they first connected. "Liam Rutherford? Are you there?"

"I am here."

The two of them struggle to make sense of this moment. Struggle to forget what they lost and be here with what they've just recovered. Then Eta-Bakara laughs. Something else Leeta could never have imagined coming from the Daht. Liam Rutherford joins her laughter. It fills his childhood room and their joy spreads throughout Winterbrook. They inhabit a world of two now, so it is quite simple for Leeta and Lucy to slip into the hallway unnoticed.

Sid is in the front hall talking on his phone when he spots the girls. He gestures to them and turns on the speaker. They gather around.

"Your mother turned you against me," Rick is saying, his voice moldy from old grievances.

"Don't go there, Dad. None of this is Mom's fault. You and I have always had different ways of seeing things and—"

"Not everything. We share a love of space! That's something good you inherited from me. Anyway, I'm getting off the phone now. Pretty much everyone's already here. Just waiting on Casey. He's coming from work. Maybe 15 more minutes. Time to start streaming now. Use the link I sent you."

Sid clicks on the link and a seven-foot aluminum foil-wrapped sphere appears on the screen, alone and provocatively out of place under a bare light bulb in Rick's barn. Rick, on the other hand, is exactly where he's always longed to be, in front of his computer, facing the camera, and hosting his own world-shaking event.

"Welcome to all members of the International Society of Alien Hunters and to the ISAH-curious. I'm Rick Rodriguez, founder and president of the Bay Area chapter. Please feel free to introduce yourselves in the chat. I see there are so many of you tuning in from different countries. Hello, Argentina! Belize! Turkey! UK! I see you, Peru! Senegal! Thank you for your ongoing vigilance in keeping our planet alien-free. You are about to see something so incredible, and I guarantee none of you will ever forget this moment for as long as you live. We'll be starting in ten minutes."

Leeta grabs Sid's arm. "I have to get my APED back from Liam."

She runs through the house. When she turns into the hallway leading to Liam's old room, she bumps right into him, almost unrecognizable with that smile on his face, like he's lit from within. He spots Leeta and glows brighter, pulling her into a warm hug. It feels nice, but she doesn't have time.

"I need my APED."

As Leeta hurriedly retraces her steps back to Sid, she talks to AYA, "Call Zertee."

"Want to hear about the conversation your parents just had?"

"No. Just call Zertee!" Leeta shrieks.

"Don't have to shout. Done."

Zertee, appears. "Is it time?"

"Soon. Sid's father will remove the aluminum foil from the pod . . ." She turns to Sid. "How much longer?"

"Five and half minutes."

"Got it," says Zertee. "I'll prepare to self-destruct the pod."

"Wait!" says Sid, "Is anyone going to get hurt?"

"Do not worry, Sid-friend-of-Leeta's. When the pod self-destructs, no life forms will be injured."

Five minutes later, Rick climbs a ladder leaning precariously against the pod. A yellow five-gallon bucket of green slime sits on the top step. When he reaches the top and starts peeling back the edge of the foil, Zertee says, "I have a read! Sending self-destruct initiation code . . ."

ZAM

Sheets of aluminum foil flutter off of what was once the cloaked escape pod while the pod collapses in on itself into a heap of fine powdery sand. The ladder topples forward, and Rick rides it to the floor where the slime mixes with the pod dust and the whole green mess oozes through the cracks of the barn floor.

The International Society of Alien Hunters lets out a collective groan that can be heard across the continents as Rick attempts to explain the inexplicable.

Dusk approaches as Zertee's spherical, transparent pod, twice the size of Leeta's single-seater, descends like a massive glowing bubble into the Winterbrook garden. Sid, Lucy, Richard, and Ruth watch in silent reverence. In spite of being the emotionally fragile and unpredictable species they are, the enormity of what is unfolding causes these four humans to forget their differences and huddle in closer. As for Leeta and Liam, they stand apart from the group and from each other as if the distance between the two of them was already 40 light-years.

The pod door opens and Zertee steps out. Leeta rushes to greet her. "Welcome to Earth, Zertee! Let me introduce you to my human family." She goes around the group from her grandparents to her father to her cousin. "And finally," she says, "this is my Sid."

Zertee bows her head, "I am pleased to meet all of you. I am grateful for the care you have given to my friend. But we must leave quickly. We have eight minutes before we have to leave here. Otherwise, the ship will return to Fure without us."

Richard enfolds Leeta in his arms. He's struggling to keep it together. Lucy joins the hug. Sid watches, powerless as his heart shatters.

Liam turns to his parents. "Dad. Mom. I know this is unexpected. But I'm going back to Fure with Leeta."

Richard cries out. He starts to lose his balance. Sid rushes forward to steady him. "Are you saying that I'm going to lose both of you?"

"Zertee, he can't go to Fure. Can he?" asks Leeta, not sure how she feels about it either way.

Zertee nods. "Yes. He can. The Daht authorized it. Come on, Leeta. Come on, Liam. We need to leave."

Leeta hesitates and looks at Sid. He is looking at her, holding back tears. Actually, they both are. He tries to send her a message from his heart, telling her without words how much he cares and how it's killing him to think this is the end. What do you say when you have only eight minutes to tell the love of your life that your heart is breaking? Sid doesn't know what to do with his face or his hands. And Leeta is imagining that she can freeze this moment by sheer will.

As for Lucy, her tears are falling freely, and she's working overtime wiping them away so no one sees. She can't believe that after all this effort to find Uncle Liam, she's going to lose him again as well as the only cousin she'll ever have.

For some reason, all this sadness makes Zertee's head throb, and she suddenly feels like escaping alone. She knows that would be against protocol, so she turns to Leeta's male human friend and says, "Sid, Leeta told me you are interested in travel outside of California and life on other planets. This pod can carry four, so if you'd like to come back to Fure with us, I have been authorized by the Daht to bring you along also."

Sid perks up as if the brightest ray of sunlight just flooded into the deepest, darkest pit. "Really? Yes! Thank you. I'm coming."

Leeta's mouth twists left. "Sid, would you still want to go to Fure if I stayed here?"

"What? No, of course not. But I don't understand. Are you seriously considering staying?"

"No. Not seriously considering. I have decided."

"No kidding?" he asks.

She shakes her head as they smile into each other's eyes, knowing they now have all the time they need.

Leeta turns to Zertee and holds out her arms to hug her friend. "Goodbye, Zertee."

Zertee steps back. "No. This is not logical. You came to find your father. You completed your mission. What else do you need to do here?"

"I completed just one short-term mission. Now I need to live like a human . . . and I can only do that here. I've always been more human than anything else, and I don't have to hide it here. Not all humans are good and kind all the time, but neither am I. I think this is really what it means to be human. To be kind and helpful and loving when you can. And when that's just too hard and you end up hurting someone, you say you're sorry and you try to do better. This is my family. I am happy I found them, and for now, this is where I want to be."

Zertee nods, slightly sad but mostly very happy for her friend. They embrace.

"When will I see you again?" Zertee asks.

"Dunno. But we'll always be friends and we can always talk."

Then Leeta turns to Liam and hands him the ring. "Give this back to the Daht. Okay?"

He nods and slips the ring on his finger.

"Have a good flight."

"Thank you, Leeta." He leans in, kisses her on the cheek, and pulls her into a hug. She hugs him back. The warmth and strength of it surprises them both, but then, it is meant to last a long time.

Liam and Leeta break it off at the same time and Liam runs toward the ship, ducks his head at the entrance, and climbs into the sphere. Unlike his Rivian, there is no clutter. All the control surfaces are sleek and clean. The seats are high-backed with adjustable head, arm, and leg rests. The seat cushion embraces every inch of his body like a warm hug and converts into sleeping cocoons. For a culture that values logic, the pod is designed for the utmost in efficiency and comfort.

"Three-hundred sixty-degree view for everyone," he says approvingly. "Nice feature. I was going to request a window seat, but no need."

Leeta and her family wave goodbye. As the pod slowly rises to the top of the garden wall, Zertee pauses for a moment to wave back at them before disappearing over Winterbrook. Liam misses the last goodbye, as his gaze is firmly fixed on the night sky.

"Well," says Richard, his voice raw with emotion. "That was something, wasn't it, my dear?"

Ruth rests a warm hand on his arm. "It certainly was." Then turning to the group she says, her voice more welcoming than any of them had ever heard, "I hope all of you will join us for dinner and spend the night. That would make Richard . . . and me very happy."

Much later, after Lucy and Richard watched old family videos starring Liam and Marcus as kids, and Sid dove into Liam's vintage collection of *Weird Science* and *Outer Space* comics, and Ruth taught Leeta how to make onion rings from scratch (Leeta agreed they were superior to anything she'd eaten in a car from a paper bag), the three friends set up their tent and sleeping bags on the grass in the center of the garden. Ruth has made them hot chocolate and blondies. Richard has given them pillows and extra blankets.

Leeta looks at the sky, identifying Canis Major overhead while Jasper snuggles in her lap. Lucy brushes her hair. Sid sketches the escape pod in the light of an electric lantern.

"So, am *I* in your graphic novel?" asks Lucy, pretending not to care whether she's in or out.

"Of course," says Sid, not looking up from his drawing. "We're all in it."

"Cool. So, how're you going to draw me?"

Sid stops working. "How do you want to be drawn?" He looks at her so intently Lucy has to look away.

"Hm. Let me think about it," she says.

"Sure. You've got time," he says. "We've got to figure out the ending of the story first."

Lucy scoffs. "None of this *we* stuff. It's Leeta's story." Then turning to Leeta she says, "You tell us how it ends."

Sid holds his breath, hoping Leeta can't read his mind and find out exactly how he'd like it to end.

Leeta looks at Lucy, purposely avoiding Sid's eyes. "I cannot tell you how this story ends because we have not yet arrived at the ending." Her voice steady, fueled by her purest Furean logic.

Leeta assumes this will end the discussion.

It does for Sid. "Fair enough," he says, strangely reassured by her non-answer.

Lucy, however, doesn't give up that easily. "But how do you *think* the story ends?"

Leeta plucks a blade of grass and chews it thoughtfully, "Honestly, I do not know yet."

The next morning the three friends settle comfortably in the Cosmos on Wheels, though they've switched seats. Sid is in the back with several grocery bags filled with their favorite food-for-the-road. Lucy is riding shotgun and Leeta is at the wheel. True, she doesn't yet have a valid California driver's license, but Sid gave her a full thirty minutes of driving instruction which was all she needed after having carefully observed enough of Angela's, Sid's, and Liam's navigational skills to understand how to operate this low-tech vehicle.

As for the future, each has only a vague idea of what might be in store for them. If they've got anything clearer in mind, none have shared it with the others. Right now, all that matters is the road ahead.

Since this is his car but he's not driving, Sid feels entitled to ask the obvious question, "Where are we going, Leeta?"

"West to the Pacific Ocean," she says. "Which is an illogical name considering that *pacifico* means peaceful in Spanish, and in fact, many tropical storms batter the islands of the Pacific. The lands around the Pacific Rim are full of volcanoes and are often affected by earthquakes. But do not worry. AYA will monitor earthquake activity and any subsequent tsunami warnings. Right AYA?"

"Sure, thing. I'm already plugged into DART."

"What's that?" asks Lucy.

"Deep-ocean Assessment and Reporting of Tsunamis."

"How'd she do that so fast?

"Because I'm always listening. So quit talking about me like I'm not here."

Lucy rolls her eyes.

"And I'm always watching. I saw that eyeroll!"

They all laugh. AYA too.

"Is the Pacific Ocean an acceptable destination for both of you?" asks Leeta.

"I'm good with that," says Sid. "It will be a good setting for some new scenes."

"Okay with me," says Lucy. "As long as we stop in Mendocino. Great shops there. And art galleries."

"How about after that?" Sid says, with equal parts worry and optimism.

Leeta smiles, catching his eye in the rearview mirror. "I want to travel, explore Earth, and just make myself at home."

AFTERWORD

IMPOSSIBLE AS IT SEEMS, it's been a year since I completed Leeta's biography, so let me bring you up to date.

Rick Rodriguez—He is still trying to reconstruct Leeta's escape pod from the sand and slime left underneath his barn floor. He tells the story of the disintegrated spaceship to anyone willing to listen. There aren't many, these days. For the most part, his alien hunter friends avoid him, as he's too unhinged even for them.

Zertee—For her role in assisting Leeta and for reuniting Eta-Bakara and Liam, Zertee has become something of a Furean folk hero. She was offered the position of Guide Leader but declined. Instead, she has gone to Trexo to find her father. In her encrypted messages, Zertee reports that the Trexans have a food called *wimlat*, which, according to Zertee, has to be better than onion rings. Leeta has her doubts.

Eta-Bakara—Immediately following her conversation with Liam at Winterbrook, she renounced her position as the Daht and tapped Sifat to be her successor. She has since reclaimed her former name and is now happily living with her beloved, working with him in ways she never could have imagined. (See Liam.)

Liam—Soon after he and Eta-Bakara reunited and re-started their lives in a place where they could openly express their love and respect for each other, they wasted no time in establishing Fure's first center for the creative arts, located in the newly constructed Art Dome. Liam serves as Director of Instruction and Eta-Bakara as Administrator. Due to the power couple's fame, for the first time thousands of Fureans are expressing and celebrating their individuality through unique works of art.

NOTE: Liam gave his cabin and all his paintings to Sid. (See Sid.) Liam instructed Sabine to work with Sid in the sale of all the paintings Sid wanted to let go of. The value of the paintings has soared as they've reached eager collectors far beyond Mount Shasta. The artist's identity still remains unknown.

Richard and Ruth Rutherford—They are both well; in many ways, better than ever. They changed their will to reflect Lucy and Leeta as their sole heirs. Since neither Richard nor Ruth plan on dying any time soon, and didn't want the girls to have to wait for the Rutherford fortune, they set up a trust which they replenish on a regular basis and which the girls put to good use. (See Leeta and Lucy.)

Jasper—Unfortunately Jasper had a recent health scare which gave Richard quite a fright. Fortunately, the MRI revealed nothing more concerning than a tummy full of blueberries. The little dog is well on his way to recovery. And Ruth has promised that from now on her blueberry lemon cake will no longer contain blueberries.

Leeta and Lucy—The cousins are like sisters, in the best sense of the word. They have been traveling together all over the Earth, including Antarctica. Their mission is to anonymously donate millions of dollars to organizations dedicated to improving the lives of humans, animals, and the health of the planet. Wherever they travel, they never fail to send beautiful postcards to their grandparents whose new hobby is tracking their granddaughters' good works.

NOTE: Leeta and Lucy have spent part of their inheritance to reverse engineer the *subyl* and get a patent. It's been six months since they brought it to market as the Big Blue Towel™. The product makes a considerable amount of money which they also pour into their charitable works.

Sid—He is hard at work on the final draft of his graphic novel, *Leeta Simtar: The Adventures of Galaxy Girl*, which will be published by Simtar Publishing Ltd. (owned by Leeta and Lucy). The graphic novel has already been optioned by an independent producer for an animated film. Leeta, Lucy, and Sid will voice their own characters.

NOTE: Leeta and Sid are officially dating. As soon as his graphic novel is finished, he'll be joining the girls on the road.

—Annie Fox, Earth, 2031

GLOSSARY

The Daht (*the daht*)—Supreme Ruler of Fure. The Daht is the sole arbiter when it comes to rules and standards of what is Furean and what is unFurean. Daht Mayeel held the position for nearly ten years. She voiced her dislike for the term "ruler," and preferred thinking of herself as a compassionate guide, lighting the way for others.

Frig (*frig*)—the largest animal to inhabit Fure, though rather small in relation to Earth's typical herd animals. *Frigs* eat a diet that is almost entirely *fwaydrun*. Their thick, furry muzzle serves as a highly effective air filter, allowing these sure-footed herbivores to inhabit the rockiest, most wind-swept regions of Fure. Interesting fact: A *frig's* keen sense of smell enables it to pick up the scent of Fure's scraggly plant-life at distances of up to 100 yards, even in a raging sand storm.

Fure (*fyur-ray*)—the largest and closest of the four planets that orbit *Kerlanti*. (The other three planets, in order of proximity to Kerlanti, are: *Hetor*, *Zarfin*, and *Yerp*.) For nearly 20,000 Earth years, Fure has been inhabited by a highly intelligent species whose original name and planet of origin is long forgotten. Fureans, as they proudly call themselves, have thrived by building domes and controlling the air quality and temperature within, by harvesting water, by cultivating edible and medicinal plants from seeds they harvest on other planets, and by maintaining a tight rein on societal standards of behavior. They've also contributed significantly to the increase in peace and prosperity on other planets by the distribution of Furean DNA.

Fwaydrun (*fway*-*druhn*)—a drought-resistant, low-light, grass-like plant that grows where no other plant could thrive. Interesting fact: *Fwaydrun* appear to have the ability to talk to other *fwaydrun* and may warn each other of the presence of *frigs*. When hearing the warning, *fwaydrun* shrink defensively down into the sand, reappearing after the herd has left the area.

Ganymede (*ga*-*nuh*-*meed*)—the largest moon of Jupiter and only slightly smaller than Mars, Ganymede is the largest moon in Earth's solar system. NASA's Hubble Space Telescope has found the best evidence yet for an underground saltwater ocean on Ganymede. Interesting fact: Ganymede's ocean is thought to have more water than all the water on Earth's surface.

Grentrum (*grehn*-*trum*)—the sandstone that covers most of the surface of Fure, either in solid rock or granular form. Interesting fact: In times of extreme famine, *sanderols* have been known to eat *grentrum* to survive.

Gurder (*gur*-*dr*)—a dome-shaped dumpling that may be stuffed with any number of different chopped seeds, boiled leaves, and spiced roots (alone or in combination), depending on the season and temperament of the cook. The name *gurder* derives from a long-deceased Furean named Gurder Setap who is said to have been among the designers of the early domes of Fure City and therein discovered her culinary inspiration. Interesting fact: There is no historical record of any Furean named Gurder Setap.

Hastip (*ha*-*steep*)—a thick, fermented drink made from crushed *korbril* roots is sweet with a slight taste of mint and an aroma of mustard. Hastip has an ABV (alcohol by volume) of 24%—roughly twice the alcohol as a glass of wine. Interesting fact: Unlike certain fermented products that increase in potency the longer they ferment, *hastip's* potency *decreases* the longer it ferments. Day old *hastip* packs ten times the punch of a tankard of ten-day old *hastip*.

Ka'aru (**kuh**-*a*-*roo*)—the traditional name for the eternally restless winds of Fure. *Ka'aru* is also referred to as *Ka*, meaning restless monster, and *Aru*, which describes the wind's low moaning sound. Interesting fact: Some Fureans believe the most perfectly chanted One Mind, One Goal, One Family sounds precisely like *Aru*.

Kerlanti (*ker*-**lahn**-*tee*)—the red dwarf star at the center of Fure's solar system. Like all red stars (the most common type of star in the Milky Way galaxy), *Kerlanti* is small and provides little light or heat to Fure. In addition, it casts a dull reddish hue over the entire surface of the planet. Interesting fact: To the naked eye, *Kerlanti* appears more orange than red.

Kiroota (*keer*-**roo**-*tuh*)—a classic Furean insult, roughly translated as "Your brain secretes *frig* excrement." Or, in more polite terms: "I am wasting my time with this conversation as you appear to have the intellectual nuance of a fistful of *grentrum*."

Korbril (**kor**-*bril*)—a small plant with clusters of thick, purple leaves, and one of the few species that thrives on Fure. *Korbrils* extract moisture from rocks by wrapping their roots around stones and squeezing, thus exerting up to 25,000 pounds of pressure per square inch. Interesting fact: An average boa constrictor on Earth can exert 20 pounds of pressure while squeezing its prey.

Mokeep (**mow**-*keep*)—a small, omnivorous mammal characterized by its fierce temperament and six rows of toxic spikes running along its back. Rarely seen, mokeep are best known for their solitary nature and propensity to eat their own young. Interesting fact: Some Furean zoologists believe mokeep may have eaten themselves into extinction.

Pertru (*pur*-*troo*)—a strong Furean expression reserved for rare occasions when one has inadvertently lost focus of the task at hand and made a mess, hopefully when no one else was around. If, however, there were witnesses, the embarrassed individual may mask their shame by covering the word with the sound of a sudden loud cough or sneeze.

Po'ost (*po*-*ohst*)—one of only three long, limbless, muscular creatures that inhabit the sandiest outreaches of Fure. *Po'osts* are normally shy, though if one is disturbed it will coil tightly onto itself before springing to heights of up to three feet, whipping the air in large circles with its venomous tail. Interesting fact: *Po'osts* have a strong craving for *frig* droppings, which explains why mature *frigs* frequently carry circular scars on their hind quarters, a sign they've accidentally stepped on a *po'ost*.

Pruvadam (*proo*-***vah***-*duhm*)—one of the few flowering plants of Fure, prized for its large, soft-shelled seeds which are often roasted, ground, and mixed with spices and used in various dishes, especially at times of celebration.

Quistel (*kiss*-*tel*)—a complex conifer with sloping branches and round leaves. A favorite food of Fureans, *quistel* is a native of *Sortin-5*, one of the seven tiny moons of *Hetor*. Interesting fact #1: Braised *quistel* tastes like chicken. Interesting fact #2: The Furean who first discovered *quistel* and brought it back to Fure became enormously popular and served as the first Daht (Daht Tzee) for 42 Earth years.

Sanderol (*san*-*dur*-*awl*)—a small, carnivorous burrowing reptile characterized by razor sharp teeth and devotion to family. *Sanderols* hunt in packs that can number up to two thousand individuals. They have a voracious appetite for carrion, but none for combat, thus they are easily frightened but annoyingly persistent.

Sork *(sork)*—an exclamation that is roughly translated as "OMG! I had no idea!" or simply put, "Wow!"

Subyl *(soo-bl)*—a multipurpose, stretchy fabric, highly engineered from a special blend of various plant fibers, resulting in a super strong, super absorbent material used for cleaning, drying spills on non-porous surfaces. Also highly effective for drying clothing, skin, and hair. Interesting fact: Some Fureans use their *subyls* as a blankie (security snuggie) during stressful times, though none will admit it nor will they admit they are ever stressed.

Tulahm *(too-**laam**)*—a traditional, cupped-hand gesture used to calm emotional reactivity in others and return them, mind and spirit, to The Group. The level of calming achieved depends on the skill of the practitioner. At its most effective, *tulahm* is a physical, hands-on channeling of the audible power of drumming and the One Mind, One Goal, One Family chant. Interesting fact: For some Fureans, the effectiveness of *tulahm* increases when they visit other planets. For some, it decreases.

Turil *(**tuhr**-uhl)*—a dried snack made by infusing a variety of thick leaves with the sweet nectar of *pruvadam* flowers. *Turil* is initially hard to chew, but will soften in the mouth over time. Interesting fact: While there are no Furean dentists (tooth decay is non-existent), many Fureans have chipped a tooth or two while enjoying *turil*.

Yralba *(yeh-**raal**-buh)*—A Furean curse word, roughly translated means "Bullshit!" Or in more polite terms "You are lying through your teeth which obviously have not been brushed for weeks."

ANNIE'S NEXT BOOK

Paige Turner and the Happily Ever After Wars**, coming in 2027.** Eighteen-year-old Paige Turner devours romance novels and gleefully dissects them on her *Happily Ever After* podcast. A recent high school grad taking a gap year, Paige now has more time than ever to work on her own romance novel. But it's not going well. She's has never actually been in love which is why her FMC and MMC can't seem to say, think or feel anything remotely spicy. When a friend suggests she kill off a secondary character to shake up the plot and turn up the heat between the two leads, Paige loves the idea and knows just who has to go—Kira, the annoying girl who keeps throwing herself at the MMC. After a late-night writing session, Kira is dead. Or is she? When Paige turns on her computer the next morning, not only is Kira still alive, she and the MMC are now in a hot relationship with no sign of the FMC anywhere in the file! How is that possible? Is there something wrong with her computer? Or did Kira, somehow, edit Paige's novel?

What happens when a character takes control over their own story and refuses to give it back to the writer? All-out war.

Subscribe to Annie's newsletter for updates at
subscribe.anniefox.com

ACKNOWLEDGEMENTS

Novel writing is a solitary endeavor. You've got to spend massive amounts of quality time alone with your characters, getting to know them and listening to their ideas about how their story should be told. Then, after months of figuring things out, word by word, it's time to invite a group of trusted people to join the game by adding their own creativity and expertise to this make-believe universe you've created.

These people listed below are my beloved team. We all worked together with the shared goal of making *Leeta Simtar* the best book it can be. It goes without saying (though I'll proudly say it anyway) this novel would not have been the same without them. Thank you!

Janna Balthasar, my editor, who has the uncanny ability to feel the heartbeat of a story and describe, so precisely, what a scene needs to fully connect with the reader.

Sarah Thomas and Tzook Har-Paz, my crazy talented cover artists and chapter head illustrators. The visual world you created for Leeta is truly out of this world.

Maria Marquis, our amazing audiobook narrator. By giving voice to Leeta and her friends you've touched hearts and opened minds across the galaxy, including mine.

Caleb and Maya Fox, my kind, smart, funny and infinitely creative grandchildren, who were always interested in Leeta's progress in her adventures and in the cover design. I can't wait until you're old enough to appreciate this story.

Andrea DeWerd and Amanda Livingston of **the future of agency LLC**, who said, "Yes we can help you market your book" when others said "No way! You should have called us six months ago." I'm grateful for your vast experience in marketing indie books and your responsiveness and good humor in taking my emails at all hours.

Steve Croft, Breakthrough Listen Project Scientist at Berkeley SETI Research Center, who graciously gave me a fascinating fact-finding interview. I so appreciate your letting me know exactly how Liam "might have" hidden his contact with an alien.

ARC team, I've never met most of you face-to-face, but I love you! Thank you for jumping on the bandwagon a full two months before publication. Thank you for your warm and enthusiastic embrace of *Leeta* and for all those early reviews.

Mark Wasserman, dear cousin, grammar maven, and eagle-eyed copy editor, without your diligence Leeta would have been bogged down in the Realm of Unnecessary Commas.

Liz Amini-Holmes, my best friend/kindred spirit, who eagerly listened as I read early chapters of *Leeta* during our virtual tea times. Thank you for always supporting and encouraging my work.

Gracie the Dog, my office-mate who doesn't mind my rereading the same scene aloud for the seventeenth time. Thanks for your company on my daily Gotta-Clear-the-Brain hike.

David Fox, my number one honey pie and partner in life. I can't possibly itemize everything you've done and continue to do to help me live my best life. Thank you ticks a box, but doesn't come close. All I can say is, I love you, David.

ABOUT THE AUTHOR

WITH 30+ YEARS as an online teen adviser, Annie Fox has helped countless teens with their friendship and relationship challenges. She has written books for kids and adults, but now she writes for teens. *The Little Things That Kill: A Teen Friendship Afterlife Apology Tour* was her debut novel and *Leeta Simtar: A Life on Two Planets* is her latest.

Annie lives in the San Francisco Bay Area with her husband, David, and Gracie the Dog. When she's not hiking with them or baking killer sourdough bread and chocolate cakes, she continues to validate the experience of young people through Q&A, and writing YA fiction with the power to open hearts and minds.

Thanks for reading *Leeta Simtar: A Life on Two Planets*. If you enjoyed this book, please consider leaving an honest review on the site where you bought the book or your favorite review website.

Sign up for Annie's newsletter at subscribe.anniefox.com
- Follow Annie on TikTok: @anniefoxauthor
- Follow Annie on Instagram: @annielfox
- Follow Annie on Facebook: @anniefox.author
- Follow Annie on BlueSky: @anniefox.com